DIVIDED LOYALTY, DIVIDED LOVE

STEPHEN NOWELL—A man of iron will driven by a dream of recapturing the youthful love he could not forget and his half-breed son claimed by a powerful Indian tribe.

MOLLY BRANT—Indomitable Indian princess, she commanded the passions of two proud men, and shaped their destinies as well.

KATHERINE SCHUYLER NOWELL—She was the prize claimed by bloodbrothers, torn by marriage, memory and regret . . .

WILLIAM JOHNSON—Sensualist, renegade, adopted son of the Mohawk nation, he was determined to lead his tribes into battle against the hated French.

KARL STIEGLER—He had taken a pledge to let nothing come between him and his bloodbrother Stephen—not war nor women. But will he be able to keep that vow?

CANADA—Uncharted, unyielding land, a challenge to all who dared to stand fast and fight . . .

THE FORGING OF A CONTINENT INTO TWO POWERFUL NATIONS!
THE CANADIANS

THE CANADIANS
by
Robert E. Wall

II
Bloodbrothers

SEAL BOOKS
McClelland and Stewart-Bantam Limited
Toronto

BLOODBROTHERS
A Seal Book / August 1981
2nd printing . . . October 1986

ISBN 0-7704-2170-9

Seal Books are published by McClelland and Stewart-Bantam Limited. Its trademark, consisting of the words "Seal Books" and the portrayal of a seal, is the property of McClelland and Stewart-Bantam Limited, 60 St. Clair Avenue East, Suite 601, Toronto, Ontario, Canada. This trademark has been duly registered in the Trademarks Office of Canada. The trademark, consisting of the words "Bantam Books" and the portrayal of a rooster, is the property of and is used with the consent of Bantam Books, Inc., 666 Fifth Avenue, New York, New York 10103. This trademark has been duly registered in the Trademarks Office of Canada and elsewhere.

PRINTED IN CANADA

COVER PRINTED IN U.S.A.

11 10 9 8 7 6 5 4 3 2

For my children,
Liz, Nina, Amy, Chris and Craig

ACKNOWLEDGEMENTS

During the writing of *Blackrobe* and *Bloodbrothers*, Books I and II of *The Canadians*, I have received help from many persons. They are too numerous to mention in one place. But there are some who must be mentioned. From Seal Books—Bantam of Canada Ltd., Gay McKellar and Susan Meisner have been very kind to a frequently pesty author. Andrew Machalski's enthusiasm for the project carried me through some rough moments. From Personal Library Editions of Toronto—hardcover publisher of *The Canadians*, Glen Witmer has been a great booster from the very beginning. From Bantam Books in the United States, Linda Price and Alun Davies have helped me whenever I asked them.

I would also like to thank Caroline Bennett Roy of Concordia University in Montreal who always encouraged the Provost and Nancy Traficante of Fairleigh Dickinson University in Rutherford, New Jersey who has continued that "tradition."

Jennifer Glossop of Toronto and Tony Koltz of New York have each served as editors for one of the volumes and have saved me innumerable errors. Without Anna Porter, President of Seal Books, this series would not exist.

I have dedicated *Bloodbrothers* to my children. They know how I feel about all of them. *Blackrobe* was Regina's. All of our life together she wanted me to write it. It belongs to her.

Prologue

"I'm not going back to Boston, Karl. My family is gone, except for one aunt, who is in no position to act like family. You are my family now—you and Socono and Sister Marie Louis. You are the only ones in this world that I have ever cared for and who have cared for me. You and I will be brothers. What is it the Abenacki do? Socono told me about it. They mix their blood and become blood brothers. Let's do it now."

Karl frowned for a moment, then laughed quietly. "Very well," he said. "I always wanted a little brother."

Stephen reached for his hunting knife and, with a fast slash, he cut the vein on his wrist and watched as the blood began to run down his arm. He reached for Karl's hand, but the Swiss playfully pulled away.

"Are you crazy?" he laughed. "Do you think I'm going to let you slit my wrist? Here, I'll do it myself." He took Stephen's knife and very gingerly pricked his vein with the point until some blood appeared. They held their wrists together and allowed the blood to mingle. They looked at each other and both became very serious. It was clear to each that what they had just done—although very boyish—was important to them both.

Part One

The Mohawk

I

1746·1749

The old man pulled the wolfskin closer to his body. Pain from the effort of closing his hands spread from his swollen knuckles up his forearm. He grimaced. The cold of winter was taking longer to leave his body every spring. Last winter had been the worst he could remember, and traveling here to Onondaga before the snows had left the valley had not been easy for a man who had already seen more than seventy winters come and go.

The morning was a busy time in the longhouse, but in deference to his position and age, no one approached the platform that had been assigned to the great sachem. His Onondaga Turtle clan cousins had done everything within their power to make the great sachem comfortable, even to the extent of hushing the naked little ones, who would normally be scurrying about the house chasing dogs and playing warrior.

He was Teoniahigarawe, great sachem of the upper castle at Canajoharie, known to the whites these many years as King Hendrick, high warrior of the most feared tribe in America— the Mohawk. Their very name had once struck terror in the hearts of everyone from Quebec up the great river to Montreal. Even Louis of France, whom Onontio in Quebec called chief, had cursed their name. The English had taken Hendrick as a young man to visit their own Queen Anne across the seas. It had increased his respect for the English that they acknowledged the importance of the clan mother. The French did not understand such things. However, now that he was much older, and had had forty more years to watch the English, he realized that his earlier respect for them had been misplaced as well. Every day the English moved more and more into the Mohawk lands. And who now feared the Mohawk? Once, the five other tribes of the Confederation had acknowledged them as guardians of the eastern door of the Great Longhouse, which stretched along the river that bore their name all the way to the lakes of the far west. Now the English lived within the doorway. Many of the Mohawk had fallen prey to the blandishments of the blackrobes and had gone off to found a new castle within eyesight of the hated Ville Marie—Montreal. If the Six Nations should go to war, he would lead no more than one hundred fifty warriors into battle. How the Seneca would mock him. But it did not matter.

The Great Council would begin with the setting sun, and then he would have to put his plan into effect. Never before had the unity of the Longhouse been so seriously threatened. Geneseo and the Drunkard of the Seneca had become the lackeys of the French. The Keepers of the Western Door, and there were so many of them, had grown fat and rich carrying their furs to Niagara, ignoring the ancient way—the way it had been done before Hendrick could remember. Going back to the time of the Dutch and after, it had been the honored custom to bring the furs to Albany, near the land of the Mohawk. But no longer. Now the Seneca thought only of themselves.

Soyeghtowa, the Cayuga, the man of the golden tongue, would speak eloquently for them. The Cayuga had become lackeys to the lackeys. Together the Seneca and the Cayuga would call upon all Six Nations of the Iroquois to make war upon the English. War was sure to be the destruction of Hendrick's people, and the Seneca knew this. They no longer cared about the good of the whole nation. They were beneath his contempt.

The old man pulled his legs out from beneath him and stretched them out. Both of his knees ached. He reached with his right hand under his robe to scratch his armpit. With spring he would have to search his body and rid himself of unwanted visitors.

The key to everything was the Onondaga—especially their sachems Otschiata and Kaghswughtioni. And the key to these men was their vanity. The Onondaga had also grown lazy over the years. They lived in the middle of the Longhouse and had been protected by the fierceness of the Mohawk and the numbers of the Seneca. They gained their prestige not as warriors but as the peacemakers of the Confederation. Their castle was the capital of the nation, where the sacred Council fire was kept forever lighted. They would not cross him and they would understand his meaning. They would dissect his

6

words to discover what it was that he truly meant. But his own people must not suspect. He would have to trick even the white man, Warraghiyagey—Johnson—who had come to live among them years earlier. Now he was like one of them and sure to be adopted as one of them. Old Brant, sachem of the lower castle of his people, was deceived by Johnson, but Hendrick was not. Johnson might speak their language and dress like them, but he was not a Mohawk. He was an Englishman, protecting English interests. His uncle was a commander of great ships like the one that had taken Hendrick to England forty years earlier. This Johnson had won over all the warriors of both castles. They screamed for the blood of the French as loudly as the Seneca called for that of the English. Hendrick could not openly resist them, but resist he must without seeming to do so.

The skin curtain of the doorway to the longhouse where Hendrick rested was pulled back. A large man, naked except for loincloth and moccasins, despite the chilliness, stepped through the entryway and then straightened himself; his broad shoulders just barely allowed him to enter without turning. His hair was jet black, as were his eyes. He waited for them to focus in the semidarkness of the longhouse. Then he discovered where Hendrick was seated and approached him.

"How is my cousin? Are you ready to address the Council?" asked the newcomer.

Hendrick viewed him with his eyes narrowed to slits. It helped him to see inside the smoky lodge. "Dagaheari, how are you, my friend? I have spoken in Council many times. It is you who should be preparing. Are you prepared to speak for the first time as a sachem of the Oneida?"

"I am not the orator that Skenandon was," said the younger man.

"Yes, we will miss him. He was a wise man who spoke well."

Dagaheari looked uncomfortable as Hendrick praised a man whom he had regarded a fool and better dead. "Skenandon will be missed," he lied. "And the Oneida have had no revenge."

"Does that mean that the Oneida will speak for war with the French?" asked the old man.

"It was a French blackrobe who killed our sachem."

"But he fled to the English, Dagaheari. You yourself know that. You tracked him and his Abenacki friend."

"It doesn't matter. He was French, and we will have our revenge on the French."

7

The old man was exasperated, but he did not let it show. "Did not burning the other blackrobe provide revenge enough?"

"We did not taste his blood," said the Oneida, growing more angry. "Mohawks interfered and ransomed the priest."

Hendrick grunted in disgust. "It is clear that the blackrobe priest had nothing to do with the murder of Skenandon. That was done by the young blackrobe who speaks our language—LaGarde. He is the one you should have been seeking."

"It was no use," said Dagaheari evasively. "He had fled and we could not reach him."

A woman brought the two sachems bowls of boiled meat. They sat eating for some minutes without talking. Finally Hendrick broke the silence. "I can help you and the Oneida, my cousins, in this matter, Dagaheari."

The younger man looked at the Mohawk quizzically. "Do you know where LaGarde is?"

"No, but I know the whereabouts of someone equally important to you. I know where his son is. And I will put the boy in your power if you promise me two things."

The Oneida said nothing, and Hendrick took his silence as agreement. "First, you must promise me not to harm the boy. He is being raised a Mohawk by Old Brant, and he is his first great-grandson."

Dagaheari spoke coldly. "Do you mean to say that our Turtle cousin, Gonwatsijayenni, took the snake into her bed?"

"That is the way it is usually done," said the old man, smiling.

Dagaheari flopped himself down beside Hendrick on the platform. His initial anger had turned inward, and now he showed only a placid exterior. "What else would you require of me?" he asked.

"I would require that you and the Oneida and the Tuscarora, for whom the Oneida speak, vote to maintain the peace in the Council tonight."

Dagaheari looked at Hendrick in amazement. His mask of indifference had disappeared totally. "But you have come to speak for war. The Mohawk wish war with the French. The Oneida and Tuscarora wish war with the French. If we can sway the Onondaga . . ."

"You have no hope of swaying our senior cousins. They will vote for neutrality. The Mohawk will call for war with the French. The Seneca will call for war with the English. The Cayuga will agree."

8

Dagaheari smiled a caustic smile. "The Cayuga have not thought on their own in many Councils."

Hendrick nodded. "If the Oneida and the Tuscarora vote with the Onondaga, then a majority of the tribes will have called for neutrality, and neither the Seneca nor the Mohawk will dare take up war hatchets in defiance of the Council. But if only one tribe calls for neutrality, then the unity of our Confederation might be broken."

"Old Brant will want your scalp, Hendrick, if he finds out about what you have told me and what you have planned."

"But you will not tell him anything, Dagaheari. If you do, then you will never get your hands on his great-grandson. And no one else but you can tell my fellow sachem any of my plans. Are we agreed that you will speak for peace?"

The old man's face remained passive. But he knew that he had triumphed. The Oneida would do as he wished them to do. He pulled his creaking legs back up underneath him once again and again grimaced. "Besides," he said, "it is not Old Brant I fear. What will Warraghiyagey do when he learns of what I am about to arrange? It is the white devil in our midst that I fear."

At that very moment in the next longhouse, William Johnson stretched out his long frame. His toes touched the edge of the end of the platform while his dark curls caught in the bark of the wood at the other end. The house was noisy and smoky. The women had kindled the fires and were pulling down dried vegetables and meats from the longhouse rafters, throwing them somewhat carelessly into the great iron pots that hung above the flames.

The girl next to him stirred but continued to sleep. Her mother hesitated to come and claim her from Johnson's platform, just in case he would wish to make love to her again. He was a good catch, this Warraghiyagey—"he who does great things."

Once the fires had been started, Johnson had tossed off the furs that had covered his body during the cold night. The stiffness in his groin clearly indicated that his body would very much like another session with the Onondaga beside him, but even Warraghiyagey found it difficult to have sex in open view of all the families who shared the house. It was bad enough at night, when only the sounds of lovemaking betrayed the activity on the sleeping platforms.

Johnson started to pull himself up onto his elbows to look about him, but his hair caught in the bark and pulled. He yelped. The girl awoke and smiled as she saw this giant of a man rubbing his head like a little boy.

"Is my brave lover afraid of pain?" she asked in her strange Onondaga dialect.

Johnson turned his gray eyes on her and smiled. He pulled back the furs that covered half of her lithe body so that he might look upon the whole of her. Most Iroquois girls would have protested the nakedness, but not this one. Clearly both she and her mother were willing to put up with almost any behavior from him if it helped to get him into her longhouse.

The man feasted his eyes on her, and his body reacted. The girl reached for him, but he pulled away. "Not this morning, my beauty," he said in an English laced with the sweet lilt of the Irish—a language the girl did not know. But she understood the motion of her lover's body as he pulled away. She pouted as he turned his back, threw his legs over the side of the platform and waited for his naked body to be ready for his loincloth.

He had much to do this day. Old Brant would begin the ceremony this morning. The sachem of the lower castle near Fort Hunter had agreed to help Johnson enter tonight's Council, and the only way was to adopt Johnson into the tribe. He stood up and pulled on his buckskin leggings and slipped the loincloth between his legs, covering himself both front and rear. He did not look back at the girl, but instead walked into the middle of the longhouse.

He saw Old Brant on the far side, sitting on his assigned platform. The Mohawk delegation to the Council at Onondaga had all been assigned to this one longhouse, except for King Hendrick. The segregation of the old sachem bothered Johnson. Had it been at Hendrick's own request, or were the cagey Onondaga attempting to work on the old man's resolve to ask for war?

Brant's English-speaking granddaughter, Molly, sat by his side and served him his cornmeal breakfast. Her baby lay in the old man's arms, and he rocked the child back and forth. It was clearly a child of mixed blood; Johnson had been amused to hear that the father was a Jesuit. He was a lapsed Catholic himself who had become an Anglican. How else did an Irishman make good in the Englishman's world? Since coming to the Mohawk country, however, he had prayed more often to the great Manitou than to King George's god.

Molly Brant smiled at him as Johnson approached their platform. It was a warm smile that turned her plain and slightly pock-marked face into a friendly, almost beautiful one. He smiled back at her.

He looked at Old Brant. "Will she be one of the maidens of the ceremony?" he asked in Mohawk.

"No," said the old chief. "My granddaughter is now one of the mothers of the Turtle clan. The maidens of the ceremony must be Mohawk virgins."

Johnson started to laugh. "There aren't any left."

Old Brant slapped his knee and howled with laughter. "Not since you came to live among us."

Johnson laughed again. "I am only finishing the work that you began, old friend," he said.

Again Brant cackled. The baby in his arms stirred from his sleep and opened his eyes. Johnson was startled to see that the baby's eyes were blue—like no other Mohawk's eyes. The child saw his great-grandfather's face and smiled. The old man was pleased. "And this little one, my friend, he will continue the work after you and I are both gone."

Molly took the baby away from her grandfather, slipped open the front of her doeskin dress and held him to her breast. The child sucked hungrily.

"That's it," said Brant. "Feed him good Mohawk milk. He will be a great warrior despite his French blackrobe father."

"His father was an Englishman, old fool," she said affectionately. "And his father was a man of great courage—much respected by the clan mother."

Johnson had heard the story of LaGarde, the blackrobe who had lived among the Oneida as a French missionary and who had killed the sachem Skenandon and then fled to the English towns. He had never spoken to Molly about him, nor had he ever head her speak of him before.

Molly looked very desirable to him as she sat there nursing her child. Her breasts were large with milk, and he could not take his eyes from them. She looked up at him and spoke in English. "This is my son, Kenonranon Brant. His uncle, my little brother Joseph, will bring him to you someday, Johnson. He will be a great warrior. Joseph tells me that you will become the Great Father of all the Iroquois. I want you to know and honor my son."

Johnson bowed to her. There was something about her carriage, the way she sat nursing her child, that was maternal and noble. He found these women so damned attractive—at one moment so blatantly sexual and the next so honorable and stately. They threw him off guard every time. All that he had learned about the Mohawk by living with them these past several years taught him to treat her now with the greatest respect. She was a Mohawk clan mother, the mother of a future warrior of the tribe. Her father, Nicus Brant, grew more and more important as Hendrick and Old Brant grew more feeble. She was a formidable girl-woman, more suited for the marriage bed than for the pleasant evening on the sleeping platform.

Old Brant rose unsteadily and smiled at Johnson. "It is time, my young friend. We must get you into tonight's Council, and if you are to speak to the Council of all the tribes, you must be one of us. The ceremony must begin." Brant signaled to the other Mohawks in the longhouse, and soon all were crowded about him.

"It is time to end the differences that exist between Warraghiyagey and ourselves, my brothers and sisters," he announced in a loud voice. "Prepare him for the ceremony."

Young braves tore at Johnson's leggings, leaving him naked except for the breechcloth he had donned earlier. A gnarled and wizened old man, a shaman of the Mohawk, approached, followed by two assistants whose faces were completely covered by grotesquely carved wooden masks. Each assistant carried paint pots in his hands. The shaman mumbled a chant that Johnson, who knew the Mohawk language well, could not translate. The priest painted the outline of a turtle on Johnson's chest, over his heart. Lightninglike streaks were painted on each cheek by the assistants. Old Brant draped a belt of wampum over his shoulders and about his neck.

By this time all of the Onondaga in the longhouse had gathered around their Mohawk cousins. They had seen the ceremony of adoption before, but never had they seen a white man so honored. They had heard of such things happening among the Seneca and the Mohawk, but not here in Onondaga, the capital of the entire Confederation, where the great mysteries of their people were preserved.

Brant spoke in a loud voice. His Mohawk dialect sounded funny to the untrained ears of the Onondaga children. Their parents hushed them, for Brant was a renouned orator; all listened to his words carefully.

"Warraghiyagey—He Who Does Great Things—is worthy to become a guardian of the eastern doorway of the Great Longhouse," said the old man. "He has lived among us for almost ten winters. He has made his castle next to mine. He has fought by my side against our enemies, the French. He has obtained better prices for our furs by interceding for us

12

with the merchants in Albany. And he has kept the white settlers away from our castles and made them pay us for the lands they take. He is a worthy brother."

All the Mohawks present grunted assent. A path was cleared and three young girls holding hands entered the semicircle.

"These three Mohawk maidens will now take Warraghiyagey to the waters to wash his skin and take from it all its whiteness."

Johnson smiled at Brant as he spoke of the maidens, but the old man pretended not to notice the white man's impertinence. The Irishman allowed himself to be led out of the longhouse and down to the shores of the lake on which the village of Onondaga was built. The young girls giggled when Johnson modestly turned his back on them as he removed his only remaining garment. But when he turned around toward them, it was their turn to feign modesty and look away.

They grabbed handfuls of sand and dirt from the beach where the great canoes were landed, and they took him by both hands and both arms and led him into the numbing waters of the lake. The women splashed water all over him and, beginning with his hair, they scrubbed him from head to toe with the sand, rubbing his skin raw. Only the coldness of the water prevented the sensitive areas of his body from bleeding.

When they had scrubbed him to the point that Johnson began to wonder if they were planning to take Old Brant's command seriously and scrub away any trace of white skin, they finally stopped and led him from the waters of Lake Onondaga back to the longhouse. On the platform where he had slept the night before, there was laid out a whole new suit of buckskins, covered with intricate and delicate decorations of porcupine quills. The maidens helped him to dress in his new clothes and then led him to face the sachem. The shaman and his assistant continued their chanting; their grotesque masks seemed to have become even more lewd. Then Brant gave him a smoking pipe and a tomahawk and placed his arm about Johnson's neck. "Now you are one of us—a brother—a true Mohawk. Let all the other five nations call you cousin."

Johnson let out a war whoop that startled even himself with its loudness. He was now a Mohawk, an Iroquois. It was the first step on his path—a path that would lead eventually to war, war against the French and the final destruction of French Canada.

13

The black night enveloped the town of Onondaga. The cooking fires in all the longhouses remained unlighted. The darkness only accentuated the myriad stars that flickered in the night skies. A brooding silence prevailed, broken only occasionally by the bark of a dog, followed by a yelp as the person closest to it chastened it to remain silent.

When the edge of the new moon rose from the waters of Lake Onondaga, casting its silver light on the ebony waters, the village slowly stirred to life. A torch, illuminating only slightly the outline of its bearer, moved toward the great center square of the town and was thrust into a large pile of wood and kindling. It seemed to be snuffed out at first, but then a low flame reappeared and the first cracks of burning pine broke the silence of the night. Before long the fire burned brightly, its light reflecting from the sides of the longhouses and casting shadows into the square.

The silence was further shattered by the beat of a single great drum, summoning the leaders of the Iroquois nation as well as the common folk to the Great Council. They came in huge numbers, most of them Onondaga from this very castle, but others had accompanied their delegates. There were some Mohawk, more Seneca and a few Oneida mixing freely with their Onondaga cousins. Some seated themselves in the tribal areas, while others joined with their Onondaga cousins from the same clans, Turtle, Wolf or Bear. When seated about the fire, they began a low chant.

The great men of the nation were present. King Hendrick, sachem of the Mohawk, was seated next to his only rival for prestige among the Mohawks, Old Brant. Opposite the two Mohawks were the sachems of the other senior tribe, guardians of the western door of the Great Longhouse, the leaders of the Seneca, the Drunkard and his associate, Geneseo. Between the guardians of the doors sat the keepers of the fire, the leaders of the Onondaga—Otschiata and Kaghswughtioni. On their right were the Oneidas, Dagaheari and Conogquieson, and on the left of the Onondagas sat Soyeghtowa of the Cayuga. The Tuscarora sachems were present, sitting behind Dagaheari of the Oneida. They would listen, but they would not speak. For they were the children of Oneida.

The drums and the chanting ceased as Otschiata rose wearily to his feet. He was dressed in his best deerskin shirt and about his middle, beginning to sag with his advancing years, he wore the sacred wampum belt of the Confederation. He spoke in a voice whose vigor put the lie to his weary appearance.

14

"My brothers of the Council of the Six Nations, the Onondaga, keepers of the perpetual sacred Council fire, with which the fire before us was lit this evening, welcome you to our Council. We have been called here by our senior brothers, the Mohawk and the Seneca, to discuss the great issue of peace."

There was a murmur of concern among both the Mohawk and Seneca delegations. Clearly, Otschiata had deliberately put the emphasis on the word *peace* instead of mentioning its alternative. It was clear to all in his first words that the Onondaga would demand neutrality.

Otschiata then continued with his formal welcome, extolling the virtues of each of the other five tribes and calling on all of the castle to make their cousins feel as if the Council were meeting in their very own villages.

Geneseo spoke next. "I thank my brother Otschiata of the Onondaga for his generosity to us," he said. "The Seneca are a mighty people. No one encroaches on the Longhouse from the land where the sun sets," he said, glaring at both Hendrick and Brant of the Mohawk. "But the eastern door has been broken in, and its defenders routed by the English. The Seneca call upon the whole of the Confederation to come to the defense of our land and drive out the English once and for all."

He sat down, and there was much nodding and grunting of approval of his words among the Seneca spectators.

Soyeghtowa, the Cayuga, rose after Geneseo. He too castigated the English, and by inference the Mohawk, and demanded a war to drive them into the sea.

"The days of the Dutch, who took no land from us, are gone," he said. "We face now the land devourers—the English. They will not cease pushing at us until they destroy us. We must destroy them first."

Hendrick's turn was next. He rose. But before he could begin to speak, William Johnson, dressed as a full-fledged Mohawk, broke through the ranks of the spectators, his new tomahawk, dripping red paint, in his hand. He raced across the great square and at the far end, barely visible in the Council fire light, he smashed the axe into a torture pole. He ran back then, his eyes looking wildly to right and left and reflecting the flames.

"I demand my right as a warrior to sing my war song," he shouted in perfect Mohawk. "And I call upon all who love this nation to join me."

There were shouts of opposition from among the crowd,

but all knew that Johnson had been adopted as a son of the tribe that very day and was within his rights to call for his war song, even if his behavior was quite extraordinary and very rude.

Johnson did not wait for permission. He began his chant, a monotone rising in intensity as he told his story.

"It was the French," he chanted, "who were the enemy of the Six Nations. It was the devil, Champlain, who invaded their lands with the hated Algonquin and Huron and who killed many brave warriors with his gun—a weapon no Iroquois had ever seen before. It was the blackrobes who followed Champlain with their baptizing waters that brought the dreaded pox with them. The Mohawk killed most, but the few that lived seduced many more Mohawk to come and live with them in Montreal. It was the French," he said, "who forced their cousins the Huron to abandon old ways and to bring the furs only to the French—a procedure that surely would have destroyed all of the Iroquois if it had persisted. The Iroquois made war on the French from the very beginning. The French invaded the sacred lands of the Seneca in the past and the Seneca resisted. But now Geneseo was an old man and the Drunkard could no longer stand straight, much less lead his people to war. The Seneca had become weaklings. They now feared the French, where once the French had fled and hidden in their villages for fear of the very name Seneca."

Geneseo rose to speak, but Johnson was not finished. His song became louder and louder. His body began a rhythmic jerking, and soon the Mohawk warriors in the audience began to beat their hands on their thighs in time with Johnson's chant. He began to dance.

"I will fight the old way," he yelled. "I will bury my hatchet in the skull of the Frenchman. I will take his hair from him to my squaw and place it on my pole before my lodgings in front of my longhouse. I will eat his heart if he is brave and I will urinate on his body if he is a coward. I will caress my French captives with the burning fire and I will smell their skin scorch."

His eyes cast about wildly as he sang and danced; his body now glistened with sweat. The rhythmic clapping had even touched the Onondaga drummers, as they were caught up in the frenzy of Johnson's dance. The drums began to beat in rhythm with the movement of Johnson's feet.

Many Mohawk warriors rose to join Johnson in front of the Council fire. They, too, joined his dance and his chant, which had become now only the repeated phrase—"kill the French."

One by one they raced toward the pole where Johnson had buried his tomahawk, and they struck the pole with their own weapons, signaling their plans to join him in his war.

Old Brant and his son Nicus also joined the dancing warriors. Old Brant began to sing his own song, recounting his past victories and his scalping of the French enemy.

All eyes turned toward Hendrick. He glanced toward Dagaheari and the Oneida. Only his eyes betrayed the amusement that he felt at Johnson's performance. He might have expected as much from He Who Does Great Things. Then Hendrick rose and joined the men of his tribe, singing his own song and dancing to the rhythm.

Johnson felt himself transformed as he chanted and danced to the drums. He was no longer the Irishman, William Johnson. The ritual bath of the morning had cleansed him. The blood of the Mohawk now flowed through his veins, and he felt a blood lust course through him that could be satisfied only by sinking his knife into his enemy and taking out his heart. His ancestors, the Mohawk, had taken possession of him. All who had died unavenged at the hands of the French screamed in his head, "Kill, kill."

The drumming grew even louder, and one by one all of the other Mohawk warriors collapsed and fell back among the spectators. Eventually Johnson was alone in the center. His chest heaved in and out as he drew great breaths. His buckskins were soaked with sweat at the armpits and the small of his back; his bare legs quivered from weariness. Finally, his voice broke and his knees began to buckle. With one last cry he shouted, "All who are men among us and who remember the ghosts of their fathers will join with me to destroy the French and the blackrobes who killed our leaders and brought their foul diseases among us." With that shout he collapsed too.

He lay for some moments on the ground, his muscles quivering. Gradually the lust left him. He knew he had swayed the onlookers but as he glanced up, he saw that none of the Oneida and Tuscarora had joined in the dance. He had failed. There would be no war with France. The Mohawk had not swayed the Oneida and the Tuscarora. They would remain neutral, with the Onondaga. The Cayuga and the Seneca might wish war with England; the Mohawk might wish war with France, but the tribes could not act, and the

17

war parties on both sides had been frustrated and dared not thwart the demanded unanimity of the Council. Before his own dance, Johnson had felt sure of the support of Dagaheari —the Wild One—who so desperately wished war. But he had not joined him. Why? Johnson knew his performance had been brilliant. It had not even been a performance, for during those moments he had been a true Mohawk warrior. But someone had reached Dagaheari and promised him more than the satisfaction of blood lust. Johnson did not know who had undermined him, but he was determined to find out.

Two young men strolled together across the grass-covered parade ground below an earth embankment. Above their heads and piercing the embankment were the great guns of the Battery of New York. Both of the young men were in their early twenties. One was of slight build, with jet black hair and piercing blue eyes. Through one of his eyebrows ran a scar that was even faintly visible on his eyelid.

Stephen Nowell had just recently arrived in New York and was discovering the harbor front with his friend, Karl Stiegler.

Karl was almost diametrically opposed to Stephen in appearance. He was blond and stocky. His muscles always seemed on the verge of bulging loose from his garments, which would have fit loosely on the bodies of most men.

The two had paused in their trip to Fort George, the Governor's residence. Nowell had a sealed letter from Admiral Peter Warren to his kinsman, James Delancey, the acting Governor. The sight of the harbor opening up before them had caused them to seek a better vantage point, and they had climbed up the embankment and stood by one of the great guns that pointed out toward the harbor. From here they could see the whole of the vast inner harbor of New York. To their left were the tree-covered hills of the Long Island shore. To their right the muddy waters of the North River poured into the green sea water, creating intertwining patterns of brown and green.

The harbor was dotted with small islands. On one, Lone Island, later called Bedloe's Island, the foundation of the harbor's first lighthouse had been laid. Off in the distance huge Staten Island created a southwest shore for the harbor. Past Staten Island, beyond their vision, were the Narrows, the only exit to the outer harbor and the great ocean beyond.

"This place reminds me of home, Stefan," said Karl in his German-accented French.

18

Stephen paused before he answered. The words came immediately to mind, but the pull of the past flooded his head with all sorts of strong images. He remembered his first vague childhood recollections—living in the Jesuit House at Louisbourg. He remembered Sister Mary Louis, who had nursed him when he was ill and protected him when he was in danger. He remembered how she died. And he recalled her death with much guilt. He remembered morning meetings on a similar embankment at Louisbourg, overlooking its harbor. And he remembered talking to Karl of his plans to become a Jesuit. He would never forget his disastrous career as a missionary. The death of the Oneida chief and his responsibility for it were burned indelibly in his soul. He recalled the siege of his home at Louisbourg and the rescue of Karl from the torture inflicted on him by the mad Jesuit, Lalonde. All of this came in one great rush to his mind and, despite his mixed feelings, Stephen smiled at Karl.

"You still think of Louisbourg as home?"

Karl thrust his hands into the edge of his breeches and rocked back on his heels as he looked out to the sea. "This harbor is much bigger," said Karl. "And the town doesn't look very French. But from this vantage, looking out toward the sea, I feel homesick for that damn fog-ridden, rock-infested island we used to live on."

"Are you sorry you came with me, Karl?"

"Not really. I hadn't much choice. The Jesuit nearly killed me, and you saved me. By living with you, sponging off your income, I've gotten my strength back. I have you to thank for being alive."

"But we are blood brothers, Karl. You remember the ceremony," Stephen joked. "I had no choice but to save you," he said with mock weariness, trying to forestall any expression of gratitude Karl might be inclined to make.

Karl was quiet for some moments. He seemed more introspective now than before his ordeal. Stephen worried about him. His health had returned, but his good-natured, fun-loving disposition had been deeply altered by weeks of the most cruel tortures. There were only occasional flashes of the fun-loving boy.

"You know, Stefan," he said. "I have not really in my own mind made the same break with France and Canada that you have made."

Stephen was surprised. "After what they've done to you? As long as I have known you, Karl, you've made no bones about your feelings against the French."

19

"I think you misunderstand me. My loyalty is to you and to the establishment of Fort Vaughan. Once we're finished, I think I will head back home to Canada. I've cursed the French, but only because they mistreated us Swiss soldiers. I didn't desert France so that I might join up with England. That was your choice, not mine."

"But you've promised to help me on the Mohawk."

"And I will. Somebody will have to speak German for you. No one will ever understand your version of my native tongue. But be aware, I do it out of loyalty to you, Stefan, not out of any love for the English."

The wind caught at Stephen's black hair and blew it into his eyes. He brushed it back with his hand so that he might look at his friend's face.

"I understand, Karl," he said finally. "But I wish it were otherwise, and I will work to make sure that we are never on opposite sides. You and I are really one."

Karl threw his heavy arm about Stephen's shoulder.

"We're a team, Stefan—you and I. No one can separate us. But Admiral Warren will have us both in irons if you don't get on with your errand to the Lieutenant Governor."

"I have Warren's letter here in my pocket," said Stephen, "and we are well on our way to Fort George. You can even see the Governor's house from up here." He turned to his right and pointed down toward the outer works of the fort, which guarded the tip of Manhattan Island. "It's no effort at all to work over from here right now."

"Let's do it, my friend," said Karl. "We have other work. Your grandfather's old servants are making preparations for us to sail in two days' time. I've much ordering of supplies to do."

"We still need some means of transportation," said Stephen.

"That's the job we left to you, Stefan. So get on with it." He gave Stephen a playful shove, which started him running down the embankment. He could not stop until he reached the bottom.

"What will you be doing while you wait for me?"

Karl laughed. "Need you ask? This is the Battery, the most notorious gathering place for ladies of the streets in all of North America. I think I'll just bide my time right here."

Stephen left Karl and walked from the Battery embankment and across the training ground to Pearl Street. He paused to allow an elegantly decorated carriage pass by. A woman was seated in the shadows of the carriage. Stephen could barely see her. But she saw him clearly. Her violet eyes examined him from head to foot. She ordered the driver to pause at the side of the road. Stephen passed behind the carriage and then walked onto the new brick-paved sidewalk, which led to the fort. She called to the driver. "Henry, I've a message for Governor Delancey. You tell his Pieter that a young man who just entered the fort and is now approaching his house is to be my escort at his ball or I won't be there."

Stephen entered Fort George through the Governor's garden entrance. He was halted by a mousy-looking, red-coated sentry, whose presence was one of the few signs in the relaxed atmosphere of the City of New York that England and her colonies were actually at war with France.

Stephen was stopped again at the front redoubt entry of the fort itself. But a letter addressed to the Lieutenant Governor, who, during the absence of the Governor in England, was actually commander-in-chief in New York, and a letter signed by Admiral Warren were enough to gain him entry into the walls of the small fortress. The sentry pointed to Stephen's left, toward a comfortable brick and stone house, when Stephen requested directions to the Governor's mansion.

James Delancey put down his copy of the *New York Gazette*. The account it gave of the capture of Louisbourg had stirred him. He was very delighted that he had used his considerable influence with the Governor to have New York send a train of siege guns to help their Yankee neighbors. As a man of French-Protestant background, he found it easier to consider helping New Englanders than it was for most of his Dutch confreres in the government of New York.

As Lieutenant Governor of New York, he dealt frequently with the Van Rensselaers, the Van Cortlandts and the Schuylers, the Albany aristocrats, with their inherited patroonships and their involvement with the Indian trade of the West. They had little liking for New Englanders, whom they regarded as dangerously egalitarian. And as more and more Yankees poured in from Massachusetts and Connecticut into their lands, demanding freehold rights, the Dutch landlords grew more and more hostile. If the French raided their damned fishing boats, so much the better. At times even the great English land barons like the Livingstons and the Morrises would speak in the same manner about the "bloody Yankees," almost as if they, rather than the French, were the enemy.

21

But Delancey knew that if the French should descend the old war route of the Iroquois—down the lakes toward Albany —all the great patroons would look toward New England for help. Only by gestures such as his in the Louisbourg siege could New York have reasonable hope of receiving such aid.

He knew he had become estranged from the New York aristocracy, however. His wife's plans for the ball next evening had been timed with his knowledge that the widow Schuyler was in New York City. She was due to return to Albany next week. Cornelia Schuyler, widow of John Schuyler, Jr., had been a Van Cortlandt before her marriage, and she was old man Schuyler's favorite daughter-in-law. What was more, her twelve-year-old boy Philip would make an excellent catch for a young Delancey daughter someday. But somehow or other he needed to achieve peace, and this opening move toward the Schuylers was an integral part of his plan.

Delancey had increased his prestige in the colony, nevertheless, by the Louisbourg success. Admiral Peter Warren had been hailed both in England and New York as the great hero of the siege, and Peter Warren was married to Delancey's sister.

But then there was that madman on the Mohawk, Warren's nephew, Johnson, who ran around naked and did God knows what with Indian women and went on war parties just like one of the savages. True, his influence with the Indians was becoming profound, far outdoing that of the Schuylers, who had for generations been New York Indian Commissioners, but even that was part of the problem and part of the reason for the alienation from the Schuylers. The animosity between Johnson and the Schuylers was greater now, for Johnson had taken the side of the settlers and the settlers' demand for freehold, even siding with the damn Palatinate Germans in the Mohawk Valley against the claims to the lands by the Dutch aristocrats.

Somehow or other he would have to smooth over the damage Johnson had done to his position without losing the advantages Johnson's influence had given the family.

There was a soft knock on the door of the study. The door opened quietly and Pieter, Delancey's black house slave, stepped inside. "There is a gentleman by the name of Stephen Nowell arrived, sir. He has asked to see you."

"Damn inconvenient time for someone to come calling," said Delancey.

"He apologizes, sir. Says he bears letters from Admiral Warren."

"Ah, Warren. Send him in, Pieter."

"Yes, sir. There is something else, sir. A message from Mrs. Cornelia Schuyler."

"Yes."

"This Mr. Nowell, sir. She wants him to escort her to the ball."

"How the hell am I supposed to arrange that?"

"The lady made no suggestions, sir." Pieter hesitated but then screwed up his courage and continued. "If she doesn't have Mr. Nowell, she says she is not coming."

Delancey exploded. "Damn the woman, damn all women."

Pieter winced. But Delancey cooled down quickly. "Tell the lady she gets what she wants—she always gets what she wants."

"Shall I send in Mr. Nowell?"

"Send him in."

Stephen stepped into Delancey's study. The leather-bound books that filled the bookcases impressed him. He had seen nothing like it in any home in Boston. The furnishings and drapes were of costly damask. The chairs were of the finest European design. The New York elite, he concluded, were richer than their counterparts in New England.

Stephen shook hands with Delancey and introduced himself as Admiral Warren's messenger and as agent of the New England merchant, William Vaughan.

Delancey took the letter from his brother-in-law and placed it on the desk.

"I have not had the honor of Mr. Vaughan's acquaintance. I have written to him and worked with him to obtain the guns for the siege."

"He is like a father to me, sir. We were together at Louisbourg," said Stephen. "And those guns you obtained for us were put to good use knocking down the walls of the west gate of the fortress."

"I am delighted to hear of it, Mr. Nowell, and I am delighted to meet one of the heroes of the siege. I am sure everyone in New York would be happy to meet one of the young heroes. My wife is planning a ball to be held in our home tomorrow evening. I would be very honored if you would attend. What a shame Mr. Vaughan is not with you. I would have liked to have him as a guest of honor as well. I have heard from my brother-in-law that Mr. Vaughan has

23

purchased a share of Admiral Warren's Mohawk Valley lands near Fort Hunter."

"Yes, sir," said Stephen. "I'll be developing and managing his farm for him. I am looking for settlers to live as tenants on the lands as well."

Delancey laughed. "Easier said than done, young man. Peter Warren's nephew, William Johnson, tried that for Peter some years ago. Tenant farming is failing in the face of freehold madness. You can't get Yankees or these Germans to think of anything except owning their own land. William Vaughan will have a long wait if he intends to get rich from tenant farmers."

"What did Johnson do?" asked Stephen.

"That savage! As best as I can determine, he did nothing but sleep with Indian women and run about the forest playing warrior. Peter Warren is disgusted with him—just keeps running up deficits on the estates. Now he has abandoned Admiral Warren's farm and opened a trading post across the Mohawk on the north side, on his own lands. He calls it Fort Johnson. My sources tell me there is always a yardful of lazy savages hanging around his front door."

"Well, I will try to do better for Mr. Vaughan, sir."

"You could not do much worse, although I must admit Johnson does have a way with the savages. They will be very useful allies against the French. But enough of this talk. Will you be able to come to my wife's party tomorrow?" he asked offhandedly.

"I would be delighted, sir," said Stephen.

"Good; the widow Schuyler needs an escort. I'm sure I can count on you."

Stephen's face fell. He did not fancy escorting any widow. But he did not know how to get out of the trap.

Delancey rang for Pieter, indicating that the interview had been concluded. The black slave entered the room and showed Stephen through the house and to the street.

Stephen was dressed in the best clothing he could scrounge from the shops in town on such short notice. But he still felt relatively shabby. He waited in the hallway of the Mason's Arms Inn on Marketfield Street, where he and his party awaited transportation up the Hudson.

The carriage that he had seen yesterday, drawn by perfectly matched chestnut-colored horses, drew up in front of the inn. A porter approached the coach door and then turned toward Stephen.

24

"Mr. Nowell, sir, it's Mrs. Schuyler's carriage for you."

Stephen walked over to the carriage door, which was opened by the porter. He stepped upon the two fold-down stairs and took his seat across from the most beautiful woman he had ever seen.

She was dressed in a black velvet evening coat, which was thrown over her shoulders and which partially covered a dazzling mauve-colored ball gown. The front of the dress was cut so low that even the rather blasé New York aristocracy would be shocked when they saw her this evening. Cornelia Schuyler was always one to build from strength in all of her dealings, and Cornelia's superb breasts were one of the strengths that she frequently called upon. Her hair was covered with an impressive white wig. The cream-colored skin of her bosom was adorned with a necklace of amethysts and small diamonds. She was about forty years old. She wore makeup but needed no enhancement. Her eyes were the color of the amethysts that she wore about her neck. She smiled a dazzling smile at Stephen, who did not quite know how even to greet her.

"Mr. Nowell, my cousin James told me you were young and handsome, but he failed to stress just how young and how handsome you really are."

Stephen bowed his head in acknowledgment and smiled back at her, although clearly overwhelmed. "It is extremely kind of you, madam, to take me along."

"Not at all, Mr. Nowell."

"Please," he interrupted. "You must call me Stephen."

"Very well, Stephen, and you must call me Cornelia. And you are my escort for this evening. A widow like myself feels so out of place at these affairs—all the young couples enjoying themselves and the older folks sitting around and watching. I am not a person who cares much for sitting and watching, Stephen, are you?"

She did not wait for his response. "Of course you're not—you're young. Well, tonight you and I will be young together. I refuse to be treated as some old lady whose time has come and gone."

As she talked, barely stopping for him to answer, the carriage passed through the darkened New York streets. They rode onto Broad Street and turned north, passing the strange-looking Dutch-style red brick houses that lined the streets. They seemed to Stephen to be facing the wrong way, with their sides facing the front. They rode up rutted Broad Street to Wall Street and crossed it, then continued on up

25

Nassau Street until they reached the palisade that crossed the island at the northern extremity of the town and passed through the gate.

But well before the palisade, an observer could tell that they were about to leave the city. The further north they traveled, the fewer houses they saw. And those houses that were situated on the roads were surrounded by larger and larger garden plots. Once outside the palisade, however, they were in rural New York. In this part of the island of Manhattan the paved streets and sidewalks disappeared and were replaced by a dirt road running northeast. Along this road the great landowners and merchants of the town had their farms, or boweries.

"How far is it, Mrs. Schuyler—I mean Cornelia," he corrected himself—"to Mr. Delancey's farm?"

"Oh, we have a long way to go yet."

He noted for the first time that she spoke English with a slight Dutch accent.

Stephen could not take his eyes off her and Cornelia relished every glance. It seemed to him that her violet eyes flashed at him as often as the amethysts that rested on her bosom.

"You must tell me about yourself, Stephen," she said. "Where are you from?"

"Originally from Boston," he answered. "But I've traveled much."

"You're a lucky boy," she interrupted. "I've been stuck here in New York since I was a child. The men of our family—I'm a Van Cortlandt by birth, you know—are educated at Oxford or at Cambridge. But we women, we are tutored at home. At least we're not turned into dumb hausfraus like the Van Rensselaers—not that they could do very much more—such stupid cows, the Van Rensselaer girls. Where have you traveled, Stephen?"

"Well, I have been to Paris and I have spent some days at Versailles."

Cornelia was clearly impressed. She switched immediately into French.

"I envy you," she said. "Is it as glorious as I've heard?"

"Every bit as glorious and as extravagant as you've heard, madame," Stephen responded in French.

"Your accent is unusual," she replied.

"I grew up in Acadia—in New France—"

"You are a Canadian? Here in New York while we are war with France?"

"As I said to begin with, I'm from Boston. I was taken by Indians as a child and raised in Canada. I have only recently returned."

"Your family must have been overjoyed at your return."

"Unfortunately, I found them all dead," he responded.

They remained silent some long moments as the carriage bounced along the badly rutted country road.

"My cousin's farm is just down the road a ways now," she said in English. "It is near the village of Greenwich."

There were other carriages on the road now, also making their way to the Delancey bowery. The Schuyler coach turned through the entry gate of the estate and followed the driveway to the main house. It was large, by New York standards. It had two floors, and a wing had been added to each side of what had been the original building. The house was of stone and of Dutch country design. Off to the left of the house, beside the barn, a giant windmill, outlined by the moon, turned its arms slowly in the evening breeze, dominating the landscape.

Stephen was unsure how this house, even though grand by provincial standards, would be capable of holding so many guests, but Stephen's view of a formal dance had been learned in Europe, where he had been educated at the Jesuit college in Paris. Provincial New York had different notions.

To a Delancey, a ball was in fact an informal gathering held in the large drawing room, stripped of its furniture. Many of the guests, dressed less well than Stephen, attended the Delancey affair as an opportunity to mingle with the great names of New York. They tended to stay along the walls of the drawing room, sipping some of Delancey's best cider. Many of these guests were merchants and their wives, who had no conception of how to perform the steps effortlessly danced by Van Cortlandts, Livingstons and Phillipses.

In the dining room and in the kitchen, there were guests who had arrived by horseback and who sat sampling the delicacies the Delancey slaves had prepared. Some of them were simple freeholders or craftsmen from the city. Delancey courted all voters in New York, rich and modest of means alike. He was the leader of the Popular Party. It was the folks in the kitchen who voted for him; the gentry in the drawing room, who were his relatives, close and distant, rarely did.

Stephen climbed down from the carriage when it pulled up in front of the main entrance to the house, and then he turned to give Cornelia Schuyler his hand. The torches held by slaves shone brightly, and Stephen could hear gasps from the

27

guests who still mingled in the front yard when Cornelia appeared on the steps of the coach. As they entered the house together, the guests of lower status seemed to melt before her as she handed her evening cape to Stephen and gracefully glided into the drawing room, almost in time with the string orchestra, which played a minuet.

She scandalized the women and disappointed the men by dancing only with Stephen. When the formal steps of the dance required her to face another partner, he found her head turned in another direction, seeking the eyes of the young man and knowing full well that his eyes would be searching for hers. When they touched hands as partners, she squeezed his tightly. When the music changed to that of the country, she insisted on showing him the steps and horrified the entire gentry by sweeping him into her arms at the end of the country jig.

When the dancing halted and food platters of pieces of roasted pork with bread and some cheeses, along with pirated French red wine, were placed at strategic spots in the drawing room, Cornelia and Stephen ate together. She said nothing. He stared at her with longing. But he was still shy. She merely smiled at his reticence and told him how charming she found him.

They danced late into the night. The craftsmen guests and the merchants returned to the city. But the guests who were related to Delancey, which included almost all of the aristocrats present, were to spend the night. Stephen was led by a house slave to an attic room, along with three young Delancey nephews. But as he started to follow the boys up the steep attic stairs, he heard Cornelia call to him. He turned back and saw her enter her room. He looked behind him. No one was watching. He followed her to her door, which was still half open. He hesitated and then scratched softly on the oak paneling of the door, as he had learned to do in France. He did so, not because of any formal manners, but because he was very nervous about the propriety of a man standing in the bedroom doorway of a beautiful woman like Cornelia Schuyler, and he didn't wish to make a loud noise.

She deepened his nervousness appreciably by calling loudly for him to enter the room. When he did, he saw that she was alone.

"Come, my shy one," she said. "Come here and sit by Cornelia on the bed."

Stephen swallowed hard and started to follow her instructions.

"No," she said, somewhat annoyed. "Close the door behind you, Stephen."

He did as he was told.

She had removed her wig already and her hair, which was even a darker black than Stephen's, fell down around her shoulders.

Stephen sat next to her on the bed. He had to pull himself up, and even though he was almost six feet tall, his feet still dangled, not quite touching the floor. Cornelia had used the tiny footstool to achieve her perch. Stephen looked into Cornelia's face. She turned her head away. She had reached the age when it had become necessary to conceal cleverly the little imperfections that had begun to appear. She did not like any man looking directly into her face at so close a range. But she knew how to divert the young man's eyes.

She had unbuttoned the back of her gown before Stephen had entered the room. Most of her bosom was now revealed. It had the desired effect on Stephen. He stared at her still, but his eyes had lowered. He felt a familiar stirring in his groin. She took his hand in hers and laid it on her breast. Now he was very aroused. He bent forward and kissed first one breast and then the other.

She grabbed him around the neck and pulled his upper body toward her, burying his face in her chest. He fumbled clumsily with the remaining buttons on her gown. She pulled his hand away, afraid he might rip off buttons that could not be replaced.

"Here, let me do it," she said. She slipped off the bed onto her feet. She kicked off her shoes and silk stockings. Reaching behind her back, she unbuttoned as many of the buttons as she could reach, but then she turned to Stephen.

"Help me with the rest, Stephen," she said, "but be careful."

He did as he was told and when he had finished, she stepped out of the dress. She was wearing only a chemise underneath. She soon tossed it aside and stood naked before him.

He moved to climb off the bed also but she stopped him. She knelt on the floor before him. One by one, she pulled off his shoes and stockings. When his feet were bare, she took them into her warm hands and began to massage them. Then she rose and began to undo his breeches and slide them off his hips. She smiled broadly when she realized he wore nothing underneath them.

He was completely aroused by now. She continued her

massage, first the calves of his legs and then his thighs. She took him into her hands and began to rub gently. Stephen tried to pull away because he knew if he did not, it would be over—all too soon. But she would not let go. He lay back and moaned, tossing his head from side to side. And then it was all over.

He waited a moment and raised himself on his elbows. He wanted to apologize, but he saw her smiling at him.

"Now, my little boy," she said, "now that we have that out of the way, we can begin in earnest. Now it's Cornelia's turn."

Stephen felt something pushing at him in his sleep. He was drifting, as if floating in the warm sea. His face, his tongue, his lips, all seem bathed in warmth. He wanted the sensation to continue, but again there was a sharp prodding against his stomach. He opened his eyes. It was Cornelia.

"Stephen," she whispered, "it's time for you to go back to your bed."

He looked up sleepily. It was still dark. She was next to him in the bed. He smiled at her and reached out his hand to stroke her breast.

"Not now," she said, pulling away.

"When?"

"When I tell you, that's when. Back in New York—tonight —after we return. You must visit me at my sister-in-law Schuyler's rooms on the Broadway—near the English church. She won't be home this evening. Now go back to your bed before someone discovers you're missing."

Stephen was not satisfied. The pleasure Cornelia had introduced him to that night was still affecting him. Reluctantly he climbed off the bed.

She started to laugh when she saw that he was still in an aroused condition. He found it difficult to walk. He dropped to his knees, looking for his clothes. His coat, breeches, shirt, shoes and stockings were both on the floor and under the bed covering.

He dressed quietly and started to leave. Cornelia called him back. He bent over her as she lay back on the pillows.

"Kiss me goodnight, Stephen."

He bent low, touched her lips to his. She forced her tongue between his lips and patted his still bulging groin with her hand.

"Tonight," she said, after he pulled away, gasping for breath.

30

He smiled at her and tiptoed out of the door into the hallway. He found the attic stairs and climbed into the loft. The three young men were sprawled all over the huge bed, and there was no way Stephen could have found any room for himself. He sat down on the floor with his back against the wall and closed his eyes. The images of the past evening flooded into his head. He smiled to himself.

Stephen arrived half an hour early for his appointment with Cornelia Schuyler. He rang the bell at the front door. Some few moments later, the door swung open. Stephen had expected that only Cornelia would be at home and was surprised to be facing not her, but a much younger woman—a girl his own age, nineteen or even younger.

"Excuse me," he said, "I hope I have the right house. Is this the Schuyler residence?"

"Yes, come in, won't you? You are expected," she said.

Stephen stepped through the door and the servant led him from the hallway into a richly furnished sitting room.

Stephen studied the girl intently. She was not tall, about five feet four inches. Her hair was a rich brown, and she wore it piled up on top of her head. Her eyes were hazel and warm looking. Her cheekbones were prominent and touched faintly with a natural red coloring. Her chin was pointy, but it gave her whole face an almost heart-shaped appearance. She smiled almost sadly at Stephen and turned away, saying, "Wait here. Mrs. Schuyler will be down shortly."

Stephen watched her leave. He found her to have a great deal of dignity and charm. Then he became annoyed with himself. What was he turning into? Cornelia had given her body to him last night. She had given him pleasures he had never dreamed of, and on the very next day he was looking longingly after her maid. But shortly afterward, Cornelia entered the study and after they had retired by the back stairway to her bedroom, Stephen forgot all about the maid.

He lay back on her bed as she brushed her black hair in front of her dressing table mirror. She looked at him in the mirror.

"Are you sleeping, Stephen?" she asked.

"Never with you about, Cornelia. You never let me sleep," he joked.

"Stop teasing. Cousin James tells me you want to bring your party to the Mohawk. I've hired a sailing packet and I want you to come north with me to Albany."

Stephen sat up in the bed.

"That would be ideal," he said. "But will you have room for my party?"

"How many of you are there?" she asked.

"There are Karl, George and Hannah—and three families of German settlers and their goods."

"Who are these people?" she asked, turning from the mirror to face him.

"Karl is my friend. He is a Swiss—a former soldier and my right arm when it comes to establishing the Vaughan estate. Hannah and George were my grandfather's servants. They go where I go."

"All right," she said, "they may come. But the Germans will have to travel separately. I have no room for them."

Stephen worried aloud for a few minutes. He could not afford to leave the Germans. It was hard to find willing tenants. Perhaps Karl could accompany them and come on later. Maybe only Hannah and George would need to come with him.

"How old is this Karl?" asked Cornelia.

"About my age—a little older."

"Is he good looking?" she asked, smiling.

"Not as good looking as me," he joked.

"Oh, well, I guess I'll have to be happy sailing upriver with only one good-looking boy in my bed," she laughed.

"What about those traveling with you?"

"They will have their own cabins. Margaret, my sister-in-law, insists on it. I think it is because she suspects she snores at night and wants none of us to know it."

"Does she?"

"Louder than any old man. The whole house can hear her. She insists on living in the family house on the Saratoga Flats patent. You wouldn't catch me there. It's the farthest northern settlement in New York. It would be the first place the French or Indians would attack if they came down from Montreal. Then there will be my children."

"You have children?" Stephen said in surprise.

"Of course. Didn't you know? I have a twelve-year-old son Philip. And I guess you met my daughter Katherine today. She answered the front door."

Stephen looked at her in surprise.

"Don't look at me like I was some old hag," she yelled, very angrily.

Stephen didn't know what to say.

32

"She's not really my daughter. She is my dead husband's daughter. Well, not even really that. She's his bastard. He insisted on legitimizing her and bringing her into our house. I'd throw the little bitch out, but my esteemed father-in-law, her grandfather, won't hear of it. He insists she live with us, right in our Albany mansion. The girl is so snotty—pretending to be so dignified, when she is no more than John Schuyler's mistake with some whore in heat."

Her tone had taken on such venom that Stephen was shocked. When she spoke of her stepdaughter, the hate poured from her and she became ugly. She caught herself and saw that Stephen was staring at her. She rose from the dressing table and walked over toward the bed. She opened the front of her dressing gown and let it slip off of her shoulders onto the floor.

Stephen was still disturbed by the attack on the girl and he was distracted. He thought the girl had possessed great dignity, and the glimpse of Cornelia's hate had scared him. But he had little time to dwell on his concerns. He gasped when he felt the warmth of her mouth on him.

Stephen left the Schuyler rooms and stepped out onto the street. He had told Karl that he would meet him at the tavern taproom on Marketfield Street. He walked down the streets, which were crowded with strollers. The sidewalks were paved with brick and set off from the street by wooden posts painted white. The streets were paved with cobblestone and sloped toward the center, where the drainage stagnated in the fall sun. There was a new sewer under Broad Street. The combination of the drainage, the sewer and the horse droppings made Stephen wrinkle his nose. He much preferred the clean air of the woods to the crowds and noise of New York.

Carriage wheels thundered on the cobblestones, splashing drainage water up toward the sidewalks. A carriage careened into a wagon of apples pulled by a vendor, sending the wagon onto its side and apples spilling onto the paving.

The apple man screamed oaths at the carriage driver and started to chase him down the street. Stephen picked up a red apple. He polished it on his jacket sleeve and continued his walk to Marketfield Street.

He was late for his meeting with Karl and the German settlers. They were not in the taproom. Stephen climbed the stairs to his room. He opened the door and stepped inside. There was a rustling in the bed. Karl sat bolt upright; his

33

blond hair was mussed and falling over his face. A red-haired girl of about eighteen sat up beside him. They were both naked.

Karl swung his feet over the side of the bed and dropped to the floor. He picked up the girl's dress and draped it over his arm. He reached for her waist and lifted her high in the air. The muscles in his great arms bulged and he held her aloft.

"Rita, Mädchen," he said, "that's all for today. My great and good friend has finally left his whore and so I guess that is a signal for me to send mine scurrying." He set her on her feet and handed her her dress. She slipped it over her head and, smiling shyly at Stephen, she walked quietly out of the room.

Karl fell back down on the bed. "I got tired of waiting, Stefan."

"I've arranged passage. I go with Hannah and George. We will go on the Schuylers' boat. I can take half our goods. You come later."

Karl's face went red. "What do you mean—come later?"

"You and the German families follow in a later boat."

"What boat?"

"I don't know yet. I'll have to arrange that."

"That's dumb, Stefan," said Karl, switching to French as he became angry. "Neither one of us should be left behind. We need your English and my German to communicate with the merchants and with our tenants. This is not like you. Why are you doing this?"

Stephen blushed under Karl's attack.

"It's the Schuyler woman, isn't it? You're deserting your friends for that woman."

"I'm not. I'll make all the necessary arrangements. I'll make it all work before we leave."

Karl walked across the room and picked up his breeches. He put them on in silence. He was angry but there was little he could do about it. Stephen was finally indulging his instincts, something Karl, unfettered by vows in his youth, had indulged for years. Perhaps it would all work out after all.

The sailing packet left the East Dock Street mooring at low tide and pushed its bow into the East River. The current picked the packet up like a piece of driftwood and forced it along, down toward the Battery and into the broad part of the inner bay. Then the sail caught the wind and the packet tacked toward the New Jersey mud flats. It came about and again the captain tacked, this time toward the northeast. By then, with the morning wind gusting and creating whitecaps on the water, they had rounded the Battery and entered the mud-colored waters of the Hudson.

The river was wide but not so wide as the bay, and the tacks were now shorter. But for the next eight hours, as they sailed north, their progress would rely not only on the wind but also on the ocean tide, as they pushed up the Hudson from the sea.

Stephen stood by the railing of the packet watching the shoreline of the city fade behind him. He held a mug of ale in his hand. He had left Karl behind, with passage for himself and their German families booked on the next Albany packet boat. He knew Stiegler had been unhappy with the arrangement. He was annoyed with the delay, but he was hardly in a position to criticize Stephen's affair with the widow. He had been involved with more women in any one week than Stephen had in his entire life.

Karl had stayed behind. Hannah and George, however, shared Stephen's cabin with him. Not that he expected to be sleeping in it—not with Cornelia on board with her own cabin.

Stephen's reverie was interrupted by a shout and a shove. A stocky boy of about twelve years went racing by him, pushing him against the railing, rushing toward the bow of the packet and out of sight. The girl he had first met at the Schuyler house came rushing up the steps from the cabin below deck, calling, "Philip, come back here right away." She was shouting and laughing at the same time. She stopped in her tracks as soon as she saw Stephen.

"Did you see Master Philip on deck, Mr. Nowell?" she asked.

"That depends," he said.

She looked at him quizzically.

"That depends on what he did," said Stephen.

She walked over toward him. "He set Bruno free."

"Bruno?"

"His snake. He set him free in our cabin and refuses to recapture him. There's no way I am going back in there until he does."

It was clear from her laughter that she wasn't all that worried about Bruno and that she and Philip had come to terms about the snake in the past. Philip was having a bit of fun with her now.

Stephen was captivated by her smile, how fresh and young

35

she looked with her brown hair blowing across her face when the river winds caught it.

The packet had tacked again; its boom groaned as it swung about, and the bow of the boat now faced the high cliffs on the New Jersey shore.

Stephen pointed toward them.

"They are like a natural fortress," he said over the wind.

"They're called the Palisades," she responded.

"It's very nice here on deck, but Cornelia will not be happy at all if she hears that I've let Philip out of our cabin. I better find him and go back below."

"He can't come to any harm. We're sailing up a river, not braving the North Atlantic."

"You don't know Cornelia." She blushed very red after she realized what she had said.

Stephen knew that his relationship with her stepmother was not a well-kept secret, even within the family.

"She's very possessive of Philip," she said.

The boy reappeared from the bow of the packet and started to walk toward Stephen and his sister warily. His ruddy face broke into an enormous grin.

"Couldn't catch me," he said in Dutch.

"Speak English, Philip. Mr. Nowell does not know Dutch. It is impolite to use it in front of him."

"Hello, Philip," Stephen said, extending his hand.

Philip shook it warmly.

"My mother says that you're a Yankee, Mr. Nowell, but you seem a fairly pleasant man. You don't speak through your nose and you don't stink of dung. Are you sure you're a Yankee?"

Stephen laughed. "You have a rather prejudiced view of New Englanders, boy. Well, maybe it was those years I spent in France or with the Indians or in Canada that made me different from the rest of them."

"Did you live with the Indians?" asked Philip, with his eyes growing wide.

"With the Oneida," answered Stephen.

"My family are the Indian Commissioners for New York," he said. "My grandfather, John Schuyler, is the most important man in New York when it comes to Indians."

Stephen said nothing to the boy, but he had heard much talk in the city of how that strange man, William Johnson, was undermining Schuyler's dominance in Indian affairs.

"Philip, you must go below now," said the girl. There was a firmness in her voice that the boy recognized. The game was

36

over. Now she would demand obedience. He looked annoyed. He wanted to continue his conversation with Nowell.

"Philip," she threatened.

"For Christ's sake," he said again in Dutch and scurried away when she raised her hand at him. He moved toward the stairs to the lower deck and the cabins.

"And find Bruno," she shouted after him.

"It's a strange name for a snake," said Stephen after the boy had gone.

"Oh," she laughed, "and what would you call a snake?"

"I don't know," said Stephen, smiling. "I guess it sounds more like a dog's name."

"It was. But Cornelia made him get rid of Bruno the dog, and so now we have Bruno the snake."

"I'd have thought she'd have liked a snake even less."

"She would if she knew about him—her—whatever, but she doesn't."

Once again the packet, coming close to the Jersey shore, had tacked and was now pointing toward the heights of Manhattan and the village of Harlem.

The girl stood next to him by the railing of the boat. The waters of the river were calmer than those of New York Bay, but still the wind churned up some whitecaps. "Those things you said to Philip, were they true? I mean about living with Indians?" asked Katherine.

"I was an Indian captive as a boy. I lived most of my life with Jesuit priests in Canada."

"You're a Papist?"

"Is that worse than Philip's Yankee?" he asked, looking into her face and smiling.

She was embarrassed by her own question. "I didn't mean anything by it; it's just I've never talked to a Papist before."

"I guess I'm best described as a former Papist. Even worse, I became a Jesuit."

Now she was truly shocked and intrigued at the same time. "You're not a priest!"

"No, I left the order and Canada well before I became a priest. I discovered who I really was, and I came back to New England. My parents were already dead, but I met my grandfather. He was very kind to me, but he's dead now. I'm trying to establish a new life for myself on the Mohawk."

"Mr. Nowell—"

"Please call me Stephen," he interrupted.

"Stephen," she began again. "You and I seem to have much in common. My parents are dead also."

"You have a stepmother."

"Yes," she said with surprising bitterness. "I have a step-mother. Cornelia doesn't like me. I don't know why. I have tried everything I can to please her. But nothing satisfies her."

She could see the disturbed look on his face and so she changed the topic.

"My grandfather is a man of great importance in New York. He rarely speaks to me, but I think he just doesn't know how to deal with his son's bastard daughter. I think he cares for me despite my background. Except for Philip, I really don't have any family."

"We seem to be two rather lonely orphans," said Stephen, looking at her. "Why don't we agree to be friends?"

"I don't know if that's possible," she said. "I don't think Cornelia will allow it."

Stephen bristled. "I don't think your stepmother will attempt to determine my friends for me."

"If that's what you think, Stephen, then you really don't know her. If she knew you and I were talking like this, she would come between us. I am nineteen years old. I have never been allowed to go to any of the dances and parties, either in Albany or in New York. My stepmother can't face the thought of a young man paying any attention to me."

"Well, I'm paying attention."

She smiled at him. "You won't for long if she discovers it."

The ship continued up the Hudson as they talked. The steep cliffs of the New Jersey side gave way to rounded hills. The river narrowed and then broadened to a great bay, or sea, as the Dutch would have called it.

Stephen and Katherine spent almost the whole morning together. He teased her, but she almost never laughed. When she thought something funny, she gave an amused smile. Stephen realized that she was enormously shy and insecure. She was almost like a child—very uncertain of herself and her skills. He stared at her far more than at the landscape as they sailed northward. He liked what he saw very much. Her skin was now rosy from the wind, but it gave her face a healthy glow. Her eyes had a softness to them and they filled with tears at the slightest suggestion of trouble or of emotional pain. Her brown hair continued to blow across her face until finally she tied it in a knot behind her head.

The cabin door blew open and Cornelia Schuyler called to

Stephen to help her come up the stairs to the deck. She was terrified of even the slightest roll of the river packet boat.

Stephen left Katherine's side and walked over to the cabin door to offer Cornelia his hand. As he turned back to look at Katherine, he saw that she had gone forward to the front of the boat and out of their sight.

"I can't bear boats, Stephen," complained Cornelia.

She was dressed in a white chiffon gown and held a white sun parasol. She was wearing rouge, and Stephen couldn't help compare its artificial redness to the natural complexion of the younger girl. Yet she was striking, and every sailor on deck turned to stare at her beauty.

"Come walk the decks with me, Stephen. Hold my arm so I don't stumble."

Stephen did as she requested. He noted that Katherine watched their path carefully, always keeping her distance until she saw her opportunity to pass by them and return to her cabin inconspicuously. But she did not escape observation.

"Look at the girl sneaking around like that. I do believe the child is touched. She is so backward. Sometimes I wonder if it is all right to trust Philip to her."

"Oh, she seems quite all right to me," said Stephen.

Cornelia looked at him quizzically but kept right on questioning Katherine's intelligence.

Stephen began to find her words annoying. "She seems quite good with your son," he said.

"When did you see them together?" she asked.

"They were both on deck earlier this morning. He's a rambunctious young man and Katherine seems to know how to handle him."

"They were on deck! That bitch!" she yelled, her face contorted with rage. "I warned her never to let the boy on deck. He could have been hurt or he could have fallen overboard—the impossible little whore."

"Cornelia," Stephen said angrily. "She has done nothing to deserve that kind of talk. Twelve-year-old boys need exercise; they can't remain cooped up in a cabin."

Cornelia turned to Stephen and looked at him coldly. "I didn't request advice from you, Stephen. When I want your advice, I will ask for it. You are my partner in bed, but you will not tell me how to run my life, how to run my daughter's life or my son's life. I want your body—not your advice."

Stephen stared at her, stunned. His face reddened with

anger. His infatuation with Cornelia Schuyler was over at that moment, as suddenly ended by a glimpse of one aspect of her as it had begun with the glimpse of another. He was only a source of physical pleasure to her. He could not condemn her attitude. He realized that he himself had shared it, that he had enjoyed her body as much as she had enjoyed his. But that would not be enough anymore.

The morning he had shared with Katherine, talking about their pasts, the time he had spent looking at her young face, was now of greater meaning to him than his moments in Cornelia's bed. He realized that he had matured just a little through this encounter. He, of all persons, had deserted his friends—his only true family—for pleasure. Maybe it was because all relationships in his life had been so transient or so rife with betrayals. But he was determined to pursue only the deeper friendships and loves. He would not respond to Cornelia's call to come to her cabin that night.

The rest of the trip to Albany moved along at a rapid pace. The winds continued favorable, even after they lost the benefit of the tides. Stephen stayed in his cabin, discussing farming plans with George, who had been old Mr. Breed's farm manager back in Charlestown in Massachusetts. Hannah, George's wife, who had cared for Stephen as an infant, busied herself about the cabin, not quite knowing what to do with herself. She had spent her life doing things, and idleness, especially enforced idleness, was foreign to her nature. Finally she began a careful mending of George and Stephen's work clothes, although they had really no need of mending. She had darned all the holes and sewn on all the patches before leaving Massachusetts. In desperation, Stephen told her to walk the deck and to tell him if Katherine Schuyler should appear.

But Katherine remained in her cabin with Philip. Cornelia would not allow another breach of discipline.

That first evening Cornelia had fretted until it had become obvious that Stephen was not coming, and then her anger became monumental. She snapped at her sister-in-law, Margaret, and she slapped Katherine hard enough to bruise her face when she did not respond quickly enough to a question about Philip's playing on the deck. Cornelia sulked the whole of the next day, remaining in her bed.

Stephen, oblivious to the uproar he had caused in the Schuyler family, attempted to keep himself busy on deck. The scenery of the Hudson Valley was spectacular. On both shores mountains came to the river's edge and inlets, where streams flowed into the great river, formed little bays. The ship could not get too close to shore for fear that the winds would be blocked from the sails by the hills. In midstream the wind blew strongly, but as a result the tacks from east to west and then from west to east were necessarily short. Because of his distance from the shore, it was difficult for Stephen to make out details. But the valley was alive with color. The fall had descended early on the lower Hudson. The red, gold and purple of the leaves intermingled with the dark green fir trees. Each of the hills, which confined the river into an ever-narrowing strip as they advanced northward, was an example of nature's lavishness.

He stood admiring the colors when suddenly he was aware of the girl by his side.

"Katherine," he said. "I'm glad we could be together again before Albany."

She turned to look at him. An ugly black mark stretched from the corner of her eye toward her nose and across her cheek.

Stephen touched her face. "What happened?" he asked.

"Nothing."

"Did she do that?" he asked after some moments of silence.

She did not look at him, but nodded yes while looking out toward the far shore of the river.

"Dammit. Can't you do something? Can't your aunt or grandfather help you deal with her?"

"Were you able to deal with her?"

Stephen looked away. "Not very well, obviously. I've just stayed away from her."

"Well, I can't. My grandfather is my guardian. But Cornelia is expected to take care of me. I want to leave and come with you to the Mohawk."

Stephen looked at her in amazement. "Katherine, you can't."

"You could take me and no one would know about it." She was crying now, tears running down her bruised cheek. "She hates me. I'm only a maid to her. I've got to get away from her. I'll do anything. I'll work for you or for the German settlers as a servant, anything to get away from her."

"If she finds you on deck, there'll be trouble," said Stephen. "Come below to my cabin. My servants, Hannah and George, are there, so no one can think badly of it."

They went down the steps and walked safely past Cornelia's cabin to Stephen's. Hannah and George wanted to

41

leave, but Stephen asked them to remain. Hannah left, despite Stephen's request. She went to the galley to get some hot water for tea. All problems to her could be resolved only by the consumption of as much tea as possible. George stood as far from the young couple as possible, wishing to give them a chance for private talk.

But they really didn't talk much. Stephen looked at Katherine's face and hated Cornelia for placing a blemish on it to mar her beauty. Katherine looked admiringly back at Stephen. His kindness to her, his gentleness in touching her and his obvious concern for her had affected her deeply. Even though she hardly knew him, she had fallen in love with him. And it was an emotion that would survive the rest of her life.

She said no more about escaping. She knew it was impossible. No Schuyler, even bastard ones, simply disappeared or went to work for farmers. Her grandfather would track her down and, once returned to Albany, she would be even less free. But someday, she promised herself, she would become this gentle man's wife and the mother of his children.

"Are you feeling better now?" he asked.

She smiled. "It was silly of me to ask you to take me away. I know it was, but Cornelia frightens me. She was so violent and hateful. I've never seen her like that before."

Hannah returned and began to make tea for everyone. When she had the brew ready, she gave Katherine a cup and smiled at her. Hannah was a childless woman who had enormous mothering instincts. She had cared for Stephen's mother as a child and had been his nurse. She had cared for Stephen's aunt, Betsy Breed, for years before Daniel Pierce, Betsy's husband, had thrown George and herself out of the house for aiding Stephen when he returned from captivity. She reached over and patted Katherine's swollen cheek, all the while clucking, "Poor dear, poor dear."

The door of the cabin swung open and Cornelia Schuyler stood at the entryway. She called out, "Stephen. Where—" But before she could finish her question, her violet eyes fell upon Katherine. "You," she gasped. "What are you doing?" Then she sneered. "You little whore," she yelled. "I've always known you'd take after your mother—an unmarried woman in a man's room."

"I'm nothing of the kind," said Katherine, her eyes flashing anger.

Cornelia raised her hand and made to approach her. Katherine seemed to shrink in the face of her onslaught. Her face reddened, her eyes filled with tears and she bit her lower

42

lip to keep it from trembling. Cornelia's assault, however, was too much for Hannah. "Who's calling who a whore?" she yelled. "You lure my Stephen into your bed with your fancy ways. No decent woman as *old* as you are would try to take advantage of a boy."

The emphasis that Hannah had placed on the word *old* had reacted on Cornelia much like an electric shock. Her face contorted into a rage and her eyes flashed violence. "Who is this bag of fat?" she yelled at Stephen.

"Cornelia," said Stephen. "I think you had better leave."

"I'm not leaving my daughter in your cabin. You're a decadent and debauched young man. God knows what you two have done already."

Stephen was angry now also. "We've done considerably less than you and I achieved together. Now get out."

Cornelia turned and stormed down the passageway to her cabin, slamming any door that got in her way. Once she had left, Katherine relaxed, but tears still rolled down her cheeks. Hannah placed her heavy arm about the girl's shoulders. Stephen took her hand in his. "I don't think you should stay here," he said. "We must go to your aunt's cabin." He led her through the door, down the hallway to the cabin opposite Cornelia's, which belonged to Margaret Schuyler.

John Schuyler's sister was a remarkable and formidable woman. When Katherine knocked on her door, it was opened immediately. The older woman was clothed in a dress of expensive but drab brown and wore a white dust cap on her head. She was about fifty years old, but her face had wrinkled prematurely and so she looked older than she was. She was thin and sharp looking. Her face was narrow. Her nose was narrow. She had almost no hips. Her whole body was narrow.

"What is it, girl?" she said rather gruffly, ignoring Stephen completely.

"May I stay with you, Aunt Margaret?"

"I thought you were sharing a room with that obnoxious child, Philip."

"I am, but I'm afraid I've angered Cornelia. I'm not sure she will let me into my old cabin and I am frightened of her."

The woman's manner softened appreciably as she listened to Katherine's story. "It was stupid of you to antagonize her, Katrina," she said in Dutch. "But I guess you are your father's daughter. It was stupid of him to get involved with Cornelia Van Cortlandt. Van Cortlandts are indecent folks. He should have married my friend—a very good Van Rensselaer girl. He might still be alive if he hadn't had to live with

43

her nagging, her demands, her infidelities." At this last remark she looked directly at Stephen, who merely smiled at her uncomfortably, not knowing what she was saying.

"If you stay with me, girl, you live by my rules—no men—" Again she glared at Stephen. "You can come with me to Saratoga for a while. I'll talk to Father for you. He'll let you stay with me until that one calms down." She nodded at the door across the hall. "We've much work to do at the Flats. We've been dawdling in that damned city for too long while Cornelia played and did other things." Again she glared at the young man. "But we've the harvest to put away, winter to get ready for. I wish this damned boat would move faster. Come in, Katrina. Don't stand outside like a boob. Come in."

Katherine stepped through the door and Miss Schuyler slammed it shut in Stephen's face.

He was shocked at first. But although he thought her gruff and rude, he could tell from her tone, if not from her words, that Katherine would be well cared for with her.

He climbed up the stairs to the deck of the packet. He walked toward the bow and strained his eyes toward the north. He too was anxious to arrive at Albany. He too had a winter to prepare for.

II

Winter, 1749-1750

The lonely echo of an axe against wood rang through the forest and smoke rose in lazy columns above the great oaks and maples that grew at the edge of the Mohawk River. Chopping down trees and burning underbrush seemed to Stephen to have been going on for an eternity.

Each morning as he awoke in the lean-to that he had built for George, Hannah and himself, he realized the time was growing shorter and shorter. Each morning the three of them huddled close together in their bedding for greater warmth against the dawn chill. And now Stephen could see his breath throughout the day, even on sunny days. His work with the axe brought sweat to his chest and back, and it poured down to the waist of his breeches; however, he dared not take off his shirt because of the chill in the air. If he rested for some time, he would begin to shiver.

He and George had hunted for the right type of trees. They could not be too thick or too thin, and they had to be straight. They felled the trees and dragged them, using the team of oxen that Stephen had purchased in Albany with Vaughan's money and that he had poled upriver on flat boats to this site. Stephen had selected a spot for the house on a low rise overlooking the river, where a slow, lazy stream flowed into the larger Mohawk. The house, when it was constructed, would be bound by water on two sides, on the north and on the west. The land on the east fell away to low, swampy ground. The house could be approached easily, by friend or by foe, only from the south.

For seven days George and Stephen worked. Most of the heavy work was accomplished by the younger man, since George was still recuperating from a debilitating illness he had suffered after leaving the Breed house years before. But George was a farmer and had cleared woodland for old

45

Jonathan Breed back in Massachusetts; he knew, with each tree that he told Stephen to bring down for the house, he was taking the first steps toward next spring's planting. He insisted that Stephen burn the underbrush, saw the limbs off the trunks and split them for firewood for the long winter. The great logs were piled at the house site. Hannah cooked their food and helped George with the splitting.

Stephen finished each day's labor exhausted. His hands were blistered so badly that each morning he dreaded the agony of opening and closing his fingers about the axe handle. His Indian friend Sonoco, the Abenacki, had helped to raise him and taught him to hunt, to fish and to paddle a canoe and how to move noiselessly through the woods. But no self-respecting warrior would undertake manual labor. The Jesuits had developed his mind but, except for household chores, they had done little about his muscles. No one had prepared him for the type of work he now had to endure.

But soon he realized that the aches in his arms and back were growing less severe and his hands were developing calluses in place of sore blisters. By the end of the second week of clearing, he was feeling stronger than when he began, and the muscles in his forearms, biceps and chest were developing rapidly.

The tree that Stephen was working on was a foot-thick maple. He was almost halfway through the trunk, using the axe and angling it just right as George had taught him. The wind roared through the half-bare branches, and leaves fell about him onto the forest floor. From behind him Stephen could hear the creak of one half-dead tree, which had fallen against the trunk of the large oak. Now, each time the wind blew, the dead tree rubbed against the oak, wearing away bark and giving off an eerie, rasping noise.

Stephen rested briefly, leaning against the oak and wiping sweat from his forehead. He tried to estimate how many more strokes would bring down the maple in front of him. He watched a chipmunk scurry across the exposed roots of the oak and disappear into the brush.

The crack of a gun shattered his reverie. Stephen picked up his musket and ran back toward the lean-to by the riverbank. Before he was halfway there, he slowed his pace. He could hear Karl Stiegler's booming voice and knew that George had signaled him of Karl's arrival.

When they saw each other, Stephen and Karl embraced. Stephen ran his hand through Karl's blond hair, mussing it.

He wanted to forget the harsh words they had exchanged in New York.

"What took you so long getting here? I'm just about worn to a frazzle. I need your muscle."

"You look fine to me, Stefan," said the Swiss. "In fact, a little hard work looks to have done you a lot of good. I've never seen you look better. It wasn't easy getting here from Albany. It was hard to find transport for them." He pointed toward the riverbank, where the German families and their flat-bottom boats, loaded with household possessions, awaited instructions.

"Those Dutchmen in Albany sure as hell don't like these Dutchmen coming upriver to settle."

"These Dutchmen are Germans from the Rhine, as you well know, and that's not what disturbs the Schuylers and the others. It's that they want freehold land."

As the two young men spoke, one of the Germans walked up to them. He was a man of about forty and clearly was the senior member and spokesman of the group. "Are we to unload here, Herr Stiegler?" he said in German to Karl.

Karl turned to Stephen. "Is this to be the site of Fort Vaughan?"

Stephen nodded.

Karl began to walk around the clearing, muttering to himself. Finally he turned toward Stephen. "Did you pick this site?" he asked.

"Why? What's wrong with it?" Stephen asked very defensively.

"Nothing. Don't be so touchy. You might just have the makings of a soldier in you. This is an excellent site for a garrison house. You have enough logs for that and more."

"George expected we would have to build houses for the Germans as well," said Stephen.

"I'd rather let them live without houses for a while and build ourselves a garrison house," said Karl. "You may have good relations with the savages, Stephen, and you may think like one of them, but with so many of the Iroquois living around here, I'd rather have me a good stout fort to live in, and I don't want any of the buildings around our own house to provide cover for any attackers."

"Herr Mueller," Karl called to the spokesman of the German group in his own language. "You and Herren Zimmermann and Menninger will stop here and help construct the fort."

47

The German nodded assent and went back toward the riverbank and his boats.

"With you, me and George, the three German men, and their two teenaged sons, we have eight workers. The women can help too. We have twelve strong workers. We can erect a garrison house quickly and then we will erect houses for the Germans at different sites."

"But if not nearby, where?" asked Stephen.

"I've been talking to these people all the way from New York. They can't afford to buy land from you, but you'll keep them loyal if you treat them as if they owned their own farms and accept payment in produce as rent. They'll want to spread out and find suitable planting sites."

"George has already pinpointed the best acres and the few meadowlands. We cut this timber from those acres and dropped it here."

"Well, that will make it easier for them. But they have minds of their own. They will have to agree."

George and the German farmers were soon fast friends despite the language barrier. The Germans were impressed with the choice of acreage, and each of the three families had soon picked a site for their farms. The Muellers were farther along the south shore of the Mohawk, where meadowland was abundant. The Zimmermanns and the Menningers both settled on the stream south of Fort Vaughan on opposite shores from each other. Once farm sites had been selected, the entire group came together to build Karl's two-story block house.

They selected the highest ground and then dug a trench about six inches deep all around the 20-foot-by-12-foot lower floor. The entire trench was then filled with arrow-straight logs, leaving a space as a doorway. Log was fitted into log at the ends, as a second and then a third level was raised, one on top of the other. The spaces between the logs were filled with a mud-based mortar. They left spaces for windows in front and in back and narrow gun holes every few feet. On the east side of the house they left an empty space for a fireplace and chimney. They had not gathered sufficient stones, nor had they any real mortar. The hearth inside the house was made of earth, while the fireplace itself and the chimney were made of boards roughly hewn from logs and then covered with mud. Once the mud hardened, it protected the wood from sparks drawn up the flue, but it still had to be watched carefully, and the potential for chimney fires was very great.

Once the seventh level of logs was firmly in place, the ceiling was the next task.

But by then, six more days had passed, and ice had begun to form every morning on the creek. The northern wind roared through the now-empty branches of the trees. Each morning Stephen expected to find their encampment covered in snow. But each day it held off for one more day of back-breaking work.

George and the Germans were fashioning logs for a roof. All agreed that there was no time to complete the house, and so they would strive to prepare it in such a way to give them maximum comfort in the coming winter and make their task easier next spring.

The roof was fashioned from logs fitted as tightly as possible over the top level of wall logs. Since their eventual goal was a garrison house, the roof logs were cut about 24 inches longer than the first floor. When the roof was completed, there would be an overhang. The second floor would extend over the first. Firing holes could be cut in the floor, adding extra defense if an enemy had gained access to the walls, cutting off the firing angle of those defending the garrison house on the first floor. The second-floor defenders could fire straight down at such enemies. It also denied attackers easy access to the roof.

But there would be no time to build the second floor. They would fit the logs together as snugly as possible and cover the flat roof with birch bark shingles, like the ones that the Iroquois used to cover their longhouses. It would keep out rain and wet snow, provided they climbed the roof when the snow piled too high and removed its weight from the logs. But fine wind-driven snow would find its way between the logs of the roof and walls. They would hang heavy blankets on the walls to keep out drafts and hope that the wind would blow as much snow off the roof as it blew down into the roof cracks and into the cabin. Blankets would also be hung over ropes to create rooms within the cabin for privacy. But all would share one large common space in front of the hearth.

But before the snows came, the Iroquois came.

Stephen and Karl were on the roof securing a 15-foot log, which the two German boys hoisted by block and tackle up to them. The three older German men and George came walking toward the cabin from the pile of great logs, abandoning the oxen. Their faces were white with fear. Karl picked up his musket, which never left his side when he worked.

"Put that bloody thing down," said Stephen. He knew what had frightened the men and he knew from just watching the warriors step out of the underbrush that they had not come to fight. They wore no paint, and Stephen knew enough about Indian warriors to know that if they had come to fight, all the whites would already be dead—caught in ambush without warning. Nevertheless, he himself was frightened that the Indians had been able to come upon them without warning. His sense of danger had been dulled by hard work.

Stephen jumped down from the roof of the cabin, while Karl fell flat on his belly and reached for his musket, trying to present as small a target as possible while at the same time placing one of the advancing Indians within his sights.

Stephen walked forward to meet the Iroquois. He called out in Mohawk, a language he had learned while he was a missionary among their cousins, the Oneida.

"What can I do to honor the brave warriors of the Iroquois nation?" He was not sure which of the five tribes these warriors belonged to, but since the closest Indian villages were those of the Mohawk, he hoped it was them he addressed. He had no enemies among them that he knew of.

He was surprised when one of the warriors addressed him in English—not that English was a strange language to many Mohawks, but this one spoke English with a brogue.

"You must be Nowell? I've been expecting you. My warriors have been watching you and reported your presence to me as soon as I returned from the Cayuga villages."

He stepped forward and offered his hand to Stephen. As he approached, Stephen realized that he was a white man in Indian dress.

"I'm William Johnson. My uncle, Admiral Warren, has informed me that you would be coming to set up a farm for Mr. Vaughan on the Admiral's old lands on the south side of the river."

Stephen gripped his hand. He felt the enormous power of the man in the grip. He was not only physically strong, but Stephen felt dwarfed by his strength of personality as well.

Johnson turned and spoke to the Iroquois. "This Nowell will give us all a good meal. He is a generous host. Wait by his fire," he said, pointing to where Hannah's cauldron bubbled away. Then he threw his arm around Stephen as if they had known each other for a long time, and Stephen felt not at all offended by the familiarity.

"How did you pick up Mohawk?" he asked. "It's a bitch of a language. You speak it almost as well as I do."

50

"I lived among the Iroquois for a while," Stephen responded.

"When?" said Johnson in surprise.

"A few years back—with the Oneida."

Karl, still carrying his musket tightly in his hand, jumped from the top of the unfinished cabin and joined Stephen.

"Who is this savage?" he asked in French.

"William Johnson at your service and no savage, I assure you, sir," Johnson responded in a badly accented French.

Karl looked Johnson over from head to toe but did not respond. Before he could, a great howl went up from where the Iroquois were sitting by the cooking pot. Hannah had been washing clothes at the stream, and when she returned to camp, carrying the bundle of clothing to dry, her first sight was of fifteen Mohawk warriors sitting about her cooking fire. She had screamed in fright and raced across the clearing toward Stephen and Karl and then halted dead in her tracks when she saw them talking to another savage.

"Dear God," she yelled. "We'll all be murdered."

Stephen walked over to calm her and was joined by Hannah's husband, George.

"Hannah, I want you to meet our neighbor, Mr. William Johnson. He has a home across the river."

"Why does he look like an Indian?" she stuttered.

Johnson walked over to them, reached for Hannah's hand, made a perfect gentleman's bow and raised her hand to his lips.

"I'm charmed to meet a fine woman such as yourself, madam. The arrival of members of your sex in our wilderness is the first sign of the arrival of civilization and the end of barbarism."

Hannah nearly cooed with delight. Now she no longer cared what he looked like. William Johnson, the first man ever to kiss her hand, had made an instant convert.

"I would be deeply appreciative," he continued, "if you could see to the feeding of my men. They are tired and hungry."

Without even looking at Stephen or George for their concurrence, she nodded yes and turned back to the fire, ready to feed an entire army if William Johnson asked her to.

Stephen chuckled. He had never seen Hannah behave in such a manner before.

"Mr. Nowell, I've come to welcome you as a neighbor, and I would hope that tomorrow you will cross the river and come to Fort Johnson and reciprocate. I will introduce you to the sachems of the lower castle, who will be visiting my home. I think it would be extremely useful for you and for me too if you were to meet them, bring them some gifts and establish a friendly relationship with them."

"Agreed," said Stephen.

"Good, then as soon as my warriors have been fed by that fair damsel—Hannah, is it——then we shall depart. Adieu, Mr. Nowell."

Johnson walked to his Iroquois and seated himself among them, allowing Hannah to feed him along with the others. She saw to it that he had the choicest cut of meat.

Fort Johnson was really not a fort at all. Rather, it was a large frame house of two stories, painted white with green shutters. It could easily become a fort by closing the shutters. On careful inspection, it was possible to see that they had been pierced to create musket firing holes.

Stephen arrived alone, after paddling himself up the Mohawk and across the stream about three miles west of the Vaughan campsite.

This English-style country house sitting in the midst of the wilderness, its front yard filled with all varieties of Indians, seemed totally out of place.

The braves sat together in small groups, talking and laughing. Some smoked tobacco and busied themselves making hunting arrows or preparing cartridge and ball for the precious muskets that some were lucky enough to own. Many of those with these weapons had received them as gifts from Johnson, endearing him to them forever.

Women and children were the majority, however. The children, while bundled in skins to protect them from the chill of the late fall wind, were running through the yard, involved in games of pretended hunting, housekeeping and warfare. Many of the boys had stripped down, tossing aside the skins and furs, which merely encumbered their games.

The women stood chatting, usually not far from a family campfire, where the stewpot perpetually boiled away.

When Stephen entered the yard, all eyes fell upon him. Several braves rose from their sitting posture, took up weapons and approached him.

Stephen called out in Mohawk that he was a friend of Johnson's. A voice from out of a group of women closest to him interrupted him in English.

"They know him not as Johnson, Blackrobe, but as Warraghiyagey."

He could never forget that voice, and when the others stepped aside, he knew that he was correct. She had not changed that much. He remembered the pretty smile on the pock-marked face. Her body had filled out, and it was now clear that she was a woman and no longer a girl. But all in all, she stood there almost unchanged from when he had last seen her, caring for those stricken with the pox at the Oneida castle of Kanowalohale. He had not seen her in almost four years, and so much had happened to him in between—probably to her as well.

"Molly," he called out. "Molly Brant."

She smiled and walked toward him. "I knew you would come back for me, Blackrobe. I knew you would never forget me."

Stephen threw caution to the wind and lifted her off her feet and swung her around with his arms outstretched, laughing with pure joy at the sight of her. It was not how one should treat a solemn Mohawk clan mother, but Molly did not seem to mind and was pleased at Stephen's happiness at seeing her and holding her again.

He put her down, and then a small boy, who had toddled after her when she had approached him, began to pound Stephen on his leg with a clenched fist, making a noise that was a cross between a shout and a sob. Great tears of anger flowed down his fat cheeks.

Molly bent down and scooped the boy up into her arms. He placed his arms about her neck and hugged her.

Stephen looked on quizzically.

"This, Blackrobe, is Kenonranon. He is my son."

Stephen's joy melted with her words. She had not waited for him. He knew that Iroquois women were not restricted to a single partner before taking a husband. And he knew that in the almost four years since he had seen her, she had matured and might well have a husband. He had no right to be disappointed, even if in fact he was.

Molly saw it in his eyes. She lifted the child away from her body and handed him to Stephen.

"He is your son too, Blackrobe," she said, smiling.

At first Stephen stared at her blankly—that one time—that one soul-jarring time. Most men had months to adjust to the fact that they would become fathers. Stephen now had to accept the fact that he was the father of this squirming brown ball of energy. He looked into the boy's red and angry face. He was not happy that his mother had given him over to this strange-smelling, strange-looking man. Stephen saw the eyes flash—the eyes of Jonathan Breed, Stephen's grandfather, the eyes of Stephen Nowell—his own light blue eyes. This was his son. This angry little Kenon—what had she called him?

"Does he have an English name?" he asked her.

She shook her head.

"May I give him one?"

"His Indian name is a strong-sounding name," said Molly.

"Let's give him an English name from scripture. Let's call him Aaron."

Molly smiled. She liked the white name. It sounded like Kenonranon, and she knew that Stephen had picked it because of the similarity.

Stephen smiled at his son. The boy stopped wiggling and contemplated the white face in front of him. He touched Stephen's face; he pulled his hair and grabbed his nose. Stephen could feel strength in the boy's grasp. Finally Aaron grew tired of this stranger and pulled away. He attempted to wiggle out of his father's grasp and go back to the security of Molly. Stephen placed him on the ground.

The father, mother and child walked to Molly's fire. She scooped some stew into a wooden bowl and handed it to Stephen. And then she did the same for herself. She picked some choice pieces of dog meat and put them into Kenonranon—Aaron's mouth. He grew angry and spit it out. He tried to pull at Molly's dress to expose her breasts.

She pushed his hand aside. "No, enough. You have teeth. It is no longer for you. Eat like a little boy instead of a baby."

The boy tried to slap her face, but she ducked out of his way, laughing.

"You spoil him," said Stephen.

Her eyes flashed angrily at his criticism. "It is the duty of the mother of sons to raise warriors and not to break their spirits when they are young. This son of yours will be a warrior his father can be proud of."

Stephen started to laugh. "You need not fear about his spirit if he inherits yours."

Aaron, realizing that he would not be allowed anywhere near Molly's breasts, toddled over toward the stranger and stuck his hand into Stephen's bowl. He yelled when the stew burned him and shoved his whole stew-covered hand into his mouth to relieve the sting.

Again Stephen chuckled. He was a rambunctious little fellow—this son of his.

The fact of his parenthood suddenly hit him. Here was a

child, not very much younger than he was when he was torn from his parents and lost his birthright. Aaron—he liked the sound of the name—the Indian name was ugly. Aaron would not lose his birthright. He was the son of Stephen Nowell. The whole world must know this. He would legitimize the boy and make him his heir. He smiled to himself. Heir to what? He didn't own anything but his name. Aaron Nowell. He would never have to wonder who he was, where he came from, not like Stephen Nowell.

"Molly, where are you living now?"

"At the lower castle of Schoharie. Sometimes, like now, I live here at Fort Johnson."

"Well, leave here. Come with me to Fort Vaughan—my new home. Bring Aaron and we will become a family, the three of us."

Molly smiled and shook her head. "You live in the white man's house, Blackrobe, with the white man's ways. Aaron will not be that. He will succeed Old Brant and my brother Joseph as sachem of the Mohawk. He must live in the Mohawk village in the longhouse to understand the people he will someday lead."

Stephen felt frustrated. He was in no position to tell Molly, who had raised their son up to now without help from him, how to rear him. Yet now that he knew he had a child, he wanted a role. He did not want to lose the boy. He did not want the boy to lose him.

"Maybe if you saw our house, Molly—it's not like Johnson's house here. It is far more like a longhouse. It's logs with a bark roof."

But she remained adamant. She sat next to Stephen and looked into his face with longing. It was clear to him that she would take him into her bed, but if she was forced to a decision between having him and or having Aaron become a Mohawk chief, Stephen would not be the choice.

The Indians in the front yard of Fort Johnson gave off a great howl when William Johnson, now dressed in the shirt and breeches of the white man, stepped out of the front door of the manor house. He waved to his friends but, spotting Molly and Stephen, he walked toward them, stopping along the way to greet old friends and pat young potential followers on their youthful heads.

"Mr. Nowell, I see you have made the acquaintance of the most beautiful Mohawk of them all."

Molly looked at Johnson in amazement. "You see this one,

Blackrobe, some great medicine man once told him that every lie he told would make the thing between his legs grow just a little bit longer. He has not been able to stop lying since."

Johnson howled with laughter, not at all offended by her jest. But very little went unnoticed by this man. He turned to Stephen after his laughter had faded. "What does she mean by calling you a priest, Nowell?"

"Part of my checkered past," observed Stephen. "Molly met me some years at at Kanowalohale—among the Oneida —when I was a member of the Society of Jesus."

Johnson looked at him in amazement. "You are the Oneida blackrobe? The one they would love to roast slowly over a hot fire if they could get their hands on him? The murderer of Skenandon?"

"I guess that's me," said Stephen sheepishly. "But it wasn't all as simple as you tell it. I had to kill the sachem or he would have killed my closest friend."

Molly interrupted, "The Oneida are fools and the biggest fool of them all is Dagaheari. I don't believe a word of his famed desire to avenge the death of Skenandon. Had he himself not insisted on burning the Abenacki, there would have been no need for the blackrobe and myself to arrange the escape of his friend, and the wise Skenandon would still be sachem, rather than the ambitious and foolish Dagaheari. He pines for the blackrobe's blood just to make himself appear bigger among the Oneida."

"I haven't a very high opinion of the fellow myself," said Johnson. "He stabbed me in the back at the last Council, and if Molly Brant vouches for you, Nowell, you'll be safe here among the Mohawk. But for God's sake, don't go west to the Oneida villages. And, Molly, you start calling him something else. Nowell, your story is one I'd like to hear, but I don't think any of the Mohawk here should be party to it—just in case some of Dagaheari's Turtle clan cousins decide he should know you're here."

Stephen turned to Molly. "Call me Stephen," he said in English.

"Stephen," she mused. "It's not as nice as Aaron, but I will call you this new name for your sake. In my heart you will always be the blackrobe boy whom I taught to speak Mohawk, who shared my bed—giving me my little warrior." She scooped up the boy, who had been standing watching Johnson in awe.

"Perhaps, Mr. Johnson, you could persuade Molly to bring our son Aaron and to winter with me at Fort Vaughan."

56

Johnson looked at Molly when Stephen called Aaron his. When she did not deny his statement, Johnson's brow furrowed slightly.

"I don't believe anyone can make Molly Brant do what she does not want to do."

Molly looked at the Irishman. "That is true, Johnson. I go where I want to go and I stay with whom I want to stay. I shall not go to Fort Vaughan," she said.

Johnson relaxed noticeably.

"I shall insist, however, that Stephen, the father of my son, come to know him. Therefore, the father is to come and live in the mother's longhouse." She turned to Stephen. "You must spend the winter with me at Schoharie."

Stephen was about to protest. He could not desert Karl, Hannah and George. They all depended on him. But the more he looked at her and the boy—the boy who would never know his origins if he abandoned him—the more his resolve weakened. There was nothing to do in the winter. The others could get on by themselves. Molly needed him more. Aaron needed him more. In truth, he needed them.

"I'll think about it," he said.

Molly smiled at him.

But Stephen detected something in the way Johnson's eyes darted from Molly back to Stephen that warned him that he resented the decision.

Karl did not hide his resentment at all. "Dammit, Stefan, you drag me off to the wilderness—away from Canada, away from my friends in the army—to help you build this place and then you desert me."

"Those friends damn near beat you to death for mutiny. I'm not deserting you. I'll be back in the spring, and I'll stay here to help until the first snowfall. Schoharie is only twenty miles south of here. It's not like I can't be reached in an emergency."

"But I'm not the leader of this group," argued Karl. "You are. We have all turned to you for decisions. In the army, officers don't leave their men in the middle of battle and go off to do other things that they suddenly find more interesting."

"I want to get to know my son."

"What's the rush? I must have a dozen sons I've never met. I never met my father. For that matter, I doubt if my mother was ever formally introduced to him. I survived. You survived with a priest and a nun for substitute parents."

"My son deserves better than what I had," said Stephen through clenched teeth.

"How the hell do you even know if the kid is yours? Are you going to take the word of some squaw who even you yourself say hops under the covers with every young buck at will?"

"The boy is my son. I recognized him," said Stephen.

Karl remained silent. He was in a rage and he was afraid of what he might say. Twice now Stephen, the dependable one, had indulged himself at the expense of others. Both times it had forced Karl, who loved to be free, to assume responsibility that Stephen had shrugged off. Well, he would do what was expected of him—even if Stephen would not.

When the first snows came two days later, Stephen packed his gear and left the cabin for the long journey to Schoharie. Karl did not say goodbye.

Cornelia Schuyler's small carriage drove by the merchant shops that lined the waterfront of Albany. The town was far more Dutch than New York. Most of its houses were Dutch style, with their sides facing the street. The street fronts of the houses of the most substantial citizens, fur merchants and patroons, were painted in pastels. Some homeowners had commissioned the painters to decorate the house façades with flowers and designs. Almost all the main streets in the town ran to the wharves. Above the town, like a brooding shadow from the past, sat the old fort, guarding the most strategic spot in British North America.

At Albany only the Mohawk falls separated the Hudson River from the Mohawk River. Down the Hudson lay New York's harbor and the Atlantic. Up the Mohawk were the Great Lakes, the heart of North America and the fur trade.

Cornelia's carriage charged down Pearl Street, splashing mud on passersby, who in turn cursed and raised their fists in anger after the coach. Cornelia loved speed and she loved to have her carriage careen through the Albany street. Today she had good reason to want to return home as fast as possible. Everything had worked as she had planned it from the moment she learned of her father-in-law's death. Within the hour, the entire Schuyler fortune would be her son's and therefore hers. It had cost her money—more money than she wanted to think about. Van Dam, the lawyer, was a thief. But it would all be worth it. The entire lot of them, her arrogant in-laws, would soon be under her control.

Cornelia entered the great drawing room of the Schuylers'

Albany mansion. She was dressed in black. She would have to wear it for months whenever she left the house—her house now. Her father-in-law had kept it to himself for years, like the greedy old man that he truly was. The men in the drawing room rose as she entered—her son Philip, Van Dam and her dead husband's brother. Katherine, also dressed in black, sat by a small cherrywood table by the front bay window. The girl was always by herself, thought Cornelia. Margaret Schuyler paced the floor. Her dark eyes glared at Cornelia as she entered the room.

"All right, lawyer, let's begin," Margaret snapped. "Read the will."

"That's impossible, madam," said Van Dam.

"Why? Can't you read?"

Van Dam pulled himself up, as if to ward off her assault. "I cannot read a will," he said, "because my client, John Schuyler, always refused to make one."

Margaret turned on him. "I saw his will signed. What kind of game is going on here?" She stared at Cornelia. "You're behind this, aren't you, you Van Cortlandt hussy?"

Cornelia's face went red. She put her handkerchief to her nose.

Then Margaret turned back to the lawyer. "The will was drawn up by your father, Van Dam. I was present when my father signed it."

"I have searched the files, madam. There is nothing."

"What does that mean?" Margaret asked warily.

"It means that this colony's primogeniture law goes into effect. When a man dies intestate, the entire estate passes to the oldest son. In this case the son too has passed on, and so the estate passes to the grandson."

All eyes in the room turned toward Philip Schuyler, who paid no attention at all to what was being said.

Cornelia raised her head from her handkerchief. "The dear boy," she said. "And he *is* only a boy. It will be years before he comes of age. All the responsibility will fall on me in the meanwhile."

"And all the money too," said Margaret. Her face seemed to grow razor sharp as she stared at Cornelia. "Van Dam, does that mean I'm penniless?"

"You get what your father would have given you as a dowry had you . . ." His voice trailed off in embarrassment.

"My father promised me that the Saratoga house would be mine."

"All real estate goes to the heir."

"Does that mean that this spoiled little—" She seemed for once at a loss for words. "—male," she said finally, "inherits my house?"

"Yes."

"I don't believe it."

"Margaret, it would be better if you came to town to live. The Saratoga patent could be leased to settlers. Come and live in the mansion with me," offered Cornelia.

"I won't live with that woman," Margaret told the world.

Katherine walked to Margaret's side. "Aunt Margaret, perhaps you should listen to my mother."

Cornelia nearly exploded with rage. "I'm not your mother. You're a bastard. There's no room in the Schuyler family for the likes of you."

"Mother," said Philip. "Don't yell at Katherine that way. She's my sister."

"Shut up, Philip," yelled Cornelia. Her anger overpowered the boy and he shrank back from her.

Katherine stared at Cornelia. Her fists were clenched and her normally rosy face had gone pale. "I'm more of a Schuyler than you. It's in my blood."

"You get out of my house, slut," said Cornelia.

"Mother, you can't throw Katherine out," cried Philip.

She looked at him and again he grew quiet.

Margaret took Katherine's hand. "We'll go together, girl. This isn't over yet. I'll get my portion, and when I do, I'll bring the Van Cortlandt woman to her knees."

She stormed from the room, practically dragging Katherine behind her. When she left, the Schuyler uncle and the lawyer crowded about the new mistress of the manor.

The snows came, but the cold winds of the north that blew across the lakes, dumping the snows in great depth in central New York, were followed by warmer, sunny days. Some of the snows melted, turning the sluggish streams into torrents of raging waters, pouring into the Mohawk.

Karl walked to the Mohawk's icy edge two days after Stephen's departure. He dared not step on the river's shoreline because he was not sure of the ice at the edge. The eastern morning sun radiated a blinding glare, and its light seemed refracted everywhere. The trees' snow-covered limbs seemed to send great, icy fingers reaching for the ground. The icicles caught the sun's light also and broke it into purples, blues, greens, yellows, oranges and reds, and then brought them all back in an instant into blazing white light as Karl glanced down the river.

He shaded his eyes against the sun because he thought he had heard a call from downriver. He could not see anything in the morning sunlight. But again he heard the call. He stared all the harder. Finally he could make out the image of a canoe and paddlers, their outlines framed in the sun's glare.

With the sun at their back, they had seen him long before and had called out. They headed the fragile craft directly for his shore. But rather than beach it immediately, the paddlers held off a foot from the river's edge and then eased it forward. The thin ice at the edge could be as sharp as a razor, slicing delicate birch bark with ease.

There were four of them, two men paddling and two women, one lying down, her head propped on a bundle of provisions. Although she was wrapped in Indian blankets, Karl could see that she was very pretty. The other woman sat ramrod straight. She was also wrapped in Indian blankets, and Karl could see now very easily that she was not pretty. It was she whose voice he had heard. She had been yelling in Dutch for the paddlers to put her and her companion ashore. Now she yelled at them to be gentle.

As the canoe was almost ready to reach shore, the older woman stood up. The canoe started to rock violently from side to side. Karl jumped forward; his booted foot broke through the ice, but he was able to grasp the woman and prevent her from falling in. When she steadied, the canoe steadied.

The woman continued to yell at the paddlers, but now she included the blond young man who held her arm.

"Why won't anyone do as I tell them?" she yelled in Dutch. "You, boy, get this damned torture machine ashore and get my old bones on dry land. We must get Katrina to shelter. She has a fever."

Karl did not speak Dutch, but it was close enough to his native German for him to understand that the woman sought aid for the girl, and it was clear that the girl was ill.

The canoe had thrust its bow into the snowbank. The paddlers tossed some parcels that had been thrown into the craft up into the snow. The old woman stepped out and sank to her knees into the wet, heavy snow. Karl bent over the younger woman. If she was ill, he would have to know what ailed her before he could endanger the fifteen lives dependent upon him up at the house. He pulled open the blankets, which practically smothered the young woman. He searched her face for pox marks. He felt her skin. She was very warm. Suddenly he felt a fist slam into his back. It was the old one, still yelling in Dutch.

"How dare you attempt to disrobe and take advantage of a young girl like that, you hateful man?"

Karl turned and grabbed her wrist before she could hit him again. He threw her off balance and pushed her harmlessly into the deep snow. Then he bent down and picked up the almost lifeless form of the girl. The blanket fell away from her and dragged behind him as he retraced his earlier steps through the snow—this time back to the house.

He could feel the heat of her body through his own jacket. She was very ill. Her face was flushed but it was hard to tell if it was the result of fever or the winter canoe trip. He looked at the flushed face; her eyes were closed and sunken, dark shadows had formed under them, making her prominent cheekbones seem even more prominent.

But Karl thought her very beautiful. Her coloring, perfect skin, small delicate nose, he found extremely attractive. He bent his ear down toward her chest as he carried her to assure himself that she still breathed. He took another enormous whack across the back for his effort. The other woman had recovered and caught up to them.

Karl ignored her yelling and reached the front door of the cabin. He called in German and in English. The door flew open and Hannah, aided by Frau Zimmermann and the other two ladies, soon had the girl under their care, undressed and immersed in goosedown quilts. Hot rocks were placed in the hearth to heat and then be placed in the bed near her feet.

As soon as Karl handed over his charge to Hannah, he turned to the older woman. Very precisely and slowly, he spoke in English to her.

"Madam, I don't know who you are or why you seem to feel it necessary to seek my help and then to beat me up. I do not speak Dutch. I speak German and French. I am speaking to you now in English, which I speak not well at all. But if you speak English, perhaps we can communicate."

"You damned big fool; you dumb ox of a man," she said in English. "Why didn't you tell me you spoke English? Once I saw you were trying to help my niece, I had no reason to want to harm you. Mind you, no man is to be trusted with any woman—much less a pretty, young and defenseless one like Katrina."

"You struck me a second time," said Karl.

"Dammit, boy, it is because you wouldn't listen to me.

62

Those two thieves I hired to get us here had just turned around and paddled back out into the river. They hadn't unloaded half the goods I brought—the bloody thieves. I was just trying to get your attention to a little robbery that was going on behind your back. But you're so dumb I'd have had to rattle your skull with a two-by-four to get your attention."

Karl felt very foolish. "I'm sorry you lost your things."

The woman waved her hand in disgust. "Never mind, what difference does it make when you've lost just about everything that matters? Losing little odds and ends really doesn't amount to a bowl of beans. Where is this fellow Nowell that my Katrina seems so stuck on? And how is the poor dear?"

"She's being cared for. She has a fever."

"Any numbskull could see that," she said angrily.

Karl ignored her insult. "My friend, Stephen Nowell, has gone to spend the winter some twenty miles from here at the Mohawk village of Schoharie."

Her face clouded, and he could tell that her spirits had fallen.

George walked over to where Karl and Margaret Schuyler were speaking. Behind him, peering from behind the blankets they had strung to create private rooms, were the German settlers' children—boys in one room and girls in the other.

George had a flask of rum. He had poured some into a mug and offered it to Aunt Margaret.

"What's this?" she asked, sniffing at it loudly. "Rum? The devil's own tonic." She downed it in one gulp and held up the mug for more.

Karl started to laugh and so did George.

"What's so funny? I'd take help from the devil himself when I'm in the kind of trouble I'm in now. No home—no money—no friends. I've been intestated near to death."

Karl thought it was his poor grasp of English that was at fault, but it was George who asked, "You were what?"

"Intestated, man, are you deaf? I've been intestated."

George looked at Karl and shrugged.

"It's that father of mine. Dumb man—damn all men—he didn't make a will or so says that cheat of a lawyer, Von Dam and now he has had the bad grace to up and die on us. Everything goes to the grandson—my house and farm at Saratoga. That little pip of a brat owns my house because my father was intestate. Nothing for Katherine—nothing for me; everything goes to Philip, which means everything goes to Cornelia. She threw us out. Damn all men, but especially damn all intestate men."

Her outburst seemed to calm her. She walked over to Katherine, who lay sleeping in the heaped-up comforters. "This girl is an especially brave young woman," Margaret said more softly. "I've come to appreciate her goodness during the weeks she stayed with me. When the bailiffs came to remove me from my home, I didn't think I could face it. I was sure it was the end. I was broken. I wanted to beg Cornelia, but my pride wouldn't allow it. Then Katherine said, 'Mr. Nowell will help us; we'll go to him.' Well, I say why not, there's no place else to go. We made good time until the snow hit. Then Katherine got sick. We're lucky to have made it here alive."

Karl went over to feel Katherine's forehead.

"Young man, keep your hands off that girl."

"Miss Schuyler, I suggest you go behind that blanket and get into the bed that was made for you. You must be exhausted."

"Donkey dust," she said. "I've never felt better." She sat, nevertheless, on one of the boxes that served as a chair, and within minutes she was snoring and gagging. She had the loudest snore Karl had ever heard.

For the next four hours Karl sat on the edge of the makeshift bed. Katherine was flushed but he was sure her fever had declined, even in the short time since she had been put to bed. Her face was very peaceful and very beautiful. He had never looked on any woman like this before. He thought her face the prettiest he had ever seen, and in her sleep there was a gentleness about her that moved him.

She became restless and turned on her side. Her eyes fluttered open. She looked frightened at the strange surroundings and by the strange man who sat on the bed looking at her. "Where am I?" she asked in Dutch, and then repeated her question in English.

"You are at Fort Vaughan, Mr. Nowell's home," answered Karl.

"Thank God, we made it," she whispered. "Where is Stephen?"

"He's not here. He's gone to winter with the Mohawks, some twenty miles from here."

She was saddened by his words. "I had hoped he would offer my aunt and me refuge."

"You will stay with us," said Karl. "While Stephen is gone I am in charge here. You are my honored guest." In his mind he knew that two more adult mouths to feed would put a strain on their supplies, but he knew that Stephen would have

64

wanted him to help her. Hell, he didn't care what Stephen wanted. He wanted to help her himself.

Schoharie was situated on the creek of the same name about twenty miles south of where it emptied into the Mohawk. It consisted of ten longhouses, each with five or six families. Defectors to the Catholic settlement of Caughnawaga near Montreal, smallpox and alcohol had reduced the once mighty Mohawk to two villages of this size—Schoharie, the lower castle, and Canajoharie, the upper castle, on the Mohawk west of Fort Johnson.

The longhouse of Old Brant, sachem of Schoharie, contained three generations of Brants—Old Brant's family; the family of his son Nicus, including Old Brant's unmarried grandson Joseph; and now Molly's new family, Stephen and Aaron.

When Stephen first arrived, Molly was waiting for him. She had prepared her platform in the longhouse with furs and skins she had received as gifts from her father and half-brothers. Stephen was greeted by Molly with Aaron in her arms at the front gate of the village. She led him to the longhouse. It had been made clear to all that Molly was to live with this young white man to determine if he would make a suitable husband for her. Nothing in the way of gifts, therefore, was expected of him. But he came prepared, nevertheless. From the stores of Fort Vaughan he had taken three muskets and one iron axe. He presented the muskets to the senior males of Molly's family. The hand axe he gave to Molly's little brother Joseph.

When Stephen arrived, Old Brant was sitting on his platform carving a ceremonial toy mask for his great-grandson. He was interested in the white man. The other members of the family were upset with Molly's preference, but Brant liked the idea of Molly taking a white husband. He did not want it to be Stephen Nowell. He had higher ambitions for her. Yet this boy had fathered his first great-grandson. He could be tolerated until his granddaughter tired of him, and he was sure that she would. She was to become a great clan mother, mother of many sons, and only one white man was worthy of her—Warraghiyagey. Besides, he mused to himself, they both were passionate people, and Johnson looked at her longingly. She was so caught up with this boy that she did not understand this need, and when she did, she would sweep aside this Stephen Nowell. He accepted Stephen's gift with gratitude—although at his age he doubted he would have much use for it. But it was a good musket, far better than the

65

one he currently owned, and what was even more important, far better than the one Hendrick of Canajoharie bragged of.

His musing was interrupted by his great-grandson, who walked straight up to the old man. He reached out for the toy, knowing full well that the old man made it for him. He was a demanding and spoiled toddler. His mother, like all Iroquois mothers, spoiled her young. But the great-grandfather, elder sachem of the Mohawk, did not have to spoil four-year-old potential warriors. It was his task to create respect for the elders.

He looked solemnly at the boy. He was solidly built. The baby fat was there. Molly fed him well. But the old man could perceive the muscle that would replace the fat when the boy matured. His skin color was a light gold, much lighter than Old Brant's or Molly's. His eyes were blue, his hair black and straight. He looked more like his father than his mother.

The boy stood before him, demanding, proud, not afraid to insist on what he thought was properly his. The old man should have reprimanded him for his arrogance, but Old Brant was filled with pride instead. He handed over the almost finished mask. There would be other times to teach him respect.

A little naked boy raced across the longhouse, back to his mother's platform, with a shriek of joy.

Stephen watched the boy race toward the platform. Molly had stepped out of the longhouse into the snow to fetch water. The boy stopped dead in his tracks when he saw that his mother was missing. Thus far he had not approached Stephen except at Molly's urging.

Stephen smiled at his son. "What have you there?" he said in English. He had decided to speak to the boy in English so that he might learn that language.

The boy held up the mask, beaming from ear to ear.

"Why, it looks just like you," the father teased.

The mask was a silly face, grinning, with the tongue protruding and hanging to the side. Stephen attempted to imitate it, pulling at both sides of his mouth and letting his tongue hang out.

Aaron squealed with delight and Stephen laughed.

The boy climbed up onto the platform. Stephen offered him his hand, but Aaron ignored it. He sat in front of Stephen and said the Mohawk word for "again."

Stephen stretched his mouth, crushed his nose and rolled back his eyes so that only the whites were showing.

Again Aaron screeched with delight. He sat closer to Stephen and demanded to be entertained even more.

Molly returned with water for boiling over the fire. The iron pot she carried was very heavy, and she had to put it down on the floor and rest before she walked to the fire. Stephen rose when he saw her enter. He walked to where she stood and picked up the iron pot with a grunt. He was amazed that a woman of her slight build had been able to lift it, much less haul it from the creek. He carried it over to the fire. He turned and smiled at Molly, but she did not smile back at him. He saw several families from other platforms laughing, and he noted that Molly was blushing with embarrassment.

He went back to the platform. When she returned to gather dried vegetables from her storage pots in the rafters, he held her arm. "What have I done to embarrass you?"

"Warriors do not carry water for women. That is women's work. When you carried the pot, you demeaned yourself, belittled me and shamed the family."

Stephen looked exasperated. "But it was too heavy for you to carry."

"Do you wish a stronger woman?"

"Molly, for God's sake, no. I want to help you, to cherish you, to spoil you. If it is all right, to spoil Aaron—and everyone around here does plenty of that. Why can't I do little things to show that I cherish you without half the world knowing about it and condemning you and me both for it?"

"Now is Aaron's time for spoiling," Molly answered. "The day will come when he will have to fulfill all that the tribe demands of him. He will be prepared for that gradually, just as I was."

"I don't really understand all of this," said Stephen. "It is so foreign to the way that I was raised by the Jesuits."

"The blackrobe way is not a good way, Stephen. Do you remember when we made love? That should have been a wonderful moment. It was the first time for you, yet when it was over you cried yourself to sleep. The other blackrobe, Lalonde, worked you like one would work a slave. Yet he was weaker than you. He was a cruel, wicked man. Yet the blackrobe way was to force you to obey him. The blackrobe mission would still be thriving in Kanowalohale if you had been in charge rather than Lalonde. Our way rewards the

67

virtuous, the strong, those who have the best interest of the tribe at heart. We have no room for the selfish and greedy. Should they become our leaders, then we will all die."

"My understanding is that Dagaheari is now sachem of the Oneida," said Stephen.

She smiled at him. "Sometimes there are mistakes—even among the Iroquois."

Stephen continued to play with Aaron while Molly cooked the supper. Nicus Brant, Molly's father, had made a kill, and the whole longhouse would share roasted venison that evening. Molly had baked some cornmeal bread and had cooked some dried beans. She fed pieces of the meat to Aaron, who had developed a voracious appetite for every kind of food after he had been weaned.

The early winter saw the night fall upon Schoharie like a shroud. The sun set almost immediately after the family had eaten. Across the longhouse another family was settling down for the night. The children were covered with furs and tucked snugly against the fur-draped back wall of the house. The combined insulation of furs on the interior and snowdrifts against the outside would keep the young warm.

The mother sat down next to the father, and he reached over and touched her breasts. Stephen had been watching them from the vantage point of his platform and immediately looked away from them. Molly saw the flush come to his face and laughed at him.

"What's so funny?" he asked rather belligerently.

"You are afraid to watch others make love," she teased.

"It's a private thing," he stammered.

She came over to sit next to him and placed her arms around his neck and kissed him. She had hoped to relax him, but it had the opposite effect. He tensed.

Cooking fires in the longhouse were burning lower, and the normally darkened interior of the house became even darker. Old Brant's current wife—a fat woman at least thirty years younger than he—waddled over to the central fire and dropped a few logs onto it. Sparks rose upward and flew out of the house, up toward the night sky. She watched for some moments to make sure that none had fallen back down to the bark roof.

The wood was not wholly dry and it gave off smoke, which soon filled the house. Stephen began to cough and choke. His eyes watered and stung. The smoke seemed to bother no one else in the house but Stephen.

Molly prepared their bed by piling furs and soft deerskins

68

on the wooden platform floor. She stepped out of her doeskin dress and lay down in the furs. She covered herself with the fur blanket made by stitching the pelts of several timber wolves together.

Aaron snuggled under the covers next to her with no preparation. Stephen removed his shoes and stockings and then stripped off his shirt. He crawled under the wolfskins next to her. She reached over and placed her hand on him. He looked into her face and grew annoyed when he saw her smug look of amusement.

"I thought my man would like to behave like a man tonight, but I don't think it will be possible if he doesn't take off his breeches."

Stephen cursed and sat up. He wasn't a prude, but civilized people just didn't parade about naked in front of other people. But he was angry at Molly's mocking tone. He pulled at the buttons of his breeches and pulled them off, forcing them inside out with the violence of his action. He tossed them into the corner of the platform. She reached over again and stroked his thigh. "That's much better," she said. She placed her hand on him and began a soft, gentle motion.

Stephen tensed again. "Molly, the boy is right here."

"Where he belongs," she responded.

"We can't just make love with our son watching."

"Stephen, he's not watching. He's asleep."

"But he could wake up!"

"So what?"

"I can't do all of this in front of the whole world."

She continued to massage him and it had the desired effect. Stephen began to relax and enjoy the pleasure that her hand brought to him. He reached over to her and began to touch her. He kissed her and slipped his tongue inside her mouth. She responded and returned his kiss passionately. Finally she pulled away, gasping.

"The blackrobe who made love to me that first time was an inexperienced boy. You, however, have become an accomplished man."

He smiled at her and then crawled on top of her. Supporting his weight by his extended arms, he looked down into her face. "I don't think I'll cry this time," he said.

But Aaron did, awakened by the thrashing movement made by his parents. Molly hushed him and quieted him down with one hand. With the other she stroked the back of the exhausted man who lay on top of her.

They remained together for some time. Finally, Stephen

rested his head on Molly's stomach. He could tell that she had fallen asleep by the rhythmic rise and fall of her stomach muscles.

He moved off of her and pulled himself up beside her. He was not sleepy yet. The winds outside the longhouse whistled through the trees with a shrillness that forced him to shudder. His eyes still smarted whenever he opened them, and he still coughed. It would be morning before the smoke cleared from the house, and then fires would be lighted and the process would begin all over again.

He looked over at the opposite platform. He could not see anything but he could hear the almost frantic sounds of lovemaking. He could feel his skin flush once again. He knew that the moans and sounds of bodies coming together that came floating across the dirt floor were no different from the sounds he and Molly had just made. He had been in Scoharie for only two days, and already he felt that he would go mad if he could not get out of the longhouse. A whole winter of confinement could not be endured.

But endure he did. He had no choice. There was nothing to do and no place to go. Stephen had brought some books with him, such as a small volume of the love poetry of Catullus in Latin, which he had purchased in New York City. He enjoyed reading the blatantly sensual poems. Here was a Latin poetry that none of his teachers in Louisbourg or in Paris had ever introduced to him. But he found reading unbearable in the smoky dusk of the longhouse. And the days that he could read outside without freezing were few indeed.

Christmas came and went without his noticing, as did the new year. He smiled to himself when he realized that he had missed them. He had always celebrated his birthday on Christmas when he lived with the Jesuits. They had assigned it to him. He assumed that someone in the community had been having fun with the similarity of his last name to the French word for Christmas—Noel.

In January the grip of winter lessened for a few days. The sun bathed the Mohawk valley, and the snows melted just a bit. Great icicles formed on the tree limbs and on the roof overhang of the longhouses.

Stephen took Aaron outside and they walked to the edge of the frozen river together. He had been teaching the boy the English equivalent of his Mohawk words. And when they found tracks at the river's edge where the ice had melted enough to allow wild animals to drink, he pointed out the various animal tracks, giving Aaron both the Mohawk and

English name for the foxes, porcupines, badgers and raccoons who came to taste the ice-cold waters.

He told Aaron the French fable of Renard the fox, which had been told to him as a boy in Canada by the priests and the nuns. Aaron loved to hear how the fox outwitted all the other animals. When he became a warrior, he said, he would be as clever as the fox in his father's stories.

Stephen was amazed at the boy's intelligence and grasp of ideas and language at so early an age. He knew that he was behaving like a typical father, bragging of his son's accomplishments, but he was genuinely pleased.

Stephen showed Aaron how to locate the rabbit runs in the snow and how to set a snare. He had learned these things from the Abenacki, Socono, when he was a boy, and he delighted in teaching his son the same things. They set the snare and returned to the river. Stephen showed his son how to test the strength of the ice. His life could depend on knowing how to survive alone and weaponless in the wilderness. His mother could not teach him these things; only his father could.

After several hours they returned to the snare, and Aaron whooped with delight when he saw the dead rabbit. He pushed out his chest and demanded his right of returning to the longhouse and placing his game before the platform of his mother, as he had seen young boys, much older than he, do in the past.

They returned to the house, and Aaron raced to the doorway and was gone. Stephen looked about him. He wanted one last look at the late afternoon sun before returning to the smoky gloom. But a great black cloud, swept by gusts of cold wind, crossed over in front of the sun. Stephen shuddered as the brightness disappeared and the renewed winter gusts pulled at his Indian blanket. He pulled it closer about him. He shuddered a second time and entered the house.

Aaron had been disappointed that his mother was not in the longhouse. Instead he brought his meat to the young woman who now shared the platform of his great-grandfather. Stephen found the boy bragging to Old Brant of how he had caught the rabbit. The old man listened to the boy with great attention. He could recall his own first kill, and he knew how important such a moment was.

Aaron looked with great affection at his father when Stephen stepped up to Old Brant's platform and stood at the side of his son. He, too, was proud of what the four-year-old boy had achieved—even if he had received more than a little help in achieving it.

Stephen looked about for Molly. She should be sharing this moment with him.

Brant watched Stephen's eyes search for his granddaughter. "She is not here," he said finally. "She has gone to Fort Johnson, at my request. She carries a message to Johnson for me."

"But she never told me," protested Stephen. "When will she return? Surely it is going to snow again. Anyone could see that with those clouds and that wind."

The old man looked away from him. He liked this black-robe, or at least this used-to-be blackrobe, with the funny English name. He did not wish to hurt him. But his grand-daughter had looked too comfortable with him. It might be hard for her to break with him when the time came to break. He had ordered her to Fort Johnson. Johnson wanted her. He could tell that. Anyone with half a brain could tell that from the way he looked at her. And Molly was a passionate, ambitious woman. If she approached Johnson without this boy she lived with, he would try to make love to her and she would succumb. Once she felt the power of the great chief, she would leave this boy to himself.

"She did not tell you because she could not find you," the old man said finally. "She will return as soon as the weather allows her. I've sent her younger brother, Joseph, with her. He is only ten but he has the heart of a bear and he can take care of her."

Stephen had spoken on some occasions to Joseph Brant, who spoke English and who was often away in Connecticut studying with the Protestant missionaries, who believed in educating the Indians. He was a very remarkable young boy, but there was a calculating coldness about him that made it hard for Stephen to believe that he was the warm and passionate Molly's brother—even her half brother.

"But Aaron will need her," Stephen protested.

"He has my woman and his grandmother, the wife of my son Nicus, to take care of him."

"No need; I'll do it myself," Stephen said, very rudely.

He took Aaron's hand and walked back to their platform. He knew, of course, that he could not cook food in the longhouse. Even the four-year-old Aaron knew of the rigid divisions of work that existed within an Iroquois longhouse. Men did not tend to the cooking. It was fine for a warrior on the hunt to cook the game he had caught when away from his

72

longhouse, but within the house preparing the food was the work of women. If he attempted it, he would disgrace himself and shame his son. He had no choice but to return shame-faced to Old Brant at mealtime and ask the help of his wife to feed Aaron and himself.

The snow had deepened now so that it could be traversed only with snowshoes. The rivers and streams, even the fast-moving ones, were frozen solid. Stephen spent his days in the longhouse, bored and angry. He was sure that his decision to live here had been the wrong one. He was angry with himself for deserting Karl and the settlers, who had depended on his leadership. He had allowed his love for Molly and concern for his son's heritage to get in the way of his responsibility. He was also growing angry with Molly for not being there. He knew that this anger was irrational. It was not her fault that she had to obey her grandfather, the sachem. But her departure had left him feeling unimportant and ignored.

The only joy to fill his days and nights was his son. They grew closer and closer. Stephen taught the boy more English. He told him stories that left the lad wide-eyed. He told him of the splendors of Versailles and Paris. He told the boy of his other great-grandfather, Jonathan Breed, now dead, who was the only member of the family who had been kind to Stephen. He told him of the great harbor of Boston, of the great sailing ships and of the wild and turbulent ocean. He told him of the grey stone walls of Louisbourg, so much stouter than any palisade the boy had ever seen.

Aaron continually questioned him. He wanted to know more and more, and Stephen's feeling for the inquisitive, bold and spoiled, but at the same time loving child, grew with each passing tedious day.

At night Aaron snuggled up next to Stephen for warmth in the same way that he had in the past snuggled up next to his mother. Stephen would place him within the protective cradle made by his side and his arm. He would keep the boy next to him until the natural restlessness of the child would get the best of him, and his knees or elbows would smash into Stephen's hip or rib cage. The father would then move away, and for the moment they would be separated. Slowly, how-ever, a sleeping Aaron would sense the loss of closeness, and gradually his body would creep closer to the huge form that was his father, and he would snuggle up again. Stephen would awaken, smile at his son and prepare himself anew for the attack of needle-sharp elbows and kneecaps.

The January thaw was followed, as it almost inevitably is, by the coldest weeks of the winter. The winds tore at the bark roof and walls of the longhouses, and even the heaviest blankets and furs hanging along the walls stirred with the drafts, which slipped through the cracks with each blast from outside. When the winds died, the cold settled down on the Mohawk. Steam rose from the rivers and streams, which had partially melted in the thaw. At night Stephen lay next to Aaron, listening to the cracking noise of the trees and cuddling deeper under the fur covers. Even with the fire roaring all night, he could see his breath inside the longhouse. But then the cold spell passed too, and the first warm, slushy days of late winter arrived.

Stephen rarely spoke to Old Brant except to ask him when Molly would be returning from Fort Johnson.

"Soon," was the only response he ever received. He was surprised when the old man approached him and asked him if he would like to join the hunting party, which would try to get some game. They were all tired of dog meat and dried corn. By March that was all that was left of the stockpile of provisions set aside for winter.

Stephen agreed when he was assured that Old Brant himself, who would not hunt, would watch over Aaron. No one ever really watched the children in the longhouse, but this strange white man had to be placated in some way. And it pleased Old Brant that the father deeply cared for the boy.

Stephen strapped on his snowshoes, grabbed his musket and joined Nicus Brant and ten other Mohawks as they set out to the southwest. They traveled lightly, unburdened by anything other than their weapons, powder-horns and small pouches containing some dried pemmican and extra shot and ball.

The wilderness south of Schoharie was in the mountains that the Dutch called the Katts Kills. They were low, rounded, tree-covered mountains like those of Isle Royale, where Stephen was raised.

The hunting party broke into smaller groups of two or three and followed the deer path from running waters into the fir tree forest along the mountain slopes. Stephen and Nicus Brant followed the tracks for several miles. The tracks were those of a large deer, probably a buck. He had left the open, deep snow for the shallower snow under the great fir trees. Everywhere there were signs of deer. The winter had been hard on them, and they had been forced to strip the bark from the trees for food. Nicus Brant signaled Stephen by hand, rather than giving away their position by speaking. Stephen halted behind a boulder while Brant moved ahead. Brant disappeared, but a few minutes later he emerged from the woods. Stephen strained his eyes against the glare of the snow. Downwind from Brant, there was a crashing in the fir trees and a giant buck with a large growth of new antlers emerged into the clearing in front of Stephen.

The animal stood majestically, its head held high, sniffing the air. It caught Stephen's scent and turned, reversed itself and rushed back into the forest.

Stephen had the animal in the sights of his musket, but before he could fire, he heard a war whoop from the bottom of the slope. It distracted him. He fired but missed, and the buck, now in a panic, tore away to the right, up the slope of the mountain, away from the musket of Nicus Brant.

Brant too had heard the cry. He rejoined Stephen without comment, although annoyed that their hours of tracking had been in vain. The two men retraced their steps back down the mountainside. At the base of the mountain they rejoined the other Mohawks and discovered the reason for the signal. The others had with them, bound hand and foot, a white man and two Indians.

Nicus Brant let out a howl of delight when he saw them. He turned to Stephen. "French fur trader and two Hurons."

Stephen was incredulous. Why would a fur trader be found this far south? He walked over to the prisoners and spoke to them in French. The man was frightened, and he was relieved to see a white man—especially a French-speaking white man.

"Are you French?" Stephen asked.

The man nodded, *"Oui,"* he said. "Yes, I'm French and from your good speech, so are you. Please get these red devils to set us free. My Hurons here and I were not harming anyone. We merely wished to bring furs to market."

"Who are you?"

"My name is Martin, Denis Martin. Our goal was Albany, and by coming in winter and coming to the mountains south of the Iroquois villages, we hoped to get there without meeting up with these devils. Obviously we failed."

"Why Albany?"

"The prices, monsieur. In Montreal a trapper like myself will get much less. I must sell to the government-licensed dealers. In Albany I am told I can become a rich man, and my friends would bring much wealth to their longhouses."

Stephen looked at the two Hurons. They looked very much like their Mohawk captors. Stephen had heard the Iroquois stories of the founding of their confederation and how their cousins, the clans of the Huron, had refused to join them and had formed a separate and powerful nation until the Iroquois, with Dutch weapons, had all but destroyed them in the last century.

The Hurons were poker-faced, but Stephen noted that their lips moved. Both men were singing. Stephen looked at Martin quizzically.

"They have given up. They expect to be killed or worse. They are close enough to your villages to be brought there for burning."

As if Martin had himself given the command, the Mohawks began shouting at their prisoners and ordered them to push forward to the north—toward Schoharie.

Stephen stopped Brant and asked him what was to be done, but Molly's father merely smiled. "They will be adopted into the tribe," he said.

The longhouse came alive when the hunting party returned with three prisoners. Inside, families from the other longhouses jammed together to get a view of the prisoners. A great fire was built and the elders gathered about it. Stephen watched, with Aaron at his side, as the two Hurons were led before the fire. Both men had been stripped naked and both remained silent.

Old Brant walked in front of them and said loudly in Mohawk, "My cousins from the North of the great seas, we have not seen many of you recently. You have not come to visit us as you did in the past, and we have not found it necessary to come seeking you as we once did. But we are still brothers. We still speak the language of our common fathers. Therefore it is good for us to show our affection for each other and to caress our loving cousins."

He took a burning stick from out of the fire and passed it slowly across the body of one of the Hurons. Pain welled up within the Indian, but he did not cry out.

"Don't you feel the warmth of my love for you, my brother?" mocked Old Brant. "With this fire you become one of us, adopted by caressing." He repeated the burning with the second Huron, taunting him in the same way. The second one bit his lip until blood poured down his chin onto his chest; his knees buckled. It was sufficient to determine his fate. The first one was the stronger of the two and would be saved for later. The weaker Huron would be the first to die.

He was tied loosely to a pole erected in the center of the

longhouse. At first Stephen did not realize what was happening. He thought the burning test was part of the cruel ritual of adoption. But when the Mohawks approached their victim with hot knives, he knew that what would follow would be a horror. He grabbed Aaron's shoulders to lead him away from the sounds of pain that came roaring from the mouth of the Huron as hot knives pierced his skin. Stephen placed his hands over his son's ears and headed back toward his platform. He found his path blocked by the boy's grandfather.

"Where do you take Kenonranon?" said the older man.

"Away, anywhere away from here," Stephen shouted. His arms were pinned behind his back by several warriors. He struggled to get away but he couldn't move.

"A Mohawk warrior must be able to face pain and death. My grandson will some day be sachem if he is wise and brave. Maybe he will die in battle. Maybe he will live to face the fires of our enemies. This Huron dies badly. He screams and cries out in pain for mercy. He is weak. We will mock him, for he disgraces his tribe. The other one will die tomorrow night. Kenonranon will watch both die. He will see what it is to die bringing disgrace on one's self and one's people. And then he will see a brave man face the fire. We will prolong his suffering; he will die well. We will eat his flesh. My grandson will eat of his heart."

Stephen was almost sick to his stomach. He had to get Aaron out of here—away from these people. Socono had been right. They were eaters of men. They were savages. But he could do nothing. He was thrust out of his own longhouse into the cold night air.

The screams of the Huron grew louder and louder until they were reduced to a hoarse croaking. Stephen covered his ears but still he could not escape the sounds or the numbing smell of burning flesh. He shivered. He would have to go indoors. He had on only his buckskin clothing. He entered the second longhouse. Most of the inhabitants had left to witness the torture of the Huron. He was startled to see Martin in the far corner of the longhouse, hands bound, sitting on the dirt floor in front of the family platform. There were no guards. He could not escape without some of the few residents of the longhouse giving a signal.

Stephen walked to Martin. The man looked up at him. It was clear that some of the squaws had already abused him. His face was scratched and bitten. All of his fingernails were missing. He looked at Stephen through pain-filled eyes.

"I can do nothing," said Stephen when he saw the pleading in Martin's eyes. "They will burn you all. They are worse than I could have believed."

"You've got to help me," said Martin, his lips cracked and bleeding. "We are countrymen. We are Canadien."

Stephen knew it was a hopeless gesture, but he pulled his knife from out of its sheath at his side. He sliced the rawhide cords that bound Martin's hands and handed his knife to the freed man. Martin grabbed the knife with both hands and plunged it to the hilt into his heart. He gasped. Blood gushed from his wound and some trickled out of the corner of his mouth. Then his eyes rolled up into his head and he fell backward, striking his head against the platform behind him.

Stephen stared at him in amazement. He had thought Martin would try to escape, but the man had been shrewd enough to grasp that there was only one way left to him to escape the pain of the fire.

Molly did not return to Schoharie until the end of March. The sun had melted much of the snow and all of the ice. A canoe could now travel from Fort Johnson to Schoharie.

Stephen had been out with Aaron, teaching him to fish. They had gone upstream from the village and failed to see her return. When they entered the longhouse, she sat there, arranging the platform just as if she had never left it. Aaron raced to her when he saw her and jumped into her arms, grabbing her tightly about the neck and squeezing, all the while yelling greetings to her. Stephen held back. There was a gnawing feeling plaguing him, until he realized what it was. He was jealous. He had had the boy completely to himself for three months and he did not like sharing him. And now even Molly seemed to be tainted like the others in his mind. The Mohawk burned and ate their victims. He had known of it from stories, but now he had seen and heard it. It was a sight and sound he would never be able to forget.

He walked to the platform and reached over the top of Aaron's head, which was buried in the crook of his mother's neck, and kissed Molly's forehead. She pulled the boy away from her and stood up. She reached up and kissed him warmly on the mouth. Stephen did not respond to her kiss.

That night they lay together as they had in the past, with Aaron cradled next to Molly.

"You seem distracted and angry over something," she said.

"I thought you would have heard about it from your family already," he said. "The blackrobe was not strong enough to witness a burning and tried to take Aaron, our son, away from the ceremony. Your father and grandfather must mock my weakness."

"They have said nothing to me," she said.

Stephen was silent for a moment. Then he turned onto his elbow and looked into her face. He could see only the outline of her features in the smoky darkness. "Molly, let's take Aaron and go to my house for the summer. I have to go back and I'll miss you both if you stay here."

"You could stay here."

"I can't. William Vaughan has paid me to develop his lands. For all practical purposes they are mine anyway. He intends to leave the estate to me. But Karl will need help."

Molly was silent for a moment. "Stephen, go home," she said finally. "But you cannot have Aaron with you. He stays with me."

"Why?"

"Because you will weaken him."

"You do believe that I am weak—simply because I would not stand by and see horrors perpetrated and people cruelly torn to shreds. You think I am weak because I am not a savage."

She grew angry and sat up, pulling the blanket in front of her to cover her nakedness. "Neither am I!" she said.

"I'm not so sure," he answered harshly. "Socono warned me about the Iroquois. What you do to prisoners is pure savagery, nothing less."

"It's no worse than what I have heard goes on in England and France. You place a rope about someone's neck and you strangle them after showing them off before the people."

"We do not do that to prisoners of war; we do it to criminals."

"I fail to see the difference. The distinction is of your making, not ours. But don't call my people or me a savage until your conscience about your people is totally clear."

She silenced him. He lay back down again. He thought quietly for some moments. There was truth in what she had said. European society was every bit as cruel as the Iroquois society, but he did not want Aaron to be confronted with the worst of either. He wanted only the best for the boy. He reached over and touched Molly's thigh. She pulled away from him.

"Molly?"

"I do not wish to make love, Stephen," she responded. "I'm with child again."

79

He sat upright. "That's wonderful," he said.

She turned her back to him. "The child is not yours. It's Johnson's."

He looked straight ahead and did not move.

She turned onto her back again and looked at him. "Are you going to call me a savage again? I told you this not to be cruel to you, but to be honest. You can count. You would discover soon enough that the child was not yours."

"Is Aaron mine?"

She looked hurt. "Yes; I'm not a liar."

He lay back down again. He was deeply angry and hurt. Long ago she had warned him that Iroquois women were free to sleep with many different men until they found and chose the one they wished to marry, but he had convinced himself that Molly had chosen him. He would not forgive her and Johnson and he would never surrender his son to them.

She reached over to touch him. This time he pulled away.

The next morning the sun was bright and the air had a touch of spring in it. Molly rose to cook breakfast. She did not speak to Stephen when she handed him a slice of venison and cornbread.

Stephen called to Aaron when they had finished. "We are going canoeing," he said to Molly. "May I borrow the canoe you came in yesterday?"

"It belongs to Johnson," she said. "Perhaps you would not wish to use something that belongs to him."

The double meaning of her words did not escape him.

"I have no objection to using his canoe," he responded.

She shrugged and walked away.

Stephen picked up his musket and powder horn. He placed sections of cornbread into his pouch and pulled his buckskin shirt over his head. He grabbed the warmest blanket on the platform and selected a second blanket for Aaron as well. He picked up the boy's shirt, leggings and moccasins and called for him to join him.

Stephen placed his son in the bow of the craft and steadied it before jumping into the stern, while pushing himself off from the shoreline of the creek. Aaron was very excited to be in the canoe with his father. It would not be a difficult trip. Using the skills that Socono had taught him when he was a boy, Stephen would simply steer with the paddle and allow the current to pull them downriver, away from Schoharie. Those who saw him leave would merely shake their heads and comment on the stupidity of the white man. Going downriver meant the hardest part of the journey was the return, when he would be more tired. But Stephen had no intention of returning.

With the first signs of spring, Karl and George uncovered the logs cut in the fall from beneath the snow and, with the assistance of the Germans, began the construction of the second story of the garrison house. The men and boys worked from sunup to sunset. With seven strong bodies working, the second story began to take shape quickly.

In the evening Karl would relax before the fire with George and Hannah. Katherine and Aunt Margaret joined them almost every night. He would watch the shadow of the flames from the hearth play on Katherine's face and stare at her until she noticed it. Then he would look away, not wanting to embarrass her.

He remembered the long watch he had spent at her bedside until her fever had finally broken. Hannah and Margaret had taken turns nursing her but Karl had never left her side.

When her fever left her, she was very weak and clearly despondent at not finding Stephen. Karl did not tell her why Stephen had gone to Schoharie, and there was no way she could have known. Every day for her became a vigil, awaiting his return. Karl began to resent her feelings for Stephen—a Stephen who did not love her and did not even know that she was in love with him.

While she regained her health, but was still not strong enough to help the other women, she began to read. Karl uncovered the box where Stephen stored the books he had purchased in New York. Most were in Latin and in Greek. But they uncovered a long fable concerning a Mr. Gulliver by the eminent Dr. Swift. Katherine read aloud at night to all who could understand English. But Hannah and George soon found better things to occupy them and only Karl sat and listened to her. At first he really didn't like the book, which struck him as absurd. Katherine would laugh at a section, and when she noticed that Karl stared blankly, she tried to explain.

"Karl, my serious one, don't you see what the doctor is saying?"

"I don't know of any wars begun over such an issue as the one Dr. Swift mentions—which end of an egg is to be opened first and which end is the top end and which end is the bottom end."

"Dr. Swift," she responded, "is talking about wars begun

for any silly reason. The war we are now fighting with France began as a war between England and Spain because a certain Captain Jenkins had his ear removed by the Spanish."

"Ears are hard to come by," laughed Karl.

Katherine joined him in his laughter. "You know what I mean."

"I think so," he responded.

Reading a chapter a night, they were into spring before the last page was finished. By the time she closed the volume, Karl was almost as fascinated by the story as he was by the woman reading to him. But with the warm weather and later sunsets, he was busy working on the house and had no opportunity to begin another of Stephen's books.

The second story of the house was almost completed when Stephen arrived. Karl was standing on the roof looking south when he saw the canoe forging ahead on the stream. He strained his eyes, and once he knew it was Stephen, he called loudly to him. Stephen responded with a war whoop, which caused everyone at Fort Vaughan to drop what they were doing and congregate in front of the house.

Karl let himself down off the roof into the several inches of snow that still remained on the ground and raced toward the river. "It's Stefan returning," he yelled.

George and Hannah raced after Karl, and the Germans walked more sedately. Katherine remained behind, standing by the front door.

"Why don't you run after him like every other damn fool in this house?" said her aunt, as she stuck her head out of the door to see what was happening.

Katherine smiled at her and instead went back into her section of the house to freshen up.

Karl gave Stephen a great bear hug. "And who is this?" he asked when Aaron very solemnly stepped out of the bow of the canoe.

"This is my son, Aaron. Aaron, this is Karl."

"Is Karl related to you?" the boy asked in Mohawk.

"Karl is my blood brother," answered Stephen. "You are to treat him as an uncle."

Aaron smiled up at the tall Swiss man. He had never seen anyone with yellow hair before. The man was huge, with great muscles bulging under his shirt. He must be a great warrior, thought the boy, and he was pleased to have such an uncle.

Hannah swooped down on Stephen's son. "What a beauti-

82

ful boy, Mr. Stephen! Why, if he doesn't have your eyes! Here, little boy, take Hannah's hand. I have something to eat in the house that you may like very much—one of my very best mince pies might be just what a boy like you—Aaron, is it?—just what a boy might like."

He only understood a few words that the woman said. But she reminded him of his grandmother and so when she held out her hand, he took it in his and accompanied her back to the garrison house.

The other settlers began to go back to their work after Hannah departed with Aaron. Stephen held George and Karl with him.

"I fled from the Mohawk and I kidnapped the boy. I don't think we can stay here. Old Brant and his son will follow me. We left yesterday. I doubt if they will begin to follow me until today. But they will come directly here. I can spend the night and then I must go."

Karl looked at Stephen as if he had gone mad.

"They'll wear you down in no time. There is no way you can be safe until you reach Schenectady, and you probably won't even be safe there. You'll have to flee to Albany."

"Then I'll do it."

"But what of our plans here, and what happens to those you leave behind? Don't you think the Iroquois will come after us, seeking revenge? Stefan, how could you? You're not thinking anymore."

"Don't lecture me, Karl. I had to get my son out of there. He has to become educated. He has to get away from those people; they are savages, Karl. I can't have the boy growing up amidst the blood, smoke, torture. It was horrible."

"For you, Stefan; the boy seems to have survived quite well without you. You made a bad mistake bringing him here. You are endangering all of us."

"I said I would get out," he said savagely.

"The Mohawks will be here tomorrow," said Karl. "Do I give them a message from you before they slaughter us? It is not just me, but it is Hannah and George and the girl you met on the Hudson, Katherine Schuyler, and her aunt. It is all of us."

Stephen looked confused for a moment. "Katherine is here at Fort Vaughan?" he asked.

"Yes, she came just after you left. Her grandfather died and your friend Cornelia threw out Katherine and her aunt, Margaret."

Stephen walked away from Karl back up the slope toward the garrison house. He found Katherine waiting for him by the front door. "Hello, Stephen," she said softly.

He smiled at her and touched her face gently with his hand. "It went away just like I told you it would."

She smiled when she realized that the last time he had seen her she had had a giant ugly blue mark just at the point at which he had touched her.

"Hannah, bring the boy here," he called.

When Aaron appeared, Stephen introduced his son to her. At first she was shocked. But then, the boy was four years old, and she knew that Stephen had fathered him well before he had come to know her. And besides, she had no claim on this man she loved. She didn't know if he had any feelings for her at all.

She looked at the boy and smiled at him. He grinned back at her, his face covered with mince pie.

Karl joined them. He had never seen Katherine look happier. She smiled and her eyes sparkled. Karl knew that, despite the fact that he had come to know this girl far better than Stephen and that he loved her, he feared he would never stand a chance against him. Katherine would look through him to catch sight of Stephen. But Karl had deeper concerns now. He was angry and frightened.

"Stefan, you haven't answered my question. I think you ought to give the boy back to the Mohawks once they arrive."

"Impossible," said Stephen, almost spitting the word out.

"You have put us all in jeopardy."

"I told you Aaron and I would leave."

"They'll catch you on the trail and the boy will return to his village. How is that an improvement over giving him back?"

Stephen walked over to the hearth, sat in one of Karl's improvised chairs and stared into the fire, saying nothing.

Karl left the house in disgust. The Germans had gone back to the difficult task of construction. All that was required now was to waterproof the roof of the second story. Karl wanted a material that would resist both water and fire. He called the workers together. "Kurt," he called. "Where is your father?"

"He is gone with my mother and sister to our own farm site," said Herr Mueller's son. "The work here is almost finished. He left me here to help you with any of the remaining chores."

"Go bring him back," said Karl. "Tell him a party of hostile Mohawks is heading this way."

The boy's eyes widened and he turned and ran to the shore of the river. If he followed the stream, he might be able to cut off his family, who were traveling through the woods.

"Everyone else into the house," Karl yelled.

Menninger and Zimmermann brought their families indoors, and both started asking questions of Karl in German.

Stephen woke from his trance by the fire and called to Aaron to come to him. He started toward the front door, but Karl blocked his path. "You're not going, Stefan," he said. "There is no way for you to escape the Mohawks. You are to stay here. We'll all face them together. We'll hold them off. I understand, I can't ask you to give up your son."

"You'll all be killed. I can't ask this of you."

"You have already, by taking the boy and coming here. We're all in this together now and we can put up a stout resistance. When Mueller returns, we'll have eight muskets firing—four on each floor, all facing south. The women must stay in the center of the house and on the floor. They'll be safe there."

"Cow chips," yelled Margaret Schuyler. "I've handled a musket since I was a girl. No Indian is going to force me to be down on the dirt floor. I'll fight with any man and I'll outfight every one of you. Katrina," she said in Dutch, "get a musket and show these Yankees and Germans how a Dutch woman fights."

Katherine nodded solemnly to Karl. "My aunt and I will each take a musket if they're available, and we'll defend the uncovered sides of the house in case the Mohawks attempt to approach the house by crossing the creek or the swamp."

Karl looked at both women with deepening respect.

Mrs. Zimmermann and Mrs. Menninger, when they heard what the Schuyler women proposed to do, volunteered to load the muskets if Karl would show them how. In the Rhineland women were rarely called upon to carry weapons.

"He's got more important things to do," said Aunt Margaret. "I'll show you how to load and I'll teach you something about firing."

They had sufficient powder and ball and extra muskets to make a real fight of it. Karl assumed command. He ordered all the blanket room dividers to be removed. They would need freedom to move about the garrison house. Kegs were filled with water at the creek, along with every pot and cauldron in the house. The furs and skins were removed from the cabin walls, revealing the firing holes from which a defender could fire with almost complete protection.

Karl assembled the weapons. They had twenty-four muskets and three pistols. Every axe and hatchet, every knife, was assembled in the center of the house on the dirt floor. It would be possible to keep up a rapid rate of fire as long as the muskets were reloaded fast enough.

The whole day was spent making preparation. When night descended upon them, they lit no fire in the hearth and all the candles were extinguished. Each man was stationed at a front window on both floors. The women and girls continued to practice reloading under the direction of Aunt Margaret, but now all were silent. The forest noises, the chirping of crickets, the occasional rustling in the bushes as predator descended upon prey, were all that disturbed the quiet night.

Karl crawled over to Stephen's window. Stephen had placed Aaron in the midst of the water kegs, whose bulk would stop almost any ball. The boy had fallen asleep almost instantly.

Karl smiled down at the boy. "He has few worries, that one," he joked to Stephen.

Stephen smiled but then looked out into the moon-drenched night. He thought he saw something move down by the creek. He touched Karl's elbow and pointed out through the gun slot in the shutter. Karl peered out into the blackness. Yes, Stephen was right. Something or someone moved and crawled up the slope toward the house. Karl alerted the other defenders, using the prearranged hand signals. He raised his hand to get their attention. When he dropped it, the lower floor would fire a volley. The second floor was to count to twenty and then fire a second volley.

The dark outlines came closer. Now they were within range. Karl's hand, held high, hesitated just before dropping.

"Hold it," called Stephen. "Don't fire. Those aren't the Mohawks. Not unless Mohawks are using blonde women warriors."

Karl stood up and peered out the gun slot. It was the Muellers. Karl went to the latch door and opened it. Herr Mueller and his family got to their feet and raced to the door. Three desperate people, husband, wife and young daughter, collapsed on the dirt floor of the house.

Karl placed his arm on the farmer's shoulders. "Where is Kurt?" he asked in German.

"Isn't he with you?" was the response.

Frau Mueller gasped and covered her mouth in horror.

"We sent him after you."

"We never saw him. We saw Mohawks in warpaint on the

86

river, and we ran back. We had to bypass their camp. They are camped on the river two or three miles west of here. *Mein Gott,* where can the boy be?"

"Never mind," said Karl without much conviction. "He's a smart boy. He'll lie low until he thinks it safe. Grab a musket and start showing your wife and daughter how to reload."

They stood on alert the whole night. Whenever the moon passed behind clouds, Stephen would tense. That would be the time to attack, when the Indians made the least visible target. As the night wore on, everyone's nerves grew more and more tense.

It was next to impossible to remain totally silent. The Germans chatted away with each other in a whisper. The ladies attempted to console Frau Mueller about her son. Surely he would turn up in the morning.

Just before dawn Karl joined Stephen at his window.

"How far south of us are the Mohawks, according to the German?" asked Stephen.

"They're not south of us at all. They are west on the Mohawk River."

Stephen puzzled over Karl's response. "That makes no sense at all. Something is wrong, Karl. The Mohawks are here too soon, and they are in the wrong place. They could not possibly be here until morning at the earliest. Yet Mueller spotted them before dark, and why this circuitous route to the river?"

"Maybe to catch us by surprise. We would naturally expect them to come directly from the castle by Schoharie Creek."

Karl never finished the thought. The predawn silence was shattered by a war scream, and a flaming arrow crashed into the upstairs wall. It struck into a crevice between logs. It flared a moment and then went out.

Margaret Schuyler raised her musket to her shoulder and sighted through the loophole. The gun seemed to explode in her hand and threw her back, away from the opening. She seemed dazed at first, but recovering, she ran back to the hole and peered out. "I got the bastard!" she yelled in triumph.

But by then the early morning stillness was shattered by a fusillade of musket fire from all sides. Lead balls smashed against the heavy logs. The young German girl started to scream. Aaron awoke and his head appeared above the top of the water kegs. Stephen yelled at him to keep his head down. The noise and the screams were enough to get him to obey.

Several Indians made a rush toward the front door. They held one of the logs from the logpile, to use it as a battering

87

ram. Herr Zimmermann and George, who held the upstairs window positions, opened the loopholes in the floor overhang and began to fire directly down on the Iroquois. One of the warriors holding the log screamed as he was hit, grabbed his chest and collapsed. Another fell, the whole side of his face smashed into a bloody pulp by a direct hit from George's musket. The other two Indians were not strong enough to pull the enormous log by themselves. It collapsed on them with the sickening crack of broken bones and crushed limbs.

That was enough to discourage the remaining attackers. Stephen, looking for any new targets, heard a call to withdraw given by the war chief. He recognized the call. There at the edge of the river, standing for all his men to see, was Dagaheari—sachem of the Oneida. Now it all made sense to him. It was not the Mohawks at all. It was his old adversaries the Oneida that Mueller had seen on the Mohawk River. But why were they here? How did they know he was here?

The sun melted all the remaining snow that day. It glowed with the summer's day warmth, creating a stifling heat inside the totally closed-up garrison house. The Indians never showed themselves again.

The defenders were weary from their all-night vigil, and Karl ordered them to take turns sleeping. Half the men and half the women went to sleep, while the other men and women kept guard. Later they would reverse positions.

Even though they had plenty of water, Karl insisted on rationing it, along with the food. There was no telling how long they would be forced to remain under siege.

Karl sat down next to Katherine.

"What's happening outside?" she asked.

"Nothing. But there will be," said Karl bitterly.

Katherine looked at him, surprised by the tone of his voice. "I'm frightened, Karl," she said. "And I understand why I'm frightened. But you're angry. That I don't understand."

Karl looked over at Stephen, who sat talking to Aaron on the other side of the room. "I'm angry with him," he said. "I'm furious with him for doing all of this to us. I can't seem to fathom him anymore. He'll probably get us all killed just because he has a son and needs to play daddy."

"That's not fair," said Katherine quickly. "I've spoken to him. He told me what went on with the Indians. I think he was right to take the boy."

Karl looked at her in surprise. But before he could say anything, Stephen called to him.

There was a scurrying at the edge of the woods. Several Oneida, now joined by Mohawks from Schoharie, whom Stephen recognized as neighbors from his own longhouse, dragged something behind them out of the woods. They let loose with war whoops and pulled their burden to his feet. It was Kurt. He had been stripped naked and painted black with pitch. They planned to burn him in full sight of the garrison house.

Herr Mueller gasped. His wife rose from the floor and ran to the window when she heard her husband. When she saw her son, now tied to a stake, she screamed hysterically.

Margaret Schuyler ran to her side and grabbed her by the shoulders, pulling her away from the window. Katherine dropped her musket and ran to help, but her aunt waved her off. "Get back to your post," she yelled. "And plug the first devil who comes into your sights. I'll take care of her."

From outside the house, Kurt screamed in fear as the warrior approached him with the firebrand and waved it in front of his eyes, singeing the blond hair that hung down over his forehead.

Stephen felt the same terror grip him that had paralyzed him in the longhouse. He could not run away from this, however. He had nowhere to escape, and now he alone was responsible for the fate of the German boy. If he had not come here, this would not be happening and this boy, who had barely begun to live, would not be screaming in agony outside; his mother would not be writhing in hysteria behind him, nor would the father be crying, tears flowing down his weather-beaten farmer's face.

He had to stop this. He rose at the window to scream to them to stop and leave the boy be. But he never said the words. A musket shot rang out from the river. The Indians began to scatter away from their victim. Several canoes loaded with more Indians—Mohawk by the look of them—had arrived at Fort Vaughan. Stephen's heart sank when he saw them, but then he saw William Johnson walking directly toward the boy, whose chin had now dropped onto his chest. He walked behind the youth and cut his hands free. The boy slumped to his knees and then pitched face-forward onto the ground. Johnson disappeared with his Mohawks into the woods.

The sun set without any further sight of Iroquois, other than those few who had pulled Kurt back into the forest. But they were there—out in the woods. They made no attempt to conceal their presence. Their fires were lit and the Council drums sounded throughout the night.

This second night no one slept. Frau Mueller wept continuously, and Karl had to physically restrain her husband from going out alone to try and retrieve his son.

Stephen sat alone, still poised at the window. Katherine had kept Aaron by her side throughout the day, and she had just put him to sleep again behind the water kegs when night came. She sat by the boy, patting his back whenever he awoke from his fitful sleep and soothing him until he dropped off again.

Stephen smiled at her. She brushed the hair back from her sweaty brow and returned his smile. She was beautiful, he thought, and the boy clearly took to her. Perhaps—but then he shook his head. He should make no plans for the future.

Karl came over to him. "I wonder what that bastard Johnson is doing," he whispered.

"They're conferring," answered Stephen. "And for all our sakes, I hope he keeps them talking or else we'll all be dead. I'm sorry, Karl, you were right. It was terribly irresponsible of me to bring my trouble down on all of your heads."

Karl said nothing. Then the drums out in the woods stopped. All was silence. All the defenders of the garrison house were alert. Every musket was trained on the woods. Torches appeared in front of the underbrush and they began to approach the house.

Johnson called Stephen's name in a loud voice. "Nowell, Stephen Nowell. Are you there?"

Stephen looked at Karl. Karl nodded. "Is that you, Johnson?" Stephen yelled out.

"Good," Johnson responded. "I'm coming into the garrison house and I'm coming alone. Don't any of you bastards shoot me. If you do, you'll all be roasting over fires before the night ends."

"Get the hell out of here, Johnson," Stephen yelled. "You can't have my son. You may have taken Molly from me but you'll never get Aaron."

Karl went to the window, shoving Stephen aside. "Come on in. No one will be shooting," he yelled.

Stephen turned on Karl in anger. But the soldier had assumed command.

When Johnson entered the garrison house, he looked about him, taking the whole place in at a glance. He knew its strengths and its weaknesses in a flash. If he had had to attack it, it would fall. But the price would be heavy and not a price he wished to pay.

Stephen stepped in front of Johnson to get a look at him. "What is it you want of me?" he asked in great anger.

"It's not me. It's the Brants. They want the boy back."

"There's more to it than that. I recognize the Oneida out there," said Stephen.

"Yes, you really got them all worked up. Dagaheari is here, calling for your blood and worse, insisting that the son of the blackrobe go with him to be adopted into the family of Skenandon—the old sachem—who it seems you sent off to his reward. Old Brant will break up the Iroquois Confederation before he agrees to that. So you see, it is not a united, big, happy family out there in the woods. It's taken me a while, but I finally figured all of this out."

"What are you talking about?" asked Stephen, still very hostile.

"Dagaheari, as you well know, my friend, is not all that bright. I had him in the palm of my hand; he was totally supportive of my plan to bring the Iroquois into war against France, and he slipped away from me. There is only one man in the whole of the Six Nations smart enough to pull that off—Hendrick of Canajoharie. He was behind it all. He told Dagaheari about Kenonranon. He told the Oneida of the presence of the hated blackrobe at Schoharie. Now I have to figure some way out of all of this so that no one else gets killed and the Confederation of the Iroquois remains intact."

He looked directly at Stephen. "That's going to require something from you."

"You can't have my son—especially Dagaheari can't have my son."

"He's Molly's son, too," said Johnson. "And you're right. There is no way that that son of a bitch, Dagaheari, is going to get his hands on Molly Brant's son. The problem is that there is no way that he is going to leave here without the boy."

"The boy stays with me," said Stephen.

Johnson's expression changed dramatically. His face reddened with anger, and in the blackness of the house this made his face seem to darken.

"Look, you spoiled son of a bitch, there is a German boy out there, a nice lad, scared witless. He has had a taste of fire. No serious damage done yet. But come tomorrow, that blackhearted son of a bitch Dagaheari is going to burn that boy, and you're all going to have to sit and watch, or at least hear it. If the Mohawk boy is not handed over, the German boy burns."

All eyes in the house turned toward Stephen. Katherine placed her arm on him to steady him. He was faced with an awful choice. He pulled away from the girl and walked over to the water kegs where Aaron slept. His shoulders began to heave and his hands went to his face.

"I can't give him up," he cried.

"Nowell, I promise you," said Johnson. "If you turn him over to me, I'll arrange for Molly to escape with him. The Oneida will not be able to blame either me or the Mohawk. I'll send her to the Onio country with the boy. Far enough away that the Oneida won't follow. Only Hendrick will guess what I've done, and even he won't wish to split the Confederation for the sake of Dagaheari's vanity. Besides, by telling Dagaheari about what went on here, Hendrick fulfills his debt to the Oneida. He owes them nothing further. Molly will have the boy safely with her, and this lad outside won't suffer the unspeakable and will be here with his folks within the hour. You have my word on it."

Stephen continued to look at Aaron. He set his shoulders. He would not give up the boy—not ever.

Katherine stood beside him. "Stephen," she whispered. "You must give up your son—at least that way, all live to resolve everything differently at a later date. If they burn Kurt, what is to stop them from coming in here as well and killing us all? Johnson's way, everyone lives."

Stephen looked into her soft hazel eyes. His were clouded with tears. She touched his arm, as if to give him all the strength that was in her. He knew she was right, just as Karl had been right. He should never have gone to Schoharie, and he should never have brought Aaron back here to Fort Vaughan. Yet the price he would pay for his errors was unbearable. He sighed deeply. There was really no choice. He reached down and gently shook his son.

Aaron awoke with a start. He smiled at his father. The boy was so different now, compared with the spoiled child he had first met. He liked to think he had been responsible for at least some small part of that change.

"Aaron, you must go with Johnson."

"Where? Are we going on another canoe trip?"

"You're going back to your mother."

Aaron smiled. He had missed Molly, but why was his

father crying? He had never seen a man cry before. Warriors never cried. His father was very strange.

Stephen placed Aaron's few possessions in his pouch and handed it to Johnson. Johnson reached for Aaron's hand, and the two started for the door.

"Wait," Stephen called out.

Johnson turned, ready to argue. But Stephen said nothing. He reached behind his neck and released the catch on the gold chain that he wore. Attached to the chain was a square gold locket with a large gothic letter *N*, for Nowell, on it. It had been his father's gift to his mother, Sarah. It contained a lock of Stephen's infant hair. It was his most precious possession. He knelt down beside Aaron and placed the locket about his neck. The boy's eyes shone with pride at his new possession. Stephen kissed his cheek.

"Aaron, remember me," he wept. "Remember you are my son, a Nowell."

The boy smiled and then was gone, swallowed up by the black night outside.

III
1750-1754

Johnson was true to his word; Old Brant assured Stephen that the boy was with his mother, but he would tell him no more. Johnson's deception of Dagaheari had placed a strain on relations with the Oneida, but Iroquois diplomacy put it to rest. Johnson even made peace with King Hendrick and, on the surface at least, He Who Does Great Things and the sachem of Canajoharie were fast friends.

Stephen grieved for weeks over his loss. Everyone at the garrison house tried to console him. The Muellers had been extremely grateful for the recovery of their son. They tried to show their gratitude by gestures and overtures to Stephen, but he rebuffed all of them; finally the family decided to move further south on Schoharie Creek to a new settlement in Cherry Valley.

The day they left, Kurt Mueller, his blond hair flattened down by brush and generous application of grease, came to say goodbye. He came to the garrison house and asked for Stephen. When he entered the front door, after knocking, Stephen took one look and started to climb the ladder stairs to the second floor.

"Mr. Nowell, sir," he said. "I'd like a word with you." He stood in the doorway, shifting his weight nervously from one foot to the other. He still had some scabs on his face from the torches of the Iroquois. He wore a wide-brimmed hat all the time now to cover them and to hide the face that his eyebrows and forelock had not quite grown back in. But now he had the hat nervously in his hand.

"Sir, I'd like to bid you goodbye," he said, his voice switching from man to boy and back again with very little control on his part.

Stephen hesitated on the stairs.

"And I'd like to thank you for saving my life. I know the price you paid for it was a heavy one."

Stephen looked at the boy and then climbed the stairs without speaking.

Katherine watched the one-sided exchange while seated next to the fire, across from her aunt. The older woman made a sour face. "That was cruel," Margaret muttered. "I don't mind blaming those who are blameworthy. But the child was not responsible. That one—the one you're always mooning over—he's the one that damn near killed all of us. He's got his nerve."

Katherine blushed when her aunt spoke of her feelings for Stephen. She rose from her place and walked over to Kurt.

"Mr. Nowell is not himself, Kurt," she said. "I'm sure he appreciates your sentiments. He does not hold you in any way responsible for what happened."

Margaret hurumphed loudly in disagreement from her seat by the fire.

Katherine ignored her. "Goodbye, Kurt. I hope your family has a safe journey and that you prosper in Cherry Valley." She held out her hand to the boy.

He blushed as he took it into his. "I'm sure we will," he said excitedly. "My father has his own farm now. We won't be tenants and Mr. Johnson has promised us protection from the Mohawks. Seems strange moving closer to them after what they almost did to me. But my family, we trust Mr. Johnson; he saved me."

Katherine smiled at the boy's excitement. "I'm happy for you," she said.

Karl stepped through the door and grabbed Kurt by the shoulders. "God, boy, you're growing like a weed," he said in German. "At this rate you'll be taller than me in a few years."

Kurt looked at him with obvious admiration. "I'd like to be as strong as you, sir."

"You will be, and before long you'll be chasing the girls all over the valley. And if you're lucky, a few of them will be letting you catch them," he chuckled. "Isn't that right, Tante?" he said to Aunt Margaret in English.

"What drivel are you trying to get me to affirm, you big lout? Speak a proper language, English or Dutch."

Karl just laughed.

"Come, boy." Margaret gestured to Kurt to come toward her. She reached into her apron pocket and pulled out a shilling coin. She slipped it into his hand. "Now be off. Grow up well and learn to treat a woman with respect. The Swiss never learned that, otherwise he might be a half-decent fellow. When you grow up, boy, think with something other that your crotch. You'll be unique among your sex if you do."

Kurt was flabbergasted by her generosity and by her frankness. He started to bend toward her to kiss her. Aunt Margaret would not tolerate the familiarity and threatened him with a long-handled pan from the fire. Kurt backed off.

"Stand off. I won't have a man—even a half-grown one—slobbering over me."

"Excuse me, Miss Schuyler," he stammered.

"Get out; you're as silly as the Swiss. You'll never amount to anything."

Kurt bowed awkwardly to her and retreated backward toward the door.

Katherine had watched the exchange from the base of the stairs. As soon as Kurt had disappeared through the door, she climbed the stairs to the second floor.

It was still one large room. She found Stephen standing, looking out the unshuttered, open window and following Kurt as he ran along the riverbank toward his family's soon-to-be-abandoned cabin.

"You were not very nice to him, Stephen." she said.

He swung around to face her. "I know. It was wrong. But I'm not very good at pretending. I resent Kurt's good fortune. It came at the expense of Aaron's."

"You don't know that, Stephen. The boy is with his mother. He loves her, and she loves him. It is you who are unhapppy."

"I can't help myself, Katherine. I will never accept the fact that he was taken from me. It's like a repeat of a terrible nightmare. My mother suffered through it with me, and now I am damned to suffer the same fate—a life of unfulfilled longing for my child."

Katherine reached her hand out toward him, deeply affected by his obvious anguish. He took her hands in his and pulled her toward him. He hugged her and placed his cheek on her soft brown hair. She smelled so fresh to him. Her soft body seemed to fit so comfortably against his. His eyes were filled with tears, but he did not wish her to see them. He placed his thumb and forefinger over the bridge of his nose, into the corners of his eyes, wiping the incipient tears away.

Stephen and Katherine were married on Stephen's birthday, June 13, in the Dutch church in Schenectady. Aunt Margaret accompanied them to the Dutch town, twenty miles to the east of Fort Vaughan. She was on her way home to Saratoga. Her lawyers in Albany had threatened to tie up the entire Schuyler probate for years unless Cornelia turned over the house at Saratoga to her.

She had disagreed with Katherine's decision to marry anyone, and she especially disapproved of Stephen. "The boy is a nice boy, but his personality is warped, Katrina," she had said. "He had no mothering to speak of as a child, and he sees in his son a reincarnation of himself. It's a mother for himself and for the boy he will be seeking all of his life. Leave him be. If you must marry, marry the Swiss. He's whole."

Katherine had paid no attention. She loved Stephen Nowell and she wanted him.

As soon as Katherine said yes to him, Stephen made plans to paddle downriver with Katherine and Aunt Margaret. He asked Karl to come with them and be their other witness. He was surprised and hurt when his friend refused. He had to help George and the others plow and plant, and he didn't have time to go. Stephen pestered him almost up to the point of their departure and Margaret, dressed in a traveling cloak, her bags piled about her, watched Stephen plead with Karl and watched the Swiss refuse adamantly.

"Leave Karl be," she said. "There'll be plenty in the town to act as witnesses. You run off in midwinter and now you run off at planting time. God knows why this Vaughan puts up with you. You certainly don't earn your keep. At least this big lout works for his pay."

Karl looked at her gratefully after Stephen left the house, hurt but accepting. He went to her and pretended that he was going to kiss her. She did not back away in horror as she typically did, and so he kissed her forehead.

"I understand how you feel, young man," she said. "I had one person I loved and who was beyond me. I know the suffering. Keep laughing. It will keep you from crying. I have been yelling since that time. It helps." She pulled his face down to her and kissed him wetly on the cheek.

After the minister had said the Dutch words of the wedding ceremony, Stephen and Katherine went to their room at the local inn. It was the same inn in which he had stayed after first fleeing from the Oneida years before. The room faced the west. Stephen looked out toward the river and followed its course with his eyes back toward the horizon, as the last pink glow of the setting sun was giving way to the descent of the blackness of night. He turned to face his new wife. She sat at the small round table covered with a white cloth and set with pewter and crystal.

"You seem distracted, Stephen," she said.

He smiled in response. She was very nervous and he wanted to reassure her. He took her hand in his.

"I was contemplating what it would mean to have a wife and eventually a family of my own."

"I'm sorry, but I've brought nothing to you. Aunt Margaret has some things that she can give us, but the real Schuyler wealth is now controlled by my stepmother. I'll never see any of that."

"I don't want any of your money. I just want you and for us to be together forever."

They were quiet for some moments, staring into each other's eyes. The room was silent. The perfumed scent of wisteria from vines outside their window was overwhelming in the warm June evening. A breeze blew the fine white curtains back, but then it died away, and the pungent scent filled the room even more.

Katherine looked at her husband lovingly. "Will I be enough for you, Stephen?" She was afraid of his answer.

"You're all I'll ever want," he said. His hand reached out to her face. He wiped the tears from her cheek with his fingers. He kissed the tip of her nose. He smiled at her and she smiled back.

There was a knock at the door. A waiter delivered a wedding dinner of squab and a white wine from France. The wine was an extraordinary expense and a gift from Aunt Margaret.

Stephen sat down next to Katherine and took her hand in his. He raised it to his lips. She smiled at him. He sat next to her and poured the wine into two fine crystal goblets. He raised his into the air in front of them. Katherine touched her glass to his.

"To our marriage," he toasted.

"To our love," she responded.

He downed the wine and grabbed hungrily at the bird. Katherine merely nibbled. She was nervous. She loved this man who had become her husband and she wanted to please him, but she was still frightened.

After dinner she asked Stephen to leave. He went downstairs to the taproom and waited for a few minutes; then he returned to the hall outside the room. He knocked softly on the door. She answered for him to enter. She was lying in the large four-poster bed. She had changed into a white nightgown with fine lace ruffles on the bodice.

Stephen closed the door behind him and walked over to her. He bent and kissed her on the mouth. Her lips trembled but she responded. He took off his coat and placed it at the foot of the bed, removed his shoes and stockings and his best white ruffled shirt. He lay down next to her on the bed. He wanted this to happen perfectly, and he knew he must not frighten her. He got under the covers and reached over and touched her face. Then he kissed her again. He stroked her neck and her stomach. Her whole body trembled now, and he patted her to reassure her. She cried out in pain when he entered her. But soon she moved as passionately as he, and although he had climaxed well before she could have felt any sense of satisfaction, she still fell asleep in his arms, a sense of warmth and comfort enveloping her.

She woke in the middle of the night, her security evaporated. Stephen was not in the bed. She sat upright, looking for him. She saw him outlined by the moonlight shining through the window. He stared off toward the west—toward the river down which his son had disappeared, a son whose surrender she had urged on the father. And she feared her love would never be enough.

They returned from Schenectady the next week, and Katherine began her career as mistress of the garrison house at Fort Vaughan. While they were gone, Karl had divided the second floor of the house into separate rooms, a large bedroom with a hearth for Stephen and herself and three smaller rooms. He announced that he was taking over the old Mueller farm site and would move there. Stephen at first seemed displeased by his plan, but there was no denying Karl.

The summer saw a good harvest. They had planted corn around the tree stumps and the cleared woodland, and wheat in the meadows by the riverbank. Karl, George and Stephen had most of the wheat. The German farmers, Zimmermann and Menninger, with farms further south on the creek, had better corn. In addition, the German families had had considerable success with their livestock. Some would be slaughtered and put away for the winter. More and more firewood was stacked next to the garrison house for the coming winter as well.

When fall arrived, William Johnson, surrounded by Mohawk warriors, visited. Stephen provided rum for Johnson and his friends. They brought corn and furs and Stephen gave them some of his supply of powder and ball.

Johnson could have handled all of the Mohawk trade himself, but for reasons known only to himself, he had decided to share some of it with Nowell.

When the Indians left that night, Johnson stayed on. He ate supper with Stephen and Katherine. Hannah had helped her cook the venison that the Mohawks had brought with them as a gift, and she had returned to her farm with some of the meat to serve to her husband. After dinner the men sat before the fire. Johnson smoked his pipe. Stephen, who did not smoke, continued to sip some rum.

"That was superb, madam," said Johnson to Katherine.

She blushed. "You must credit Hannah with most of the success," she responded modestly.

"Nonsense," he answered. "In an open house such as those of our frontier, no mistress of the house can either hide her faults behind her cook or claim credit where none is due. I saw the effort you put into filling my belly, madam; I thank you. How does your husband remain so slim with such excellent cooking?"

"We don't eat meat all that often, Mr. Johnson," said Katherine. "Stephen has been working so hard at the harvest that he has had little time for hunting."

"I daresay it will do him little harm, but surely a woman in your condition could use all the meat she could get."

Katherine's face went scarlet, but Stephen stared blankly at Johnson. "So you've gone and made yourself a new papoose to make up for the one you lost, eh, Nowell?"

Johnson broke off. "Good God, man, don't tell me I've blundered into a little family secret. I just assumed, well, a man of some experience would notice the shape of a woman's figure—oh, damn, I guess I've done it."

Stephen rose and walked over to Katherine, "Is it true?" he asked.

She nodded, clearly ashamed that he had discovered it in this fashion.

He leaned down and kissed her gently. "I'm very happy," he said.

"Happy," yelled Johnson joyfully. "Why, the birth of little ones in the house is the source of the greatest joy. I propose a toast. Nowell, fill my glass and get some more for yourself. Mistress Nowell, you too must come over here and join our toast. Don't take too much, mind you; you must watch out not to harm the child."

While Stephen filled the three mugs, Johnson lifted his into the air. "To the new heir of Fort Vaughan." The husband and wife joined him in the toast.

They sat quietly for some moments. "How is your harvest?" Johnson asked finally.

"Excellent."

"It will have to be," said Johnson. "I believe that hostilities will be renewed with the French in the spring. They have built a fortress at Crown Point, a strategic point on Lake Champlain, north of here. Next they will attempt to descend down Lake George. It's like a knife thrust in the heart of the Mohawk and our routes west. I'm determined to stop them, and I am determined to build us a post on the western lakes as well. I'll need the help of men like you, Nowell. Next summer doesn't look like it is going to be a time for harvesting. It looks like the return of war. And this time, by God, it will be the last war. France must not be allowed to retain a foothold."

Stephen started to laugh. "That will require a drastic change in attitude on the part of His Majesty's government, Mr. Johnson. For your England has treated events in North America as unimportant. We captured Louisbourg. They plan to give it back. How can they expect us to take their war seriously when they treat us in this manner?"

Johnson leaned forward and looked at Stephen. "The time is coming, Nowell, when England must make up its mind to seize an empire here. It will happen, and men like you and I will be the masters of that empire. Great men under the crown."

Katherine interrupted with an offer of tea.

Johnson spent the night and then returned with his Mohawks to Fort Johnson the next morning.

Katherine had expected Stephen to be angry with her for not telling him earlier that she was with child. It had been an embarrassing way for him to discover it. But that night when he came to bed, he had not mentioned it. He had kissed her goodnight and then had turned his bare back toward her. She stroked his back and placed her arm about his waist. She wanted him to touch her, to make love to her. He sensed her need but did not respond. He turned and faced her finally.

101

"We must not do anything to hurt the child," he said.

She did not know about such things, but she thought the other women had spoken of intercourse until just about the last month. But then perhaps she had misunderstood. Stephen knew so much more than she.

A week after Johnson left, Socono and Kip arrived at Fort Vaughan.

Katherine was hauling water from the creek and turned to look up to the house. The Indian was standing directly behind her when she turned around. He was tall; his head was shaved except for a small tuft of hair; he was shirtless and wore only a loincloth. But her eyes riveted on the scar on his face. He was so ugly. She screamed. A white man carrying a musket in his hand and a heavy pack on his back came up behind the Indian.

"Dammit, Socono, you're so goddamned ugly, I can't even let you do simple things like say hello. Excuse me," he said to the terrified Katherine. "My name's Israel Kip. This here bug-eating redskin is Socono. He's Abenacki and not very happy about being in Iroquois country. We're looking for one Stephen Nowell."

Katherine finally became less frightened. "I'm Mrs. Nowell," she said.

"Well I'll be damned—excuse me, Mrs. Nowell. Socono, this is Stephen's squaw."

The Indian looked her over speculatively. Then he smiled, placing his hand on his belly, patting it and sticking it way out in an exaggerated imitation of Katherine's condition. He spoke rapidly in a language that Katherine did not understand. It was clear to her that Kip pretended to know what had been said, but he paid no attention to the Indian.

Stephen came running down to the creek. He had spotted them when he returned from the fields for his lunch. He hugged both of them, clapping Kip on the back with great familiarity. He treated the Indian with greater dignity.

"Katherine, these are my friends. Corporal Kip and I were together at Louisbourg. Socono, as you know, just about raised me. He is my Indian father."

That night Karl came for dinner, as did Hannah and George. The garrison house rang with laughter and they drank far into the night. There would be no work the next day.

Kip and Socono had decided to trap in the woods north of the Mohawk in the Adirondacks. Stephen went to Johnson and got him to agree to protect them from any Iroquois hunting parties. In return they agreed to keep their eyes open for any French activity in the northern part and to warn Johnson should the French move south.

Stephen left the garrison house and joined his friends at their camp in January. Katherine wanted to beg him not to go. She was due at the end of March and she was frightened to stay alone. Stephen wanted Karl to join him but Karl refused, saying he saw little benefit in giving up the enforced laziness of the winter for the hard work of trapping. Stephen claimed he wanted and needed the extra cash that furs would bring, but Katherine always suspected he went off into the woods expecting that somehow or other the wilderness would give up its secrets and his son would be found.

Amy was born on March 2, before Stephen's return. Katherine was alone in bed on the second floor of the garrison house. George and Hannah had moved into the house for the winter since Stephen was gone, but that night Hannah had returned to her own house for just one day and night to put everything in order. George had left just before sundown, with the message that he would return before bedtime. He had to speak to Menninger about tapping some maple trees in the first days of the coming spring. Before he could return, the pain hit her. It began in her back and gradually worked its way around to the front. The pain was worse than anything she had ever experienced in her life and, although the occurrences were far enough apart to indicate that it would be some time before the baby came, Katherine still panicked at the thought of being alone in the house. She sat up in the bed and tried to breathe deeply, hoping that would relieve the excruciating pain that gripped her whole body. She broke out into a sweat. She tried to stand. She had heard that Indian women delivered their own children, that they walked and walked before the baby appeared. The next pain nearly forced her to collapse. She grabbed the bedpost and gripped it until her fingers hurt.

She heard the front door open and close. She called out, "George! I'm up here; please help me. The baby's coming!"

It wasn't George. It was Karl. "Katherine, my God, let me help you," he called out. He bounded up the stair ladder. She had fallen on the bedroom floor. He picked her up and carried her to the bed. He ran downstairs and found some soft cloths and some warm water.

He bathed her face and sat with her. As each pain racked

103

her body, he held her in his arms. "Stephen," she screamed in anguish. "Help me."

"It's all right, Katherine," Karl soothed her.

"Stephen, hold me," she called again. He took her into his arms. She sobbed and he stroked the back of her head.

He knew he would have to help her deliver the child. He didn't know what to do. He hoped there would be no complications and it would all happen naturally.

She stiffened with pain once more and then she screamed. Karl knew that things were moving faster. He had seen soldiers in pain, and he could deal with it. He folded a cloth and forced her to bite on it. She gripped his hand so hard that her nails dug into his flesh, causing it to bleed. Then the bed was suddenly soaked with fluid. He went to the linen chest and pulled out dry bedding. He pulled at the stained sheets and threw them on the floor. Again pain gripped Katherine. Karl held her hand.

"I can feel the baby coming," she said through gritted teeth.

Karl brought candles and placed them on a small table at the foot of the bed. He lifted her gown to check the progress. The baby's head was showing. The woman screamed again and this contraction forced the head free. Karl placed his hand on the baby's head and began to lift gently. The shoulders of the child, and then the whole body, slipped free.

Katherine had fainted. It was a girl. Karl tied the cord and then cut it with his knife. He washed the baby in warm water. She began to cry, filling her lungs with great gulps of air. He dried off her body and then wrapped her in the soft cotton cloth he had taken from below. He placed her in the crook of Katherine's arm.

He took some water and washed Katherine's body, removing the bloodied sheets. He was glad she remained unconscious. She was such a modest woman, and the knowledge that a man had touched her and washed her would have been very painful to her.

When he had finished, he sat beside her, holding her hand. She awoke, her eyes fluttering in panic, and then she saw him sitting on the bed beside her. She looked over at the baby and smiled. Then she looked up at him quizzically.

"It's a girl," he said softly, smiling at her.

She beamed. She looked so beautiful to him—this woman he loved. He had experienced with her the greatest moment in life, the giving of new life. He had felt her suffering, pain racking her body. He had held her next to him and come as close to that experience as a man could. Even before her, he had touched the baby, held her tiny body in his giant hands. They were as much his—this woman and this baby—as they were anyone else's.

"You must get word to Stephen," Katherine said finally. "He'll be so pleased."

Her words destroyed his moment. He had looked upon her longingly. But she was not his. She was Stephen's. He would get word to the father of the child, but he would always remember the moment.

When Stephen returned from trapping, he was surprised to find that Amy had been born. He took down the old Bible that he kept on the shelf above the hearth. He wrote her name and the birthdate carefully. He baptized her himself, using the Latin words he had studied as a boy. Katherine had been shocked to find that he still retained some Papist habits, and she was further shocked that the totally irreligious Karl Stiegler had been the one who had put Stephen up to the baptizing—pestering him to get it done.

When she questioned him about it, he replied that Amy had to have a proper beginning with all the proper trappings if she was to grow up to be a fine lady.

IV

1754-1755

Katherine sat in her bedroom brushing her brown hair before the precious mirror that Aunt Margaret had sent upriver to her from Albany. Stephen was downstairs sitting before the hearth of the garrison house with Karl. They did that every night, going over the day's activities and planning for tomorrow. Occasionally George would join them, but more and more the older man was moving into retirement. She heard Karl laugh. She loved the sound of his laugh and wished she could hear more joyful sounds from her husband these days.

She put down the brush, turned from her dressing table and climbed into bed. Stephen would sit up reading after Karl left and he would come to bed only after she fell asleep. She lay back against the pillows and listened to the sound of the two men talking down below.

Katherine was not oblivious to Karl's feeling for her. She had known from the moment of Amy's birth and from the way he had treated the child. He was far more like her father than Stephen had ever been. She heard them still talking downstairs. Soon Karl would come upstairs with Stephen before returning to his cabin. He would kiss Amy goodnight and then leave. It was his ritual. He doted on the girl. He had held her hand when she had taken her first steps. She called him *Alte,* or "old one" in German, which struck Katherine as funny since the Swiss was barely thirty years old.

Every Sunday morning Karl would come to the garrison house for breakfast. He and Stephen would sip coffee and eat fine bread and fresh eggs that Katherine would prepare. Hannah and George would join them after breakfast and, except for the months of deep winter, Karl would take Amy by the hand and they would walk the farm, checking on the progress of each animal. It was a strange sight, this enormous man with the great muscles and the little girl, her tiny hand lost in his giant one.

She heard the creaking of the stairs as the two of them, one slight and one heavy, came up.

Stephen entered the room. She pretended that she was asleep. She usually was asleep at this time. She heard Karl walk into Amy's room and then leave. Again his footfalls were treading below. She heard the front door slam and the latch fall into place.

She was rarely up this late. The moonlight streamed through the window. Stephen undressed. His body had changed very little over the past five years. His muscles were not prominent like Karl's, but he was hard and strong. His shirt was off and he slipped off his breeches. He put the nightshirt, which Katherine had laid out on the bed, over his head and walked over to the window staring out into the moonlight. His lips moved and Katherine knew that he was praying.

He climbed into the bed next to her. She continued to feign sleep. She wanted him to make love to her but she knew it was hopeless. They had rarely made love since the night when Johnson had first pointed out her pregnancy to him almost four years ago. She was angry with him about this. When she had attempted to speak of it, she became tongue-tied. Proper young women did not speak of sex or the lack of it with their husbands. But she felt cheated and angry. She wanted more children. Obviously he did not. He ignored the one he had, allowing his best friend to play substitute father, all the while pining for the one he could not have and who was not her child at all.

"Are you awake?" Stephen asked her.

She turned and looked at him. "Yes."

"Karl left earlier this evening and then he returned; there's word from Johnson. The French have moved south. The Iroquois have told him that the English have suffered disaster on the Monongahela, at the forks of the Ohio. Virginia troops under a Colonel Washington have been forced to surrender to the French. The whole Virginia, Pennsylvania and Ohio country is aflame. French Indians are all over the back country and have taken up the war hatchet."

Katherine's attention was riveted on the words *Ohio country*, and she knew that the very mention of it had upset her husband. It was there that Molly was supposed to have taken Aaron.

She had been sleepy before, but now she was wide awake. What did it mean for them?

107

"We have to stop them," said Stephen, "before they reach our settlements here. Crown Point isn't that far away. If they take control of Lake George, we'll be under constant attack. Johnson has great power with the Iroquois, but if they perceive England to be weak and France to be stronger, they'll protect him and leave the rest of us in this river valley to our fate. Johnson's organizing an army to stop them—Yorkers—Yankees and Indians. Karl and I will join."

Katherine was frightened. She reached over to Stephen. He took her in his arms and held her. He stroked her back until she fell asleep.

The town of Albany was booming. Never before had its modest Hudson River waterfront along Pearl Street seen such activity. Two armies were being organized. One, under William Johnson, consisted of New York militia as well as militia from Connecticut, Massachusetts and New Hampshire. In addition Johnson secretly received aid from the Mohawks. The Onondaga Council had again decreed neutrality, but Johnson was able to recruit Oneida and Mohawk by paying bounties to individuals. He hoped to have over 200 braves before he moved north against Crown Point. Johnson had also been appointed superintendent of Indian affairs for the northern tribes by the commander-in-chief, General Edward Braddock.

But for all his advancement, it did not mean that William Johnson had no rival for power. The second in command under Braddock was the Governor of Massachusetts, Sir William Shirley, and he too was in Albany.

It was Shirley's task to organize an army to attack the French fortress in the west—Niagara—and Shirley too had New England militia. Moreover, he wanted Indian assistance. Johnson and Shirley had developed a distinct dislike for each other and Johnson would not use his influence with individual warriors to assist his New England rival.

With two armies to provide for, Albany merchants were growing fabulously wealthy. Cornelia Schuyler had entered her father-in-law's business firm shortly after his death and she had done a credible job. Someone, she argued, had to take care of Philip Schuyler's interests. He was a handsome boy, and as a man he would be heavy-set like his father. As an older man, he would in fact be fat, but Cornelia smiled when she thought of him. He would keep the girls of Albany happy, for he had inherited her sensual nature. Her profits, and therefore Philip's profits, from this war would be extensive, particularly if she could break into the war trade.

She had visited William Johnson as soon as he had come to Albany. She had offered to share with him her contact with the New England merchant, Daniel Pierce, and any war contracts that might be derived from him. She still remembered the way he had looked at her, sitting across the parlor in his headquarters from her, smiling that languid smile of his.

"You are really an extraordinary woman, Madam Schuyler," he said softly. "But then again, Cousin Delancey warned me of your parts."

"What about my parts?" she asked.

"He said they were gorgeous," said Johnson, now openly leering at her.

"He only knows the half of it."

"Would it be possible for me to know the whole story?" he asked. "There's a room in the back, where perhaps we could negotiate."

Cornelia rose. "Let's begin," she said.

Johnson got out of his chair and took her hand. He led her to the back room. The room contained a double bed covered with Indian blankets.

"Is it true," asked Cornelia, "that you run naked with Indian women?"

"Never in winter," he replied, drawing her body up close to his. He kissed her mouth and she parted her lips hungrily. He unbuttoned her dress in the back, and as it fell away from her body she pulled away from him and stepped out of it.

Johnson walked to the bed while removing his coat and shirt. He loosened his breeches and then sat on the bed. He pulled off his boots and removed the breeches.

Cornelia stood a few feet from him, admiring his body. "My God, you're a beautiful man," she said. She stepped up to him and touched his chest, tracing the scar left by a bullet wound that had grazed his stomach and left its mark.

He turned onto his stomach. "There's a better one on the shoulder," he said. "An Ottawa arrow went in there."

She placed her finger in the inch-deep wound. "That's exciting," she said, laughing.

"I didn't think so at the time," said Johnson. "But now let me see your scars."

She pulled her chemise up over her head.

Johnson rose from the bed. He cupped her breasts, and,

leaning his head down, he took one of her nipples into his mouth. She shivered.

"You're cold. I can take care of that." He picked her up into his arms and then laid her down on the bed. He covered her body with his own and then began to kiss all the sensitive spots. She was aflame with passion for him before he was finished. She took him and guided him into her. She gasped with the pleasure that continued to build and to build until she thought she would burst.

When they had finished, they lay on the bed, breathing heavily. "I think I have been wasting my time with boys," she said.

Johnson smiled. "You are very accomplished, Mrs. Schuyler. Although I do believe a Mohawk woman could still teach you a thing or two about giving. With you it's all receiving."

"I like to receive," she said, with an edge to her voice. "And I believe it is the same with you. I would like to conclude our deal."

"No deal, madam. This was it. You had me. I had you."

"It could be better."

"I know," he said. "But you fail to understand me, Mrs. Schuyler. I will get in bed with you. I'll take my pleasure with you but I'll not steal with you."

"It's not stealing," she said angrily.

"What do you call it, then? I buy your goods at inflated prices and you slip me part of the profits. I want no part of that."

She rose from the bed and grabbed her clothing. "You're a fool, Johnson."

"About money, yes. But there are compensations," he said, thrusting himself up off the bed and approaching her.

"You're a pig—a stupid, savage pig," she screamed at him. She threw on her dress and stormed out of the room.

Johnson started to laugh. He wondered how she would manage to button the back of her dress without someone's help. She had been angry enough to storm out into the street with her bodice falling down in the front.

That encounter had been enough to shut out the Johnson camp. Johnson had taken over Indian affairs from the Schuylers and, although he had fought bitterly with James Delancey in the past, Delancey, who was still Lieutenant Governor of New York and the enemy of the Dutch merchant aristocracy, had seen the benefit to himself in the Johnson tie and had made peace with his in-law. But an enemy of Delancey's could well be regarded as a friend of William Shirley, and Cornelia hoped to break into the war trade by the opening that the Shirley camp provided. The key to Shirley was his chief suttler—Daniel Pierce of Boston.

She had never met the man, but they would meet today in her Albany residence. Cornelia sat propped in her bed. It was well after ten in the morning and she had not yet risen. Her fellow merchants would have been at their respective desks and offices for well over two hours. They thought her lazy. She rarely showed up at her establishment before noon. But she had discovered that her sex, while barring her from some places and some discussions, gave her other advantages that could be better exercised from her own bedroom.

She would receive this fellow Pierce downstairs, however. It would not do to come on to him too strong—that is, until she knew him better. She would bribe him of course; he was said to be fabulously wealthy, and if he was in army supplies, he had to be corrupt.

Cornelia got out of the bed. She slipped out of her linen and lace nightgown and stood naked before the mirror. Her figure was excellent still. There were some stretch marks on the lower stomach muscles from carrying Philip. They would never go away. But they were a minor disfigurement that would also never grow worse. She would have no more children. She ran her hands over her flat stomach and cupped her breasts. They were large but showed little signs of sagging. She bent forward to look more closely into the mirror and to search her face. "Dammit," she cursed. "It's always the face that goes first." Little lines about the eyes and the mouth cracked the makeup she wore, and which she wore rather heavily now.

She rang for her maid. She needed her clothes laid out and her hair done. This was one of the few times that she missed the little bitch, Katrina. She had had her uses. She had always been very good with Cornelia's hair. The German ox she now employed was clumsy and stupid. "Gretchen," she yelled when there was no response to the tiny bell she kept by her dressing table.

She heard a shuffling in the hall. "Gretchen!"

"*Ja*, Frau Schuyler," the maid said as she opened Cornelia's door.

"I'm meeting with an English gentleman this morning and I must get ready. Where have you been?"

"Downstairs, madam; Fraulein Schuyler is visiting and wants to see you."

111

"Margaret? Is she in Albany? I wonder what she wants. Not more of Philip's inheritance, I hope. Send her up, Gretchen; we'll talk while you do my hair. Hand me my dressing gown."

Margaret Schuyler came into Cornelia's room with a determined stride. "Prepare your guest room, Cornelia, I'm staying!"

"Why, Margaret dear, don't tell me you're abandoning the house I've loaned you at Saratoga."

"Loaned me! Damn you, woman, the house is mine. I have father's sworn public statement to that effect. Our lawyers agreed, and you had better not try and take it from me again or I'll wipe your face in the mud of the street down below. Probably would do you some good. We could get all that gop off your face. Might make you look less like a cadaver."

Cornelia ignored her. "The Saratoga property is yours for life. Then it comes to Philip."

"Brat of a boy," she bellowed. "I'll leave Saratoga to Katherine."

Cornelia was exasperated. "Margaret, you didn't come here to argue the will. Why have you left Saratoga?"

"That devil Johnson came, sent your son-in-law and that Swiss fellow Stiegler to warn me off. I'm too exposed, they said, and in too much danger of a French attack. Not enough rangers around to scout the woods, and I hope Johnson leaves his Mohawks home; they're less than useful these days. So you have a house guest until further notice."

Gretchen left the room when the front bell was rung, leaving Cornelia's hair only partially arranged.

"Here, let me finish that," said Margaret.

Before Cornelia could pull out of the way, Margaret Schuyler had a healthy section of Cornelia's hair in her hand. She yanked it, causing Cornelia to yelp in pain. "Margaret, what the hell are you doing to me?"

"Putting your hair into a decent woman's bun. It's about time you began to look like something more than a slut."

Cornelia flushed with anger. "You fantastically interfering old witch. Find your room and stay in it. Daniel Pierce will write me off for having married into a family of mental misfits if he meets you."

"Who the hell is Daniel Pierce?"

"Only about the most important man in Albany today," was her response.

Gretchen returned, sticking her head into the room. "Mr. Pierce, madam. He's downstairs."

112

"Good," said Cornelia. "Margaret, you go to your room and stay there until after Pierce leaves."

Pierce sat in the parlor, waiting for Cornelia. The room was an elegant one. The woodwork on each door frame and on the mantelpiece was exquisitely carved, and the molded plaster of the ceiling was designed in delicate rosettes. All were painted white. The upholstered furniture was in gold and blue with the Schuyler family crest woven into the fabric. The floors were of oak, stained dark brown.

Pierce was impressed. The Schuylers were monied people —yet people currently involved in trade like himself.

He was sixty years old now, and there was little difference between the color of his powdered wig and his real hair. His complexion was pale. His nose was long and its length was exaggerated by the wire-frame spectacles he wore on the tip of his nose. In fact, he had left off wearing his formal wig and allowed his own hair to grow long. His face had several deep lines in the forehead and about the mouth. He was aging, but it did not really concern him. He felt well and his interests grew daily.

He had married into the Breed family and turned himself from a small-time fur trader into the richest merchant in New England. True, initially much of that wealth had resulted from his interests in the firm of Breed, Nowell, and Pierce and had come from the drive and determination of Sarah Nowell. That firm was now dissolved, and his two partners were deceased, by his hand. But what his former partners had never known was that his own private fortune had far surpassed the wealth he had obtained from their joint ventures.

He had been in the pay of the French government for years—taking payment in the form of carte blanche in the Montreal fur trade. He owned one of the largest licensed fur-trading operations in all of New France. In return, he used his position as a member of the Massachusetts Governor's Council and as a confidante of William Shirley to send the most sensitive information on to Quebec. He was especially well placed now that Shirley was so highly regarded in North American military operations.

During the last war he had been one of the Governor's inner circle. True, his stock had fallen in Quebec when he was not able to prevent the capture of Louisbourg, and he had been forced to keep a very carefully lowered profile after his nephew Stephen Nowell and that interfering sot William Vaughan had accused him of spying. For two years he had drawn on none of his Montreal profits. He had merely let them accumulate. But ten years had passed since the Louisbourg fiasco. Nowell was somewhere in the New York wilderness, probably living like the savage he was. Vaughan, when he wasn't drunk, still made charges and still had influence with New Hampshire men, but Pierce did not bother himself with worn-out adventurers like Vaughan. He was a figure from the past.

Shirley had placed him in charge of the purchase of supplies for his army. His associates in Montreal and Quebec had placed him in charge of insuring that Shirley's army never reached Niagara and that Johnson's army never made it north to Crown Point. He was relatively confident that he could handle the Shirley question, but Johnson was not relying on New England merchants for supplies. Instead, he dealt with local Albany factors. This was why the meeting with Mrs. Schuyler was so important. Her reputation as the most corrupt of the Albany crowd had attracted him to her. He was sure she would be loyal to the interests of her class. He could not pull her into the French camp—at least not yet. But he could make a deal with her for the purchase of the most inferior quality materials for both armies at exorbitant fees. They would both grow rich with enormous profits, and the armies would collapse in the middle of the wilderness, wretchedly supplied and feebly fed. He had achieved at least that much with Braddock's crowd in Virginia—only superhuman efforts would carry them to the forks of the Ohio, and if by some miracle they got that far, they would be in no position to fight, or so he hoped. Mrs. Schuyler need know nothing of the politics. She would leap at the economics of the scheme.

Cornelia entered her sitting room. Pierce rose to greet her. He was overwhelmed. She was strikingly beautiful. Her black hair showed no signs of graying; her violet eyes seemed incredibly alert. He felt that little that she truly wished to know could be kept secret from this woman. She was wearing an extremely low-cut dress, especially considering that this was a morning meeting. She revealed far more than was proper—or necessary.

Pierce had little interest in bare bosoms. He had all appetites under control—except his greed for money.

"Good morning. It's Mr. Pierce, I presume," said Cornelia.

"Madam, please excuse the wretched hour of my call. I hope I have not inconvenienced you too much."

"Not at all, Mr. Pierce, provided that our meeting brings us both benefits. In particular, Pierce, if it brings us both profits for our businesses."

"I think you and I will hit it off quite well, Mrs. Schuyler."

"It's Cornelia."

"Daniel."

"Now, Daniel, how can you and I help each other make money and supply the army?"

"Well, Cornelia, there are a number of ways. . . ."

For the next fifteen minutes Pierce outlined schemes for the purchase of rejected meat and bread and the resale at inflated prices to the army through Pierce's office. Kickbacks to him would be required, but in return Cornelia Schuyler would get exclusive contracts from Pierce. Her firm would play the same role, he hoped, to Johnson's army that his did to Shirley's. Both armies would suffer as a result and neither would achieve their goals. Mrs. Schuyler never mentioned to Pierce that her influence with William Johnson was not significant. She hoped either to improve that position or to dupe Pierce into thinking that she could play an important role in undermining the Johnson expedition. In either case, she hoped to use Pierce to obtain her own ends.

The campfire had gone out on its own at least two hours ago. Stephen lay on the forest floor, wrapped in his Indian blanket. His stomach hurt. He had had cramps ever since he had eaten dinner. The food had been too little and already spoiled.

The first rose lighting of the sky would appear on the eastern horizon within three hours. Everything and everyone was enveloped in the grey-black of an early morning ground fog. The silence of the forest was broken only by the soft snore of Karl Stiegler, who lay beside Stephen.

Stephen was wide awake. He tried to make out Karl's face and could barely see the outline of it. His friend snorted, turned on his back and rolled to the other side, facing away from Stephen. He mumbled something in his sleep but Stephen could not make it out.

Karl had been restless every night since they had left Fort Vaughan to join Johnson's army. In Albany, while Stephen worked to raise volunteers and then to organize a ranger company, Karl, who was the real soldier, had stayed in their tent, brooding. Stephen wasn't quite sure what had upset him. Probably it was the renewal of war. Stephen knew that Karl's sentiments were divided. He lived now with the English, and the French had abused him horribly, but Stephen could not forget the many times Karl had insisted that his loyalty was not to England, but to Stephen Nowell and his family. Karl had told him again without hesitation that he had come on Johnson's expedition against Crown Point only for Katherine's sake—to protect her and Amy and their home. What Karl did not say to Stephen was that Katherine had come to him and begged him to accompany Stephen, to protect her husband from danger. Karl could not refuse her. But Stephen had done his recruiting without Karl's help, and he had done it in the name of Mr. William Vaughan, their mutual employer. Stephen recalled his and Karl's reunion with Vaughan. Johnson had been waiting for the New Hampshire ranger militia to arrive before leaving Albany. Most New England men had arrived by river packet after assembling in New York City—but not New Hampshire men. They had trekked overland, over the mountain, to Albany. Johnson had cursed them heartily because they were late, and he had feared that they might not arrive at all.

Stephen had visited Aunt Margaret's house in Saratoga to see if all was in order, and he sat on the front porch of her house, enjoying a rest before returning to town. Then he heard a booming voice singing a seaman's song. He knew the voice instantly. He rose from his chair and walked quickly out onto the road to Albany, which proceeded in the opposite direction only a few hundred yards north.

Out of the woods at the end of the road came William Vaughan, and following him, about a hundred wearied mountain men from the back country of New Hampshire.

Stephen ran forward, waving his arm in the air. "Willie," he yelled.

Vaughan stopped, and when he recognized Stephen, he ran forward. The two men embraced. Stephen was laughing with delight. "You didn't warn me you were coming."

"What, lose a chance to slap down a Frenchman? I wouldn't miss it. I am surprised at you, boy; I had thought you would be asking me what kept me away so long—not why I came."

He pushed Stephen to arm's length. "Let me look at you. Dammit, you look more like your mother, my Sarah, every day, and you've filled out a bit. You've got a few muscles you didn't have before."

"You've added a few new ones too," said Stephen, punching Vaughan lightly in his well-developed middle section.

116

"A little too much good living—not that my investments in your venture on the Mohawk is spoiling me."

Stephen flushed. He was embarrassed by the failure of Vaughan's estate to bring in handsome profits—or any profits at all, for that matter.

"Stop blushing, Stephen; God, you've not changed in that. I should have a farthing for every time you've blushed in your short lifetime. I could retire without worry about Fort Vaughan."

Stephen smiled back at the large man in front of him. Vaughan had been his benefactor, just as Stephen's mother, Sarah Nowell, had saved Vaughan from a wasted life of alcoholism. Vaughan had been his mother's lover and, after her death at the hands of Daniel Pierce's henchmen, Vaughan had all but adopted Stephen as his son. They had not seen each other in almost ten years, but they had written often, and Stephen felt as close to this giant of a man as ever.

"I've brought some friends of yours along with me." He turned as he spoke; coming up the path from the woods onto the Albany road were Socono and Israel Kip.

Again, Stephen was delighted. He had seen these two woodsmen many times over the last ten years since they had served together at the siege of Louisbourg. Kip was always a joy to be with, and Socono and Stephen's relationship had created a bond of tragedy and love that neither man could break, even if either one had wanted to.

"Damn my eyes, Socono, I think that's Stephen," yelled Kip as he approached. "Hey, Nowell, it's us."

Again Stephen threw his arm about the white man, while grabbing the forearm of the Indian with his free hand. "God, I'm glad you're all here," said Stephen. "It wouldn't have been right without you."

Stephen turned toward the Abenacki. "Has my brother been well?" he said in the Indian's own language.

"My little brother has not forgotten how to speak the tongue of my people."

"Could I forget how to sleep or to eat? It is the language of my soul, Socono."

The Indian smiled at him. The great scar in his cheek, burned into it by the white man's hatred, the scar that had cost Stephen's father his life and Stephen himself years of anguish, was made even more prominent by the Indian's broad smile.

Now everyone who meant something to him would be by

117

his side—everyone, that is, except the most important person, his son Aaron.

Again the Swiss soldier began to snore, but this time more loudly. Stephen started to smile. It was clear that Karl would never make an Indian scout. Every brave in the lake country would know when he was around, just as soon as he fell asleep at night. Stephen was tempted to wake him. But then there were no Indians around at the foot of Lake George, where they were camped. Stephen corrected himself. There were Indians, of course. The Mohawks who had come with Johnson. There was Hendrick and some one hundred braves from Canajoharie. There was Nicus Brant and another hundred from Schoharie. And there was Dagaheari and a handful of Oneidas. Johnson was sure that Hendrick could not be trusted. He had given to Stephen the task of spying on their Indian allies.

Stephen had seen his old enemy from Kanowalohale, Dagaheari, for the first time since the attack on the garrison house. The Oneida had said nothing to him but merely glared at him with his terrifying black eyes.

Stephen reached over and shook his friend's shoulder.

"What's wrong?" asked Karl, almost instantly awake. His soldier instincts had not faded with time.

"You were snoring," said Stephen, laughing.

"What the hell's wrong with that? I always snore."

"We're supposed to be an advance party of scouts. We would need an artillery barrage going on over our heads to cover the noise you're making."

"Jesus Christ," said Karl, flipping onto his stomach. "It's not even dawn yet. Why don't you go back to sleep and then you won't have to listen to me."

They were silent for a few minutes and then Karl began again—softly. Stephen would have gone to sleep himself, but suddenly his forest instincts took over. The ground fog could block his vision, but the dampness in the air did strange things to sound. He heard motion that he could not see and normally would never have heard. Someone was moving through the forest, creeping away from the lake shore and moving east.

Stephen rose to his feet. Johnson had been right. The Mohawks seemed to be deserting the camp. There was no sense in alerting Karl. He was useless in the woods. Stephen crept forward through the underbrush, following his instinct, feeling the ground in front of him to avoid stumbling and alerting the pursued.

They were careful, and he was hard pressed to follow them. But he did follow them, and closely. They were Indians; he was sure of that. No one else but an Indian or someone like himself, trained by Indians, could have made so little noise in the dark. But they could not be hostile Indians. They clearly had come from Johnson's camp. Had the general sent out Indians without alerting his white scouts? He thought not. They were deserters.

Stephen was sure there were about ten of them. They were making good time and they were practically noiseless. They continued for some miles to the east. They were heading toward Wood Creek, a long, narrow extension of Lake Champlain that stuck like a knife toward the Hudson.

Johnson had constructed a fort, Fort Edward, on the bend of the Hudson south of the headwaters of Wood Creek to protect the settlements along the great river from French attacks, coming from the lake and the creek. Then he had decided to approach Crown Point via Lake George. A wagon road was hacked out of the forest from Fort Edward to the southern end of Lake George—their current campsite.

About halfway between the English camp and Wood Creek, the Indians that Stephen followed became bolder and began to walk almost uncaringly through the forest. Stephen knew that they expected to meet someone else, and that in this way they were alerting their contacts to their arrival.

There was still an hour to go before the sun rose and began to burn off the fog. Without the protection of the blanket of grey mist, he would have to stay much farther away from them, but given the noise they were now making, they would not be hard to follow. Then they stopped. Stephen was alerted by the silence. Should he creep forward or should he stay still? Had they heard him and were they now lying in ambush? Or had they made contact with those who awaited them? He had little choice. He had come this far. It made little sense to come creeping to a halt and know no more than when he began. He got onto his hands and knees and inched forward. He felt in the leaves in front of him for any obstacles. His heart was pounding. Sweat began to break out on his forehead and in his armpits, sweat caused not by hard work but by his fear of detection.

Then he heard voices. He exhaled softly. He had not been heard. Instead, the Indians had met with those who expected them. Stephen crept closer. The words he heard were in Mohawk, and he recognized the voice of Nicus Brant.

They sat about a small clearing, wrapped in blankets to keep out the morning cold. There were about twenty Indians. They did not rise to speak, as was the formal custom of the Iroquois. It was difficult for Stephen to know who said what, but it was clear to him that he had stumbled onto something of great importance.

"We greet our brothers from our old river home," said a voice from out of a blanket.

"Greetings also to you of Caugnawaga," said Nicus Brant.

"Why have you asked for this meeting and why have you demanded that we deceive our white brother Onontio, the French Governor, and his brother Dieskau by coming to this meeting with you?"

Nicus' voice rose, as if he were about to deliver a formal oration. "These are sad days for the Mohawk. We will be forced to fight and kill each other. Break with your priests and come home to our castles. Join with our brother—He Who Does Great Things—and make war on the French. They have always been our enemies. Since they first arrived on the Northern River and came to our lakes and attacked us, they have always been our enemies. They gave wealth to our enemies the Abenacki and the Huron. They tried to take the fur trade from us and inflict their priests upon us. Join with us and fight them."

"The priests are our fathers, and they have brought us to the home of the Good Jesus—the church. We will not join you. But neither must we fight each other. Mohawk must never wage war against Mohawk. Go home; leave the English. The French army is close at hand. The English do not even know they are here. When they look for you, we will lead them into the woods and we will become lost and give many apologies."

Several of the warriors began to laugh. Nicus waited a moment and then stood up. "That is the only solution," he said. "These two armies are blind. We Mohawks are their eyes. They will never find each other and no Mohawk will be forced to face a brother Mohawk in anger."

There were solemn nods about the circle. The warriors rose. Several who were related closely to each other embraced, but soon the two parties separated and went in opposite directions, back toward their separate armies.

Stephen sat motionless until all the Indians had disappeared. He was shocked by what he had heard. It did not

120

surprise him that Mohawks would place loyalty to each other ahead of devotion to either the English or the French cause. But what did shock him was the news that the French army under Baron Dieskau was at Wood Creek. Johnson had received no word at all about that. The French, instead of waiting for the English assault on Crown Point, had themselves taken the offensive and were within striking distance of either Johnson's army at Lake George or at Fort Edward and of the settlements on the Hudson. He had to bring that news back to camp, and he would have to be as careful getting back to English lines as he had been in discovering this meeting.

Stephen's report to Johnson was confirmed that night by the arrival of a wagon master from the Fort Edward road. He had been captured by the French and had escaped. The French were on the move against Fort Edward. Only a handful of militia defended it. Johnson would have no choice but to turn back to defend his supply base. On the next morning he would set out on the road back to Fort Edward.

He had at first listened to Stephen's report without comment; a trembling of the nerve just below his right eye betrayed his anger, however. "Thank you, Nowell," he said bitterly. He rose from his camp desk and began to walk about his tent. He wore the uniform of a British general, and Stephen thought he looked frightfully uncomfortable in it. Stephen had rarely seen him in anything but Indian garb. He slammed his fist into the desk. "I don't deserve this from them," he said. "Not from Hendrick and the Brants. I forgave that damned old man once before after he gave me his word and then betrayed me. I'll not forgive him again. I'll put him to the test once and for all."

The next morning at dawn Johnson brought all the Mohawk leaders before him. King Hendrick led them before the general. Hendrick wore the ancient military coat that had been given to him in England many years before in the reign of Queen Anne. He looked old and tired. His face was drawn and haggard, and the muscles of his chest had turned to fat and sagged badly. His middle had grown enormously, whereas his legs were skinny. His stomach was sour and he broke wind or belched with great regularity. Yet this almost comic figure had an air of dignity about it.

Alongside King Hendrick stood Old Brant. He too looked old and weary. He had determined to remain behind. He was too old and tired to trek off into the woods seeking Frenchmen. Nicus would go in his place and uphold the family honor.

Dagaheari, the Oneida, stood directly behind Old Brant. It was for vigorous younger men like him to wage war.

Johnson got up from his camp chair and began to address the Mohawks in their language. "My brothers, the French have descended the lake and are nearby and threaten Fort Edward. It disappoints me that my eyes have failed me and that I have not known of their approach before this. But I have determined to march ahead to meet them."

Hendrick flashed a quick look of surprise in Old Brant's direction. "How do you know these things, Warraghiyagey?" he asked.

"Word came in late last night. We march now."

"We are not yet prepared for war," said Old Brant. "We have not yet consulted the omens."

"I march to war," yelled Johnson very rudely. "If my brothers wish to join me, I will honor them by giving them the van. If they wish to remain behind like old squaws, they may remain behind and cast bones and read entrails. But Warraghiyagey goes to war."

"As does Dagaheari," yelled the Oneida. "How about my cousin of the Turtles, King Hendrick?"

The Mohawk chieftain seemed almost to grow taller. He looked at Dagaheari with disdain. "I was killing the French when you were still staining the floor of the longhouse with your baby piss," he said to Dagaheari. "I will lead my warriors into battle," he said.

"How, old man?" answered the angry Oneida. "Your knees are weak and stiff; your arms cannot wield an axe. In fact, there is not a part of you that isn't stiff except for the one that needs to be."

Some of the Mohawks began to grumble and moved threateningly toward Dagaheari. The Oneida had harbored his hatred of Hendrick and the Mohawk for years, ever since they had tricked him and allowed Kenonranon and his mother to escape him. He thoroughly enjoyed this opportunity to humiliate the great sachem of the Mohawk.

Johnson saw trouble brewing and intervened. "Of course, great Hendrick will lead all of the Iroquois into battle. If he cannot walk, he will ride. I will give him my horse."

When the English column set out toward Ford Edward, the day following Stephen's scouting and conference with Johnson, they set out with the Mohawks, Hendrick atop Johnson's mare in the van. Vaughan's New Hampshire rangers, including Stephen and Karl, followed. The sun was up and warm as they left the camp in double columns, moving toward the east. The sunlight was bright, reflecting off the lake with a glare that blinded them all. Karl grumbled that they should have set out either earlier or later. This was clearly the worst time to be moving east, with the sun low in the sky and the enemy supposedly in front.

Stephen walked along next to his friend. William Vaughan rode as well, leading the New Hampshire rangers. Kip was directly behind Stephen, and Socono walked behind Karl.

Some Massachusetts and Connecticut militia had tried to force Socono up front with the other Indians; after all, Johnson had ordered all Indians up front. But Vaughan would not hear of it. Stephen had alerted him to the deep-seated hatred that existed between Dagaheari and Socono and between the Iroquois and the Abenacki.

As they moved forward from the camp, they entered a deep gulley, which ran between mountain slopes on either side. Here the sun problem disappeared. It was dark and desolate. Direct sunlight would not penetrate until the sun was very much higher in the sky, no longer blocked by the high peaks.

They had moved several miles into the gulley when Hendrick halted his horse. A voice speaking Mohawk came out of the gloom. "Why do our brothers come painted for battle?"

Hendrick sat taller in the saddle. "Why did not our brothers of Caugnawaga lead the French astray and then turn their backs to the direction of Canada, as they promised?"

"Our general and our priests are not easily fooled—any more than is Warraghiyagey," the voice responded.

"We must then ensure that no fighting takes place between us," said Hendrick.

"We will allow the mighty Hendrick and his warriors to pass through this ambush," said the voice. "We will attack only the whites."

Dagaheari raised his musket and fired in the direction of the voice. "No more Mohawk betrayals," he yelled.

Instantly both sides of the gulley burst out with musket fire. Indians fell. Hendrick was struck by a ball. The mare was killed instantly and fell to the ground, throwing the heavy Indian onto the ground on top of her. Hendrick rose to his feet; blood poured out of his chest. He staggered away from the dead horse into the underbrush. No one would see him here. Tears of pain and of sorrow streamed down his painted face. He crashed noisily through the underbrush, but with all the firing behind him, it didn't matter. No one could hear to follow him.

He pushed aside a small balsam tree and staggered into a clearing, which rested on a slope of the mountain. As he entered the clearing, he saw women and children. They were hiding behind rocks and trees. It was the encampment of the Caugnawagas. He fell forward in a heap. He lifted himself onto his elbows and he looked at them. The women started to come toward him. They had knives in their hands and they giggled. Hendrick's heart sank. He was to die at the hands of squaws and children. But it did not matter. Far worse had happened back in the gulley. In this clearing he would die without dignity, but back behind him, his nation, the Iroquois, had died.

As soon as the musket balls began to pour into the ranks of Indians and New Hampshire men, William Vaughan got down from his mount and joined Stephen, Kip and Karl. Socono had already disappeared into the woods beside the trail. The Mohawks had panicked and fallen back upon the New Hampshire men. Vaughan grabbed Karl's shoulder. "You, Stiegler, rally the men and begin a retreat back to camp. Stephen, come with me. Let's see if we can rally the savages."

It was no use. Hendrick had disappeared. Stephen saw Nicus Brant running in the woods, trying to get his men to change directions, but the unthinkable had happened. Mohawks, even though they were Mohawks from the Catholic missions, had fired and killed other Mohawks.

Stephen looked for Dagaheari, but there was no sign of him. He would be a marked man. The Mohawk would never forget his actions or forgive him for this day.

Vaughan ducked behind one of the many boulders that were strewn about the gulley. Stephen rushed to his side and fell behind the rock just as a musket ball made a splattering noise above his head as it struck the rock.

"We better get out of here," said Vaughan. "I think Stiegler has gotten the militia back down along the path out of the enemy's range."

"Have you seen Kip?" asked Stephen.

"He ran off into the woods with Socono," said Vaughan. "Don't worry about those two. They can take care of themselves. Let's try to make it back to Stiegler's line."

The two men rose together and began to run back toward

the west, down the gulley path. They could hear musket balls whizzing over their heads and by either side of them. An answering fire from the direction in which they ran passed over their heads also, as their friends tried to provide covering fire.

Then Vaughan fell. Stephen halted his dash and turned around. The large man sat holding his knee, pulling it up toward his body. "Don't stop, Stephen, keep going. I'll be all right."

"Like hell you will," yelled Stephen. "You can't walk, much less run. Put your arm around me. We'll go together."

"We'll both be killed. Keep moving."

Stephen grabbed Vaughan's arm and pulled him to his feet. The older man's heavy arm fell about Stephen's neck and the two began to move forward again.

Then suddenly Vaughan's weight became dead weight. Stephen saw blood pour out of the wound on the side of Vaughan's head. Blood gushed down on Stephen's face, neck and shoulders. He staggered under Vaughan's weight and tripped forward, falling flat on his face. He was dazed for a moment. Vaughan's body had fallen on top of him. He had to throw him off and drag him toward safety. Stephen was close to exhaustion. His breath came in great gasps. He heaved upward and forced Vaughan's massive body to hit the ground next to him with a thud. Stephen looked into Vaughan's pale face and felt the side of his neck for a pulse. Vaughan was still living. Stephen tried to yank him upward and haul him over his shoulder into a carrying position, but Vaughan's two-hundred-pound frame barely moved. Stephen was flushed from the effort and flushed with anger that this man who had been so good to him would probably die right in front of him because Stephen was too weak to save him. Again he heaved Vaughan's body. It moved. He drew it up toward his body and, bending low, he let Vaughan drape across his back and shoulders. He placed his hand under Vaughan's thigh to hold him in place and then staggered forward.

He heard balls winging by him, smacking into rocks and trees and ricocheting in all directions. He moved as fast as he could, but everything seemed to slow down. Each step forward seemed to take an eternity and his goal—the line of fire established by Karl—seemed to be getting farther and farther away. Finally he fell again. Vaughan's body again fell on top of him. But now he didn't care. He didn't have the strength to begin all over again. He couldn't get to his own feet, much less carry William Vaughan. Suddenly he felt Vaughan's body lifted off him. He turned around. It was Karl. He had lifted Vaughan off the ground with one great effort and held the man in his arms.

"Get up, Stefan," Karl yelled. "Get moving—forward."

"I can't."

Karl nudged Stephen in the rear with his foot. "Get your ass in motion, soldier," he yelled in his best corporal's voice. "I promised Katherine and I promised Amy to get you home alive, and that promise I don't take lightly."

Stephen got up on his hands and knees. He breathed in a gulp of air and then rose to his feet. He started to run, knowing full well that if he stopped he would never be able to begin again. As fast as he ran unburdened, he could hear Karl keeping up with him, carrying the bulky form of William Vaughan. Stephen stumbled, but this time he fell into the arms of a New Hampshire ranger. They had made it safely back to their lines.

As soon as William Johnson heard the firing of muskets in the gulley, he determined to turn his campsite into a fortified defensive position. Every supply wagon was overturned to make a barricade running in a great semicircle, anchored on each end by the shores of Lake George. As the New Hampshire men and Mohawks came falling back into the camp, they found the safety of this small fort and climbed through the narrow openings between wagons with relief.

Karl dropped the still form of William Vaughan gently on the ground before the surgeon's tent. Stephen collapsed beside Vaughan's body. As he looked beside him, he saw Israel Kip sitting, breathing heavily. A surgeon's orderly knelt before Vaughan. "It's only a superficial head wound. He's unconscious from the blow. But he will recover."

"He'll recover if we take him out of here," said Kip. "He's lost a lot of blood. Most of it is on you, Nowell. First thing these bastards will want to do is bleed him. Take him to where the New Hampshire boys can look after him."

Kip grabbed Vaughan under the arms and Karl grabbed his feet. Stephen followed behind until they found the New Hampshire campsite. Here William Vaughan was among his own and would be cared for.

Johnson seemed to be everywhere. The wagons were now in place, but individual boxes and cartons had been piled between wagons to form a more effective barrier; time was running out. They were already under fire.

The Caugnawaga and French Canadian volunteers had placed themselves in the woods that ringed the campsite clearing. They fired at long range and without great effect at Johnson's "fortress."

Johnson came up to the New Hampshire rangers. He took a look at the unconscious Vaughan and then turned to the others. "Who's in command here?"

Kip scratched his head. "Well, we took a vote making Willie Vaughan our colonel. We never did get another vote to see who would take over if anything happened to him. So I guess no one is in charge until we have another election. Hardly have time for that now."

Johnson looked exasperated. "You," he said, pointing to Karl, "you used to be a soldier."

Karl nodded yes, but before he could remind Johnson that he had once been in the French army, Johnson continued, "Good; you are now militia captain—battlefield commission. Let them worry about voting after the battle. Now get these men on the line."

As he spoke, a musket ball crashed into his hip. He yelled and grabbed Kip for support. But he stayed on his feet. "Goddammit," Johnson yelled, "I can't afford to be wounded. Get me over to the surgeon's tent. I need this ball removed so that I can continue."

Karl began to yell at the New Hampshire men. "On the line," he shouted. "The French are coming."

Stephen found a place behind the heavy wooden crate. Kip wedged himself next to Stephen after returning from the surgeon. "How's Johnson?" Stephen asked him.

"He's hurting. They got the ball out of him. It took a lot of guts. He just gritted his teeth and let them probe and then yank. That's a brave man. He wouldn't take no rum or anything. He said he had to have a clear head. He's resting in his tent, with word to get him on his feet and outside once the French attack."

All was quiet out front now. The Canadian and Indian contingents had halted their fire. The only noise was that of troops marching. The tread of booted feet, muffled by the soft ground of the forest, and the jingling of equipment could be heard quite clearly in the English encampment.

They came narrow file out from the gulley and then spread out before the English position. These were the troops of the regular French army. They were dressed in uniforms of white, with black leather boots. Each man's musket was crowned with a long bayonet, many of which caught the sunlight and flashed into the faces of the colonials behind the wagons.

"Will you look at that!" said Kip with a low whistle.

The French marched in precise formation and turned on command into three long lines, facing the English wagons. They stood there in silence. Their commander, Marshall Ludwig August, Baron Dieskau, strode to the front of the line.

"That's the one," whispered Kip. "He's the one we aim for when we get close enough. Always get the officers. These monkeys can't fight without someone telling them what to do."

Stephen nudged Kip. "Where are the Indians and Canadians from this morning?"

"Can't see any of them. It may be the big monkey doesn't want them to steal any glory from his regulars."

Dieskau waved his sword in the air, and a cheer rose from the ranks of his troops. They marched forward all along the line. When they came within musket range, they kept up a steady barrage by having the first line kneel and fire and then having the second line pass through its ranks and step forward. They continued advancing, kneeling and firing in this manner, creeping ever closer to the English. But as the ranks came closer and closer they were thinned.

Kip was yelling at Stephen, "Don't let the bastards get up too close. These men will run if someone comes after them with a bayonet. We must stop them outside the line."

Again the sounds of musket balls passing overhead were heard. But this no longer frightened Stephen. He looked for Karl. The new captain was about five places down the line from Stephen, encouraging the men. Even above the sounds of the battle, Stephen could hear him yell, "Aim carefully. Pick your target. Don't fire blind. Make every shot count." His face was flushed but Stephen could see that he exuded confidence, and without even an introduction, these New Hampshire men trusted him. After the battle they would worry about local politics and pick a new leader, but right now, in the heat of the battle, they were happy to have a professional soldier as their leader.

Karl left that group of men and approached Stephen and Kip. "Keep your head down, Stefan," he said. "You're getting careless. When you get careless, you get killed."

Stephen just smiled.

Kip let out a yelp. "I got him. I got the bastard chief monkey!"

Stephen and Karl both raised their heads and took a look out onto the field. It was true. Dieskau had fallen, and a group of officers had taken him into their arms and hauled him back toward the woods, away from the battle.

"Where's Johnson?" asked Karl. "I think it's time to counter. The French are tired and they're hurt. Johnson should order us forward."

"But Johnson's hurt too," argued Stephen. "Let's just do it."

Karl thought a moment and then nodded. "Let a chance like this slip by and you lose the battle and probably your scalp. New Hampshire men," he yelled, "the French are ready to retreat—out after the bastards."

The rangers cheered and, as one body, they rose from behind the wagons and cartons and poured out onto the field. All along the line the militia joined the New Hampshire men, thinking the order had been given to charge.

The French ranks shuddered, as if hit by a shock wave, and then they broke; discipline collapsed. After almost an hour in the open field, being shot at by experts, and after seeing comrade after comrade shot dead next to them, seeing this horde of savage-like Americans charging toward them was too much. They ran for the safety of the woods, where their retreat would be covered by the Indians and the Canadians.

Stephen and Kip ran side by side across the field. Stephen tried to keep an eye out for Karl, but he had lost sight of him. They entered the edge of the woods. They stopped running now and became more cautious. The shadowlike forms of Indians could be seen. They had been unwilling to assault a fortified position, and now they had no intention of staying to fight a rear-guard defense. The Canadians had argued with them to no avail. Both groups would join the regulars and retreat to their boats on Lake Champlain for a hasty return to Crown Point.

Kip went off to the left and was soon out of sight. Stephen moved ahead carefully. He was more at home here in the woods. Karl came crashing through the underbrush behind him. He was out of breath from racing across the field. "Stefan, we must get the men to fall back. We've routed them. But they will surely set up an ambush ahead, hoping that we will become overconfident."

There was a stirring in the bushes in front of them. Karl raised his pistol and fired into the bush. There was a scream and then a cursing in German.

129

Karl looked at Stephen and then both men crept forward to push the bushes aside. There sat a bloodied Baron Dieskau, his back against the side of a tree, abandoned by his troops.

He looked at the two men and then began to complain in French. "Why have you two shot me again? I am harmless, wounded, unarmed." His knees were wounded but bandaged. Karl's pistol ball had pressed into his hip, but it was not bleeding too badly.

"We shot you," said Stephen, "because you're the enemy and we had no idea whether you were armed or not."

Despite his pain Dieskau looked at Stephen in surprise. "Your speech is very good. You are a Frenchman."

"I studied in France. I was a Canadien. Now I live with the English."

"Well, Canadian, I think little of your countrymen after this battle. They refuse to join the assault. They are the cause of my ruin."

"They refused to join the slaughter, you mean. My former countrymen are no fools. If the English take Canada, as someday I believe they must, if we are to have peace in North America, they will take it because you Frenchmen, or whatever you are, refused to listen to them."

"No more arguments," said Karl. "Baron," he said in German, "I will help you back to the English camp if you promise not to try to escape."

"Escape! How in God's name could I do that? My legs, man, you have destroyed my legs. Do you think I can sprout wings? I am captured by numbskulls who speak all the languages of Europe."

Karl hoisted Dieskau over his shoulders as he had hoisted Vaughan earlier. The general yelled with pain and then fainted. "Well, at least he'll be quiet on the return trip. Come back with me, Stefan."

"No, I'll wait here for Kip. He won't be long. The French are gone. There's no more to do here."

"Take care. Remember, I promised Katherine."

"Karl, I can take care of myself in the woods."

"That's for sure," laughed Karl. He turned, gave his burden a hoist up higher on his shoulders and left.

The woods were quiet now. One could not have guessed how they had rung with musketry only minutes before. The quiet was almost deathly. There were no birds singing. They had all been frightened off. Only the mosquitoes were undaunted by the sounds of war. Stephen slapped at one, which

130

had landed on his face and had drawn blood. A little trickle of blood began to drip down the side of his cheek.

He sat down on the leaf- and moss-covered ground. He would never know what instinct forced him to turn, but it saved his life.

He saw the tomahawk come crashing down toward his head. He had only enough time to raise his arm. He felt the jolting pain as the steel axe slashed through his flesh, and he heard the sickening sound of snapping bones. He swung himself around and lashed out with his foot. The Indian tripped and fell, with thrashing arms and legs, on top of him. They were face to face and Stephen looked into the hate-filled, black eyes of Dagaheari.

He grabbed Stephen by the throat to choke him. "The blackrobe dies now," he said through clenched teeth. "The Oneida are avenged and I will take your head back to Kanowalohale to show all that Skenandon can rest in peace. His murderer has felt an Oneida axe."

Stephen felt himself slipping into darkness. The Oneida had cut off his breath, and the pain in his arm was becoming excruciating. With the last burst of strength, he brought his knee up sharply into the Indian's groin. Dagaheari shouted in pain and rage. His spit hit Stephen in the face, but he relaxed his hold on Stephen's throat. The Indian staggered to his feet. He looked eight feet tall to Stephen as he lay helpless on the ground. Dagaheari's chest was heaving in and out from the struggle. He reached for the hunting knife at his side. He sneered at Stephen. "Before I kill you, Blackrobe, I will tear out your heart while you still live and I will eat it before your eyes."

A musket shot broke the silence of the forest. Dagaheari buckled at the knees, a look of surprise filled his face and then his eyes went blank and he fell face forward. Stephen saw Socono and Kip standing over him. He saw Socono bend down over Dagaheari's body and remove his scalp. He knew then who it was who had fired the killing shot. But he remembered no more.

What followed was always like a long nightmare to Stephen. He remembered rum being forced down his throat. He gagged and vomited it up. His coat and shirt were torn off him; he felt himself lifted onto a table while great strong arms grabbed his arms and legs. Then came the pain. His left arm seemed to become the focus of all the pain that was possi-

131

ble in the world. The knife dug into it, pulling back flesh. He screamed for them to stop it, but it went on. Next came the sound of the saw biting into bone. His muscles jumped. He tightened and strained all of his muscles to get up off the table. Yet the hands that held him down prevailed.

Next he remembered the jolting of a wagon along the wilderness road to the Hudson. Each bump, each rock forcing the iron and wood wheels to jump into the air filled his whole body with more pain. He remembered being so hot, kicking off blankets with his feet; his whole left arm was on fire with fever. He could feel it from shoulder to fingertips. Rough male hands grabbed him then and lifted him out of the wagon into a boat. The river flowed south and the journey to Saratoga was quick. He remembered hearing the voice of Aunt Margaret, and he felt her softer touch and the smell of fresh linen bedding. But still the pain and still the burning up inside.

He saw her sitting behind the cool waterfall. It was the waterfall of the pool back at Louisbourg. She was naked. Her brown skin dripped with the spray from the falls. She smiled as he approached her. She was holding something in her arms. It was their child—Aaron. He reached out to touch her. But she pulled back. She thrust the child at him. He took it into his arms. He smiled down at the child. Then he gasped in horror. The child's body was burned, flayed. Its tiny arms and legs were pierced with hot knives. Live, burning coals had been placed in its eye sockets and had burned straight through into its skull. Stephen started to scream, "Aaron, Aaron—my son."

Katherine came to Saratoga from Fort Vaughan with Karl. One look at his anguished face had told her that the situation was desperate. She was at Stephen's bedside on the flats of Saratoga two days later. He was red and flushed with fever, and he repeated only one word over and over again, the English name of his Indian son. His eyes opened and he looked up at her, unseeing. He tried to move the stump of his left arm to turn his body. He seemed unaware that the arm was gone. Katherine reached over and turned him onto his right side. She grabbed for the pillows and placed them against his back and rump to make him more comfortable and to prevent him from rolling back onto the stump and making it bleed again.

Her fear was that his arm would become infected, and if it

got worse she knew she would lose him. She sat and watched his agony and was helpless. She could wash his face and she could wash his body. She could make sure that he was covered with blankets to prevent chills. The doctors could come and sniff at the stump and place compresses on it and bleed him to remove infectious vapors from his system. But she saw life slipping away from him.

Amy sat in the room playing. She wanted her father to get up and play with her. Karl took her by the hand and led her outside for a walk down by the riverbank.

Margaret leaned over and placed a cool cloth on Stephen's forehead: She shook her head and gave a worried glance at Katherine. "The boy suffers so. I think only one thing will ever satisfy him. He has to see his son once again. I think if he doesn't, he'll surely die, and soon."

"But we have no idea where the boy is."

"One man does—Johnson. Go see him and find Stephen's son. It's the only way we'll keep the father alive."

The victory at the battle of Lake George, as it came to be called, had brought instant renown to William Johnson. He was the toast of America and of England. His capture and generous treatment of his counterpart, Baron Dieskau, was well received in France. It was said that the Mohawks had wanted to burn Dieskau in revenge for King Hendrick, but that Johnson had intervened personally and had defended the marshall's life by placing his own at risk. The ultimate and unexpected glory came with the King's award, the title of baronet. Now He Who Does Great Things was also Sir William Johnson, Bart.

He was recuperating swiftly from his hip wound and at the same time working against the rumors spread by members of the Shirley faction that he had spent the whole battle in his tent and that real glory should go to others. In this war of words, Johnson once again proved victorious. Shirley was recalled in disgrace. Johnson had won a battle, and England, particularly after Braddock's disaster in Pennsylvania, needed a hero who won battles.

Johnson's suite of rooms in an Albany inn was constantly crowded with wellwishers and favor-seekers. Katherine arrived at the outer room of the suite unannounced, accompanied by Karl.

A clerk dressed in black, with only a white ruffled collar to break the drabness of his appearance, attempted to halt them and block their path to the general.

133

Karl shoved him aside with one thrust of his heavy arm. "You go in, Katherine," he said. "I'll wait out here with this gentleman."

She walked into Johnson's private chamber. He was seated at his desk working on papers. He looked at her from behind a pair of spectacles. He took them off quickly. Very few people knew that the woodsman was now nearsighted.

"Well, neighbor, it is always good to see friends from back up the river. Mrs. Nowell, it is good to see you. How is your husband?"

"Not well. In fact, I believe that I shall lose him."

He rose from his desk and walked over to her, placing his arm on her shoulder. "Can I be of assistance?"

"That's why I came. He keeps calling for the boy, his son—Aaron. I believe that if he could see the child once again he would either get well or die in peace." She began to sob. "But I can't stand seeing him suffer this way."

"How has he reacted to the loss of his arm?" Johnson asked.

"He isn't even aware of it."

Johnson frowned. "The boy's mother is vehemently opposed to your husband seeing him. She is a strong-willed woman."

"But she must have loved Stephen once. She could not want to see him die in this manner."

Tears streamed down Katherine's cheeks.

Johnson raised her face to look up at him, and with his other hand he took a linen cloth from his desk and dried her tears. "I suppose it would be possible to obtain a favor from Molly Brant for Stephen, in return for a favor from Katherine to William." He smiled at her.

At first she did not understand the implication of his suggestions, but when she did, she froze. She should never have left Karl out in the other room. Had he been present, Johnson would never have come to the realization that he was alone in his bedroom with a beautiful woman.

"Sir William," she said coldly, "I hope you have not misunderstood my intention in coming to see you here. I love my husband and I wish only to help him."

"And I, madam, love Molly Brant, but I have children by other women and she has them, obviously, by other men. There is no harm done. Why don't you just relax. I'll serve us some wine, and you send that German brute back home; we'll talk about Aaron Brant."

134

He reached down and touched Katherine's breast; then he bent forward and kissed her passionately on the mouth. She did not resist him, but neither did she respond. He took her hand and led her toward the bed. He sat down on it and she stood in front of him.

"Dammit," he said finally. "React! Do something! Scream for your German boy to help you! Or rush into my arms and make love with me. But don't just stand there and stare at me."

She turned on him angrily. "What do you expect of me? Only you can get me what I want. I need the boy to keep my husband alive. Only you can get me that. If the price I have to pay is to sleep with you and have you slobber all over me, then I'll do it, but don't expect me to enjoy it. Go ahead and take your will with me. I need something from you. Take your needs from me."

"Christ almighty," shouted Johnson in disgust. "God save me from virtuous women." He rose from the bed and walked past her to the desk. He picked up the quill and began to write on a piece of paper. He signed it and then turned to Katherine, who still stood by the bed. "Here, take this to Fort Johnson. The boy is there, as is his mother. They have been there for several months. Molly Brant is now mistress of Fort Johnson. She will allow the boy to go to Saratoga to see his father if I ask her to."

Katherine walked over to him and took the paper into her hand. "Thank you," she said and then turned to leave the room.

"Mrs. Nowell," Johnson interrupted before she could leave. "Please don't think too harshly of me. I would never have taken you by force."

"But you would have taken me if I had agreed."

Johnson shrugged and then smiled. "And I would right now, or at any other time, should the opportunity present itself. I am, madam, a very passionate man."

Katherine merely nodded and then left the room. As soon as she saw Karl, she rushed over to him and he put his arms around her. He knew she was frightened and she trembled. "What's wrong, Katherine?" he asked.

"Nothing," she responded. "Quickly, let's get out of here; I've got this paper. If you or Kip or Socono could go back up the Mohawk to Fort Johnson, we can bring Stephen's son here very quickly. That's the only thing that matters now."

Karl looked at her quizzically and then looked at the door

135

of Johnson's room. The door opened as he stared at it. Johnson himself appeared. He bowed at Karl and at Katherine.

Katherine took Karl's hand in hers and led him out of the suite and down into the street. The wagon ride to Saratoga would be a rough one, but with Johnson's note in her hand, Katherine had some hope that all would work out.

Stephen lay in the bed, propped up on pillows. His face was still flushed with fever and his eyes seemed glazed; he stared straight ahead. The boy walked into the room, crowded with his father's wife, child and friends, both red and white. He stood tall before the bed, to gaze into the face of his warrior father. He remembered the face. It was older looking and haggard, but it was the same face. This was the man who had told him the beautiful tales of the animals of the forest and had helped him to hunt his first game. His mother always praised his father to him. She had told him that his father was a white and would always remain one. He would never understand the ways of the Iroquois. This was why she had been forced to leave and take him with her, away from his father. He Who Does Great Things, his new father, understood the Iroquois ways, even if he too was white.

The white squaw, wife to his father, signaled him to step forward, to come closer to the bed and to the man.

Stephen looked at the boy. At first he merely stared, but then a look of comprehension came to his face. "This is my son?" he asked, his voice croaking.

The boy was tall and sturdily built. His skin was a golden color and his hair was jet black and straight. He stood in breechcloth and leggings; beads were worked into his hair. Only his piercing blue eyes betrayed anything but Indian ancestry.

Stephen tried to place his left arm about the boy's shoulder. He looked down at the bandaged stump, surprised. He had been aware of his loss for some days, but he could not get used to the idea. He reached over with his right hand and touched the boy. "Aaron, you've grown tall," he said in Mohawk. "Are you as clever as the fox?"

The boy smiled, flashing his white teeth. "I hope to be so one day, Father. But I am not yet a man. It will take more time."

"You are already as wise as the owl if you know that as a boy," said Stephen.

Again Aaron smiled at him.

136

Stephen seemed to drift off to sleep for a few minutes. But the boy did not move from his side.

Aaron looked hard into his father's face. His mother had told him to respect his father but to be wary of him.

The man's eyes opened. "Are you happy, Aaron?"

The boy smiled. "My uncle Joseph and I hunt. I have killed a deer and I dream of hanging bear claws about my neck. Joseph teaches me also to read and write and speak your language, Father. He will be a great chief of our tribe, and I will fight with him beside He Who Does Great Things. We will kill the French and the Abenacki."

"Would you come to live sometime with me?"

The boy looked at him. He knew if he said yes, he would please the man and perhaps help him to regain his health. But it would be a lie.

"No, Father. I'll not lie to you. I'll not live with you, ever."

Tears started to run down Stephen's cheeks. He closed his eyes again. He seemed to be asleep once again, but still the tears flowed. Finally, his voice, so feeble it was almost a whisper, said, "I love you, Aaron."

"I love you too, Father."

This time Stephen fell asleep, and his breathing came regularly.

The boy stepped away from the bed and walked toward Katherine. She smiled at him. "I think your father will recover. If he does, I will always credit you with saving him."

Aaron responded in good English. "I hope you are right. I hope my father will live."

He reached behind his neck and undid the clasp of the gold chain he wore. He took the locket in his hand and pressed it into Katherine's. "I don't believe I will ever see my father again," he said to Katherine. "I will obey my mother's wishes and I will become a Mohawk warrior. Please return this talisman to him. It is a white man's symbol. I know that now. I wore it out of respect for a great warrior. But I am a Mohawk. It should be worn by his white son."

Katherine wanted to refuse, but she knew it was no use. This eleven-year-old boy had enormous strength of character. She took the gold locket. The Gothic letter *N* was showing a bit of wear.

Katherine turned and called Amy to her side. "This is your sister, Amy," she said. The boy merely looked at the young girl and said nothing. After he left, Katherine had every

137

intention of placing the locket around her own daughter's neck.

Aaron turned from her and left the house. A canoe sat waiting for him on the river. He climbed in, and the paddlers dug with all of their strength into the water. The canoe leapt forward to midstream. The boy looked back at the farmhouse above the mud flats. He wiped the tears from his eyes.

Stephen's fever broke the next night. The doctors now predicted that he would recover. Katherine sat with him morning and afternoon, and when the turn for the better came, she broke down completely. Margaret Schuyler had to help her from the sick room into Margaret's room, which Katherine now shared.

The next morning, Stephen awoke at dawn. Socono sat on the floor by his bed. Margaret would not allow him in the house, but at night, after Margaret had fallen off to sleep and alerted the whole household to that fact by her enormous snores, Katherine would sneak out and open the door for Socono.

Stephen saw that his friend was not asleep. He smiled at the Indian and spoke to him softly in Abenacki. "I don't remember much, old friend, but I guess I owe you my life once again."

"The devil Dagaheari would have killed you, just as he would have burned me at the stake had you not interfered. He is dead now. The world is a better place without him. I am deeply sorry, little brother, about the arm. The white man's medicine is brutal but effective. Had one of our people suffered such a wound, he would not have lived."

"Perhaps I should not have wanted to live. I can never really hold a musket, to hunt or to make war; I cannot paddle a canoe. None of the things you taught me will be of much use to me now."

"The little brother begins to whine like a child—like a spoiled child. You have your life; live it. Do not pine for what might have been."

"Did you see Aaron?"

"Yes; he is a fine-looking boy. He will be a great warrior. I should have put my tomahawk in his head to protect my people against such a warrior."

Stephen looked at Socono worriedly, but he knew from the amused look on the Abenacki's face that he had been joking. "He's gone again, hasn't he?"

Socono nodded.

Stephen turned his face away. He did not wish the Indian to see the tears in his eyes.

"Little brother, you have another child and a woman who cherishes you. Return that love and do not waste it on one who can never return it."

The Indian rose to his feet. The sun had begun to rise, and he knew that the witch who owned this lodge would soon come from her bed and begin to cast curses on him, should he be in her way. He had a great fear of the powers of Margaret Schuyler.

He touched Stephen's forehead and nodded gravely. "You will recover now," he said. "I will begin to teach you all over again about survival in the woods with only a good right arm." He stepped out of the open window onto the veranda and was gone.

Vaughan arrived shortly after Socono left. He entered the room and filled the doorway. Stephen looked up at him from the bed. "You're on your feet, William; did you see my son?"

"No, I didn't. I'm sorry; I'd like to have known Sarah's grandson. I guess I owe you my life. You and Stiegler. You Nowells seem always to be getting me out of trouble."

Stephen looked at his bandaged stump. "I don't think I'll be doing much for anyone in the future."

Vaughan stiffened. "Look, Stephen, there is still much to do. Your mother died at the hands of Daniel Pierce. I can't prove it, but I'm as certain as I can be. And he stole everything your mother had set aside for you—Sarah Nowell's legacy, the money that she set aside in your name. Pierce has been trying to get his hands on it ever since Sarah died. He can't. The trust is iron clad. He can't break it. It belongs to Stephen Nowell and to no one else. It goes to Betsy Breed, your grandfather's sister and Pierce's wife, after fifteen years, and then to charity if she is not living. You've only got to wait a few more years, and then, right after Betsy Breed inherits it, she's a dead woman. He'll do her in like he's done in all of the Breeds. You have got to stop him, and you've got to get your hands on that money. It's yours, your woman's, your daughter's."

"And my son's?"

"Him too; the legacy of Sarah Nowell has to come to her kin and you've got to make sure that it happens."

"What about you, Willie?"

"Me? I'm all bluster. I've been all bluster ever since she went. It's been over ten years and still I dream of her—her strength, her energy. Those years we had were my heaven. It was kind of unfair taking me from hell, putting me in paradise and then sending me back again."

"You never talked much about the money before. Why didn't you tell me more about it?"

"Would it make any difference?"

"Well, knowing the money was there and that it will probably go to Pierce might have been enough to force me to try and get even with him."

"I was afraid of that. I knew the only way he could be caught—a musket ball in the heart—and I was afraid they'd hang you, boy. I couldn't face that."

Stephen lay there silently for some moments. "My mother's money is not getting into the hands of Daniel Pierce, William. You can rest assured of that."

Vaughan sighed and leaned back in his seat. "Good, now I favor a little breakfast for you and me."

Katherine fixed Stephen's breakfast in the kitchen. She wanted it to be especially nourishing. She had eggs and bacon and cornbread ready for him when Karl knocked at the kitchen door. She smiled when he entered. "He's going to be all right, Karl. He is cool this morning and even better, he is hungry."

He smiled at her. But then he grabbed her arm as she turned from him. "Katherine, I've wanted to ask you. What did Johnson say or do to you the day in Albany when we went to seek his help?"

"Oh, it's not important now," she responded.

"It is to me. Did he harm you?" He squeezed her arm without realizing it.

"No," she yelped, "but you are."

Karl dropped her arm instantly. "I'm sorry," he said. "But I could not stand the thought of his touching you. And now the story has been spread about by that pig dropping of a clerk of his that you slept with Johnson to get the boy to come here. Your stepmother has gone all over the town spreading that story. She's seen everywhere with that scum Daniel Pierce. He's the one who robbed Stephen of all of his wealth. Johnson must come out immediately and deny it."

"Don't be a fool, Karl; a public denial would merely fuel the gossip. Let it die. It's not true."

He turned from her and walked out of the kitchen, but she was frightened by the look of anger on his face.

140

The Mohawk River ambled along in the afternoon sun of late September. Its level was low. There had been little rain that summer. The heat had settled down over the valley and everything had slowed its pace, even the river. But one figure stood out in contrast. It was a lone man paddling a canoe feverishly against the current, traveling up the river away from Albany and Schenectady.

Karl had removed his shirt while he worked, and his fair skin had been burned by the sun. His large muscles rippled as he paddled. His face had the same look of anger on it as it had when he had left the kitchen in Saratoga.

He pulled upriver past George and Hannah's farm. It was all but abandoned now. George had taken over Stephen's garrison house for the duration of the war. There was smoke coming from the chimney of the garrison house. Karl could first smell it and then see it, even before the house itself became visible. He passed the garrison house without stopping.

Sweat poured off him. He had made much progress since bypassing the falls at Albany and setting out on the river. His chest and back muscles were sore at first, but now that he had gotten into the rhythm of paddling those pains had subsided. As he paddled, the work did not have the usual numbing effect that repetitive action normally had on him. Instead, as he approached his destination, he became angrier. He had to defend the reputation of Katherine Nowell. She was Stefan's wife, Amy's mother—a woman he had come to love more and more with each passing year. Stefan could no longer defend her. He was barely capable of staying alive.

It fell to him, Stefan's closest friend, his blood brother, to do what had to be done.

He continued upriver, passing his own farm, the old Mueller house, and again he did not stop. Several miles farther upriver, Fort Johnson came into view. He angled the canoe to intercept the north bank of the river just below the fort. There were various other houses along the riverbank and along the Schenectady road, and there was a large meeting house for the tribes. The Mohawk and Oneida made more councils now at Fort Johnson than they did at Onondaga.

Karl landed the canoe and walked directly toward the fort. There were two red-coated sentries at the door, but both recognized Karl as a militia officer and allowed him to enter without challenge.

Now he was lost. He did not know where to go. He heard

141

the voices of the women on the second floor. He had heard before that Johnson had all of his children, by wives and mistresses, living here with him, and that his daughters had been raised as proper young British ladies. He hoped that he would not have to look for Johnson on the second floor.

He saw an orderly come down the hall toward him. He carried an official-looking dispatch case. He ignored Karl, sniffing almost disdainfully, and turned to his right through a set of double doors. Karl followed him. The orderly had gone through another set of doors into a sitting room—office. Karl followed and stood face to face with Sir William Johnson.

The orderly raised a cry as Karl reached across the desk and grabbed Johnson by his ruffled stock, pulling him up out of his chair. He smashed his fist into Johnson's nose. He felt the cartilage snap against his knuckles, and blood shot out of the general's nostrils. Johnson staggered backward and fell over his chair, crashing against the floor and sliding head first into the wall behind him. He pulled himself up onto his elbows and shook his head, spraying blood in every direction.

Karl moved around the desk and stood before Johnson, who had now struggled to his knees. Johnson's fist slashed out and struck Karl in the stomach. Karl buckled at the knees and staggered backward. He kicked at Johnson's face, but Johnson caught his foot, holding him and twisting him off his feet. Karl fell onto the hard oak floor with a crash. He set all of Johnson's papers on his desk flying in different directions.

As Johnson's orderly ran from the room, screaming "Assassin," the general jumped on Karl, who lay stunned on the floor. His knee came grinding into Karl's groin. Karl screamed and reached for Johnson's face with his huge hands. His nails dug in, but it was difficult to hold on because Johnson's face was covered with blood from his nose. Karl's thumb slipped from Johnson's gory cheek into his mouth and the general bit it with all his might. Again Karl screamed. With his free fist, he again smashed Johnson's face. The force of the blow snapped Johnson's head backward, and he fell off Karl. Karl got slowly to his feet. His head ached and his groin ached. He staggered forward to slam Johnson once again, but suddenly his arms were pinned behind him. He struggled to get free, but then something crashed down on his head and he blacked out.

He was only out for a few seconds, but he was in the firm

grip of two Iroquois warriors, who held him in a chair while a third bound his feet tightly. Johnson was sitting back at his desk. An Indian woman held a cloth soaked in water and administered it to his nose to stop the bleeding.

Suddenly Johnson brushed the Indian woman's hands away. "Is he awake?" he asked. He started to laugh. "My God, Stiegler, I haven't brawled like that since I was a boy back in Ireland. That was wonderful." Then he grew serious. "Now then, suppose you tell me what it was all about."

"That was for Katherine Nowell," Karl said. "I'm only sorry I didn't hurt you more."

At the mention of the name Nowell, the Indian woman stared at him. "What have you done to Stephen's wife?" asked Molly Brant.

"I haven't done anything, for Christ's sake," said Johnson.

"That's not what they're saying in Albany," Karl shouted.

"Dammit, man, do you believe every rumor that runs wild in a garrison town like Albany?"

"You forget, Johnson, I was there that day. I saw her when she left you. She was upset and frightened."

"And why not? Her husband lay dying—his arm amputated and probably infected. You forget my response. Molly and I sent Kenonranon to his father."

One Indian interrupted, speaking in Mohawk. Johnson waved his hand, as if to dismiss him. Then he turned toward Karl. "Nicus Brant, my good friend, would like to take you out and burn you for attacking me. I think that would be excessive. But I don't think at my age I would want you around, jumping me from behind. By God, if this were ten years ago, I would not hesitate to take you on. I'd break every one of your bloody bones at least twice," he chuckled.

Then he turned to Brant. "No, Nicus," he said in Mohawk. "We will not kill this man. You are to take him to Albany, however, and see to it that he no longer has free access to Fort Johnson. That is, if you don't want Molly to be a widow and your grandchildren fatherless."

He turned to Karl. "I don't know if you will believe me, Stiegler, but I did not harm Mrs. Nowell. Not that I wouldn't have done anything I could, but she would have no part of me, and I would never take a woman against her will. She is a fine woman. Stephen should be grateful that he has her. And I guess he should consider himself lucky to have a loyal friend like yourself. Although for my sake, I wish you were not quite so loyal." This last he said touching his smashed nose tenderly.

Karl stepped onto Miss Schuyler's veranda. Margaret herself answered his call.

"My, aren't we formal!" she said when she saw him.

"Miss Schuyler, I'd like a chance to see Katherine, but I don't want to have to talk to Stephen. Can you ask her to step out here?"

She dropped her usual tough mannerisms and stared at Karl quizzically. Then without a word, she turned away from the door and disappeared back into the house.

The veranda was enclosed with trellises, and all sorts of flowering vines grew on them. There was a profusion of colors and smells. The buzzing of bees was everywhere in the late September afternoon.

The door opened again and Katherine Nowell stepped onto the veranda. "Karl, I'm so glad you're back. I was worried about you when you left. You seemed so angry."

"I'm not angry any more," Karl said softly. "Katherine, I'm leaving."

She looked at him and smiled. "Good; someone has to go back home and prepare for winter, and I'm not sure Hannah and George are up to it any more."

"I'm not going back to the garrison house or to my own cabin. I'm going back to Canada."

Katherine's eyes opened wide in surprise.

"I've always warned Stephen that I would return once I felt that my duty and loyalty to him were over. Now it's time. Baron Dieskau has been very kind to me. Before he left Albany for New York and France, he left a letter of introduction to his successor in New France. I will ask for and receive a commission in the French army—a gift from Dieskau for saving his life and carrying him back to our lines."

Katherine stared at him silently. Finally she touched his arm. "Karl, I don't know what to say. Stephen will be very unhappy. I don't know if he will be able to handle things now. He has said several times to me that now he will be even more dependent on you."

"He has Socono and he has Israel Kip and he even has Mr. Vaughan, now that he has recovered. And I suspect Vaughan could be induced to spend the winter on his own estate. But not me. I'm going home."

"We always thought your home was with us. Amy will be crushed. Her Uncle Karl means so much to her."

Karl looked away. "Katherine, don't do this to me. It's hard, very hard."

144

"But I don't understand."

Karl turned to look back at her. "You don't understand. No, you never did. Katherine, I've been in love with you from almost the very first day I ever saw you. But you've never understood. I helped you deliver your child and I always thought of Amy as our child—yours and mine. After all, I spent more time with her and I loved her far more than her father has."

Katherine was shocked by Karl's outburst. He spoke softly, but there was an overwhelming emotion in his words. His face was flushed and his eyes were filled. He reached out and took her hand in his. "Come with me. I worship you. Stephen ignores you. Even now, lying in bed, he talks to Socono and Kip far more than to you. I don't wish to hurt you, but Stephen Nowell lost his heart to Molly Brant and their son years ago. If she had been a proper white girl, if he hadn't been such a prig about proper upbringing, they'd still be together, begetting more little papooses. He'll never get over her, Katherine, and he'll never love you—not like I love you. He'll never be the father to Amy that I've been."

"Karl, be quiet. Don't say any more," said Katherine. "You've already said too much."

"No, I've been quiet too long. I love you, Katherine. Get your things and get Amy and come with me back to Canada."

"I love Stephen. I always have, Karl, and I always will. I can't leave him—especially not now."

Karl lowered his head. He had always known what the answer would be and had protected his fantasy by never asking the question. Now that dream—of Katherine and Amy with him—was destroyed.

Katherine reached out and touched his flushed face. She brushed his straw-yellow hair off his forehead with her hand. "You're a friend. I need you as a friend. I can't face life back home without you there, giving me your strength."

"No more," he muttered. "I can't take it any longer. I can't be in the same room with you, knowing I can't touch you the way I want to touch the woman I love. I can't face sleeping in the same house, knowing that you are in bed with him in the next room. I want you in bed with me. But I love Stephen and when I have these thoughts I feel shamed. I feel disloyal to my friend. But I'm human. I can't take any more."

He lowered his voice to almost a whisper. "It was wrong of me to ask you, Katherine. Please forget I ever said anything."

He turned away from her and stepped off the veranda. He began to run down the path toward the river.

Katherine reached out for him when he first pulled away from her. Her hand continued to clutch the empty air as she watched him rush to the waterfront and climb into the boat. When he was finally gone, she lowered her hand and turned and entered the gloom of the house.

Part Two

The St. Lawrence

V

1756-1757

Stephen, wearing his nightshirt, sat in a soft chair in front of his bedroom window. He knew that Katherine would be entering the room shortly with a basin of water, some soap and a cloth. The hot September sun poured into the room through the open window and he was sweating. He had finally gotten over the feeling that his left arm was still there, and no longer did he feel aches and pains in an arm that had long since been buried. The stump was healing well, according to the doctors. His body was repairing itself, but his mind was deeply troubled.

He bitterly resented Karl's leaving. The only thing Katherine had been able to tell him was that he had returned to Canada at Baron Dieskau's suggestion and that he was joining the French army. Why, Stephen wondered, had Karl deserted him when he needed him so badly? How was he to work Vaughan's estate? He was a cripple. He needed Karl's strength. Everything he touched seemed to go sour. His friends left him. He lost his son. His wife surely would have to grow weary of his complaints. Certainly she must find him ugly too. At least Vaughan had remained. After he recovered from his wound, William had taken over the garrison house at Fort Vaughan. He left instructions with Stephen to join him there with Katherine and Amy just as soon as he was able to travel. But Stephen had serious doubts in his own mind. He did not want to accept any more gifts from his benefactor. If he could not work for Vaughan, he saw no way he could accept a position from him.

The door opened and Katherine entered the room. She walked over to Stephen and sat on the carpeted floor beside his chair. "Time for your bath, sir," she said, smiling at him.

She started washing his feet and legs. He stood up and she

pulled the nightshirt over his head and off his body. Involuntarily he turned slightly away from her to hide the stump of his left arm. It was so ugly. He hated the sight of it. He sat back down in the chair when she had finished, and she brought a freshly laundered nightshirt over to him and helped him to get into it.

"Stephen, I don't think you should remain undressed like this. The doctors say there is no reason why you couldn't go outside or ride with me to the village. We have so much to do at Fort Vaughan and so little time to prepare for the coming winter."

"Perhaps I could grow a new arm," he said bitterly.

She looked at him in exasperation. "Stephen, I know you've been hurt and you've been ill. But you're alive and you're recovering. Do you plan to spend the rest of your life sitting in this room feeling sorry for yourself?"

"I doubt your aunt would put up with me that long, Katherine. I think my days at Saratoga are numbered. She's beginning to make cracks."

"We should be going to Fort Vaughan."

"I'm not going to Fort Vaughan and accept charity from William Vaughan. I've taken enough from him in my life already."

They were interrupted by a shout from the riverfront. Stephen recognized the voice. It was the voice of Israel Kip. Within a minute his imposing form filled the frame of Stephen's window. He was stocky and would become fat when he grew older. Already his hair was thinning.

"What have we here?" he bellowed. "I thought you'd be trying out one-handed wood-chopping techniques."

Stephen looked up at his friend wistfully. "Hello, Israel."

"Hello yourself," he said. "Katherine, why is your man still in his nightshirt? It's past noon. Have you been dallying late abed these days?"

Katherine blushed. In her heart she wished it had been true, but she remained quiet and merely smiled at Kip.

Stephen was the one who responded. "I've not really recovered yet."

"What ails you?" asked Kip.

"Well, nothing sensational. I have only one arm, or hadn't you noticed?"

"You're weak as a baby from staying in bed and having females pamper you. No offense, Mistress Katherine."

Aunt Margaret burst into the room. "Who the hell is yelling in my house?" she demanded.

150

"I'm doing the yelling," he shouted back at her.

"And who the hell are you?"

"Israel Kip," he responded.

"And what, sir, in the name of God, is an Israel Kip?" she asked.

For once in his life, Kip seemed stumped and at a loss for words.

Katherine interrupted. "This is Stephen's old friend, Corporal Kip, Aunt Margaret."

"Well, why can't he come up to a front door and knock like decent folk? Here, you." She motioned to Kip. "Come around to the front door and behave like a civilized white man, even if you don't smell like one."

Kip rather sheepishly smelled himself and then stepped away from the window and did as he was commanded.

"My God," said Katherine. "Kip may have finally met his match."

Stephen smiled at her suggestion.

"He was making sense, Stephen," she said.

Stephen ignored her and looked out the window to where Kip had been standing.

Kip entered the sick room through the door, followed by Aunt Margaret. He walked over to Stephen and grabbed him by the right shoulder, carefully avoiding his left side, just in case he was still in pain. "I've come to meet Socono. He said he would be back in September. We planned to winter together again," said Kip.

"Is that savage coming back?" asked Aunt Margaret. "I'm locking your window at night, Stephen, if he does. I know you met him in my house anyway. But I'll not have heathens with their stench and their vermin coming into a decent Christian home."

"Socono ain't got vermin," interrupted Kip. "Heathen he is, mind you—a bloody Papist. But I've decided not to hold that against him. He don't flaunt it around none, and he don't abide them priests no more. Then again, he don't have much use for our ministers either. Now when it comes to vermin, I've got some pretty good specimens growing on me right now."

Margaret screamed. "Out of this house! You filthy bastard! Out!"

Kip looked amazed.

"You don't come back in until you've washed with soap in the river." She grabbed Kip's ear and led him like a little boy out of the room. He shouted, "Bathe? You mean submerge my body in water and put soap on it? Do you want to kill me, woman?"

Stephen and Katherine sat in amazement. Kip was the bane of the existence of all physicians and surgeons, and he had strong arguments against bathing, but he was all bluster in the hands of Margaret Schuyler.

Socono arrived the next day; Margaret would not let him into her house. To Katherine's amazement, Stephen got dressed and met with the Indian on the veranda. But Socono always demanded strength from Stephen, and he could not bear to fail his friend. Socono would not remain seated on the porch. "Come with me," he said to Stephen. Stephen followed him down to the riverbank. Socono got into his canoe and motioned Stephen into the back. Stephen started to protest, but the Indian merely stared at him disdainfully. Stephen shut up. This Indian, who had been his teacher from the time he was a little boy, would take no excuses. He had been contemptuous of complaints then, and he regarded them no differently now.

Stephen got into the canoe and picked up the paddle in his hand. Socono began to paddle the canoe. Stephen allowed his paddle to drift in the water. The Indian turned back to look at him. "I did not plan to give my little brother a ride," he said sarcastically.

Stephen grew angry. He only had one arm. What did Socono expect? Well, if he couldn't paddle, at least he could steer. Stephen changed the angle of the paddle and the canoe veered to the right. Up front Socono smiled, but he did not turn around. Before long Stephen had worked out the technique of switching the paddle from one side of the canoe to the other. He discovered that by gripping the paddle in the center of the handle, he could control it much better and could actually aid Socono in paddling the craft, in addition to steering it.

After they had paddled down the Hudson several miles, Socono pointed to the shore and Stephen again changed the angle of the paddle. They beached the canoe and the Indian allowed Stephen to drag it further up on the riverbank by himself.

"We must hunt some game," he said to Stephen.

"With what?" asked Stephen.

Socono handed him his hunting knife. "I've taught you much, little brother. I taught you to track and to stalk game.

You are as good at that as I am. But you forget that in addition to the bow and arrow, I taught you to use a knife—for throwing. One needs only one arm to use the knife or the tomahawk. You and I will hunt together and each of us will use only one arm. We will not go hungry."

The afternoon hunt with Socono proved the turning point in Stephen's recovery. He never looked backward again. He adjusted to life with one arm. The Indian had taught the boy. Now he taught the man. At the end of the month, Stephen took Katherine and Amy back to Fort Vaughan. Socono came with them. Kip remained behind at Saratoga. Socono was to return and meet him there before they took off to trap.

Vaughan had put the garrison house in excellent shape, but he too had no intention of remaining on the Mohawk for the winter. When Stephen and his family arrived, Vaughan was packed and ready to return. He would go back to Albany and leave for Boston before winter set in.

Before departing, he took Stephen aside and insisted that he walk to the riverbank with him.

"Why don't you stay the winter, Willie?"

"Because I've already been out of Boston too long. You forget the kind of competition I have to face. Daniel Pierce and his cutthroats will have me bankrupt before the winter is out if I stay away. You take care of that woman of yours. She reminds me a great deal of your mother. She has courage and spirit."

Stephen looked at Vaughan with surprise. He had never seen Katherine that way. Loving and tender, no doubt, but meek and shy were the words he would have used to describe her.

Socono had decided to accompany Vaughan back to Albany, and he was already in the canoe. Stephen walked over to him and grasped his hand. "Goodbye, Socono; I will see you in the spring."

"Goodbye, little brother. I hope your winter will be better than mine. I think our friend Kip has finally fallen in love like a young pup. He follows the she-witch around. I think she has cast a spell on him. I don't think he will trap with me this winter. I think he will stay in the lodge of the squaw."

Stephen started to laugh. They were an unlikely couple— the untamed soldier of fortune—fur trapper and the perennial spinster man-hater.

Vaughan joined Socono in the canoe, and the two men

153

pulled away from the shore, out into the river. Stephen stood along the shore, waving and watching until they disappeared beyond the great bend.

In October William Johnson made a visit to Fort Vaughan. He was accompanied by seven Mohawk braves. Katherine and Amy were playing after supper. George and Hannah had left their farm and planned to stay with Stephen and Katherine in the garrison house for the winter. George had nodded off to sleep in his chair while Hannah busied herself in the kitchen. Stephen stepped outside the house to check on the barn where he kept his oxen and two milk cows.

He walked toward the barn along the leaf-strewn path. He knew the Mohawks were watching him from the underbrush as soon as he stepped onto the path. He called out in Mohawk, "My friend, Johnson, are you leading this band of spies?"

He heard Johnson's laugh. "Dammit, Nowell, you're very good in the woods," said Sir William, stepping out from the cover of a small clump of fir trees.

"Why this surprise approach, Sir William?" asked Stephen, switching to English.

"Well, my scouts have reported to me that you have recovered and are living a normal life. I need someone to do a job for me. But I was afraid that if I came right out and asked you in front of your family, that good woman of yours would step in and talk you out of it before I got the words out of my mouth. Just let a man get hurt and a woman will try to turn him into an infant."

"No need to worry about that with Katherine. If she had had her way, I would have been forced out of bed and out of the house long ago."

"I'm surprised," said Johnson. "My girls—that is, my daughters—have tried to turn me into a vegetable since Lake George."

"What's the favor you spoke of?" asked Stephen.

"Not a favor—it's a job. I'll pay you for it and pay you well. It's the war, Nowell; it's not gone well. Except for our victory this summer, it's been a disaster—Braddock ambushed and killed, his army routed; Lord Loudoun sailing around the Gulf of St. Lawrence off Isle Royale without attacking Louisbourg; Shirley never getting anywhere near Niagara and having to abandon his attack; even my force never made it to Crown Point, and now word is that the French have seized and burned Fort Oswego on Lake Ontario."

Stephen nodded in agreement. "You're right. We failed on every front."

"What I propose is to alert the new government—which must surely take power after this summer's events—I want to alert them to my plans for North America. I need a spokesman in London, a hero of the battle of Lake George who has access to the ministry, who advocates my kind of campaign. Give me control of the war. Give me the money for gifts and I'll turn every tribe on the frontier against France. We'll invade Canada with enough of my brethren here to destroy French power in North America once and for all."

"You want me to go to England?"

"Quite right, Nowell, I want you to go immediately, before the winter sets in."

"But my wife and child—I can't leave them here unprotected."

"You're right. I'll take care of them. Not at Fort Johnson; that wouldn't be safe enough. I'll take them to Lake George to our new fort. I've garrisoned it with regular British troops from Shirley's old command. We've named it Fort William Henry, after one of His Majesty's younger sons. I'll see to it that she gets one of the officer's cabins all to herself. Some of my people will come here and watch the garrison house for you."

Stephen considered for a moment. At first he thought Johnson's scheme was madness. But then he began to have seconds thoughts. He had not looked forward to the inactivity of the winter. The prospect that Johnson offered to him was exciting. The security of his family would be provided for. They would be living inside the strongest English fortification in the entire area. He did not think George was up to taking over the farm, even during winter, and he could not handle any heavy manual labor himself.

"I'll have to discuss this with Katherine," he said. "I'll have to get her agreement. But I think I'd like to go."

They shook hands and then Stephen walked back toward the house.

After he left, Nicus Brant stepped out of the underbrush and stood next to Johnson. Johnson smiled at him. "Nicus, my friend, I believe we found the solution to our problem. The blackrobe will go across the sea to England. Molly and Kenonranon can live safely at Fort Johnson without fear that Nowell will find them and upset everything all over again. And he just might help us with the new Prime Minister."

Brant looked at Johnson with admiration. "And Warraghiyagey will have the opportunity to see the lady of the blackrobe."

"Oh, no," said Johnson, touching his nose. "One attempt was enough. The men who love that woman play rough. Mistress Nowell will go to Fort William Henry for safekeeping. Besides, I believe Molly would do worse to me than the Swiss bastard ever did if she learned I cheated on her." Molly Brant's father merely smiled in agreement.

They lay in bed together that night. Katherine reached over to touch Stephen. She found that his nightshirt had rolled up about his hips when she placed her hand on his bare rump. "Are you sleeping?" she asked softly.

"No."

"What's wrong?"

"I've been thinking. Johnson has asked me to go to England for him."

"When?" she asked, her body stiffening with concern and surprise.

"Right away."

"Are you going?" she asked with an edge to her voice, in anticipation of his response. She knew he would go.

"He's willing to find an officer's quarters at the new fort at Lake George for you and Amy. You can bring Hannah and George also. His people will take care of the garrison house for us."

"You're going then."

"Yes."

She took her hand away. "You're just going to leave us as easily as that."

"Katherine, you and Amy will be safe."

"It's not a question of security. I want my husband by my side for a change. I don't want him running off doing what William Johnson wants. It's bad enough that man cost you your arm. I don't want you to go." She grabbed the pillow, punched it with her fist angrily and then flopped her head back down upon it with a thud. Stephen had never seen her angry before. But it would not deter him; he was determined to go.

The ship nosed its way gently against the wooden piles. Lines were tossed and it was made secure against the dock. Sailors tossed a gangplank with a huge thud onto the dock below, but even this noise was almost drowned out by the babble of sounds that filled the Southwark wharf front.

Across the Thames, the dome of St. Paul's glistened in the sunlight and the bells of London's many bridal-cake steeple churches pealed out, almost in opposition to the ugly screams of the docks on this side of the river.

Stephen Nowell pulled his cape about his body more tightly. The London winter chill he found even more cutting than the cold blasts of the Mohawk Valley. It reminded him more of the damp chill of Isle Royale. He reached under his cloak to check the empty left sleeve of his coat. He had become used to life with only one arm. But he had developed a habit of checking the sleeve to make sure it was pinned against the coat and did not hang down, empty and ugly.

He walked down the gangplank onto the wharf. His trunk would be sent on to his lodging later. His inn was in London itself, and he would have to arrange for a boat to take him across the river.

Longshoremen pushed against him in the rush to get up the gangplank and sign on to the job of unloading—the *Greenwich*, James Delancey's own brig out of New York. She carried mostly furs and naval stores from the New York forests.

The longshoremen had to vie with fishmongers on the wharf yelling the price of their wares. In addition, the wharf was covered with prostitutes and pimps, pickpockets and cutpurses, merchants and proper ladies, all mixed together, the great and the small of the capital city of the great English empire. The noise was deafening.

Stephen checked his pocket on his left side once again, but this time to assure himself that Sir William's letter was safe. He walked back down along the dock, looking for a boat. A boatman grabbed his coat. "London?" he asked.

Stephen nodded yes.

"That will be a shilling," said the boatman with the strange accent of London.

Stephen knew the price was many times inflated, and he started to walk away and find another boatman.

"What's wrong, your lordship?" asked the boatman.

"I didn't ask for a night's lodging," said Stephen. "All I want is to be taken across the river. I'll walk to the bridge and walk across the river before I'll pay your price."

The boatman lowered his asking price by half and Stephen accepted. The boatman smiled, for he was charging more than twice the going rate.

Stephen sat in the back of the boat, huddled down low against the cold river wind, as he was rowed across the

Thames. The water was choppy and the spray chilled him. He would find his lodging and then take his letter to the residence of the new Prime Minister, William Pitt. Johnson had written to Pitt before it was known that Pitt would be in power. Sir William had concluded that Pitt's appointment was inevitable and extremely fortunate.

Stephen's inn was in the city of Westminster and not at all far from Pitt's London residence.

After the boatman left him off on the London side of the river, he found a carriage to take him to the inn. It was on a narrow side street near the riverbank. As he entered the front door of the inn, he heard his name called. "Stephen, darling, is that really you?"

He knew instantly who it was who spoke.

He turned around. "Cornelia, my esteemed mother-in-law."

Her face turned hard. The forced smile disappeared immediately. "Don't connect me with John Schuyler's bastard."

"You refer to my wife, madam."

Again Cornelia Schuyler grimaced. "That is something I must simply chalk up to your lack of taste. Imagine going from me to her."

Stephen wanted to respond concerning the ease of passage, but he saw no reason to insult her further. His cloak slipped off his shoulder, and he saw her eyes widen with surprise when she noted his pinned-up sleeve.

"Fortunes of war," he said rather flippantly. "Or should I say misfortunes?"

"I had heard that you had been wounded. I didn't know it was that serious."

"I get along."

Cornelia looked at him. Her violet eyes stared at him. She thought of the boy who had made love to her—the strong, healthy body. It saddened her to think of him less than whole, just as the ravages of aging saddened her when she looked into her morning mirror.

"Your Uncle Pierce is with me in London, Stephen. In fact, he stays at an inn just down the road from this one. I am staying here at the same inn as you, I gather."

Now it was Stephen's turn to look at her in surprise. "You and Pierce—together? How? What has happened to my Aunt Betsy?"

"The same that happened to your beloved Katherine. She stayed behind at home. And it is not gallant of you, Stephen, to ask about my relationship with a man."

158

"I don't have to ask. You're living with him, aren't you?"

"You just asked."

"My God, Cornelia, that man is a monster. He murdered my father and mother and my grandfather."

"Don't be absurd, Stephen. He is one of the most prominent men in New England. He is here pleading former Governor Shirley's case with the Prime Minister."

At that moment Daniel Pierce entered the foyer of the inn. His hair was whiter now and he wore his eyeglasses with the steel frames at all times. He recognized Stephen instantly. He halted in place; his face went white but he regained his composure quickly. He came over to Cornelia. He had her black cape over his arm. "Are you ready to leave, my dear?" he asked.

"Uncle Pierce, we meet again," said Stephen.

Pierce looked at him with disdain. "I told you before, years ago, sir, that I regard you as an imposter. You are not entitled to address me as Uncle."

"Family squabbles," laughed Cornelia. "It seems, Daniel, that you and your nephew get along about as well as his wife and I do. We're all just one big happy family." She threw back her head and laughed sarcastically.

Pierce grabbed her by the elbow and steered her out the front door of the inn into a waiting carriage. The innkeeper's servant slammed the door and the horses leapt forward and pulled the carriage away from the door.

"What the hell is he doing in London?" cursed Pierce. "That boy dogs my path."

"It's obvious, darling Pierce," said Cornelia. "He's Johnson's man. Just as you're Shirley's."

"I'm no one's man but Pierce's," he said fiercely.

"I stand corrected. You're quite right. You may well be the most self-interested man I have ever known."

"You've not suffered, madam, from your connection with me."

"Hardly. The tie has been a boon to business. I have never done so well before. My only fear is that the war will end before I have become truly rich—so rich that Van Rensselaers and Delanceys and Livingstons, anyone in New York, will live in envy and in fear of me."

Pierce smiled. "The war won't end, Cornelia. Not if I have my way. The Prime Minister must be convinced to continue the present policy of sending armies to America."

"So that you and I can feed them."

"In a manner of speaking," he said with a chuckle. "We

dine with Abercrombie tonight. With any luck, Pitt will appoint him to the New York command."

"He's such an ass," said Cornelia. "How could a bright man like the Prime Minister place any trust in him?"

"He doesn't, but the army's system of seniority will prevail. Abercrombie will command."

"What about Johnson? Which, of course, brings us back to your nephew."

"He's an imposter."

"Don't pull your bloody tricks with me, Pierce. Stephen Nowell is who he says he is. You may not wish to say that publicly, but don't attempt that nonsense with me."

Pierce merely smiled.

"He is here to represent Johnson. From what you say, he's thwarted you before. What if he gets Pitt's ear?"

"No matter. What can Johnson ask of Pitt? Probably greater scope for himself. But who does Johnson command? A handful of moth-eaten Mohawks. Let Nowell prevail. The war will drag on, no matter what. We'll get the contracts for Johnson's Indian blankets, muskets and gifts to the tribes."

Cornelia smiled and snuggled up closer to Pierce. "I do like the way your mind works, Daniel." She thought for a moment about Stephen—about their time in New York. Yes, she liked the way Pierce's mind worked, but she remembered a distinct preference for his nephew's body.

Pierce looked out the window of the carriage into the darkness beyond. Cornelia had proved a useful partner. Her New York contacts had been invaluable. But she knew nothing of his ties to France. She would never know. The war would go on, but not because he wanted the loot and profiteering, but because his greatest income, the fur trade license issued by the governor of New France, had to be protected. No one but Stephen Nowell and that bastard sot William Vaughan had ever guessed. He was not about to allow Nowell to place his neck in the noose.

Stephen watched his uncle and mother-in-law disappear into the night. He stared for some moments. It was a combination of persons he had not foreseen and had no inkling of until this very moment. He knew of Cornelia's successes as a merchant in Albany. He knew too much about Pierce's successes. They were working together, and that boded ill for England and for the American cause.

His rooms had been reserved and the innkeeper was expecting him. There was a message for him from the Prime

Minister's office, inviting him to Pitt's residence in two days' time. He wondered if he would meet Cornelia and Pierce there as well.

He did not. He rode by carriage the short distance from the inn to the Pitt residence in Westminster. The sun was setting as he left, but he still had a view of the sprawl of the city of London. Stephen could not help but compare it to the Paris of thirteen years ago. The French capital, although bustling with people, had seemed to be a city of poor, unemployed artisans and students, of crowded narrow streets and ancient buildings. But London seemed new; everywhere there was new construction. The wharves were alive with shipping and people loading and unloading ships. The shops were everywhere, and they were crowded with the goods of the empire. New houses sprang up. Smaller, modest homes of the middle-class shopkeepers crowded next to the Georgian mansions of the aristocrats. The air was heavy with the smell of burning coal, which more and more came to be the fuel of this new creature, a city and nation of shopkeepers. Already great fogs sweeping in from the Thames and the sea mixed with the coal smoke to create the circumstances that would plague the city for the next two hundred years.

The Prime Minister's house was an unassuming one not far from the government offices at Whitehall. There were several carriages standing outside the residence when Stephen arrived. He stepped from his hired coach, presented his invitation to the footman at the door and entered the house.

The hallway ran for almost thirty feet toward a series of white wooden doors. There was music coming from one small suite of rooms to his right. He was conducted to one of these rooms.

The room was occupied by four persons. There was a tall, elegantly dressed civilian whom Stephen recognized instantly as the Prime Minister, William Pitt. In addition there was a general of the British army, replendent in red coat and gold braid, and there were two women. One of them Stephen did not know, and he assumed that she was the Prime Minister's lady. The other woman, dressed richly in a gown of blue silk, he knew well from his sojourn at Versailles as a boy.

"Mister Nowell," William Pitt said, bowing in Stephen's direction.

"Prime Minister," responded Stephen.

"I don't believe you know anyone here. My wife and General Lord Howe and his companion Madame DeLuynes."

161

Manya swept across the room toward him. "Etienne," she said in French. "It is so good to see you again." She held out her hands toward him but then clumsily pulled them back when she saw the empty sleeve. "I am so sorry," she said with some shock.

He smiled at her. "I am used to it now."

William Pitt looked at both of them. "I gather I was incorrect, Mr. Nowell; you do seem to know at least one of us."

"Please excuse me, Your Excellency," said Stephen, switching to English. "The Princess Wroblevska and I are old friends, going back some years ago.

"Madam Pitt," he continued, "it is an honor to meet you." He kissed the hand she held out to him. "Lord Howe," he greeted the general with a bow.

"Please be seated, Mr. Nowell. My wife and I are quite pleased that you have made the acquaintance of the widow DeLuynes in the past. I gather from your use of her maiden name and title that you knew her before her marriage."

"Before and after."

"Please be seated, Mr. Nowell. My wife has arranged a brief interlude of music before our meal."

Everyone was quite correct, but Stephen could not help feeling that he had walked in on a private joke or that he had been the topic of conversation. He felt uneasy.

Stephen sat next to Manya. He wanted to ask her what she was doing in London, but he had to remain quiet as a quartet of musicians began to play their violins, cellos and violas. Manya smiled at him on several occasions, but most often she listened intently to the music.

It gave Stephen the opportunity to study her. She seemed to have changed very little in the years since he had last seen her. Her yellow hair and fair complexion were the same. She had grown slightly heavier about the middle and her bust had filled out. She was still a strikingly beautiful woman.

Finally the music stopped, but not before Stephen had stifled several yawns. He looked around nervously after the first one but saw Lord Howe's hand covering his mouth; the general looked at Stephen in surprise and then began to laugh to himself. Stephen smiled back.

The dinner that followed was lavish. The table was set with silver, china and crystal. The cutlery was designed with scrolls and tiny roses and was made of the finest sterling silver. There were three different wines, all of them French, served along with a squab followed by beef baked in a pastry shell.

Stephen was seated between Manya and Mrs. Pitt. He was able to pay appropriate attention to the hostess, but as soon as he was able, with politeness, he turned his attention to his friend. "Manya, I could not believe my eyes when I saw you in the sitting room."

"You don't know how surprised we all were. We expected an envoy from the dreaded Johnson who would be a naked, painted half savage. Instead we find someone who would be at home at Versailles."

Her English response was difficult to understand and so Stephen switched softly to French.

"It's probably terribly impolite to speak French, perhaps even unpatriotic, but I have to speak with you. What are you doing here in London and with Lord Howe?"

"I suppose," she said, "the proper word is that I have become his paramour. There was little prospect in France for an unmarried, widowed princess from Poland and little hope that my cousin, the Queen, could do anything for me. Pompadour now completely dominates the King. She has little to fear from Maria Leczinska or her family. She bears us no ill-will, but so great is her power over Louis that no one need concern themselves with ingratiating themselves with the Queen or her party. Thus no husband for the Princess Wroblevska. I met Lord Howe in Paris between the wars. And now I live in England and I live well. He provides for me and I think he loves me."

"But do you love him?"

She merely smiled. "Once before I chose between love and security, Etienne. I chose a title instead of a handsome boy from Canada. I gave up happiness for security. I gained neither. At least this time I have security."

Stephen was saddened by her statement. He searched her face but she hid any emotions well.

"You really did not answer the question, Manya."

She laughed.

"And what of Michal?"

Manya smiled. "Unchanged. My brother still fights for Poland. We've been cut off except for rare letters since the beginning of the war. But I believe he is still well. He fares better than you, I believe," she said, looking at Stephen's empty sleeve.

163

"It was at Lake George. I was with Johnson."

"I can tell from the look on your face, Etienne, that you have suffered much. It shows when you speak about it. Tell me, not of the war, but of your life. Are *you* happy?"

"The boy you knew in Paris, Manya, discovered much about himself. You saw me at Louisbourg. You knew of my break with France. After the last war I moved to New York colony. I married and I have a daughter."

She smiled at him. "I'm so happy for you."

"I have a son, too. But he is not my wife's. He is the child of an Indian woman whom I met before the war. I never see him now. His mother and I are no longer friends." He spoke with such obvious pain that her smile disappeared.

"You two must stop gabbing away in the language of the enemy," interrupted Lord Howe. "Though for the life of me I am beginning to wonder if something might not be wrong with me. I'm beginning to understand Manya's English."

His smile was infectious and Manya blushed. He looked at her adoringly.

Mrs. Pitt arose. "I believe, Princess, that the gentlemen have much to discuss."

The three men rose and remained standing until Mrs. Pitt and Manya had left the room.

"Mr. Nowell, the Prime Minister tells me that you are some sort of envoy for Sir William Johnson," said Howe as they sat down.

"Nothing official, My Lord," said Stephen. "But yes, Sir William asked me to come to London and present his views."

"Which are?" asked Howe.

"Sir William believes that the time has come for the total destruction of New France. He believes this can be accomplished by sending him sufficient funds to buy the loyalty of all the tribes, eastern and western even, and turn them once and for all against France. He believes it is possible to destroy French power through the Indian nations. He has their loyalty and he will destroy New France."

There was silence for some moments. Then Pitt started to chuckle. "Leave it to William Johnson to come up with a plan that would not only conquer the French, but would leave him the richest, most powerful man in North America. Johnson is an incredible schemer. Lord Howe, what think you of the noble baronet's scheme?"

"It's utter poppycock," said the general. "The days of Indians winning wars in America are over. Other than as scouts, they are more often in the way and no help at all.

Quite to the contrary, we need more European-style campaigns."

"Like Braddock's or Baron Dieskau?" interrupted Stephen.

Howe looked at Stephen patiently. "Ah, you are no country bumpkin like we thought. You will note, Nowell, that I said that Indian scouts are very worthwhile. Braddock stumbled into an ambush because he had none. It's like walking around blind. But we now need regular troops, artillery, siege trains and a navy. With those, New France will fall."

"But it is interesting to hear the view that we should be pushing for victory in Canada," interrupted Pitt. "Just a few days ago, General Abercrombie and this fellow Pierce from Boston were pushing a piecemeal go-soft-and-slow policy. They believe the French are too strong and have a stranglehold on the continent. They wish us to concentrate troops in the major cities but to concern ourselves more with the European campaign. That woman who was with him, Howe, wasn't she striking? Schuyler's her name."

"Mrs. Schuyler is my mother-in-law and grandmother to my daughter Amy," said Stephen rather maliciously. He knew how Cornelia hated to appear old in any way. He knew that the word would be out and she would be asked about her grandchild. He felt slightly better about her insulting of Katherine for having done it.

Pitt sat back in his chair and poured himself a glass of port wine. He smiled. "I'm glad to hear both points of view, and I'm afraid that both of you are right. Strategically, the time has come to fight France where she is weakest, and that is in North America. The time has come to strip her once and for all of her empire. In that I agree with Johnson. But, Mr. Nowell, Lord Howe was right in his tactics. We can have no more massacres. The forts of North America will fall more readily to cannon than to tomahawk, and I plan to allow Howe the opportunity to prove he is right. Just as soon as I am able, I plan to give him a command in America. We will strike at the lifeline of French power, the forks of the Ohio, Niagara, Louisbourg, Crown Point, Quebec, Montreal, and they will all be ours."

"I'll never see a command, Prime Minister. I am too junior in rank. Already the supporters of General Abercrombie are streaming to the King to demand that he have the Crown Point command."

"I'll handle the King," said Pitt.

"While you're at it, get him to give command to the bright young men of the army. We must break down the Duke of

165

Cumberland's crowd, which has strangled us with their seniority system."

"His Royal Highness, the Duke, is the King's son, My Lord. The King is not likely to overturn a system long supported by his warrior offspring."

"You'll need men like Colonel Amherst and Major Wolfe or no campaign in America will bear fruit," said Howe. "And you need men like my little brother William, and you'll need navy men like my other brother, Dick."

"I'll get them all," said Pitt. "Most of all, I'll get you, My Lord."

Stephen sat quietly through this exchange. Then Pitt turned to him. "Please don't feel that you wasted your time by coming to us, Mr. Nowell. But I am already as convinced as Johnson that the time to strike is at hand, and it has been too long delayed already. But it will be the British army and navy that destroy French power in Canada, not Johnson's savages."

Stephen tossed in his sleep. He found it more and more difficult as he grew older to sleep in strange beds. The pillows were large and the bed itself was covered by a great down-filled silk comforter. But still he was unable to sleep.

He had returned from dinner at the Prime Minister's residence and gone straight to bed after drinking some warm milk. He could not finish it and had left half of the jug on the nightstand by his bed. He was discouraged and at the same time relieved. He had carried Johnson's message to England and had found little interest in its content. Yet he was encouraged by the fact that at last England's government was giving priority to events in North America. No longer would they give away the fruits of victory as they had done at Louisbourg in the last war. With any luck at all, the days of French power would be limited.

Stephen was startled by a soft knock on the door. It was late. At first he thought he had been mistaken, but then the knocking came a second time, accompanied by his name called softly in French.

Stephen stripped off the bedcovers, stepped down off the bed and went to the door, opening it hurriedly.

"Manya," he whispered.

"I had to come and see you," she said as she stepped into the room's darkness.

"Won't Lord Howe protest your coming into a strange man's bedroom?"

166

She looked at him. "You and I are not strangers, Etienne."

He looked into her eyes and saw the longing there. He thought back to Versailles, to when they were both children. And the feelings he had for her then came flooding back.

"I had to come, Etienne; security is never really enough. I want to be loved finally by someone I love." She was crying. He lifted her face up to look at it. The room was in darkness and he could only see the outline of her face. He bent down and kissed her. She opened her mouth and kissed him back hungrily.

She broke away from his grasp finally, out of breath. She stepped back and dropped her cloak to the floor. She was still wearing the blue gown she had worn at the dinner party. She then reached behind her back and began to undo the long row of buttons on her dress.

"Manya, are you sure you want this?" Stephen asked.

"I was sure at Versailles when I was only sixteen. I was sure at Louisbourg when I saw you there. But I never did anything about it. I loved you, Etienne, for years, and you said you loved me. Don't tell me now whether or not you still do. You have a wife and children. Just don't say anything to me right now. Just love me."

She had undone all of the buttons and the front of her dress had fallen away from her breasts, covered now only by a white cotton undergarment. She stepped out of the dress completely. Then she walked over to the bed. She tried to light the candle, which sat unfirmly tilted in the wooden candle holder by the bedstead.

Stephen walked to her and reached for her hand. "No light," he said.

"I'd like to watch you," she said. She began to lift his nightshirt up about his middle to raise it above his head.

"No, Manya," he said. "Leave the nightshirt. You don't want to see my body. The arm is ugly and maimed."

But she would not stop. She lifted the shirt off him.

He turned to hide his left shoulder from her.

"You could never be ugly, Etienne," she whispered. She turned him to face her and then kissed his left shoulder and continued to kiss his arm until she reached the spot where it disappeared.

She could not see his face, but his whole being was in revolt. She was so beautiful. She should not be seeing, much less loving, his ugliness. He raised her head to look at her once again.

"You're as beautiful now, Etienne, as you were as a boy. Let me feel more." She reached for his groin and began to stroke him.

"I'm impressed," she said, laughing. "Is this the weapon that conquered the mighty Mademoiselle Sophie at the Latin Quarter?"

Stephen started to laugh. "Where did you hear that story?"

"Why, every woman at court with a brother or lover at College Louis le Grand had heard of Etienne LaGarde, who made Mademoiselle Sophie plead for mercy."

Stephen's embarrassment and shame were gone completely now. He laughed heartily. "Well, it wasn't quite like what they all said. Sophie faked it to make me look good. I never touched her."

"Well," said Manya, gripping him tightly in her hand. "That was Sophie's loss."

Stephen sat on the bed and pulled Manya up beside him. "Do you really want to sleep with me?" he said. "I don't want to do anything to hurt you or Lord Howe. From the way he looked at you tonight, it is clear he adores you."

"And I'm fond of him. He is a fine and good man, and after this—I don't want to deceive you, Etienne—I shall go back to him, but I want to make love with you finally. We should have done this sooner. I want to have you in reality for a change, instead of having you in my fantasy."

He touched her breast and side. He lay back down against the pillows and pulled her down on top of him.

When they had finished, Stephen fell asleep. He lay facing her, his mouth slightly open and his faint snore sounding louder than it really was in the night quiet of the room. Manya rested her head against his chest, and she could feel the beat of his heart and the slow rising of his chest with each breath. She was content lying there. She kissed his chest, and he stirred slightly in his sleep and placed his hand on her bare hip.

She had lied to him about the arm. It was ugly and she grieved that he had suffered such a loss. She smiled when she remembered the feel of him inside of her, however. Sixteen years earlier, as a girl, she could have had this man all to herself. She had rejected him to become a French duchess and a woman of power. Now she was mistress to an English lord and more.

She would go back to Howe and leave this sleeping man next to her once again. But this time she had not cheated herself. This time, if only for the night, he had been her lover.

She pulled her face away from him. "Even his skin smells sweet," she said aloud. She slipped off the high bed onto the floor without using the footstool. Her chemise was on the floor. She picked it up and slid it over her head. Her dress was on the far side of the room. She couldn't see it. The moonlight coming through the window created an alley of light, and all of the rest of the room was made darker by contrast, but she knew where she had left the dress. She bent low, feeling around for the garment with her hand.

She was startled when the door of the room squeaked open and light from the hallway mixed with the moonlight coming from the window. She stepped back into the shadows. She knew Stephen was expecting no one. He would have said something. Was it burglars? She watched the form of a man tiptoe from the door toward the bed. As he arrived halfway, he entered into the shaft of moonlight and she saw a knife flash. She screamed in French, "Etienne! *attention!*"

The assassin was startled by her cry and stopped dead in his path. The hesitation saved Stephen's life. Her scream awakened him. He sat upright in bed. His eyes adjusted to the darkness, and he saw his assailant immediately. He kicked the covers off his naked body and leapt to the floor. The man came at him, the knife held high and ready to strike downward into his exposed flesh.

Stephen knew he would have to act quickly. He grabbed the half-empty jug of milk and hurled it at the man, striking him in the face. The assailant was blinded for only a brief few seconds, but it was long enough for Stephen to duck out of his path and into the shadows. He stuck out his leg. The knifewielder tripped over it and fell onto the floor with a great grunt. Stephen stepped forward and kicked the man in the side of the neck. The blow was absorbed on his sole and heel. The man's neck struck the foot of the bed and he was knocked unconscious.

Manya rushed to Stephen's side just as he knelt down to pick up the knife, which had clattered to the floor.

"Who is it?"

"I don't know. Get a light from the hallway. We'll light the candle by the bed and get a look at him."

When they had a light to shine in his face, Stephen did not recognize the assailant, but Manya gasped. He turned to look at her, but she looked away from him. The assailant began to stir. Stephen stuck the needle-sharp point of the blade into the man's throat until he drew blood. His assailant's eyes

169

opened, and as soon as he became aware of the pressure in his neck, his eyes widened with terror.

"Don't finish me off, your worship," he said in his Cockney accent.

It was the imaginary title of honor that triggered Stephen's memory. It was the boatman from the Thames.

"Why did you try to kill me?"

"I wasn't trying to do nothing of the kind," the boatman protested. "I was just trying to relieve you of your purse."

Stephen pressed hard, and blood began to run down the blade of the knife toward the boatman's eyes.

"Etienne, don't," Manya cried.

The boatman began to panic and to plead. "Please, your worship, don't do it. I tell you I was paid five pounds, more money than I have seen in a month of rowing."

"Who?"

"I don't know him. He had a funny accent—I think an American chap. He told me if I killed you he'd pay me five pounds more after the job was done and after you was buried."

Stephen pulled the knife away. He slipped it, handle first, under his arm, grabbed the boatman by his hair and hauled him to his feet.

Manya stepped back into the shadows.

The man pulled away from Stephen with all of his might. His hair slipped through Stephen's fingers. He ran toward the door. Stephen grabbed the knife and paused to throw it.

"Don't, Etienne," Manya shouted.

Stephen hesitated long enough to make it impossible to throw at the fast-fleeing target. He turned and looked quizzically at the princess.

"You would have killed him," she said finally.

"He would have killed me."

"I don't think you would like the task of explaining all of this to the bailiffs and sheriff's men. Let him go. He was small fry."

"You're right. He is. But I know who the big fish is."

Stephen walked over to the bed and found his nightshirt. He slipped it over his head. He stepped in the milk that had fallen on the floor. And he cursed. His anger was growing. If Manya had not come to him this evening and agreed to spend the night, he would be dead, the victim of a cutthroat.

He turned toward Manya. "I know who is behind this," he said with a quiet that belied his true emotions. "It's always been Daniel Pierce. That's the bastard who paid to have my father and mother murdered. He's the one, goddamn me if it's not true, who killed my grandfather. It's always been him. He's in London. He's with my mother-in-law and he wants to get rid of me. He's always wanted it. He hopes to deny me my inheritance. Hopes! He's succeeded. He'll never rest, though, until I'm dead, unless I get him first."

He looked for his breeches.

"Where are you going?" asked Manya. "You can't go looking for him now. If you go after him in the mood you are now in, you'll be paraded to Newgate and hanged for murder. You may get away with killing a Thames boatman, but you'll not get away with murdering a prominent Boston merchant."

Stephen hesitated and then walked back to the bed. He pulled himself up on it. "It's always impossible. Pierce always gets away with murder while those who would seek justice are paralyzed."

"I didn't say you couldn't get rid of Pierce, only that it would be foolish to do it in a fit of temper. Why does Pierce succeed? Study that and emulate."

"He succeeds," said Stephen bitterly, "because there are never any witnesses to what he does, because he has no conscience, no soul."

"In other words, he plans his crimes. If you wish to match his deeds, you must match his wits."

"I have no desire to match his deeds."

"That's not how you argued a few minutes ago."

"Well, I've calmed down. I don't wish to murder in cold blood like he does. But I do want him to pay for his crimes. Quite frankly, I don't much care to be ducking assassination. I want an end to it and I want it with justice."

Manya had completed dressing and she walked over to Stephen and turned her back to him. Absentmindedly, he began to rebutton the long rows of silk-covered buttons on the back of her dress. She swept up the golden hair that fell about the nape of her neck and piled the hair on top of her head. She took some hairpins, which she held in her mouth, and deftly placed them so that her curls remained elegantly pinned up. Only some small blonde curls remained uncontrolled and protruding from the upsweep of hair; they fell back down onto her long, thin neck.

She turned and faced him. "I think I can help you, Etienne."

He smiled sadly at her. "How?" he asked out of politeness.

She smiled coyly. "Well, at least I can take your mind off Pierce." Then she reached over and kissed him on the lips.

It was a mistake for her to have gone to all the trouble of getting redressed.

Daniel Pierce knew that his plot had failed before the night was over. He had waited for the boatman by the river with a loaded pistol in hand. The reward was not to be an additional five pounds but rather a lead ball in the brain. The boatman never returned. A man as greedy as the potential assassin would have returned if he had succeeded. Pierce could only conclude that he had failed. Now he would have to be extremely cautious.

He returned to the inn where he was staying. He climbed the short flight of stairs to a second landing and entered his room. The candle in the room was still lighted and Cornelia Schuyler, in a very revealing nightdress, was sprawled across the single bed.

"Cornelia," he hissed. "What the hell are you doing here?"

Cornelia opened her eyes and looked around, startled for a few seconds. She saw Pierce and smiled. "Why, Daniel, you were abroad so late, like a dutiful wife I've been keeping the home fire burning for the return of my man."

"You're not my wife, however, and I can ill afford any scandal."

"Oh, posh!" she said. "London does not recognize scandal. My God, the King is in his dotage and the whole city knows he's screwing every woman at court who is willing to be pawed by the senile old boar. The Princess of Wales is a bitch in heat over her dear earl. And you're worried because two colonials might be spoken of as having had an affair. Dammit, Daniel, no one in the city would give a snail's balls for the news."

"I don't want you implicated in my dealings."

"You mean you don't want me getting any of your profits. You're such a greedy man, and you are so sexless. I do believe you would put the feel of money ahead of the feel of my body."

"You and I have had our moments, Cornelia."

She sighed and got off the bed, picking up her dressing gown and cape from the floor. "Yes, we've had our moments. But I suspect that this is not to be one of them." She slammed the door behind her.

"Good riddance," he said aloud. She was becoming a tiresome woman. He laughed to himself. Did she really think he would put her ahead of money? There was no woman in the world who could claim his affections. Well, there might

172

have been, if things had worked out differently. Sarah Nowell had been a remarkable woman. She was his peer as a merchant and uncommonly handsome. But she had had all the misplaced loyalties of a Breed—her family. She trusted incompetent drunks like William Vaughan while rejecting him, Daniel Pierce. And he had had her murdered. Her father had been no better. He had even trusted Eben Warren, their joint solicitor. Pierce himself had had to smother the old man with his own pillow. His wife, Betsy Breed, at home in Charlestown, was really a prisoner in her own house. She had been ill when he left. He feared to find her in the churchyard when he returned. With her dead, the Nowell trust would go to charity. The Breeds—every one of them gullible to the end. He laughed aloud when the thought struck him. Their biggest fault was that they had all trusted him. And now it was the turn of young Nowell—every bit a Breed, with all their stupid loyalties.

He had to remove him. Too often in the past, Nowell had stumbled across his plans and caused him to fail, or at least not to succeed to the extent that he felt he should. Nowell had escaped his threat, but he would not get away the next time. There was too much at stake.

From early before the last war he, Daniel Pierce of Boston, had been the source of information for the French government in Quebec concerning New England's plans and preparations. He was the master spy—right in the heart of the Council of Massachusetts. He had more than compensated France for the wealth that poured into his coffers in Boston and into those of the dummy company he owned in Montreal. Almost singlehandedly thus far in the present war, he had undermined English efforts. Because of him, Braddock was dead; because of him, Shirley, his supposed mentor, was now in disgrace. Not only was Niagara untouched, but the only western English fort at Oswego lay in ruins. Only that wild bastard, Johnson, had managed to outmaneuver him and only because the French Indians and Canadians had proved themselves cowards. With more courage, Johnson's forces would have been routed as easily as Braddock's.

He was engaged now even more closely with the French intelligence forces. He regarded it as typical of the French that their entire operation in England was headed by a woman. After all, was not the King of France himself tied to the apron—or perhaps better, to the corset—strings of the woman Pompadour?

It was clear that Pitt was determined to turn the tide in

North America. He was determined to conquer New France. New troops, new leaders, all were being readied. Daniel Pierce's task would grow more and more difficult.

The woman had provided him with exact numbers and with much of the plans for the next campaign. She had assigned to him the task of thwarting the plan regarding leadership. He himself had led the campaign, calling upon ministers. Sir William Shirley and Lord Loudoun, former commanders-in-chief, had agreed to attempt to thwart the appointment of Lord Howe. American objections, many of them coming from counselors like himself in New England and from powerful families like Cornelia's in New York, had guaranteed that the fop, Abercrombie, would command, not the competent Howe.

There was a scratching at the door. He was startled. It was too late for visitors and it seemed clear from Cornelia's attitude that she had no intention of returning. Well, maybe she had changed her mind. She was a very changeable woman, and by God, was she sensual.

He opened the door. "Cornelia?" But it was not Mrs. Schuyler.

"You," he said. "What are you doing here? It's late and no proper woman would be visiting a man's room at this hour."

"Well, I'm not a proper woman," said Manya in her heavily accented English, closing the door behind her. "I'm His Most Christian Majesty's chief servant in England, and you work for me."

Pierce walked away from her and returned to the washstand in the corner of his room.

Manya followed him. "It was foolish to attempt to kill him, especially when you err."

He looked at her in surprise. "How?" He caught himself. "I don't know what you're talking about."

"Don't play games with me," she hissed. "It's a serious business we're in. When my workers fail," she bluffed, "they don't run and hide. To me they come. The boatman works for France. He has been assigned to cover Nowell. You were told that, and you were told that you could use him, but no one told you to kill Nowell. I want to know why. How does France gain from killing Nowell? And don't give me the obvious statement like France gains from the death of any one of its enemies. The gain must balance the risk."

Pierce did not respond at first. He turned his back on Manya. "I'm not used to taking orders, much less taking orders from a woman. I've been on my own in Massachusetts

174

for almost twenty years, and I have done more than my share. France would have been chased from Canada long ago but for my efforts. I don't have to answer for anything to you."

"You do when you use my people and open us to exposure. Exposure, as you must be aware, is fatal."

"Goodnight, madam," said Pierce.

Manya's face flushed with anger. She was on the verge of shouting at Pierce but realized the hour and the place were not right. There were other ways for her to control him.

There was another knock on the door. Manya looked at Pierce. "You are expecting someone?" she said.

Pierce's face had gone pale with fear. "It might be Nowell." He reached under the washstand and pulled out a dueling pistol. He cocked the hammer. The click of the mechanism sounded loudly in the stillness of the room.

"Daniel, are you awake? I'm coming in." It was Cornelia.

Manya quickly moved to Pierce's bed and draped herself across it.

The door swung open and Cornelia entered. She took in the scene with the sweep of her cold eyes. Her face contorted into a sneer. "I gather you and your whore would rather be alone," she said. She turned and slammed the door.

"Dammit, woman, now look what you have done to me. She'll never accept this. She'll leave me flat. And I'm not guilty of infidelity."

"No, only to your wife," quipped Manya.

Pierce ignored her. "How could you do this to me?" he complained.

"It was the necessary and the obvious solution," Manya responded offhandedly. "Your problems do not interest me any more. Since we have a divorce, you and my bureau, you claim you take no orders and I respond to you that you get no help. No protection from me."

"I'll expose you," said Pierce.

"A merchant's word against the word of Lord Howe's lady? A lady who dines with the Prime Minister? You will not be believed."

She walked to the door and opened it. "Leave England, if you wish not to hang, and remember the arm of England reaches across the sea to your Boston also."

She stepped to the door. She closed it softly and walked down the hall. When she reached the end of the corridor and the top of the stairs, she turned around and looked behind her. The hallway was empty and dark, as were the stairs in front of her. She whispered to herself in Polish. "My gift to

175

you, Stefan, is Daniel Pierce. He will flee London now and sail for New France. It is the only safe place for him. Maybe with him gone, your rightful inheritance will come to you. I love you, Stefan—now the man but still so like the aimless pup of a boy. Au revoir, Etienne."

VI

1757-1758

The dirt road followed the shore of the river along the north bank of the Isle d'Orleans. It rambled over knolls and through patches of maple and fir trees, connecting farms whose fields ran right to the river's edge. The spring thaw had left great puddles in the low point of the road, and the drier parts were rutted by wagon wheels in the mud.

Karl kept off the side of the road, trying to keep the mud and cow dung off his military boots. It had taken him some time to get used to wearing the uniform of the lieutenant of artillery, a uniform he had learned to hate while serving as a common soldier at Louisbourg in the last war. But letters of recommendation from Dieskau to General Louis Joseph, Marquis de Montcalm-Gozin de St. Veran had a prompt response.

Karl still did not love France. But he loved Canada. He was glad he had left Stefan. He still felt the dull, painful ache in his heart when he thought of Katherine.

Karl had been welcomed in the city of Quebec and had been granted the promised commission and a place on the general's staff. France was remote to him, but Montcalm was not. The general had taken him under his wing. As part of the King's plan to settle soldiers in New France, Montcalm had awarded Karl a farm in the parish of St. Pierre on this island in the middle of the St. Lawrence, a few miles downriver from the town of Quebec. The land was not the best farmland available. It was on an island and more difficult to reach than other soldiers' farms, but Karl had never owned any land in his life before and he was elated. This day he had come to Isle d'Orleans to inspect his "estate" and to occupy his house for the first time.

Down the road he saw a small boy rounding up cows inside a fenced pasture. The boy had swung open the board gate and the cows, on their own, had begun to come out on to the road and head home toward the barn for the night. He was a boy of slight build, with black, curly hair. He was dressed in the rough, homespun shirt and breeches of the countryside.

Karl's great steps outdistanced those of the boy, and before long he had joined the herder at the rear of the procession. The cows moved more rapidly as they recognized the path toward the warmth and fodder of home, yet still they reminded Karl of a group of ladies turning to gossip about each other, particularly those in the front commenting on those bringing up the rear.

"Does this whole herd belong to you?" he asked the boy.

"No, monsieur," said the boy. "But some belong to my father, Henri Gingras, and some to our neighbor Millard. The best cows are Gingras' cows because I care for them better and I feed and milk them. I am Antoine, son of Henri."

"I'm glad to meet you, Antoine. I'm your new neighbor, Lieutenant Stiegler."

"You must have the old Fortin farmhouse and the land. It's a good house and good land, but it has lain fallow for years. It will take much work to restore it. You must stop by our farm on your way to your own and meet my family. My father and mother have eight children. I am the youngest. Maybe you will want to get help from us on the farm. My brothers have little work to do."

Karl laughed. "Little work? I just left another farm. No farmer has little work in the spring. This is the planting time."

"It's too early to plant. You must come from south of here. Your accent is strange."

"I've lived on Isle Royale with the Acadians and I've lived among the Bastonois."

"Among the heretics? The curé will not care to hear of that."

They walked quietly for the next few moments. Only the jingling of the cowbells tied to the neck of the cows broke the silence. They came to the top of a small hill. Karl could see across the north channel of the river. On the far shore the Montmorenci River plunged over its falls to drop into the St. Lawrence. Great clouds of mist rose from the churning water at the bottom of the falls. A hawk circled the cloudless blue sky above them. Karl stopped to watch the bird and at the same time to take in the view of the falls. Below the knoll and stretching right to the riverfront there was a cluster of small

178

buildings. The Gingras house was constructed of stone and had a roof built to allow the heavy snows of the winter to slide off or to be blown off by the great wind that came out of the frozen wastes of the north.

"Your house will be just like ours," said Antoine. "Only not so large. It is about a mile and a half farther along. You also have fewer acres than us."

"I don't need as much as you. There is only one of me. Tell me, will I be able to see the falls from my windows like you can?"

"Perhaps," said Antoine. "I've never looked to see."

There was a shrill whistle from the barnyard of the Gingras farm. Now the cows broke into a trot.

"They recognize my father's call. I will have to drive the others on, but I think you should stop here and visit with us. My mother will be angry if she does not meet you."

Karl said goodbye to Antoine and walked toward the Gingras house.

"Papa," yelled Antoine as he drove on the Millard cattle. "We have a guest. Tell Maman I'll be back for supper."

The front door of the Gingras house flew open as Karl approached it and a mass of people piled out. Madame Gingras was a slight woman with brown hair and sharp nose and chin. Her daughters, all five of them, ranging from twenty-three to sixteen, were prettier and younger versions of the mother. Henri came out of the house last. He and his two sons were small men, especially when compared to Karl, who towered over them. Gingras and his sons all had pipes in their mouths, but what truly startled Karl was that the women were also smoking. Never before, either in Europe or in America, had Karl seen women smoke.

"*Bonjour, mes amis,*" said Karl. "My name is Lieutenant Karl Stiegler. I am your new neighbor. My farm is the abandoned one beyond the farm of the Millards."

The girls hung back from the crowd, which gathered about Karl. The boys were somewhat awed by the size of the stranger but were putting up a good front. But the girls were proper girls, instructed in the catechism by the curé. Although it was not proper for them to show it, they had each scrutinized Karl carefully. He had a farm just down the road; he was a gentleman and officer and, what was just as important, he was very handsome. Each Gingras girl had mentally led him from the curé's altar to the marriage bed.

It was Madame Gingras who put an end to the posturing and the gawking. "Monsieur, you must stay for supper.

179

Rejean," she yelled at one son. "Catch up with Antoine and make sure he invites the Millards to a *fête* at our farm. We must celebrate the arrival of a new neighbor."

Henri offered Karl a pipe of tobacco as soon as he entered the house. Karl went to the fireplace and spread his hand before the hearth. It was beginning to get chilly now that the spring sun was setting low in the western sky. He took a lighted taper and lit his pipe. The house was soon filled with the rich aroma of pipe tobacco, smoked by all of the inhabitants.

Karl was given the place of honor before the fire. The men of the Gingras family sat about the fire while the women disappeared into the kitchen. He liked these people. They were warm and generous to him, a stranger. They were full of joy, and their joy filled him with a sense of peace.

"How are things in the town?" asked Henri.

"Much preparation for the campaign to come this summer," answered Karl.

"Where will the marquis strike this time?"

Karl merely smiled. He had his suspicions, but he was not free to speculate about such matters with civilians.

Henri did not wait long for Karl's answer. "I wish the army would stay put in Canada. In the old days we would have peace with New York and the Bastonois even when there was a war between our kings. We were all better off in Canada in those days. Now we have French nobles who general our armies with regiments from France. They go south and sting the English lion. But the lion will not stay put forever. One day he will turn on us, and then pity us all. We Canadiens, we understand. Vaudreuil, the governor, he understands these things; he is one of us. He was born Canadien, but Montcalm, he is one of those Versailles prigs."

"I work for the marquis, Monsieur Gingras. He is a fine man and a great soldier."

"Who cares? He does not understand Canada. Nor will France stand by us when the English finally come. We will be on our own. We were better off when we and the Bastonois made our own peace. But now with Louis' soldiers here and the English king's soldiers to the south of us, nothing will ever be the same again."

Henri's two sons nodded in agreement.

There was a shout from the yard as Antoine returned, accompanied by the Millards, husband, wife and two teenaged sons.

It was clear from the way two of the Millard men eyed two of the Gingras daughters that in a few years there would be closer ties between the two families, but the boys were soon outraged by the way their chosen ones ignored them and attempted to attract Karl's attention.

The male Millards soon joined the group about the hearth and soon added their smoking pipes to the general gloom of the house. Madame Millard disappeared into the kitchen with the carcass of a large brown and white rabbit thrown over her shoulder—the Millard contribution to the *fête*.

Gingras removed a stone from the chimney. He stuck his arm into the cavity and pulled out a large bottle of French brandy.

"We must celebrate the arrival of a new neighbor to the parish of St. Pierre. The old Fortin farm has a new owner."

They drank the brandy in one gulp. Gingras refilled the mugs and they were emptied a second time.

"I'm not sure *owner* is the right word. I hold it from the Seigneur."

"So do we all, but that means very little—a few bushels of corn, some help with his crops—that's all the service we must give. The Seigneur, our lord, puts only a light burden on us. He is a Canadien like us."

"I'm Swiss by birth," said Karl.

Gingras had poured a third mug of brandy for Millard, Karl and himself this time. He ignored both Millard's and his own son.

"You can't help that," he laughed. "Now you are of the parish of St. Pierre. We will be grateful to have a soldier among us when the English come."

"You must not speak in so defeatist a tone, Henri," said a voice from the doorway.

The men turned and saw a tall, gaunt-looking man in a black cassock.

"Father, come join us in a drink," said Gingras. "Lieutenant Stiegler, this is our curé, Father Cardinal."

Karl bowed. His head was reeling from the brandy. "Your eminence," he said.

The curé's face turned red and the men started to snicker.

"I'm not a cardinal, lieutenant," said the priest angrily. "My rank is curé. My name is Cardinal."

Karl smiled broadly. His normal caution was reduced by the alcohol. He disliked priests in general, and he was very sure he disliked this very haughty one in particular. "Forgive me, curé," he said, emphasizing the title. "I thought from the look of you that you were more important."

The others gasped, but the priest merely smiled. "Lieutenant, you are a newcomer here, I gather."

"Yes," said Karl. "I am now the holder of the old Fortin farm."

"Good," said the priest. "I suspect I will be seeing you at mass this Sunday. We can talk about your tithe then."

"I'll pay the tax, priest, because that is the law, but you'll wait a long time to find me at mass," said Karl.

"You are a Catholic, are you not, Lieutenant?"

Karl merely smiled, and Gingras shoved a mug of brandy in the priest's hand. "Some brandy, Father?"

"You are a Catholic, Lieutenant?" repeated the priest, ignoring Gingras.

"But of course," said Karl. "I am Swiss by birth, but I hate the heretics."

The priest smiled. "I am so happy to know that. It would never do to allow Protestants and their infectious heresies in New France. If I had even the slightest suspicion, I would take it to the Seigneur and maybe even the Governor."

"Rest assured, Father, I am no Protestant."

The priest bowed at Karl. "We understand each other, Lieutenant."

Gingras produced a keg of beer he had made very recently. The brandy had all been drunk, and now Gingras prepared to tap the keg. Chairs and tables were pushed aside. Antoine took the fiddle from the wall and struck up a tune. Karl thought the beat had the jiglike rhythm of some Scottish tune he had heard while serving with the English. The men clapped and several began to sing. Millard stood and danced his jig in the middle of the floor while the other men clapped in time with Antoine's fiddle. Then Gingras sang a song. His last line was repeated by the others in every instance. Karl could hear the voices of the women and girls in the next room joining in with the tune. They sang and they danced for what seemed like hours to the hungry Karl—all while drinking the beer.

Madame Gingras and Madame Millard entered the room finally, carrying a huge iron pot between them. The aroma of the pot they brought was mind-numbing. After the two women placed it on a large maple wood table, the room filled with the smell of roasted meats, an aroma that overcame even the pungent tobacco fumes. The two women were followed by girls who carried platters of boiled potatoes, cornbread, and maple syrups and sugars.

Madame Gingras lifted the lid off the great pot, and steam rose to the roof beams, to a chorus of "ahs" from the whole house. The great *tortier*—pigeon stew containing also a whole partridge, a cut-up rabbit and moose meat—was ready for serving.

Karl picked up a plate and stood in line to be served by Madame Gingras. He looked into the pot for a choice piece of meat. Madame Gingras noticed his puzzled face. "I like the rabbit best," she said. "Try some."

He saw the rabbit's whole head in the pot. Antoine, who was standing behind Karl, reached over his shoulder with a knife and deftly pierced the rabbit's eye and pulled it from its socket. It disappeared into his mouth.

"Antoine," shouted his mother. "That's rude." She swung an arm at him, but he ducked neatly aside and laughed.

"There are two eyes, Maman. Offer the other one to our guest."

Karl shook his head. He was not up to rabbit eyes. But he was hungry. He took a piece of moose meat, a partridge leg and a mug of cool beer. He sat in a corner of the room, making sure he stayed clear of the curé. Marie, the oldest Gingras daughter, came and sat next to him as they ate. She asked him about the army and about Quebec. It was clear to Karl that she was embarrassed and very shy. She had been forced by her mother to sit with him. She was plain, and it was clear that Madame was worried that her oldest daughter, surpassed in beauty by her younger sisters, would be very hard to marry off. Karl talked with her politely for five minutes. But he noted that she grew more relaxed and familiar. He rose and excused himself and walked over to where the curé sat. He decided that the company of the priest was less dangerous.

The city of Quebec was divided into two levels. Along the flat bank of the St. Lawrence, where the St. Charles entered into the great river, was located the lower town. Here were found the docks, the wharves, the warehouses of the merchants and the shops of the craftsmen. Towering above the narrow, winding streets was the upper town—crowned with the spires of Le Château, home of the government, as well as the spires of the seminary and the houses of the religious orders.

The upper town was surrounded by a great stone wall,

running from the cliffs above the St. Lawrence on the south to the sloping ground above the St. Charles on the northwest.

The Marquis de Montcalm's headquarters were in Le Château. He had arrived in New France the previous year, to replace the captured and permanently disabled Baron Dieskau. It was a post that he had sought for years—an independent command with a serious commitment of men and supplies from the throne.

Montcalm was a handsome man, short but with strong features. He wore a powdered wig and the white coat of a general officer of the French army. He was enjoying his independence and his success. Last summer, in a lightninglike strike, he had destroyed the English fort on Lake Ontario at Oswego. He had struck and destroyed the fortress even before the fabled Sir William Johnson had been able to respond with his red devils.

Spread before him on his desk were his maps for this summer's venture. Lake Champlain was like a giant road striking at the heart of the English and Dutch colony of New York—and New York was the key to English America. Seize that colony and you divided the English in two. New England would be severed from Virginia and the other southern colonies. But before seizing the colony, one would have to take the town of Albany and then proceed from Albany to New York City. Lake Champlain was a French lake today, with a fort at Crown Point in Montcalm's hands and a new fort just constructed at the point where Lake Champlain and Lake George joined.

Now, with access to Lake George, a second route, joining with Champlain but driving even farther south than Champlain, was available to the French. Lake George was still an English lake, with the English fort, Fort William Henry, built by Sir William Johnson, dominating it at its southern terminus. That fort Montcalm would not allow to remain standing. This year's campaign would require two steps. First the French must insure control of Lake Champlain. The English must not be allowed to attack Crown Point. Lake George as a road to the north must be denied them. Montcalm was sure of the way to achieve this. He would first strengthen his new fort, Fort Carrillon, or Ticonderoga, as the Indians called it. Secondly, he would destroy the English fort at Fort William Henry, and with its destruction, the path to Albany would be cleared.

There was a knock on the door. "Enter," said the marquis. Karl entered the room.

"The Comte de Levis is outside, sir," he said.

"Ah, Lieutenant, I'm glad you've arrived. How is your farm?"

"It's exhausting me, sir. I've never worked so hard in my life. The only thing worse than trying to restore abandoned land is trying to convert virgin forest into farm."

"I gather you've done both."

Karl merely smiled. He had told almost nothing of his experiences after leaving Louisbourg to the French. He trusted Montcalm. In fact, he had grown to love this nobleman who had almost a fatherly interest in his well-being.

"My neighbors have been very generous to me, sir. I feel more like a Canadien with each passing day."

"Yes, you're lucky—fabled Canadien hospitality. My nephew Charles arrives today from France. I hope you will extend a bit of it to him. Certainly I've felt very little of it," said the marquis. "Especially from my political overlord, the Governor."

"Are you involved in another battle with the Marquis de Vaudreuil?"

"I don't believe that Vaudreuil and I will ever see eye to eye. He is Canadien and, although devoted to the King, he listens to the Seigneurs and even to the habitants. They would prefer to leave well enough alone and not launch attacks against the English. But I have my orders and my duty to the crown. I must destroy the King's enemies wherever I find them. It is ironic, Karl, because all through my military career I've had the reputation of being a master of defense. Most of my career I've performed only adequately when I move from the position of defense. It is against my nature to attack. I like to have my men behind something, protected."

"I've been a common soldier myself, sir. I know that soldiers prefer to be protected and down behind something."

Montcalm laughed. "I suspect that it is not only the common soldier who prefers such protection. But on this occasion, I must attack. I have my regiment—regulars from France—and there are the Canadien troops. I don't know how Vaudreuil will instruct them and whether he even can. Will they be trustworthy? And then there are the Indians that the priest provides us. Them I don't trust at all. I trust even less the western Indians, who don't have the controlling authority of priests."

Karl nodded in agreement. "Don't trust the Indians. We must have them only because Johnson will have them as well. The Canadiens will defend their homes until the last, but I would not have much hope for the success of thrusts into New York if they depended on Canadien militia."

"You're right," said the general. "Now send in Levis. We have much planning to do."

The flotilla of canoes and *bateaux* had sailed from Crown Point in the morning. The sky had a summer heat haze that made it appear more white than blue. The tree-topped mountains blurred into the white haze. It was difficult to define where the sky began and the mountains ended. The waters of the lake were almost grey-black and reflected the afternoon sun's rays with a silver glare.

Karl stayed close to the marquis for most of the journey south. Lake Champlain continued to narrow. Montcalm, in the first boat, was searching for a promontory of land on the west side of the lake. At this point a small creek flowed into Lake Champlain. The creek originated in Lake George and flowed into Lake Champlain after some rapids and a small fall. Across the lake, on the east shore, a low mountain dominated the lakefront. On the west shore the mountains were taller and looked down upon the French fleet like great frowning bears.

The Caugnawaga Mohawk standing in Montcalm's boat pointed toward the shore. "This is Ticonderoga," he said to the general.

Montcalm checked the map that was spread out in his lap. He nodded in agreement. "Yes, Fort Carrillon. Charles," he said to his nephew, "give the signal to my aides, Bougainville and Stiegler, to drop in back and pass the word that we are to proceed to that promontory." He pointed toward the west shore. "We proceed with great caution. We would not want to run into any of Sir William Johnson's wards lurking in those woods before we made it safely to the fort and to our camp."

They landed without incident, and then the general put them all to work improving the fortress—all except the Indians, who soon mysteriously disappeared. Logs were felled, trenches dug, redoubts laid out. Scouts were sent off to the south toward Fort William Henry. The English did not react, although Montcalm was sure that the Mohawks had warned Johnson of the French presence at the northern outlet of what to that point had been an English lake.

Late in July, when the fortress at Ticonderoga had begun to take shape, Montcalm again gave the word for them to

186

reload the *bateaux* with supplies and, strapping several *bateaux* together, he hauled some thirty cannons and mortars south with him. Miraculously, the Caugnawaga and the St. François Christians reappeared, a thousand strong, along with another thousand from the western tribes. The canoes and *bateaux* navigated the stream, which flowed above the fortress and followed its course into the clear waters of Lake George.

They rowed south for two days, and toward evening of the second day they came into view of the stockaded English fort, made of wood and earth. They beached their boats outside cannon range and sent out their Indian scouts to prevent any English sortie before they could organize their siege.

The English remained within the fort, which was close to the lakefront and surrounded on two sides by marshes. Above the marshes, on high ground, protecting the road to Fort Edward and the Hudson, they had established a second fortified camp. The position was a strong one but not strong enough to resist persistent artillery.

Montcalm had taken his aides, Bougainville, Gozin and Karl, to reconnoiter the English position. He stood on the slope of the hill on high ground, behind the English camp—between them and Fort Edward. He snapped his glass shut and turned to Bougainville. "The Comte de Levis will fortify this point and prevent any succor from William Johnson," he said. "The Indians should camp here as well. We will reduce the fort by regular siege. Our artillery will be brought closer and closer to the fort by constructing zigzag trenches, bringing our guns into position and providing protection to our flanks."

"That will be difficult, sir," said Charles Gozin. "Look how the forest has been burned away. The landscape before the fort is strewn with tree stumps. Most will have roots. It will be hell digging through them."

"The English will open fire with their cannon sharply. I believe my men will appreciate the cover," Montcalm said, smiling at Karl.

The Comte de Levis, Montcalm's second in command, arrived on the scene. The two leaders greeted each other warmly.

"It is the wish of monsieur that I encamp here?"

Montcalm nodded.

"As you order. I believe, however, that you should meet with the Indian chiefs. I don't like the way they are behaving, the western tribes in particular. When I first arrived here, several English attempted to scout this camp. They were captured and beaten."

Montcalm's face went white.

"Also," continued Levis, "an Iowa chieftain was killed. They have placed his body sitting upright on the hill above and have surrounded his body with buffalo robes. They intend to bury him sitting there and they plan to slaughter the remaining captives in his honor."

"Monsieur le Comte, ransom the prisoners immediately and send them off to Montreal with the next supply canoes."

"It will not be easy to get them out of the Iowas' grip."

"Promise anything," said Montcalm, with anguish plainly drawn on his face. "But get them into our hands. I'll meet in council with the tribes tonight. In the meanwhile, send me the chiefs."

Some moments later several richly painted and feathered Indians approached the general. Karl's eyes widened with surprise when he recognized Socono among them. The Abenacki looked at Karl stoically. He would leave it to the Swiss to betray him or not. Karl kept silent. What was the Indian's game? Whose side was he really on?

Socono did not speak. Rather, it was the chief of the Mohawks of Caugnawaga and Two Mountains who addressed Montcalm bitterly. "Father, we are in great distress."

Montcalm looked very concerned. "Why are my children upset?"

"Father, we are far more experienced with fighting in the woods than you. Yet you do not consult us in making your preparations to destroy the English."

"My son speaks wisely," said the general. "Tonight I will seek the advice of all the chiefs in council."

The Caugnawaga seemed pleased that the war chief of the great King was so easily persuaded. But he continued, "The great guns—when will we hear them?"

"Within three days, all thirty-one guns and the bomb mortars will rain death upon our great King's enemies."

Again the Indians seemed pleased.

"But until the guns fire," said Montcalm, "I expect your warriors to live here with my brother, Levis, maybe preventing Johnson from relieving his brothers trapped in the fort."

"Warraghiyagey will not set foot here," said the Caugnawaga. "We are two thousand strong. Our brothers who persist in taking up the hatchet for Johnson will not dare venture out

188

against us. Warraghiyagey is helpless against the might of Onontio, the governor of Canada."

"My father Onontio, Vaudreuil, and my father's King are in the debt of my children."

The chiefs left. Karl did not dare signal or attempt to speak to Socono. But he desperately wished to know why the Abenacki was with this army. He looked for him after the conference but Socono had disappeared.

When the cannons first fired, Margaret Schuyler jumped with surprise, overturning the teacup that sat on the small table by her side. The first shot did no more damage to the fort than to spill an old lady's tea.

"Foreigners," she shouted. She got up from her chair and walked to one of the two bedrooms. Both Katherine and Amy were asleep. They took a nap almost every afternoon now.

"The two of them would sleep while the whole fort collapsed about them," she murmured. "Where the hell is that man? He is never around when I need him. I have to know what is going on."

The front door flew open and Israel Kip walked in, almost as if he had heard her complaint.

"Ma'am, the French have begun their shelling."

"Do you think I'm deaf? I can hear it. Where have you been?"

"I've been at Colonel Monro's headquarters. You see, ma'am, when you want to know what is going to happen, it is best to snoop on them what makes it happen. This Monro fellow is a Scotsman. I suspect he is a fighter. He expects this fellow Webb at Fort Edward to send reinforcements. Johnson has gone to join Webb with all his Indians. Monro expects to be relieved."

"You sound dubious."

Kip looked at her blankly.

"You don't believe it will happen. Damn, I don't know why I allow an uneducated nincompoop like you to hang around me."

Kip looked hurt, which infuriated Margaret all the more. But then Kip shrugged off her insult. "Yes, I'm dubious. I'm dubious that Webb will move his arse out of Fort Edward. I'm dubious Johnson can get his Mohawks to fight against any Caugnawaga that may be here. I'm dubious that Webb will allow Johnson to move against the French. I'm dubious that this fort can hold out for more than a few days and I'm dubious that I should be here at all."

"You're going to run out on us?"

A look of disgust crossed Kip's face, and he opened his mouth to speak, but before he could respond, the thunder of French cannon splintering wooden palisades drowned out any words he might have uttered.

Amy cried out in her sleep and Katherine appeared at the door of her bedroom.

"It's begun," she said.

Margaret nodded.

"Kip," said Katherine, "what will the colonel do? Will he accept French terms?"

"He should," said Kip. "But knowing these professional soldiers, he won't. He'll have to get a healthy number of us killed before he can surrender. Otherwise it would ruin his career. These soldiers are funny folk. It's not bad to lose and surrender, so long as a lot of your men are killed. But show a spark of weakness by avoiding casualties and you're finished. I'm dubious"—he looked directly at Margaret—"I'm dubious he'll surrender until we've had a good fight, and certainly not until after we've got a good number of friends to bury."

Margaret paced the floor. "I don't know why that one damned poor excuse for a husband sent you here."

Katherine looked at her, shocked. Her bluntness normally was overlooked, but this time Katherine felt her aunt had gone too far. Stephen had sent them to William Henry because it was the safest spot in the colonies. He could not have foreseen this French attack. She glared at Margaret.

Her aunt ignored her. She continued her pacing. "What do you think of the savages that are with the French?"

Kip looked at her and a deep frown crossed his face. "They're a worry. From what I can make out, they're Socono's types, Papist savages plus some plain heathens from the west."

Margaret fretted. "They'll murder us in our beds if they get in here. Monro is right to fight."

The firing continued for a week. With each passing hour it became more accurate. The English ramparts were wrecked. The earthworks had collapsed and the wooden palisades were a shambles. All that remained was for the French to charge in and enter the breached fortress. Then, as suddenly as they had begun, the cannons grew silent. A party of French officers under a white flag appeared in front of the collapsed walls. Colonel Monro and his officers were to be presented with terms.

Charles Gozin and Karl Stiegler were blindfolded just outside the gates and allowed to enter. They walked, led by the English officers, until they came to a small table, which had been set in the middle of the mortar-shelled, pitted dirt yard. Monro, his head bandaged, sat alone at the table. Several officers stood a distance behind him. They were close enough to hear the exchange. Most of the residents of the fort stood farther behind the officers.

The blindfold was removed from Karl's eyes. The glare of the sun hurt them, and he reached up and shaded them with his hand. At that moment he heard his name called, and his eyes searched beyond the colonel and his officers. He recognized the voice instantly. What was that woman doing in the fort? He saw her try to force her way forward. "I know that boy," she protested when several officers restrained Margaret Schuyler from running forward to greet Karl.

"Get your hands off me, you buzzards," she said as she was dragged backward. "Karl," she yelled, "Katherine and Amy are here too."

Karl was shaken by her news. For days he had been directing cannon fire into a fort where two of the only three people in the world whom he loved were dwelling.

Charles looked at Karl quizzically.

"It's Aunt Margaret. She is a Schuyler, aunt of the wife of my best friend, Stephen Nowell. She says Katherine Nowell is here."

Charles looked at Karl in surprise. "You know Nowell? Is he the one who called himself Etienne LaGarde?"

"Yes, why?"

"I knew him at school. We were roommates at College Louis le Grand. You say LaGarde's wife is here?"

Monro had watched the exchange with interest. Karl pulled his eyes from the disappearing Margaret and focused them on the colonel.

"Friend of yours, Lieutenant?" he asked. "Pardon me, I assume one of you is English-speaking and that is why your general has sent such low-ranking officers to parley with me."

"Yes, sir," said Karl, stammering slightly. "She is a friend."

"You spent some time in our midst, then, sir. Seems a bit inappropriate for you to respond to our hospitality in this harsh manner."

"I have come to offer my general's compliments, sir. The officer who accompanies me does not speak English, but he is the nephew of the Marquis de Montcalm—Charles Gozin. My name is Lieutenant Karl Stiegler, aide to the general."

191

Monro's effort at lightheartedness was a façade. He was a beaten man. He had no word of any aid, and he knew he could not hold out very much longer. And just the day before, in a grand gesture, Montcalm had sent to him an intercepted message from General Webb, which indicated that the English could send no succor to Fort William Henry. Any terms this young blond-haired lieutenant offered him he would have to accept. He could not be responsible for the slaughter that would occur when the French, the Canadians and their Indian allies broke into the fort.

"What are your general's terms, Lieutenant?"

"You have the honors of war, sir. A gallant defense requires generous terms. You may retain your weapons, but you must surrender your ammunition, and you must leave the fort. You will be given free passage, first to the encampment on the rise above, which must also surrender, and then a free passage to Fort Edward. All, of course, must give parole not to participate in any further hostilities for eighteen months unless an exchange is arranged."

Monro sat stunned. He had not expected so much from Montcalm. But it was clear that Montcalm wanted William Henry and not its garrison. With his new fort at Ticonderoga, and William Henry destroyed, it would give France control of the lake. Lake George would again become Lac St. Sacrement. The way to the Hudson would be open, and only Fort Edward would stand between the French and Albany. But Monro had no alternative.

"Tell your general that I must consult with my officers but, given the results of our last council, I can give you a tentative yes. Thank the marquis on behalf of the officers and soldiers and residents of the fort. As you must realize, it breaks my heart to surrender my command to the enemies of my King, but I find some solace in surrendering to an officer as gallant as your general."

Within the hour the British flag had been lowered and replaced with the fleur-de-lis. Karl pushed his way through the crowd of soldiers. Their families and camp followers had crowded onto the parade yard. There were wagons loaded with belongings. Women and children sat on top of them, holding down the bags and packs of family possessions. The road to the fortified encampment on the way to Fort Edward had only recently been cut through the wilderness, and it was still rough.

The noise and confusion were staggering. Karl had hoped

to find Aunt Margaret and Katherine immediately. He asked several wagon occupants, but his French uniform put them off and they would not respond. He started knocking on doors at the officers' quarters on the far side of the parade ground. Then he saw Israel Kip at the end of the line of doorways.

"Israel," he called.

Kip looked at him and then nodded when he recognized Karl. He walked over toward him with that gangling lope he had developed through the years in the forest.

"I've come for Katherine and Amy. I'll place them under my special protection."

"They're going to need it," said Kip somberly.

"What do you mean?"

"I mean that Socono came to me last night. He's with the Abenacki from St. François. He says his people and the Caugnawaga and the Iowa that you fellows brought here with you are steaming. They can't understand the surrender. How can you let us walk away—no scalps, no plunder? They're working themselves into a frenzy. You had better get back to your general and warn him that he'll have a slaughter on his hands if he don't do something."

"Why is Socono here?"

"Smart bastard, ain't he? You're never quite sure where he'll turn up. But I've known that Papist savage for too long not to take his advice. He said to watch out for the Indians. Since we was made to surrender our weapons by Monro, I ain't got much with which to defend Stephen's womenfolk."

"The English column for Fort Edward has already started to leave the fort," said Karl. "It is too late to try to warn Montcalm. We'll have to try something else."

Kip took Karl by the shoulders and pushed him through the doorway into Katherine's house. She was standing by the fireplace, tying a shawl about Amy's shoulders. The child was annoyed with her mother's efforts. "Amy, you obey me," said Katherine. "We may be on the trail at night and you'll wish you had it around you."

"I don't need it, Mama. It's hot," she said angrily, stamping her foot.

"You do as your mother says, young lady," said Karl firmly.

The child looked up at him and then a great smile flashed across her face. She broke away from Katherine, trailing the shawl behind her on the ground. She leapt into his arms.

"Alte Karl," she said, hugging him.

Katherine stared at him in surprise.

Karl held on to Amy and lifted her high into the air. As he lowered her, she clung to his neck and he supported her body with his arm and shoulder. He walked over to Katherine, and bending, he kissed her on the forehead.

"I've missed you, Karl," Katherine said. She stood up and threw her arms about him, almost crushing Amy.

"And I, you," he responded, laughing.

They stared at each other for several long moments. He clung to her. She was crying.

Aunt Margaret stormed to the door of her bedroom. "Katrina, aren't you ready yet?" She stopped when she saw her niece in Stiegler's arms. She saw Kip still standing by the door. "Israel, why are you just standing there? What did that bag of vermin, Socono, tell you?"

Kip shuffled his feet uncomfortably. "Miss Schuyler, you've got to stop insulting the Indian. He just might have saved our lives. He said not to join the column but to go out the sally port and make it to the woods on our own."

"What's going on?" asked Katherine.

"The Indians with the French intend to attack the column," said Kip.

"But we've surrendered and given up our weapons. Aren't we under the protection of the French government?"

"Tell that to them savages," said Margaret angrily. "Damn, I know I never should have handed in my musket," she cursed.

"I have my sword and a pistol," said Karl. "I don't think they'd dare attack someone in my company."

"Don't bet on it," said Kip. "They'd as soon take your hair as they would mine. They'd blame it on some of Johnson's bandits."

"Well, we can't simply stay here," interrupted Margaret. "Let's get out while we can. Katrina, Amy, let's go."

"I'm coming with you anyway," said Karl. "Kip, do you know the way to the sally port?"

The woodsman nodded and headed out the door.

The five fugitives weaved through the crowds of people making their way toward the great gate of the fort. Kip led them behind the fort magazine and then down a flight of stairs to a level below the palisade. This part of the fort was deserted, and Kip opened the trap door and dropped through. He disappeared for some few moments; then his smiling face reappeared up through the hole.

"The way is clear," he whispered.

Amy went next. Karl lowered her into Kip's arms. He set her down on the dirt floor of the tunnel. Karl grabbed Margaret by the waist, and she struck him in the chest. "I can get down without the help."

He smiled at her and ignored her protest. She was lowered kicking into Kip's waiting grasp.

Next Karl lowered Katherine. When Kip stepped aside, Karl jumped down into the hole.

Kip had already made his way to the entrance of the tunnel. The others quietly gathered behind him. They had now to cross a clearing of about two hundred feet, and then they would reach the comparative safety of the woods.

"I'll cross first," said Kip.

"No," interrupted Karl. "You're the woodsman. The others will need you if they are to make it to Fort Edward with their scalps. I'll go first. If I make it, then send Katherine and Amy next, then Margaret and you last."

Kip was nervous but nodded in agreement. What Stiegler said made sense. Karl got up from his crouched position and began to run a zigzagged pattern across the open meadow. He made it to the woods and disappeared behind the bushes.

Katherine took Amy's small hand into hers. Her heart was pounding, but she dared not show her fear to the child. She got to her feet and pulled Amy along with her. She tried to emulate Karl's running pattern, but halfway across the field she was short of breath. She gave up the zigzag and made straight for the bushes behind which Karl had disappeared.

When she was about ten feet from the edge of the forest, she heard an Indian whoop. She turned her head to the right and saw three painted Indians breaking into a run in pursuit. She stumbled headlong into the bushes and fell. Amy collapsed on top of her. Karl pulled them both to their feet and began to push them through the underbrush.

Amy started to cry, but Karl clamped his huge hand over her mouth. Holding Katherine's hand in one of his and grabbing Amy about the neck and shoulders, with a hand on her mouth, he charged like a bull through the woods. He knew the Indians would follow him easily, but if he headed toward the French camp, he thought he might be able to save Katherine and Amy.

They raced ahead for about five minutes. Amy fell once, and Karl picked her up and threw her onto his shoulder. He knew the pursuers were closing in. He could hear them. They made no attempt to conceal their pursuit. The fugitives reached the edge of the woods once again. The next meadow sloped down toward the wagon road to Fort Edward. All along the road, as far as he could see, the English inhabitants of Fort William Henry trudged single file toward the Hudson.

Karl's heart sank. He had failed his beloved. Now all he could do was join the march, a march that Socono had warned was doomed to slaughter.

But Katherine had no intention of joining the English march. She pushed Amy ahead of her toward a hollow formed by a white birch that had fallen on top of a great boulder. She pushed Amy in the cavelike opening and hissed at Karl to follow her. Then she ducked into it herself.

Karl hesitated only a moment. Katherine had made the decision. It was already too late to make a dash for the temporary safety of the marchers. He followed her under the branches of the birch. The Indians would discover them, of course, and then he would fight to save those he loved.

Katherine lay on the ground. She covered Amy's body with her own. Karl handed her his pistol. He knew she would not hesitate to use it to protect her child—or their child. Amy was as much his as she was Stephen's, even if she wore the gold Nowell locket about her neck. He quietly drew his sword out of its scabbard.

The pursuers had suddenly grown quiet. There was an eerie stillness about the forest. The only sounds were the trudging feet of the retreating English, the occasional neighing of a stricken horse, or the thump of a heavy wagon wheel hitting an obstacle; all these sounds came from the distance, vaguely, like the sounds of reality as one awakens from a dream.

Karl heard the Indians finally. They were approaching the edge of the forest. As soon as the sound of the fleeing had ceased, they had become suddenly cautious. They murmured to each other in sounds that Karl could not understand. They were searching the underbrush. Any second now a painted face would peer into the opening, and he would strike with his sword. At least he would get one of the bastards.

Karl's body stiffened as he saw a moccasined foot appear at the side of the boulder. But then suddenly, from the trail below, came the sound of an Indian's war whoop, and several muskets were fired. The foot disappeared. Then there were war whoops close at hand and the sound of feet again crashing carelessly through the underbrush down toward the fighting.

Karl breathed a sigh of relief. They were safe. He placed his hand on Katherine's back. She looked up at him. The terror was still in her eyes. He took the pistol from her hand.

He poked his head through the opening. Out of the corner of his eye he saw the painted body of an Indian, and he saw the gleam of a steel tomahawk descending. He had no time to aim. He fired the pistol blindly at the blurred form, which was charging at him. The ball struck the Indian in the middle of the forehead and went crashing into his brain. He crumbled at the knees and fell forward. The tomahawk fell harmlessly with a clank onto the side of the stone boulder.

Katherine stifled a scream. Karl called to her that he was all right. He went to the edge of the meadow to search for the dead Indian's companions, but they had already raced toward the scene of carnage below. From both sides, at several intervals on the long line, the Indian allies of France were attacking the unarmed prisoners of France.

Suddenly Katherine was standing at his side. Her hand went to her mouth when she saw an Indian grab a woman by her long brown hair. There was a flash of a knife in the sunlight. The woman's mouth opened in a scream that they could not hear on the ridge above.

Katherine looked away and put her head onto Karl's shoulder. She started to weep.

"Mommy, are we safe?" Amy called from the shelter.

Katherine shook herself and wiped the tears from her cheeks and eyes. She sniffled, throwing her head back. "Stay there, Amy," she ordered. "Yes, we are safe. Uncle Karl has saved us."

Karl dragged the body of the Indian deep into the woods in case his comrades came back looking for him. He did not know what else to do. The Indians were on a rampage. They would kill anyone who stumbled across their path. They would get into the rum supply that the English army would surely be carrying and become ten times more dangerous. He decided to stay exactly where he was. Tomorrow he would find his way back to Montcalm's camp, and he would take Katherine and Amy with him. He would not turn them over to anyone who could not protect them, and surely the English had not been able to protect themselves.

He made his way back to the opening and crawled in. Amy had fallen asleep and Katherine sat beside her, stroking her black hair.

"Her hair is so like Stephen's," she said.

Karl tensed and looked away.

Katherine moved away from Amy's side and sat next to Karl. "I've offended you by mentioning my husband's name. He is your best friend."

Karl's face looked pained. "Yes," he acknowledged. "He's my brother. We've shared everything. Even to loving the same woman."

Katherine looked into Karl's face. She wanted to touch him, to stroke away the pain that was so obviously expressed in his face. She pushed his hair off his forehead. "You're wrong, Karl," she said softly. "Stephen doesn't love me. He never has. I've loved him. So in that you've not shared."

"I love you, Katherine."

"I know."

"It's not fair," he said, his face contorting. "He doesn't love you and yet he has you. I can't abide life without you and I'm alone. When I was a boy, I slept with dozens of women. There was no love involved, just pleasure. Now I can't even look at anyone else." He laughed bitterly. "On my island, the girls throw themselves at me. I can have my pick, provided I take her to the curé and marry her. I don't look twice."

Katherine laughed. Her smile, the sparkle in her eyes, the way she held her head—it was too much for him. He bent down and kissed her on the mouth. She started to pull away from him, but he grabbed her shoulders and pulled her body toward him. She stopped struggling, her mouth opened and he slipped his tongue into it. She responded passionately. He kissed her for some moments and then he lowered his hand and touched her breast. She snuggled close to him. He started to unbutton her dress. She pulled away.

"The child," she protested.

Karl ignored her statement. "I want you, Katherine, and you want me."

She looked up at him. She took his hand and pressed it against her breast.

He smiled at her. He knew that Amy would continue to sleep.

He woke in the middle of the night suddenly, aware of her absence. He looked about him in a panic. He could see the dark form of Amy, still sleeping peacefully. He crawled on his knees to the entrance of the shelter. She was standing with her arms folded about her against the chill. She leaned against the side of a boulder.

"Katherine," he called softly.

198

"You're awake," she responded.

"What are you doing out there? It could be dangerous. The savages will be drunk and roaming the woods."

"If they're drunk they've crawled into some shelter to sleep it off," she responded. "I couldn't sleep."

"Was it my snoring?"

She smiled sadly. "No."

"What?"

"You have to ask? I've just been unfaithful to a man I love very much."

Karl sat back on his heels. The wind picked up and the dead birch whose branches formed the shelter seemed to moan.

Karl looked at her for some moments. He loved her passionately. He had just tasted the sweetness of her mouth, and felt the ecstasy of release within her body. He had succeeded in fulfilling a dream that had seemed totally unobtainable just yesterday. And now he had to face the possibility that expressing his love would be the source of Katherine's devastation.

"Katherine, I took advantage of you. The fear, the Indians, it was all too much for you. Please forgive me."

"That's nonsense," she said harshly. "I wanted you; I wanted your body. It had been so long. No, I have come to grips with my own feelings. I love Stephen, I can't deny that, and I love you, Karl, and I can't deny you what I so desperately want for myself—the closeness of a man who loves me. I'm so very confused."

Karl looked at her in astonishment. "You love me?"

"Yes, I do," she said. "I have for some time now. I guess it began when Amy was born and you were there. I think I realized it first when you left. I was desolate without you. It was the first time since the time you carried me from the canoe into our home that you weren't by my side when I needed you. You were my strength. With you gone, I was like a child."

He stood up and walked over to her. He put his arms around her. He didn't want to say it, but he knew he had to.

"And what of Stephen?"

"God help me, I love him," she cried. "But he doesn't love me."

He bent down and kissed away her tears. She kissed him on the lips. The wind stirred the leaves of the trees above their heads. A cloud passed swiftly before the moon, blocking its

199

light and then freeing it just as quickly. They stood there holding each other, bathed in the white light of the moon.

As Katherine and Amy disappeared into the bushes and the three Indians pursued them, Kip placed his hand over Margaret Schuyler's mouth. She bit him.

"Why the hell did you do that?" she hissed at him.

"You bit me," he said in astonishment.

"You stuck your hand in my mouth; what did you expect me to do?"

"I thought you would cry out and draw their attention to us," said Kip.

"I'm not that crazy or that brave. Sometimes I think there's not much to choose between them. I just hope the boy can handle them."

"He has a sword and a pistol," answered Kip. "But he's like a wild boar in the woods. He'll never escape by sneaking through."

"What do we do now, Kip?" asked Margaret.

"We wait. We wait until it's dark, and then we make it safely to those woods and you and I make our way to Fort Edward."

He could see she was terribly upset and fearful for Katherine and Amy.

"I think they'll make it, Auntie," he said, without much conviction.

She nodded in agreement.

They sat in the tunnel for three hours, only occasionally speaking. Just before sunset they heard the chirping of a squirrel, and Kip was suddenly very alert. He responded, much to Margaret's amazement, with the same sound. From out of the bushes stepped Socono, carrying two muskets. He approached the tunnel and Kip rose to meet him, knowing full well that Socono would not be so brazen had he not scouted the area first. He grabbed Margaret's hand and pulled her up out of the tunnel entrance.

Kip went to Socono and grabbed him by the shoulders. They spoke in their strange combination of English and Abenacki.

"It's Stephen's wife and daughter," said Kip. "They fled into the woods with Stiegler. Several Caugnawaga followed them."

Socono looked even more serious than normal. "There has been a massacre, as I warned you. The French tried to stop it, but they were ineffective. There are many English dead and wounded. The tribes have taken much booty and many prisoners."

"Dammit, that's no way to fight," cursed Kip.

"My friend is mistaken," said Socono. "That is the best way to fight. We Indians are few in number, compared to you whites. We cannot fight as you do, marching straight into the fire of the musket. We are too few to have the casualties that you are willing to have. Then again, when our enemy is defenseless, having surrendered his weapons, we can ill afford to let him walk away unharmed. For he will then return another day to destroy us."

Kip rolled his eyes skyward. "You're a damn Papist heathen, Socono. You always were and you always will be. Just let's hope that Stephen's kin haven't fallen victims to heathen thinking and killing."

Socono frowned. "My brother Stephen was a good and brave boy. He is a good man now, but he is not always a wise man. He should not have left his woman and child during a war to carry messages beyond the seas. Perhaps it was his arm. Perhaps, I think, it goes deeper than his arm."

"Will you two stop making ugly sounds and tell me what we do now," said Margaret angrily.

"Next," said Kip, "Socono looks for Karl and Katherine and Amy. You and I make our way to Fort Edward."

When daylight arrived, Karl was able to get his bearings. There was smoke, heavy smoke, rising above the trees to the north. That would be the fort, put to the torch by the French. Montcalm's headquarters would be on the slopes beyond the fort. Karl woke Katherine and Amy and got them moving through the underbrush. The sun was warm and the birds flitted in the tree branches above their heads. Karl walked first, to break the trail and to hold the branches so that they would not snap backward and strike Amy, who followed closely behind him.

They walked briskly for two hours and then broke out into a clearing, filled with the tents of the French army. Most of the tents were in the process of being dismantled. With William Henry in flames, there was no longer any reason for Montcalm to remain at the southern end of the lake. He would soon return to Ticonderoga.

Karl caught sight of Charles Gozin and hailed him. Gozin approached him and then bowed to Katherine.

"This is Madame Nowell," Karl said in French.

"Etienne's wife? Please convey to her my best regards; I

will see to quarters for her. Is this Etienne's daughter also? What a fellow he is with women, lovely women."

Katherine looked at Karl with no small amount of puzzlement. "What is he saying?"

"He says you're very beautiful."

She blushed. She knew she was not looking her best. She had not slept well and she was dirty from their ordeal. But she was vain enough to run her hand through her hair and to try to straighten it.

"Charles will find you and Amy a tent and some fresh clothes. I must make my report to the general. You go with Charles."

Katherine took Amy's hand and followed Gozin. Karl watched them disappear between the rows of tents. Amy was laughing and chattering with her mother, yesterday's ordeal already forgotten.

He walked to Montcalm's tent. The sentry on duty snapped to attention. He knew the general's aide well and made no effort to bar his entry.

Montcalm was seated at his camp desk, his head held in his hand. His coat was draped over the back of his chair. When he raised his head to see who had entered, it was clear to Karl that he had not shaved.

"Stiegler," he said. "Where have you been? Have you seen the slaughter? The savages—the goddamned savages—they murdered defenseless people. Did you see any of it? I tried to stop them. I even went into the madness myself."

Karl said that he had seen, but only at a distance.

"Those women and children, the wounded, I went out this morning to see for myself. I'll never forget it for the rest of my days." His eyes were red, and it was clear to Karl that he had been weeping.

"I never believed they would behave so. The Canadien officers assured me they were under control." He shook his head, as if to clear his mind.

"Never again, never will I employ those savages in an army under my command."

"Sir, you must not be this upset. Most of the English have made it safely to the fortified encampment, and they will be conducted to Fort Edward."

"But I gave my word, the word of a French officer and nobleman, that they would be safe. My honor is besmirched. I will never be able to deal with the enemy without this black mark hanging over me. And I will never forget those corpses, maimed, scalped, all because they put trust in my word."

He stood up from the table and walked angrily toward the entry of the tent; Karl, blocking his way, quickly stepped aside.

"I have a good mind to send my regulars into their stinking camps and let them feel French steel. But the Governor, the vaunted Onontio, would never approve."

"It was not your fault, sir." Karl tried to assuage Montcalm's anger. "You tried to stop them. You'll forget about it."

Montcalm stopped at the entry and looked out into his camp. "You're wrong about that, cher Karl. I'll never forget about what happened at William Henry, nor will history forget it. What should have been remembered as a triumph of French arms and a high moment in the career of this general will be remembered instead as a massacre of the innocent. But we go on. Your report, Lieutenant."

"I rescued two of the prisoners, sir, mother and child. They are very close to me. The child is my godchild. I prefer not to send them to Fort Edward, especially now that the Indians have mutinied. I would prefer to take them to Ticonderoga and even Quebec for exchange, once my friend Stephen Nowell, the woman's husband, returns from Europe."

Montcalm sighed. There seemed to be no escaping yesterday's nightmare. He looked at Karl and waved his hand in dismissal. "As you wish, Lieutenant, as you wish," he said.

Kip and Margaret Schuyler caught up with the tail end of the retreating column as it reached Fort Edward. They had met with Socono, who had assured them that Katherine and Amy had not been among the casualties. He said also that he thought they had escaped but that he could not yet be sure. When the column reached Fort Edward, General Webb provided shelter in tents for the refugees. Word spread quickly in the camp about the awesome dispute that had occurred between Webb and Sir William Johnson. Johnson had demanded that Webb march to the relief of Fort William Henry and Webb had refused, implying that he did not trust Johnson's Mohawks to secure him from the dangers of ambush. He argued that his inferior force made it impossible for him to confront Montcalm's much larger army. As soon as Margaret heard that Johnson was in the fort, she insisted that Kip take her to see him.

The two of them walked across to the other side of the fort to the general's quarters. Johnson's lodgings were easily distinguished by the number of Mohawks who sat on the dirt in front. Margaret went straight to the door. The two sentries barred her way by crossing their muskets. She ducked under them and, before the sentries could turn around, she was inside.

"William Johnson, you son of a bitch," she yelled at the top of her voice. "You find me my Katherine and my Amy."

There was a rustling in the back room, and then Johnson, wrapped in an Indian blanket and obviously wearing nothing else, came out of the room, closing the door securely behind him.

"Miss Schuyler," he said, not at all flustered by his lack of proper clothing or her ranting. "I assume you want something from me."

"You horny toad, you've got some wench back in that room, haven't you? From the looks of that blanket, I would say she's redskinned too."

"Miss Schuyler, may I call you Margaret?"

"No."

"Miss Schuyler, I searched for Katherine Nowell and her child. My informants, and they are the very best, tell me that they were not killed and that she has in fact showed up in the French camp, in the company of a young French officer whom we both have had the honor to meet."

"How come you moved so fast on this?"

"You forget, madam, that the Nowells are my neighbors, that Stephen is working for me and that it was my suggestion to send the virtuous Katherine to Fort William Henry for safety. I owe it to Nowell to at least keep them in view, and they will be viewed. When Stephen returns, I will be able to tell him where his wife and child are, so that he may return them to where they belong. It is the least I can do for friends. That idiot Webb outranks me. If he did not, Fort William Henry, my fort—I built the damn thing—would still be standing, with the British flag flying, and Montcalm and his barbarians would be back in Canada."

"I don't see much difference between his barbarians and yours."

"There is a difference, madam. Mine obey me. Now, Miss Schuyler, may I serve you in any other way, or may I go back to my horniness, as you so quaintly put it?"

Margaret mumbled to herself.

"What is it you're saying?"

"You can get me a preacher," she said loudly at last. "I finally found a man worthy of me. I am determined to bless him."

The winter sun set early on the river in February. The ice was solid, at least a foot thick, and it was possible to walk from Karl's island to the mainland on the north side of the St. Lawrence. Upriver to the west, the lower town of Quebec at the foot of the cliffs was already in darkness. In contrast, the golden rays of the sun struck the steeples of the Jesuit house, the cathedral and the Ursuline convent, which sat majestically on the heights above the river.

Katherine Nowell walked along the river edge. The ice was white here, and it was frozen to the very river bottom. She stared out at the whiteness of great wind-driven drifts of snow, which made crazy-quilt patterns on the river ice. She was startled by the beat of wings. A pure white snow owl, his daytime sleep disturbed by her presence, rose into the air like a wind-driven swirl of snow. He flew only a few feet and settled on a great boulder whose top was above the river level. Here the bird perched and glared with sleepy eyes on the woman intruder. Her mind wandered back over the past months.

Katherine had been in Isle d'Orleans since the late summer. Karl had convinced her to stay with him, at least until Stephen could return from Europe and reclaim her. She was torn by her love for both men, but after the massacre she felt safe with the French army during the day, and safer still in Karl's embrace at night.

She could not justify her actions to herself, and she knew therefore that she would never be able to justify them to Stephen. But at first she didn't care. She threw caution away and reveled in the pleasure that Karl's body gave her.

They had joined the French withdrawal to the fort of Ticonderoga. Most had wintered there, but Moncalm and his immediate staff had returned to Canada. Katherine and Amy accompanied Karl.

She and Amy both had enjoyed the late-summer row north on Lake Champlain to the Richelieu River. When they arrived at the rapids at Chambly, Katherine thought of Stephen for the first time in days. She could not help but recall the story he had told her about his first passage over these rapids with the Oneida, Dagaheari, who later cost Stephen his arm. She tried to picture the very spot where his canoe had capsized and he had saved the life of his Mohawk companion.

She felt an overwhelming sinking feeling when she thought of her husband. She loved his eyes; the scar that ran through one eyebrow; his dark unruly hair; his almost beautiful face; but she hated his indifference. She shook her head, as if to clear the memories from it. She was glad when they passed the rapids and the sound of the rushing waters gradually diminished in her ears.

They arrived at Quebec four days after entering the St. Lawrence at Sorel. Karl had taken Katherine and Amy immediately to Isle d'Orleans. He did not go directly to his own farm but stopped instead at the Gingras farmhouse.

Maman Gingras took Amy under her wing immediately. "What a beauty," she said in French to the uncomprehending Katherine. "The child's hair shines. The brown and red and gold highlights and the brown eyes, so large, with eyelashes that are so long they almost curl. She'll break the boys' hearts."

"This is my new wife and her daughter," Karl lied to his friend.

"Oh, so young to be a widow and left with a child. Such a sad story. You're a good man, dear Karl."

Karl smiled and, squeezing Katherine by the shoulders, he drew her closer to him. "No," he said. "I'm a lucky one."

"We will have a party," said Madame Gingras, "to honor Karl's new wife. Henri," she yelled to her husband, who was barely visible in the fields down toward the river shore. *"Une fête,"* she howled.

He waved back at her, and they could see him calling to his two sons, who worked at the harvest with him.

The party began as soon as Gingras and his sons returned. Maman went to the smokehouse and returned with a great ham. The table was placed in the yard in front of the farmhouse. Soon it was piled with freshly baked breads and rolls and a great earthen jug of beans, cooked in maple syrup and flavored with smoked bacon.

The Gingras children crowded around their father as he sharpened a murderous-looking butcher's knife. He carved the ham neatly into thin slices and passed them to his wife. She had built a wood fire, and she held a large skillet over it in which brown butter was melting. She sautéed each piece of ham immediately and placed it on a piece of toasted bread. On each piece of ham she placed a spoonful of sour cream.

Henri beamed as he handed the plates to his guests and his children. "Taste this," he said to Karl, "and give the new wife and her pretty little girl an extra large piece. This comes from France, from my wife's family, the LaPortes—ne'er-do-wells for the most part, mind you. But this *jambon* will melt in your mouth. It almost makes being related to them bearable."

Madame Gingras slapped him on the back of his head so hard that it almost knocked the pipe out of his mouth and onto his plate. "You're lucky any of us would take you, Papa," she laughed.

Katherine was enjoying their smiles and good humor, even if she did not understand what they said. Amy, after eating her ham and beans and downing a whole pitcher of fresh, creamy milk, ran off, tagging after Antoine, who headed for the pastures to drive home the cows.

After dinner and profuse goodbyes, Karl and Katherine set out in Henri Gingras' hay wagon, with Antoine and Amy bringing up the rear. They drove the rutted dirt road along the river shore until they came to the top of the knoll overlooking Karl's stone house. Katherine sat with her arm through Karl's. He allowed the horses to pause as they looked down. This had become his home. His hope was that she would share it with him.

The house sat in a grove of white birch trees. A small stream ran by it and then wound its way into the great river beyond. The house was stone, with a chimney at each end and a steep shingled roof. Gingras had sent another son ahead to prepare it, and a column of smoke curled lazily from a chimney, rising until it was grabbed by the breeze and scattered into the darkening sky.

That night Katherine lay in Karl's arms in his soft bed. The air had grown chilly; even in late August the leaves would begin to show splashes of reds and yellows among the green. They needed a quilt on their bed at first. But soon the warmth of their bodies made them feel languid. Karl stroked her naked breasts and then kissed them gently. She had her hand behind his neck, twisting the soft hairs at the nape between her fingers. She loved his fair hair, and she loved to feel the strength of his shoulders and arms as he held her. There was such power in his body, and she felt protected by his strength. They loved with an almost violent passion and now he rested, exhausted, balanced on that fine line between awareness and sleep. His mouth rested on her and his lips moved in tiny, almost automatic sucking kisses. But she was alert, rested, grateful and almost peaceful.

She heard a stirring in the bed in the next room, and her daughter cried out. Katherine moved carefully away from Karl, trying not to awaken him. She picked up her petticoat from the bench near the bed and put it on. She went to Amy's side and found her weeping.

"Amy," she called, stroking the child's back and trying to wake her gently from her dream. "Mother's here," she said softly, whispering into her ear.

Amy's eyes fluttered open and she tried to focus in the darkness. She knew her mother's closeness from the warm, fragrant smell of her.

"Mama," she called. "It was a bad dream. It was the Indians chasing us. Alte Karl saved us, but he could not save Papa. Papa got lost in the forest and we couldn't find him. We have to find him," she said, almost in a panic.

"Hush, Amy, it was a dream," said Katherine, drawing her child's hands to her breast. "It was a dream. Your father is across the ocean in England. He is safe there."

"Promise me, Mama," said the child. "Promise me that Alte Karl will look for him and find him. Then we can all be together again."

Tears started to flow down Katherine's cheeks.

"Promise me that," begged Amy.

"I'll have to ask Uncle Karl," she said finally, sniffling and drying her eyes with her hand.

Amy smiled. "Then I can go back to sleep; Alte Karl always tries to make me happy."

Katherine rose to her feet after the girl had fallen off to sleep. She crept back into her own bed and slipped under the warmth of the quilt. Karl snored softly. She reached over and kissed him gently on the mouth. He stirred in his sleep and then opened his eyes. He smiled at her. "Have a heart," he joked. "I need a little time in between. You're an insatiable woman."

Katherine blushed, even in the darkness. She wanted to tell him what Amy had said, but she couldn't. She could not bring herself to destroy his happiness. Instead she placed her hand on his cheek. He took it into his own and raised it to his lips. He kissed the palm and then began his low snoring once again.

That had been six months ago, before the leaves had turned to fire and had fallen in swirls, as the winds came out of the mountains beyond the city and the river. The great St. Lawrence could not be seen for days; mists enshrouded it as it gave up all of its accumulated summer warmth. The stove and fireplace in the stone house roared; log after log was tossed onto the fire. Katherine was colder than she could ever remember being. When the wind finally blew all the mist from the river, it was solid ice and had remained that way ever since.

She continued to look out across the frozen river. The sun was almost gone now. But its last rays glittered off the boulders at the falls, covered with frozen spray. She felt her stomach. It had visibly increased in size in the last month. When she had told Karl that she carried his baby, he had actually done a little dance of joy. She knew he saw it as a further tie to him—a tie she could never break. He was right, of course. Just as Amy was her tie to Stephen.

VII

1758

The islands that dotted Boston's harbor were rich with spring foliage. The light green new leaves on the wild cherry trees mixed with the bright yellow of forsythia blossoms and brought all of the islands alive with spring color. The breeze blew steadily, bending the young branches of the bushes as if they were paying forced obeisance to the gods of the sea, and crowning the dark, cold waters of Boston's outer harbor with whitecaps.

The *Artemis*, out of London, was only hours from her berth along the Boston wharves, but she had to tack again and again in the face of the wind from the shore. Stephen shuddered as the bow struck the waves with a thud and sent spray back across the railing toward the center deck of the ship, where he stood. His anger was not much different from the slow, cool rage he had felt last fall when word from his family had first reached him. He had received a letter from Sir William Johnson which, by a fluke, had arrived before official publication of accounts of the disaster at William Henry. Johnson had assured him, as did Aunt Margaret two weeks later, that Katherine and Amy had survived and were prisoners of the French. He had panicked at first when he heard of their capture. Aunt Margaret's letter telling him that it was Karl who had helped them had overjoyed him. But in early winter, as he set his plans for a return to New York, he had received a letter from Quebec, passed him via Paris by Manya, who had special connections at Versailles. It was this last letter—a letter from Katherine—that had changed everything.

When the letter arrived, he was sitting in his rooms at the inn. He knew he should have returned to America as soon as he had gotten word of Katherine's capture. His work for Johnson had been concluded in failure months before. But with Katherine and Amy in Quebec, he had no one to return to. He had used that also, he readily admitted to himself, as an excuse to stay with Manya.

They had seen each other often. Every time she could get away from Lord Howe, she made tracks to his rooms. They had made love just minutes before the landlord knocked on the door with Katherine's letter. When the knock came, Manya had giggled and pulled the covers over her head so that she would not be seen.

As Stephen read the letter, he began to search for the easy chair by the fireplace with his hand. He had to sit down. Manya saw the look of distress come over his face. She rose from the bed and sat on the arm of the chair by his side.

Katherine began by informing him that she was no prisoner and that she had stayed in Quebec of her own volition and would remain there until the war was over. Then and only then would she confront the decision she would have to make. She loved Stephen, she said, but she loved Karl too.

Stephen slammed his fist containing the letter into the arm of the chair opposite Manya. The letter fell from his hand, and Manya reached down and picked it up. She started to read.

"She's taken Karl into her bed," he said incredulously. "Maybe she needs a man with two arms."

Manya started to laugh. "Oh, how you pity yourself," she said. "This Katherine woman behaves like a queen. She must have two arms when one is good enough for a Polish princess?"

"It's not funny," he yelled. His anger grew with each passing moment. "How could she betray me?"

A look of astonishment came over Manya's face. "Oh, my Etienne," she said, "don't tell me you have picked up Jesuit hypocrisy. How can you complain of her betrayal just after making love to me?" There was a twinkle in her eye, and astonishment gave way to amusement. "Your wife behaves no worse than you."

"Manya, if that is all you can do—excuse her—you're no help. Why don't you go back to Lord Howe?"

She rose from the arm of the chair and walked to where she had left her undergarments and dress.

When she was dressed, she went to the door and turned to him. "I wonder what His Lordship would feel about you if he knew I cheated on him with you."

She opened the door and walked out.

Stephen's anger continued to grow, but he realized he did

211

not wish to take it out on Manya. He called her name, but she did not return. He did not see her again before leaving London.

As he stood on deck he still felt that same anger. His wife had rejected him. His best friend—his blood brother—he chuckled aloud bitterly when he thought of that relationship —his blood brother had betrayed him. They were together and he was alone.

The wind whipped at his greatcoat and blew his black hair. He rubbed the scar that ran through his eyebrow and that now ached as the cold wind battered his face. He really should go below, he thought, but he would become seasick even in this light swell if he did. "Katherine," he said softly. How could she have done it? How could she have betrayed him for Karl? Again the laughing face of Manya flashed before his eyes.

He could have forgiven Katherine an affair. He thought again. Maybe he could have. But for her to have left him to live openly with his best friend was intolerable.

The *Artemis* finally slipped behind Nantasket and the whitecaps disappeared. They would still have to tack into the channel between the islands, but then the wind slackened. Stephen banged the railing of the ship with the palm of his hand. He would get her back. "Goddamn me," he swore aloud. He would arrange all his affairs and then he would go to Quebec and claim his wife back from that Swiss bastard.

His anger with Karl was monumental. Karl he had trusted with his life. It was Karl who had befriended Katherine and Amy. Now Stephen's head told him it was all a plot for Karl to wiggle his way into Stephen's family. But his heart told him it was all untrue. Karl loved him. If he loved Katherine too, it was part of a tragedy that would now have to be played out.

He stared at the distant outline of the town of Boston and, across the channel, the town of his birth, Charlestown. He could see the hill on which his grandfather Breed had built the family home. He tried to recall his feelings on first viewing the Breed homestead some fourteen years earlier. How old had he been then—nineteen? So much had happened since. He was thirty-three now. His coat slipped off his shoulder, revealing the pinned-up sleeve. He grabbed his left shoulder with his right hand and pulled the coat back up, holding both collars together against his throat to keep out the cold.

He had much to do in Boston. All of his affairs would

hinge on his meeting with his Aunt Betsy. He had written her from London. She had responded that she would welcome a visit from him.

He would have to go below and pack his trunk. The steeple and hills of Boston were now clearly visible. His journey was almost at an end.

The carriage climbed to the top of Copp's Hill with little difficulty. Stephen leaned out of the window to get a better view of the old Cromwell's Head Inn at the base of the hill just in front of the Charlestown ferry slip. He would spend his nights at the old inn. The carriage began to descend the steep hill; the driver tried to apply the brakes and called upon his horses by name, urging them to hold back and slow down.

As the carriage pulled to a halt before the inn, a black man with enormous arms and shoulders opened the door and pushed a small stepping stool in place for passengers to descend. He offered his hand up to Stephen, then pulled it back when he saw Stephen's sleeve. Nowell grabbed the frame of the door with his right hand and leapt to the ground.

"Josiah," he said, "it's good to see you again."

Stephen enjoyed watching the change in the black man's expression as it mellowed from blank hostility to recognition and then radiated into a warm grin.

"Mr. Stephen," he smiled. "I didn't recognize you—the arm—how? Mr. Vaughan told me but I forgot."

Stephen grabbed Josiah's arm. "It doesn't matter. I get along now. Is Mr. Vaughan in his rooms?"

"Yes, sir. He hardly don't go outside his room no more."

"Is he drinking, Josiah?"

The black man struggled within himself. Loyalty to Vaughan was almost ingrown in the man, but he remembered that he spoke to another as devoted to Vaughan as he was. "Mr. Stephen, he is drunk most of the time. Except the morning. He refuses to drink in the morning. But come high noon, he starts, and he doesn't stop until he falls down on his foolish face."

Stephen shook his head. He looked down toward the ferry slip. "Do you still help old Hudson cross the river to Charlestown?"

Josiah shook his head. "No, sir, that Mr. Pierce bought the ferry company and then he fired Hudson. That was almost four years ago. Old Hudson died before the winter was out. He's buried atop the hill there," he said, pointing to the cemetery on Copp's Hill.

Stephen cursed. He had been fond of the old bald-headed ferryman who had given him the initial clue to his family when he had first visited Boston. "Another grudge to settle with Pierce," he thought aloud.

Stephen knocked on the door to Vaughan's room. He heard a violent crash and a blood-curdling curse. Stephen pushed on the door. It was unlocked, and it flew open. He saw Vaughan sitting on the floor, holding his head. His chair had fallen over backward. He was completely naked and very drunk. A young girl, dressed only in a chemise, rushed by Stephen and out into the corridor.

Vaughan looked up. "Well, there goes my Hope," he slurred.

"Oh! It's not that desperate, Willie," laughed Stephen.

Vaughan's eyes tried to focus on him. Then he recognized Nowell. "Stephen," he shouted. "By Jesus, it's you. Let me get up and give you a proper greeting."

He struggled to his feet and staggered against the over-turned chair, banging his shin. "Damn all chairs," he shouted. "First it cost me Hope and now it has practically cost me my leg."

He looked at Stephen. "Sorry, my boy," he said, belching. "I should not joke about losing limbs with you here."

"Think nothing of it, Willie. But what's this about losing hope? You're not that badly off."

"Badly off? Christ, boy, I just lost the girl I was planning to bed—Hope Clapp. Can you believe that name?" He howled with laughter. "I call her 'Hope Not.'" He slapped his thigh and banged his foot on the ground.

"I was trying to prove to her that I could stand on my head," he said. "I got this soft cushion on the chair and I was almost balanced perfect; then the damned leg gave way when you came barging in and Hope flew out the door."

Stephen smiled. He knew Vaughan was having fun with his pun.

Vaughan grew serious. "You understand, Stephen, I meant no disrespect to your mother by taking this wench to bed, but I have my needs. It's not like I love her or anything. There was only one love." He belched again.

"William, I think I owe it to the memory of my mother to sober you up."

Vaughan walked to the bed and collapsed upon it. "Boy," he said wearily, "she did that once. But I'll never be a sober man until I revenge her. I should have walked into Breed's

214

house across the strait just as soon as you and I figured out who had done her in, and I should have put a bullet into Pierce's balls just to watch him suffer for a few moments, and then I should have put a second one into his brain. If I had had the courage to do that and be willing to swing for it, then it would have all been over."

"You'd have lost hope," Stephen teased.

Vaughan started to laugh.

"But there's no need for you to hang for killing Daniel Pierce, Willie," said Stephen with some feeling. "He's exposed. He's fled."

"I know," said Vaughan. "But fled where?"

"My sources tell me he is in Quebec or in Montreal, somewhere in Canada."

Vaughan sat upright on the bed. He had lost his considerable girth, and the skin hung loosely about his middle. He slammed his massive arm into the pillow. "It may as well be China."

"Not at all," said Stephen. "You and I both know that General Amherst is preparing a Canadian campaign this summer. It must begin with Louisbourg. You know a bit about seizing that place."

Vaughan smiled at Stephen. "That was a great moment, wasn't it, boy? You and I showed them Frenchies a few things, didn't we?"

"You can do it again, Willie."

Vaughan shook his head. He grabbed the flab of his belly and held it in both hands. "I've gone soft—too soft," he said.

"Willie," said Stephen seriously. "I need your help. It's my Katherine. She was taken at Fort William Henry and she is held in Quebec. I want to get her back. But I am committed to William Johnson and Lord Howe and New York."

"You mean that asshole Abercrombie?" interrupted Vaughan.

"Howe's second in command, and Pitt has assured me that he'll be in actual command of the troops. I want you with Amherst in case he seizes Louisbourg early and goes on to Quebec. I plan to be with our army when we strangle New France, but I'd like you there in my place if anything moves faster than I can handle."

Vaughan thought for a moment and then lay back on the bed, sighing deeply. "Oh, shit," he said with resignation. "Here I go again. Stephen, get Josiah to being me a tub of cold water. Your mother sobered me up once before with cold water. Now it's you. One of these days I'm going to turn

215

to drinking and there won't be a Nowell to sober me up. That will be the end of Willie Vaughan."

As Stephen climbed the slope up to the top of Breed's Hill, he turned to look back at Boston's hills and steeples. He could not have known that years before, his father, Samuel, had often done precisely the same thing. The city sparkled in the early evening sunlight. But the sun was so low in the sky that the hill's shadow cast a purple pall over the streets of the north end.

He was nervous about his meeting with his aunt. So much depended upon it. He heard the sunset gun from the castle in the harbor below and knew that the British flag would now be lowered.

The nail-studded oak door loomed before him. Once before he had approached it, so full of hope, only to have it dashed to pieces by the ambitions and intrigues of Daniel Pierce. Then Jonathan Breed, his grandfather, who had been willing to acknowledge him, had still been living. But not for long. That same day Breed had perished, a victim, Stephen was convinced, of the hand of Daniel Pierce.

Stephen walked to the door of the farmhouse, raised the knocker and let it fall. There was only silence. He raised it again and banged it down with his fist.

Betsy Breed, her hair now white and her face wrinkled, answered the door herself. She looked at Stephen's face intently. "Stephen," she acknowledged.

"Aunt Betsy," he responded.

"Do come into my house." She led him into the front parlor and stood before the leaded, paned windows with her back to him. When she turned, he saw great tears filling her eyes and coming down her cheeks. "I am so sorry, my boy." She sobbed and threw her arms around his neck. "I am so sorry it took me so long to hold you in my arms. I've been such a fool, and for so long."

Stephen did not know what to say and so he remained silent, patting her shoulder with his hand.

"You suffered so, boy," Betsy wept. "Maybe if I had been strong enough to stand up to Daniel, I could have saved you both. Now my husband is branded a traitor and has fled to the enemy, and my Sarah's boy, my beloved Sarah's son, has been shunted aside, abused and maimed. I am such a weakling."

"Aunt Betsy, none of it was your fault. How could you have known about Pierce?"

"How could I not have known? I lived with him as his wife for years."

"He's a devious man."

"An evil man," she interrupted with anger. "He betrayed his country, his people, for greed."

Stephen let it rest at that. He had not the heart to tell her that he suspected Pierce was responsible for the deaths of Samuel and Sarah Nowell, as well as Betsy's brother Jonathan. Such knowledge, he felt, would unbalance her mind. He pitied this woman who had denied him his birthright through her own weakness.

"I want you to know, Stephen, that I have asked my lawyer to transfer your mother's trust fund to you. I've informed him that, as the heir to that trust, I have acknowledged you as Sarah's son. I can do no more as long as my husband lives. I have initiated divorce proceedings. He has abandoned me." She sniffed, her head held high. "And from the evidence provided me from London, he has been unfaithful. I have no doubt that all of his possessions in Boston will be placed at my disposal. Everything Sarah left you and everything my brother Jonathan would have left you is now yours. You are a rich man."

Stephen was astonished. It was far more than he had expected. All he had hoped was that Betsy would provide him with an income, but instead she had converted to him the fabled Nowell trust. He would have thousands. He would be one of the richest men in Boston, should he choose to live there.

Betsy looked into his face longingly. "Stephen, I hope that makes up for some of the harm I have done you."

Stephen placed his arm about the old woman's shoulder. Her white head rested on his chest and she sobbed.

"Aunt Betsy," he said comfortingly, "it would have been enough merely for you to have said, 'Yes, you are Stephen Nowell.' All else astounds me."

"I knew you were Stephen that day when Mr. Pierce chased you from me. I should have listened to my brother —to my own heart. But now, at last, I have my Sarah's son at my side. It will help mend the wound that Pierce has given me. He used me. God help me, I knew it all the time. But I loved him—please don't hate me, Stephen, if I say it. I still love him."

Stephen stroked her hair. "He was never worthy of a woman like you, Aunt," he said.

She stopped and pulled a white handkerchief embroidered

with small pink roses from her sleeve. She wiped her nose and eyes. "You're right," she said with force. "He wasn't worthy of any decent woman."

She sat in the window seat and then, remembering that Pierce had courted her there, she rose and went to the upholstered rocker in the far corner. "Promise me one thing," said Betsy to Stephen.

Stephen looked at her quizzically.

"Send back Hannah and George. I need them. I've been very lonely."

"I'll ask them to return as soon as I get back to New York," responded Stephen.

"You're a good boy, Stephen," she said, looking into his eyes. She shook her head. "You have my brother's eyes," she said finally. "And your mother's hair. How could I have allowed that man to deny you?" She started to sob again.

Amy Nowell had learned French with great speed, thanks to the almost complete devotion she had for Antoine Gingras. He was thirteen years old—a man in her eyes. His voice had changed, or almost changed. He had a fine line of a moustache, which his brothers teased him about but which Amy held in great reverence.

It was Antoine who, nevertheless, caused her her first pain about Alte Karl and her mother.

Katherine had warned Amy very early that she would have a brother or a sister, and when her brother was born Amy was delighted.

She was frightened when Maman Gingras and Madame Millard arrived and chased her from her mother's room. When she heard her mother's moaning and her screams, she ran from the stone house out into the spring night, clasping her ears with her hands. She ran into Antoine, who had fetched his mother in the hay wagon at Karl's request.

"What's wrong, Ugly?" asked Antoine, with his usual term of endearment for her.

"I was afraid for Mama—she hurts so."

"Stupid," said the boy. "It's just part of having a baby."

"What do you know about having babies?" asked Amy haughtily.

"A lot more than you," he responded. "My mother has had eight."

"I'm sure you remember her having them all. I do believe you are the baby of the family." She put heavy emphasis on the word *baby*.

"Well, at least I know how you get them," said Antoine. "Karl put his thing inside your mama and made her pregnant."

"Oh, no," she said. "Your sister says only the mama and the papa can do that or God will be very angry. The curé told her."

"That's just what I said," he responded.

"But my papa is far away," she said.

"Your papa is dead. The new baby's papa is Karl."

"He's not dead," said Amy with venom.

"Of course he is," answered Antoine. "How else could Karl and your mama get married?"

Amy started to cry, but then she grew angry and began to shout. "My papa is in Europe. He is not dead." She struck out at Antoine, but he ducked beyond her reach and laughed at her.

Katherine lay exhausted in the bed. Her face was pale, and little beads of sweat again had broken out on her forehead, even though Maman had wiped it a few moments before. The two women were bathing the baby and wrapping him in a warm cotton blanket. Karl entered the room and took the child from Madame Millard; he placed his son in Katherine's arms.

"Our son," she said, looking at the child, "is a healthy boy—fair like his father and pretty like his mother."

Karl laughed. "Boys are not supposed to be called 'pretty' and babies never are pretty."

"Amy was," said Katherine.

"Amy was unique," he responded.

"I missed you when our son was coming. I wanted you there like with Amy."

"That was special, Katherine. These two ladies are the experienced ones. If something had gone wrong, I would have panicked. These two old crones chased me out; they threatened to leave if I didn't go."

Both of the older women smiled at him when he nodded in their direction, oblivious of his unflattering English description.

"What will we call him?" Katherine mused. "It should be a family name. My father's name was John. My brother's name is Philip. How about your family?"

"I don't know my father's name," said Karl sheepishly.

Katherine had never questioned him on this topic before.

He blushed. "I used to joke about it when I was younger.

219

The fact is that my mother didn't know my father's name either. But the general has been like a father to me. I would like to name our son Louis Joseph after the Marquis de Montcalm—Louis Joseph Stiegler, my son—the first native-born Canadien of a long line."

She knew at once how important the name was to him, and she smiled in agreement.

Three weeks later Karl took Katherine, Louis Joseph and Amy to Sunday mass at the parish church in St. Pierre for Louis Joseph's baptism. Father Cardinal celebrated the sacrifice with great solemnity before the entire parish. After the last gospel, Karl rose from his pew and carried his infant son to the baptismal font. Cardinal turned to the congregation and then shouted at Karl. "Halt!" he cried out in a thunderous voice. "That child is a child of sin. He must not be brought to the altar of God to receive the redemptive waters of our Savior unless the parents—the fornicators—repent."

Katherine stared uncomprehendingly at the priest, but Karl's face flushed instantly.

"What did you call my wife, priest?" he said, with a deadly softness in his voice.

"She is not your wife. You two have attempted to deceive us, but God has exposed you—your deception has been uncovered. You two have sinned. The child is a bastard. The woman is an adulteress. Her whorish behavior must not go unpunished."

Katherine now became frightened. She turned toward Madame Millard, who sat next to her, and asked in her halting French what was wrong. She did not understand when Madame Millard pulled away from her and looked in the opposite direction.

Karl was now almost in a blind rage. He gently leaned his son on his shoulder and walked toward Cardinal.

"You son of a bitch," he said. "What did you call my Katherine? Why just her, why not me also?"

"You are as guilty of the sin as she, but I know she has a husband. I am not sure of your status. God has his ways. When it came to my attention that there was some question about your marital status, I questioned in the city. Captain Gozin, the marquis' nephew, knows this woman's husband and was shocked to hear of her infidelity."

Karl would have struck out but for the presence of the baby in his arms. Instead he walked back to his pew and took Katherine by the hand. Amy followed. She was terrified, having comprehended far more of Cardinal's tirade than her mother.

The priest shouted at them as Karl led his family down the aisle. "Observe the sinners," he said. "They are unrepentant. They are cast into the fires of hell. No one, not one of you, may associate with them. They are to be as lepers. Unclean."

The priest's voice rang through the church and pounded into the brain of Karl Stiegler. He grieved for Katherine, but his anger against the priest overwhelmed his sense of embarrassment for his woman. He turned to Cardinal. "As God is my witness, priest, if I could see you die in blood, I would gladly die in peace."

His curse rang through the church, and most of the parishioners crossed themselves to ward off his words. Karl stormed out the front door and joined Katherine and Amy in the churchyard. He handed her their unbaptized son. Taking her by the arm, he started along the river road on the long walk back toward their farm.

They were about halfway home when the Gingras wagon caught up with them. Henri slowed the horses as he came up to Karl. With pipe clenched between his teeth, he spoke, biting so hard on the stem that he was in clear danger of snapping the pipe in two. His oldest daughter Marie was weeping, holding her cheeks where the faint marks of a palm print could still be seen. Antoine walked behind the wagon. He too was weeping and rubbing his rump.

"Monsieur Stiegler," said Henri. "My family has done yours a great wrong. Your daughter, Amy, very innocently told my loud-mouthed but sore-bottomed blockhead of a son that she thought her father still lived and was in Europe. He blabbed his information to my pious daughter, Marie, who in her zeal for virtue in others, perhaps expects the world to be as virginal as she seems destined to remain. She ran to the priest with the news. You must forgive us; we have wronged you."

"Your children told no lies, Monsieur Gingras," said Karl.

"Oh, I suspected that. My children do not lie—but neither do they mind their own business."

"You wish to continue to associate with us sinners?"

"You will need us as friends, Lieutenant. The curé has great power in this town. You will be ostracized by all."

"Why not by you?"

"Maman and I follow different rules. Don't get us wrong. We are good Catholics. We love our church, our religion, but Jesus told us that men would know his followers by how they loved one another. It is our way that is the Christian way—not the curé's."

Karl smiled finally. His muscles, tensed by anger, suddenly relaxed. He told Katherine what Henri had said. Katherine reached up to the driver's seat and kissed him on the cheek. Maman started to sputter. "Save those for a fine man like Karl," she said, "not an old goat like Gingras. Here, pass me that baby." She took Louis Joseph into her ample arms and cooed at him. "Come to Maman, little one," she said. "Maman knows how to baptize just as effectively as the priest."

When Stephen stepped off the packet boat from New York at the Albany dock, he stared about him in amazement. The town was alive with soldiers and with all the additional paraphernalia that inevitably accompanies armies. There were suttlers' supplies lying all over the docks, only casually guarded by militia. The red coats of the army and royal marines mixed with the blue of the navy, the green uniforms of ranger troops and the motley, homespun array of the colonials. Off Pearl Street, in a small corner, tents for camp followers had been erected, and women busily bent over cooking pots or walked to and from the Hudson to wash and dry linens.

Stephen had thought that Albany had bulged in preparation for Johnson's campaign against Crown Point in 1755, but the chaos then had been minor compared to today.

He had planned to stay that evening at the Albany Inn, a place where he had labored for a winter as a boy, but he was now sure that all the sleeping accommodations would have been seized by officers from the Abercrombie expedition. He was surprised to hear his name called over the din on the docks. A young man whom he did not recognize was calling, "Stephen Nowell!"

He was just out of boyhood, with fat, ruddy cheeks, brown hair and brown eyes. There was something familiar about him, but Stephen could not place him. He was dressed in the uniform of a New York militia officer.

"Stephen Nowell! don't you know me? It's me, Philip Schuyler—Katherine's brother."

Stephen smiled in recognition. The boy had grown considerably since that day aboard the packet to Albany and the few times he had seen him in Cornelia's mansion in Albany.

"Philip, it's good to see you. You're with the army?"

"I'm on leave from the front. The army is pushing up Lake George toward Ticonderoga. We will attack within the week.

I've been sent home to get married. Miss Van Rensselaer and I will become husband and wife tomorrow."

"Well, my congratulations; war seems to make young people rush into each other's arms much faster."

Philip blushed. "Since you are my brother-in-law, I guess it does no harm to tell you. We sort of rushed into each other's arms before the ceremony. That's why I had to come back; the young lady is very pregnant." Philip laughed rather smugly. "But I was always going to marry her anyway. It might as well be now, but I am going to miss the attack on Ticonderoga with the honeymoon and all."

Stephen shook his head. Cornelia had spoiled him beyond endurance. His attitude was insufferable, but he carried it all off with such charm that it was difficult to be angry with him. He took privilege as if it were his due. He was unaware that there were young men without his privileges who had left pregnant girlfriends at home, who would have to await their return to make it all legitimate—provided they returned at all.

"Have you heard from my sister?" asked Philip.

"Only that she is well and in Quebec."

"Have you attempted to ransom her?"

Stephen shook his head. "I intend to travel to Quebec myself and speak with her."

Philip decided that the topic was too sensitive to continue, and Stephen decided to change the subject. "What does your mother think of your marriage?" he asked.

Philip laughed. "Oh, Cornelia was livid. She had to go to the front to General Abercrombie personally to get me released so that old man Van Rensselaer didn't come after me with a horsewhip."

"Abercrombie is at the front? I thought Howe was to have field command."

"Haven't you heard? Where have you been? Howe was killed last week in an ambush near the head of the lake. Abercrombie had to rush from headquarters here to take field command as well."

Stephen was shocked. He had liked the young nobleman, and he felt deeply for Manya. Once more her security had been shattered, and he pitied the English troops now advancing on Montcalm, the master of defense. His face went ashen.

"You didn't know, did you?" said Philip.

"No, I was aboard the packet and word had not arrived in New York before I left."

Philip nodded. "The army was devastated. We all were. We

had come to respect His Lordship. He was an inspiring leader."

Stephen looked at Philip—so young, so brash. "Go to your young lady, Philip, and spend as long with her as you can."

"Oh, it's all been arranged, sir. I have to be off. Shall I tell Cornelia that you're in Albany?" he asked.

"No, I think she will be too busy with the wedding and all. I'm off to Saratoga to see Aunt Margaret."

But Philip was already running down Pearl Street as he answered. Stephen said aloud, "Stay away from Abercrombie, boy, and live to see some sort of future. With Howe gone, many of you will see no tomorrow."

Stephen's visit to Saratoga to Aunt Margaret's house on the flats had been a brief stopover. He had to see Margaret and Kip together to come to the realization that they were really married. She was older than Kip by fifteen years; she was a man hater; and he was the perpetual foot-loose woodsman, with an explanation for everything. Yet it seemed to work. Marriage had mellowed Margaret; her instant anger against all men had dissipated slightly. Israel was truly fond of the woman and had spent the entire winter in the house at Saratoga. It was the first time he had neither trapped nor gone to war.

When Stephen questioned Margaret about Katherine and Karl, however, that old look of steel, like the one that had come upon her the night she had helped fight off the Iroquois at Fort Vaughan, came into her eyes and she turned on Stephen with vehemence.

"You abandoned her and her child to their fate, Stephen Nowell. You were never there when she needed you. It was always Karl. She had to turn to him."

Stephen's blue eyes flashed at her. "So you admit that they behaved as lovers?"

"I admit nothing for someone else. Ask her. Ask him. But I sure as blazes hope they did. I hope they grabbed a little happiness from each other. Surely she got little enough of it from you."

She placed an arm about Kip's expanded waistline. "I've had some loving from this man and I wasted years. Should have had me a few dozen before I had this one. I've got no basis for comparison."

Israel blushed. But Stephen in his anger missed this rare occurrence. The man who was embarrassed by almost nothing was shy before Margaret Schuyler Kip.

"I still can't believe Katherine would do this to me," said Stephen, "and even if she has, I want her back. I want Amy back. I've already lost one child. I cannot accept the loss of a second."

"As I said," answered Margaret, "you had better address that pretty speech to your wife, if you can find her."

Stephen left the Schuyler house and stood on the veranda. Israel broke away from Margaret's side and walked over to Stephen, placing his arm about Stephen's shoulder.

"You can find her, Stephen. She's got to be in Canada someplace. Go see Sir William; him and his Mohawks will know where she is, and you can always send word for Socono to come. I'd go myself, but I doubt if my new missus would tolerate it. She'd expect me to bring her along and she's had enough excitement for a little while."

Stephen smiled at Kip. "You stay with her. Margaret is a fine woman. Much of what she said to me in my heart I know is right, but I have to find Katherine, and I can't help but feel betrayed by her and by Karl even more."

With Aunt Margaret's condemnation still ringing in his ears, Stephen set forth on the Hudson by hired boat. His goal was the bend in the river at Fort Edward. Everywhere he looked, *bateaux* loaded with soldiers, supplies, heavy guns and kegs of gunpowder were heading north on the river to the fort. He had never seen such traffic before, but there seemed to be a pall on everyone's activities. The news of the death of Lord Howe had cast an ominous gloom over all of their preparations. No one truly believed that the assault on Ticonderoga could work—not without the brash and brilliant Irish peer to lead it.

When Stephen arrived at the Fort Edward landing beach, he went off looking for the quarters of Sir William Johnson. He asked a corporal of the New York militia for directions and soon found his way. As usual, Mohawk warriors sat in front of the building and Mohawk women cooked over outdoor fires in the yard.

Stephen entered the front door and stopped in the doorway. She was standing alone before the unlit fireplace.

"Molly," he called softly to her.

She turned and looked at him with her soft, brown eyes. She looked at his missing arm. "The gift of Dagaheari, I am told," she said in Mohawk.

"Not a gift," said Stephen. "It was paid for in full."

"He was a fool all of his life. You, Stephen, will be

225

honored by the Mohawk for life and reviled by our brothers the Oneida for putting an end to the foolishness of Dagaheari."

"It was not I who killed him, Molly. It was the Abenacki Socono."

"Then he too shall be both revered and hated."

There were some moments of silence. Stephen felt awkward before this woman whom he had loved, with whom he had fought so bitterly. He could not avoid the only topic that still bound them together. "How is our son?" he asked finally.

Her face brightened almost instantly. "He becomes a man," she smiled. "His voice is now a man's voice. He has the skills of a great hunter. My brother Joseph teaches him the ways of the warrior, and I believe he has inherited his father's courage and his mother's wisdom."

Stephen laughed bitterly. "You did not say his father's wisdom."

Molly's face grew serious once again. "His father has knowledge—not wisdom. You know much, Stephen, but it was not wise of you to take my son away from me. I would probably not have stayed with you because you could not adapt to the Mohawk way of life, and because I grew to want Johnson more and more, but I would have remained your friend, and I would not have removed Kenonranon from you completely. But when you took him away, I was terrified that I had lost him forever. I got him back because my father and grandfather were outraged also. But I could never trust you again. I sent him to you in your illness because Johnson has power among the whites. You could never have defied his will among your own people, and by then my son was able to make his own decisions; I knew where his heart lay."

Stephen nodded. "I loved him so. I still do."

"And if you had been wise, rather than merely courageous, you could have known him as I do."

"How is your grandfather?"

"Dead—not long after the news of Hendrick's death."

"I'm sorry."

Molly merely nodded acknowledgment. "My father, Nicus Brant, grows more powerful, and my brother Joseph will someday be the greatest warrior of his people."

"Is Sir William about?" he asked.

"Johnson is at the commander's quarters. He is very angry these days—ever since Lord Howe was killed. He does not get along with Abercrombie, and I think he feels the campaign with the French is already doomed."

226

"He's right," said Stephen.

At that moment the large frame of William Johnson darkened the doorway. Stephen turned to look at him. He saw Johnson's eyes dart from Stephen to Molly and back again. Stephen realized he was suspicious and nervous about the two former lovers being in the same room alone. It was clear he attributed his own unfaithfulness with other women to Molly and to Stephen.

"Nowell," he said loudly. "Good to see you back."

"Sir William, I'm glad to be back, and I'm sorry that I was not successful in convincing the government to fight your kind of war."

Johnson shrugged. "Never really thought they would be bright enough to see it my way. Now we have that fool Abercrombie leading us against Montcalm. It will never work. I'm withdrawing and continuing on in the west. That's where this war will be won or lost."

"Sir William," interrupted Stephen. "My wife and daughter, do you have any word on their whereabouts?"

"I'm indeed sorry about the Fort William Henry fiasco, Stephen," said Johnson. "But they are safe. They are in Quebec, living on an island downriver from the fortress itself. They're safe."

"I must go to them."

"Well," said Johnson, "if you join Abercrombie's forces you'll be an old man before you get to Quebec. I intend to join the force striking at Niagara. Once we take that fort, we cut off the west from the St. Lawrence and we stop the flow of furs, which is the life blood of New France. Then my Mohawks and I will strike at Montreal, but from the west."

"But that will all take too long as well," said Stephen.

Johnson shrugged. "Then you should join up with Amherst. He is striking at Louisbourg. If I remember your story correctly, that was your old territory. After Louisbourg always comes Quebec."

"Well, that would be the quicker route to Quebec."

Johnson laughed. "Word is that Jeffrey Amherst never did anything quick in his life." He put his arm about Molly and squeezed her to him. "That must be just fine for Mrs. Amherst. Don't you think so, Molly?"

Molly feigned disgust and pushed herself from his grasp.

"Yes, I think you will get to Quebec faster via the Louisbourg expedition, but only because of that skinny fellow, Wolfe. He'll be with Amherst and he'll drive the general crazy with his tactics. He likes to attack, attack, attack and attack some more. He'll push Amherst through Louisbourg and on to Quebec, even if he has to do it all by himself."

There seemed to Stephen to be a certain irony in his contemplating a return to his home city on Isle Royale.

Johnson came across the room and took Stephen's hand in his. "We've had our arguments in the past," he said, "but I hope you know I've never meant you any ill will. I saved your folk from the Iroquois back on the Mohawk that one night. It cost you your son. But it gave him back to Molly here, and she and Joseph are doing a fine job on that boy. He is becoming a very fine young man. And I led you on our expedition to Crown Point and it cost you your arm. Then I sent your wife and daughter to Fort William Henry, and now they have been captured by the French. I don't think I've been a happy influence in your life, Nowell. Moreover, I took Molly from you. I'm sorry. Without Molly there would be very little of value in my life."

Molly walked to Johnson's side. She took his arm and began to lead him toward the back room of the log cabin. "You're tired," she said. "Stephen, he has been up all night arguing with the white general. Abercrombie is a stupid man and does not understand what the simplest-minded of our people already understands. Johnson is a great leader and could show them how to chase the French from these lands forever if they would only listen to him."

Stephen saw Johnson's shoulders sag, and for one moment he glimpsed what Johnson would look like as an old man. It dawned on him, then and there, that it would not be Johnson who conquered New France. He was a tired man—a man whose command of the tribes would be rewarded. But the general fresh from England, with heavy artillery, siege trains and regular troops, would never allow an irregular with his Indian hordes to reap the glory that they all coveted.

"Goodbye, Nowell," said Johnson. "This woman, she leads me around like a child. But she's right. I'm very tired." He turned slowly from Stephen and, holding on to Molly for both support and comfort, he went through the doorway into the back room. As they entered the room, Molly turned and looked at Stephen. Stephen could not determine if the look was one of wistfulness or just plain sadness. But he knew that the look was the last unguarded one they would ever exchange.

Ships left Boston for Louisbourg, with a stop at the new port town of Halifax, with great regularity once the second siege of the great French fortress had begun. Stephen had taken the packet back to New York City and then traveled aboard a merchant ship from New York to Boston.

In Boston he had visited with his aunt once again, and they had both signed the papers placing him in possession of the Nowell trust. At last Sarah Nowell's money was in her son's hands. In addition, Betsy Breed, now legally divorced from Daniel Pierce the traitor, made Stephen Nowell her only heir. In an eyeblink, Stephen became one of the richest men in all of Boston, possessor of the Nowell trust and heir to the Breed fortune.

Stephen left orders for the purchase of several merchant vessels as a gift for William Vaughan and set sail on a supply ship, the *Princess,* traveling from Boston to Halifax and then on to the army's position outside Louisbourg.

The moment he had waited for for so long came so swiftly that it took Stephen by surprise, when the papers declaring him to be Stephen Nowell, son of Sarah and Samuel and grandson of Jonathan Breed, were filed and accepted in Boston court. From the time when his father, who lay dying in a canoe on the shore of the St. François River, had said to him, "You are Stephen Nowell," twenty-eight years had passed before he had been able to make that assertion legally. As he signed the papers, he smiled bitterly to himself. Now that the world had recognized his claim to his birthright, he had no one to pass that claim and his wealth on to. He must make Katherine return and share his rights and his wealth with him. She would understand; after all, she too had been denied once because she was not the daughter of her father's wife, which was no fault of hers. She deserved to share his good fortune with him.

The coast of Isle Royale was bathed in a thick fog when he arrived in Gabarus Bay. There were almost no ships visible at all. Captain Sawyer, the master of the *Princess,* would take no chances and kept well off shore. But still Stephen could hear the roar of great guns. The fires from the town could not penetrate the denseness of the fog, but they illuminated the wall of vapor, turning it into hideous shades of yellow and orange.

During the night, a windless, starless night, as they lay off the shore of the island, the roar of the guns ceased, while the glare of the fires grew more intense. To the west, where Louisbourg lay, the dark night gave way to light, like some crazy reversal in nature, as if the sun had changed its course and risen in the west.

In the late morning, the wind picked up and began to break up the fog. Captain Sawyer tacked to get back into the bay. Stephen stood at the railing of the ship, as he had since early morning. Suddenly, from out of the great fog bank, a massive form loomed above them. It took Stephen several seconds to identify it as a great warship. The helmsman of *Princess* was quicker, however. He swung the wheel violently and, since the ship had some small headway, she responded quickly and avoided a collision.

Stephen could see the open gunports of the other ship as it passed within a few yards of where he stood. As the ship's stern came into view, there was enough light for Stephen to barely make out the name *Arethuse*. He jumped back from the railing and ran toward the captain, who had come up on deck from his cabin.

"She's French—a French frigate," said Stephen.

"My God!" yelled Sawyer, "the French fleet is out of Louisbourg. They have goddamned ships of the line in that harbor. The frigate is a scout. Let's get the hell out of here."

Sawyer ordered the helmsman to allow the ship to run before the wind toward the south, away from Louisbourg. She sailed for the rest of the morning without seeing another ship.

Toward noon the watch called out that he could see a sail to the south of them. Given the direction from which it came, Sawyer was willing to approach the newcomer, thinking it was sailing from either Halifax or Boston.

It turned out to be neither, but a small sloop of war, *Triton*, from the West Indian station, joining the fleet off Louisbourg. In the company of a ship of war, Sawyer regained his composure. He warned the lieutenant in command of *Triton* that he thought the French fleet had escaped, and the two ships crept cautiously northward back toward Louisbourg.

Once again they entered Gabarus Bay. This time it was free of fog and empty of ships. They tacked out of the bay, beyond Flat Point and Black Point, and approached the entrance to Louisbourg. The harbor was filled with ships, each of them crowded with sailors. But there were several burned-out great hulks scattered about the harbor, as if cast aside by an angry god. What filled them all with relief was the sight of the British colors flying from the lighthouse on the point, from the island battery in the channel and, most importantly, from the ramparts of the King's bastion, The Citadel, the fortress of Louisbourg. Louisbourg had fallen a second time.

When *Princess* arrived at the wharf at the foot of the totally destroyed circular battery, she was swarmed over by seamen, sent by the admiral to unload the precious supplies she carried.

Stephen leapt the last foot from the gangway to the wharf and walked through the wharf gate into the town. It was ruined. Not a house stood and Stephen, who had been raised in the city, had difficulty recognizing the streets. The Jesuit house where he had lived and worked was a pile of rubble. The convent where Sister Marie Louis, who had been like a mother to him, had served as a porter could not even be dignified by the term rubble. It had totally disappeared. The wooden marketplace had been burned to its foundation. In reality, only the walls of the city and the bastion of The Citadel remained recognizable to him.

Stephen hoped to find William Vaughan, and the only place he could think to look for him was at The Citadel. It was the second time in his life that he had seen the British flag fly over the seat of French government on Isle Royale. The last time, it had been given back to France, and he had no great hope that the same would not occur this time as well.

The corridors of The Citadel were filled with red-coated officers. General Amherst had established his headquarters in the old Governor's residence. His brigadier, James Wolfe, had moved into The Citadel as well. Word spread quickly among Wolfe's own men that his health was so poor that Amherst had ordered him out of his field tent and indoors.

Stephen asked at Amherst's office if anyone knew the whereabouts of William Vaughan, but he had no luck. The officer at the desk was a sharp-faced lieutenant with a sinus condition, which made all of his words seem to flow directly from his nose. He barely looked at Stephen when he informed him that he was not in charge of the refugees' bureau.

"Mr. Vaughan has been with the expedition since it left Halifax."

"So have several other civilians," was the response.

Stephen knew the man was right, but he resented his manner. He left the office and stepped out into the corridor. There was a long line of residents of the town standing before the newly established suttler's office. The residents had been without food for days, and no new supplies could come in

231

from the deserted countryside. The inhabitants of Louisbourg would have to depend on the British military and naval forces for their food.

Stephen recognized the priest before LaGarde saw him. He was white-haired now, and his face showed wrinkles about the eyes. There were deep lines curving from his nose down about the sides of his mouth. He was painfully thin, and it was clear to Stephen that he had not eaten in some time.

"Father," he called softly. "Father LaGarde."

The priest looked up in surprise when his name was called. He looked at Stephen, but he obviously did not see as well as he had in the past.

Stephen walked over to him. "It's me, Etienne," he said in French.

The priest squinted. He reached out his arms to touch Stephen and then came to him, placing his arms about him.

"Etienne, it is so good to see you again, to touch you. Your arm—you have suffered, my son."

"I still suffer, Father. I look for my wife and daughter, who have been captured and taken to Quebec."

"Oh, the war, look at what it has done to us. Look at our town—ruins—our house is gone. Father Mercier, he would have been the only one left from your days with us. He was killed in the final bombardment. They're all gone now—Gregoire, Mercier, Brother Richard."

"You didn't mention Father Lalonde."

"Ah, that one. He left us years ago, and we have not heard from him since then. But he was very sick, Etienne. You cannot blame him for what he did to poor Karl. He was so ill."

At the mention of Karl's name the anger began to flood Stephen's mind once again.

The priest continued, "Look at what this war has done to you." He held on to the empty sleeve. "That innocent little boy, *mon cher* Etienne." His eyes filled with tears. "Now they tell us we will not be allowed to remain here. We will be shipped out like they did to the Acadians. You were not here then, Etienne. They rounded the people up in the church and pushed them into ships like cattle. They dropped them all along the coast so that their 'Nova Scotia' would be British, not French. Now they will do the same to us on Isle Royale."

Stephen was filled with pity for the priest. He could remember now only the kindness of the father's care, the love he had given him. The deceit was banished from his mind.

"Can I help you in any way, Father? I remember the last

232

time that we spoke. I was very harsh. I blamed you for many things. I am older now and, I hope, a bit wiser." He hesitated over the last word, remembering what Molly Brant had said to him.

"I asked you to forgive me for years of deceit, for not telling you that you were English, for allowing you to grow up with us and not sending you to your family in Boston."

"And I refused you."

"You had right on your side. The Society, at my own suggestion, had instructed me to violate what my conscience told me was right. I had never faced that dilemma before. I loved you, Etienne, and that complicated everything. Once I knew that I should tell you the truth, I feared that my years of silence would so anger you that I would lose you for good. I was right. I did lose you."

"I forgive you now, Father. Can I help you?"

"I would like to rebuild our house, but they have told me not to start, that we will not be allowed to live here, that they plan to destroy Louisbourg. I can't believe that," said the priest, shaking his white mane and laughing. "It took so long to build it. They just can't destroy it that simply."

Stephen reached into his coat pocket. He had several gold coins; he took them out and pressed them into LaGarde's hand. "I want you to take these and to take care of your needs, Father."

The Jesuit looked down into his hand and smiled at Stephen. "You didn't keep the vow of poverty either," he said.

Stephen smiled back. "No, Father, I kept none of the vows or the rules that you taught me. You take this money and buy some food for yourself. Where are you staying? I'll come visit you and we can talk."

"I found a tent," said LaGarde. "I share it with one of the officers in the navy. We all thought we would be safe with the great ships in the harbor, but only the *Arethuse* put up a fight, and she alone escaped. All the others were burned after the sailors were taken off to help man the guns in the walls."

"The *Arethuse* is a ship I've come in contact with," said Stephen. "Where is your tent?"

"By the old hospital, the hospital where they brought you as a boy when you first came here."

"I'll find the place later. Goodbye, Father."

LaGarde had already turned to his neighbors on the line and shown them the coins Stephen had given him. "We are fortunate today," he said. "Now there'll be food for all—especially the children."

Stephen knew instinctively that once again his old mentor would go to bed hungry that night.

Stephen found William Vaughan when he went to Brigadier Wolfe's headquarters down the hall. Vaughan was well known there, and he was expected to return to consult with Wolfe. Stephen was sitting in the outer office when Wolfe himself entered the room. He was a painfully thin man and it seemed almost miraculous that his spindly legs could support even his reduced frame. His hair was red and scraggly, and he was losing it. His hairline was receding rapidly. He had almost no chin at all. But when he came into the office and his clerks jumped to attention, the electricity in the man's personality could be seen. "Be seated, men," he called. "We have a ton of paperwork to get out, all the things that we ignored while we took this place. Where are General Amherst's orders for the day? Have they been posted? Who has control of the refugee problem? Has anyone seen William Vaughan?" He fired the questions in clipped, precise English. He turned to Stephen. "Who is this gentleman?"

"My name is Nowell, sir, Stephen Nowell. I too am waiting for William Vaughan."

"He's a man worth waiting for. He helped me capture this place."

"He and I had some experience at that back in 1745," said Stephen.

"Is that where you suffered your loss?"

"No sir, that was at Lake George with Johnson."

"You are obviously an accomplished soldier, Mr. Nowell, and, if you served with Vaughan, a brave one. He would not have any other kind about him." He then turned from Stephen and entered his office.

Vaughan came storming into Wolfe's office about half an hour later. He grabbed Stephen and squeezed him. He was so agitated that first Stephen thought he might have been drinking again.

"Stephen, my lad," he said loudly. "I've caught the bastard. I've got him and I'll hang him."

"Who?"

"Pierce—goddammit, I've got Daniel Pierce. He's under arrest. I have to get to Wolfe to put him on trial."

"Where did you get him?"

"Right here in Louisbourg. He had been living here. The attack took him by surprise—he and his boss from France, a

Polish lady, a princess, head of all French spying. They were both here."

Cold fear gripped Stephen. "Did you capture the Polish princess as well?"

"No, she got away. Got herself on a ship called the *Arethuse*. It broke out of the harbor just before the capitulation."

Stephen was shaking. Pierce and Manya. It had to be her. They were plotters together. She had worked with him? Had her love for him been all a deception? Was she involved in the plot to kill him? Had she even set it all up?

Vaughan interrupted Stephen's thoughts. "You don't seem happy that I've got him at last, boy, and that he is going to swing. I've got the order for his arrest and the evidence against him they turned up in London. That all came from Sir William Howe, who serves under Wolfe. His brother was Lord Howe. I'm sorry to hear that the man was killed, but before he died he sent copies of the evidence against Pierce to his brother in case Pierce should turn up, either in Louisbourg or in Quebec. And now I've got him."

Brigadier Wolfe ordered a military trial for Daniel Pierce to begin the next morning. William Howe, whom Stephen had not known but would have recognized from his resemblance to his older brother, presided, along with two junior officers. Vaughan insisted that Stephen be present, although he was not comfortable with the thought of seeing Daniel Pierce again.

Pierce was led into Wolfe's own office, which was to serve as a temporary court, by two red-coated sentries, who stood on either side of him. He looked pale and shaken and stopped dead in his tracks when he saw Vaughan and Nowell.

"Place the prisoner before my desk," said Howe.

When Pierce had been properly positioned, Howe picked up a piece of paper and began to read. "Daniel Pierce, sometime resident of Boston, in the colony of Massachusetts, you are charged with betraying secrets of His Majesty's government to the King's enemies and thereby committing treason against His Majesty. How do you plead?"

Pierce whispered, "Not guilty."

"Speak up!" said Howe.

"Not guilty," said Pierce in a louder voice.

The prosecutor rose and faced Pierce. "Mr. Pierce, is it true that during the last war you communicated with the government of France through the Provincial of the Society of Jesus, then in Montreal, René Desmarais?"

"No."

"Did you not agree to serve as an agent of the government of France while serving on the Council of the province of Massachusetts, in return for a license to operate the fur-trading business out of Montreal?"

"I deny that charge, sir."

"Please accept in evidence the following document, captured by Mr. William Vaughan and left behind by the chief agent of the French government here in Louisbourg. There are copies of this same document provided to the court by the presiding officer, Sir William Howe. It is a copy of an exchange of letters between the then governor of New France, the Reverend Desmarais and the Minister of Marine in Paris. These papers identify Pierce as having made such an arrangement."

"Bring those documents forward, Lieutenant," said Howe. They were passed among the members of the court. "What is your defense against these accusations, Mr. Pierce?"

"They are forgeries!"

"They seem authentic enough to me," said the captain sitting beside Howe.

"My French isn't good enough to understand what is being said here," said the other officer.

"We need a translation," said Howe.

The prosecutor passed two sheets of paper to Howe. There were some moments of silence as the translations were read.

"Seems conclusive enough to me," said Howe aloud. "Do you have any more to say, prosecutor?"

The prosecutor indicated that he did not.

"Pierce, what have you to say for yourself?"

Daniel Pierce's face went red with rage. He turned toward Vaughan and Stephen. "It was all trumped up by those two. They made it all up. One is an imposter who had tried to get his hands on my wealth, on the wealth that rightfully belongs to my wife."

"Your ex-wife," said Stephen. "My aunt has divorced you and recognized me as her heir."

"Sir," interrupted Vaughan. "Pierce has been the evil genius behind most of what has gone wrong in Massachusetts over these last years, and he certainly has been the cause of sorrow in my life and in Mr. Nowell's life."

The officer appointed to represent Pierce stood to object. But Howe anticipated his objection. "I don't think this is pertinent to the case. We have before us a direction from the Crown that one Daniel Pierce is a traitor, to be seized and to be tried when apprehended. This man admits that he is the said Pierce. We have evidence that the Crown was correct to so charge him." He leaned over and spoke to his colleagues quietly. Then he turned back to Pierce. "Pierce, this court finds you guilty and sentences you to hang, sentence to be carried out tomorrow morning at dawn."

Pierce went white with fear and his knees buckled. He had to be supported by the two sentries who stood on either side of him.

"I appeal to the King," he called out.

"Which King, Mr. Pierce—that seems to be the issue."

"This is a farce. This is not justice," he screamed as he was dragged from the office.

"He's right," Stephen said to Vaughan.

Vaughan merely shook his head. "It's a damn sight more justice than he gave to your grandfather and to your mother, my Sarah."

"But he had no chance to present a defense."

"What defense did he have?"

"I don't know, but he should have had an opportunity."

"Bullshit," said Vaughan. "I'm getting up early tomorrow morning to see him hang, and I'm going to ask to kick the ladder from under his feet."

The drums beat a low tattoo when the first bright light of dawn arose in the east. Troops were lined up on both sides of the courtyard of The Citadel. Pierce was led out into the yard, followed by a minister of the Church of England. He blanched when he saw the gallows—the heavy frame of wood with a rope hanging from it, a stepladder set up underneath it. Beside the gallows a plain wooden coffin lay on the ground.

Pierce stumbled forward, his face contorted by fear. He turned, as if to run back to the safety of his cell. Guards grabbed his arms and tied his hands in back. He was hustled forward toward the gallows. He screamed as the black hood was placed over his head. His body was physically lifted onto the ladder and the noose placed about his neck. The priest prayed, but his prayers were interrupted by the sobs that came from beneath the hood. The priest stepped back and, with little seeming concern, William Vaughan approached the ladder. He placed both his hands upon it and he yanked. Pierce's body fell free for a quick second and then there was a sickening, horrible snapping sound. His feet danced spasmodically for a few seconds and there was quiet. The captain of the guard gave the command, and the soldiers lining the courtyard turned as one and began marching back to their barracks. Only a small death-watch group remained. After an hour of watching Pierce's lifeless body sway, first one way and then another, in the breeze, they placed the coffin directly under his body. A soldier climbed up the ladder and released the rope with his knife. Daniel Pierce fell with a thud into the pine box.

William Vaughan wrapped his coat closer about his body to keep out the chill. He would go home to Stephen now to tell him that it was all over, and then he would find himself a warm fire and a bottle of rum.

VIII

Summer, 1759

When the first great ships came tacking up the river, the people of the island panicked. They believed that les Anglais had finally come.

Antoine Gingras raced from his father's farm to warn Katherine and Amy. Karl had left the island weeks before and was working with most of the regular troops to build the fortifications across the river on the Beauport shore, between the St. Charles and the Montmorenci Rivers.

Antoine's father and brothers had also been called out by Governor Vaudreuil to help defend Quebec. The heretics— the hated Anglais—were coming to destroy them.

But by the time Antoine arrived at the Stiegler farm, he had pulled back on the reins of the hay wagon. The ships were clearly visible close to the shore. They were French. A supply fleet had arrived in the St. Lawrence ahead of the English invasion. There would be great rejoicing in the city this night.

He found Katherine nursing her child, sitting in a chair on the covered veranda of her stone house, watching the ships. When she saw him approaching, she took the baby Louis Joseph from her breast and covered herself.

"Katherine," he called to her. "We're saved. Those ships are French. Maybe now my father and brothers can come home and Karl can visit you here again."

She smiled at him. "Antoine, I think you are tired of being the man of the house." Although she teased him, she hoped he was right and that the English would not come now.

She dreaded their arrival because she knew in her heart that Stephen would be among them, and that he and Karl must then confront each other.

Amy came from the house when she heard Antoine call.

"Hello, Ugly," he said offhandedly.

She stuck her tongue out at him and called him "pig." Her French was now as fluent as Karl's, whereas Katherine still stumbled over words and knew little of the local slang. She did not understand the exchange between the boy and her daughter. It had all taken place too fast.

Amy, at ten, had reached a gawky stage in her development, although it was already clear that Antoine's nickname for her would no longer be appropriate in a few years. She still tagged after him, no matter where he went, and had an almost slavish devotion to him. She continually bombarded her mother and Karl, when he was at home, with the precious name of Antoine Gingras. But she would never give him the satisfaction of allowing him to know she revered him.

Antoine turned the wagon in the road. "Maman wants to know, Mrs. Katherine, if you wish to come over to our farm to stay. She says you must be lonely. But to tell you the truth, I think it is Maman who is lonely without Papa. My two sisters who married the Millard boys went with them into the town when they were called up. There are only four of us now at home."

"Four is a big enough family, Antoine," laughed Katherine. "I don't want to leave this house if I can help it. I've been so happy here."

He clucked to the horse, which now faced home, and the animal moved quickly down the road. Antoine stood in the driver's seat and called back toward Katherine, "You come if the English approach, do you hear? We have a boat. We will get across the river safely if they come. You can leave Ugly behind if you want. She's English anyway." He sat down, laughing loudly.

"I'm not English," Amy yelled after him. "I'm not the enemy. Am I, Mother?" she turned and asked Katherine, when Antoine was out of shouting range.

Katherine merely shrugged her shoulders. "You're not anyone's enemy," she said, avoiding the thrust of the question. Then she sighed with relief when Amy didn't pursue the issue.

The English came some days later. At first, there were only the ships that had attempted to cut off the French fleet and had missed it, but then, later in the summer, the main body of ships arrived, along with an army under the command of the recently promoted Major General James Wolfe.

Karl came back to Isle d'Orleans the same night that the English arrived. Katherine lay in bed with Louis Joseph by her side, in the cradle his father had made for him. Amy was sleeping in the same bed as her mother. Katherine had expected Karl's visit, and all had gone to bed with their warmest clothes on. Katherine had a bag of food and changes of clothes already packed.

Karl crept into the house without making a noise. The dog they had kept to warn of strangers caught his scent and, recognizing him, made no racket. He stepped into the bedroom and placed his hand on Katherine's mouth. She awoke with a start, her eyes filled with fright, but when she saw his face she calmed down and he removed his hand.

"Karl, what's going on?"

"It's the English. They have landed on the island and they're making their way toward this village. They will be in St. Pierre shortly. We must get you away."

He awakened Amy, and Katherine scooped up Louis Joseph into her arms. Karl took Amy's hand and, grabbing Katherine's bag of provisions, he headed for the front door of the house.

Amy began to balk. She wanted to take the dog. Karl would not hear of it. He scolded Amy and told her they must be quiet and the dog would give them away.

They went out into the night. Out on the river, giant ships were lit by lanterns—a careless act in time of war—showing contempt for the power of the French to retaliate. But it gave Karl the opportunity to see boats loaded with troops headed for the island shore. The English would land on Isle d'Orleans.

Antoine had left Karl when the road swung away from the shore toward Karl's farm. He passed on to bring the lieutenant's warning to the Millards. Monsieur Millard was considered too old for service in the militia, and he had remained on the farm, angry at being rejected. Antoine felt he would have difficulty convincing him to evacuate like the general had ordered.

He approached the Millard farm and he knew something was wrong right away. The Millard dog had the keenest hearing of all the dogs on the island. He had never reconciled himself to Antoine's daily invasion of his territory with the Millard cows. In the past, Antoine had made a game of invading the farm to see how close he could get before being "caught." There was no noise this night.

There were lights visible in the windows of the farmhouse, and now Antoine could hear voices. He saw two dark forms lying on the ground in front of the house. He crept closer. He wanted to run in the opposite direction, but he took a deep breath instead and crawled on his hands and knees up to the dark hulks.

One was the Millard dog. His head had been split open with the blow of a tomahawk. Brain matter lay scattered on the ground. The second and larger form was the body of Millard. His throat had been cut and his belly ripped open. The ground around him was covered with gore. From the contortions of his body, it was clear that he had suffered greatly before the merciful knife had been drawn across his neck.

Antoine vomited. His blood rushed to his head and pounded in his temples. He could feel the increased beating of his heart.

There was a scream from inside the house. Antoine got to his feet to run away, but he could not. He recognized Madame Millard's voice in that scream. He turned back toward the house and crept up to the window. He had expected to see Indians, but they were white. There were six of them. They had Madame Millard stretched out on her own dining table. Each of her limbs was pinned down by a man, while one raped her and one watched. They were dressed in the green uniforms of the dreaded American Rangers.

Antoine panicked completely and began to run. He was sure he would be heard, but the Rangers were too intent to hear him. He raced to the road and continued to run back past the Stiegler farm—back to the temporary safety of his home.

Karl, along with Louis Joseph, Katherine and Amy, walked along the road to the Gingras farm. All was quiet. Karl whistled softly. From out of the bushes Antoine appeared and behind him, his mother and sisters.

Karl grabbed the boy's hand and mussed up his hair. Antoine looked very somber and very scared, and Karl wished to bolster his courage. But it had the opposite effect. The boy began to weep.

"Antoine, what has gotten into you? I need you to behave like a man tonight, if we are to get off this island."

"The Millards," he said. "The Rangers have killed him and they have raped her. I didn't try to stop them. I was a coward and I ran away."

"How many of them were there?" Karl asked.

"Six."

"Don't fault yourself, Antoine. I would not have had the courage to face six animals alone either. You did the right thing to come back and guard your mother and sisters until I could get here. But now you must pull yourself together and help me get our families safely behind our lines."

The boy sniffled and then nodded his head in agreement.

"Come," said Karl. "I left the boat hidden in the bushes along the road toward the village."

Karl led and Antoine brought up the rear. They moved along the road through the blackened night. The moon and stars were hidden by a low-hanging cloud cover, and it was impossible to see more than a few feet in front of them.

When they were halfway down the road to the village, they became aware of a glow in the sky behind them. Antoine called to Karl in surprise. "Lieutenant, what is that?"

Karl looked around and just shook his head and continued to walk forward.

"My God," said Maman Gingras. "It's the Millard farm. The pigs have set it ablaze. Why would they destroy like that?"

"Why would they slaughter and rape innocent people?" interrupted Karl. "It's all terror tactics. The English feel they can break the will of the Canadiens to fight for France if they frighten us. We can't give in to them. Don't look back, Katherine. Our house and farm will be next, and then the Gingras farm will follow."

He placed his arm around Katherine's shoulders and urged her forward. The baby stirred in her arms and then fell back to sleep.

"I don't want to look back," she said and pushed ahead into the darkness.

In about ten minutes' time Karl's little group of refugees came to the small landing beach where he had left the Gingras boat.

As he removed the branches that he had placed on top of the craft to camouflage it, he heard a twig snap in the bushes to his right. The entire group froze in place. A black form approached them from out of the deep gloom of the night woods. The blackness of the form was outlined by the glow of the sky from the burning farms.

"Bless you, my children," said the form. It was Father Cardinal.

"I found this boat when I arrived here earlier. I waited for you to return so that you might take me across to the city."

"I thought you might wish to stay behind and give succor to

243

your flock, priest," said Karl, his voice dripping with sarcasm.

"Madame Gingras, you are a good Catholic. I am sure you can persuade the lieutenant of the importance of my coming with you to Quebec."

"I can see the need for a priest on this island to help the dying," she said in response.

It was clear that the priest was deeply frightened. People must have come to him with stories of the atrocities. His demeanor was one of calm resignation, but even in the dark Karl could almost feel the panic taking hold of the man.

It was Katherine who interceded for him. "Karl, if you have room in the boat, we must take Father Cardinal with us. Priests will be special targets for the Rangers. We cannot leave the man to that kind of fate."

Karl grumbled but, when Katherine made the request, the issue was settled. The branches were off the boat, and Karl and Antoine started to push it out into the river. Cardinal started to step into the stern, but Karl viciously pushed him aside. "The women go first," he hissed, "and then you find yourself a place near an oar. You'll row just like Antoine and myself or, so help me God, I'll push you overboard in the middle of the river."

They rowed cautiously out into midstream. The glow from the burning farm illuminated the sky all over the island. In addition, the flames silhouetted the great ships of the English navy. Again and again they saw small boats like theirs drop into the water and push away from the giant hulks of the transports. And each of these boats was filled with uniformed soldiers.

They tried to keep upstream from the English. The channel currents pulled at them, and they found themselves within hailing distance of one of the vessels. A shout was heard. "Boat to starboard, sir."

"Ahoy, who goes there?"

Karl quickly shouted back in English. "Picket boat; hold your fire."

"What picket boat? Identify yourself. What's the password?"

"That does it," said Karl. "Everyone grab hold of an oar and pull together—together now, pull."

The boat almost leapt in the water and surged away toward the north shore of the St. Lawrence.

"Marines," shouted the lookout aboard the English warship. "Enemy boat to starboard—prepare to fire."

244

"Get down low," yelled Karl. "They're going to fire on us."

The night was silent except for the grunts of the men and women rowers and the loud splash of poorly coordinated oars in the water. Suddenly the silence was shattered by the crack of muskets fired in a volley. Father Cardinal stood up in his seat, grasping his neck. Blood gushed from his mouth. Then he fell sideways into the waters of the St. Lawrence and disappeared.

Katherine, who had been holding Louis Joseph in her arms, placed the baby, who began to scream with anger, on the floor of the boat and grabbed Cardinal's oar. Feverishly she began to pull, anything to get out of range before the Marines reloaded.

Most of the next volley roared over their heads or smacked into the water beside them. They continued to pull madly in their efforts to escape. Karl stood up in the rear and, using his oar as a rudder, he steered the boat out of the light of the reflected flames into the dark shadows. Another volley fell harmlessly off to the right. The Marines had lost sight of them. They were safe.

Karl sat back down and picked his son up out of the puddle of water in the bottom of the boat. He hugged him against his chest and tried to comfort him.

"Hush, little man," he whispered. "You must be a man now too and keep quiet."

The baby looked into his father's face and, although the darkness prevented him from seeing Karl, the sound of his voice was enough to make him smile.

Katherine continued to row, but all now had reduced their pace. It was an easy row to the Beauport shore. But French sentries would be on the alert for possible British attack. They did not wish to be fired on by their own troops.

Karl leaned forward and touched Katherine's shoulder. "Are you safe?" he asked.

She looked back at him over her shoulder. He could see she was weeping. "The priest," she said. "If I had let you leave him behind, he might still be alive."

Karl grabbed her shoulders tightly. "Don't do that, Katherine, my love," he said. "He might be alive or he might have ended up as a bayonet target for some British troops. He took his chances. We all did. He lost. Now I must see to it that we don't."

He stood up once again and hailed to the shore in French, giving Montcalm's password for that night.

The next morning it became clear to the French leaders that the English were present in force. From their entrenched positions on the Beauport shore, they could view the St. Lawrence, which was alive with British warships and transports.

Montcalm arrived at the center redoubt of the entrenchments to view the enemy. Karl had just come back from Quebec, where he had left Katherine and the children at the home of Dr. Arnoux. Katherine had already volunteered to serve as a nurse. Karl joined his commander and his aides, Gozin and Bougainville.

"My God," said Montcalm. "I'm indeed glad that Governor Vaudreuil sent our relief fleet upriver beyond the city to Sorel. I've never seen so many warships in one place at one time. They would have destroyed us utterly if we had attempted to challenge them."

"The English are establishing their base on Isle d'Orleans," said Bougainville.

"With that fleet there is no way to attack them."

Montcalm smiled and put down his spyglass. "Monsieur Bougainville, rest assured I have absolutely no intention of attacking the English. It is General Wolfe who must attack me, and I truly hope that he tries. Counting the small garrison in the city itself, I have almost 14,000 regulars and militia in these trenches. I have entrenched the bluff along the shore from the falls of the Montmorenci to the junction of the St. Charles and the St. Lawrence, and I have placed in them redoubts; I have carefully planned the crossfire. If the British attack, they will be decimated. If Wolfe decides not to attack, we merely wait. This is, after all, the end of June. By September our opponents' navy friends will become more and more agitated. By October they will leave, with or without Monsieur Wolfe. Our Canadien winters, gentlemen, will ultimately settle this issue. We wait—no matter what happens."

"That will be a difficult policy for our esteemed Governor," said Charles Gozin.

"I can handle Vaudreuil," said the general. "In this crisis he will take orders from me, if only to avoid responsibility for any defeat. Any victories, of course, he will claim for himself."

There were chuckles from members of his staff.

"Sometimes, I realize, it is difficult for me to say anything positive about Vaudreuil, gentlemen. He and the Canadien troops in general are superb woodsmen and bush fighters without peers—outdoing Indians at their own game. But in this type of warfare—the formal siege—Vaudreuil and his Canadiens will be next to useless. We'll have to keep an eye on them at all times. And we must base all our actions on our regular regiments from France."

Karl could not remain silent. He had heard much talk among the militia when he had returned Maman Gingras and Antoine to Henri and his other sons. "General Montcalm, the Canadiens are demoralized as it is. They were convinced that no English fleet could navigate the river, but here they are."

Gozin, who rarely addressed Karl directly because he disapproved of Karl's arrangement with Katherine, jumped into the conversation. "The reports are that the English captured Canadien river pilots and forced them to bring the ships upriver."

"General Wolfe has made it very clear that he intends to conduct a campaign of terror among the Canadiens," said Montcalm. "I would not be surprised if he threatened the pilots with torture if they did not guide him."

"I can testify to the terror," said Karl. "Last night it began on Isle d'Orleans—murder, rape, house burnings. He is determined to break the Canadien will to resist."

"We will hold out," said Montcalm. "Last summer I held to the defensive at Ticonderoga. The English attacked again and again. I held my position. The fort on Champlain is still ours. Let Wolfe attack me and the results will bolster our Canadiens' desire to defend their homeland."

In the days that followed, however, Karl's trust in Montcalm's policy was shaken. Wolfe seized the heights of Levis across the river from Quebec and began to build a battery to fire on the town. Vaudreuil sent a force of militia to drive off the English, but they were themselves routed. Within a few days, English guns capable of destroying the lower town of Quebec were in place and began firing.

Wolfe next seized the high ground on the left flank of the French entrenchment—across the Montmorenci River and falls. He had now divided his army in three parts, separated by water. No one single part was able to come quickly to the aid of the other. But Wolfe was convinced that if even a third of his force could meet the French in an open field of battle, his third would emerge victorious. His dividing of his forces was intended to tempt Montcalm to leave the security of his trenches and come out and fight, but the Frenchman would not be tempted. Only at the end of July would Montcalm agree to an even vaguely offensive action. Vaudreuil launched a fireship attack on the English fleet, which failed. Finally, the 31st of July, Wolfe could take it no longer. He decided to attack.

Karl was at Montcalm's headquarters. Word arrived that the English were on the move. The English line of battleships and frigates had come in close to the mud flats on the Beauport shore and had opened a barrage against the entrenchments.

Karl accompanied Montcalm on the road from his headquarters on the Beauport creek to the left flank of the entrenchment, which was under attack. When they arrived at the headquarters of the Comte de Levis, they found that the English had beached two transports on the mud flats about half a mile offshore.

Levis joined Montcalm and his staff. "General, I am not sure what our opponents are up to, but I believe they plan to attack two redoubts at the foot of the bluff."

"That would be foolhardy in the utmost," said Montcalm. "The redoubts are covered by a crossfire from the entrenchments on the bluff above them."

"Correct, but I believe the English intend to do just that."

"Even if the redoubts fall, I want no counterattack," said Montcalm.

Levis nodded in agreement.

"Wolfe will send men to ford below the falls at Montmorenci. It can be done at low tide—right now," said Montcalm. "No matter; we have them in a crossfire if they come from that direction too."

"General," said Karl, "the weather is about to break." As if to emphasize his remark, a streak of lightning crossed the sky, followed by a clap of thunder. Some heavy, warm drops of rain splattered on the shoulders and heads of the French officers gathered around the general.

"Levis," asked Montcalm, "will your Canadiens hold?"

"Watch," was all that the second in command would say.

The English poured out of the transport onto the mud flats and began to advance against the redoubts. In the van were green-uniformed American Rangers, followed by Grenadiers —the heros of last year's Louisbourg campaign. Bringing up the rear were Frazier's Scots, carrying huge broadswords and screaming the yell of the Highlands—a sound not often heard since Culloden.

"They attack bravely," said Montcalm.

The fire from the redoubts began, and the front rows of Rangers were cut down like rows of wheat before the scythe.

The British artillery from redoubts across the Montmorenci began to open fire on the mud flats as well, but with little or no effect.

The rain fell even harder, and it became impossible for Montcalm to see the course of the battle. "Lieutenant Stiegler," he ordered, "go below and find out what is happening."

Karl climbed down the embankment and began to run down the bluff toward the besieged redoubts. He passed the lines of Canadian militia and got close enough to the mud flats to see the Highlanders climb to the top of the French position and fall on the defenders, with swords swinging. The Canadians who survived the swords came pouring out the back and tried to climb the grassy knoll to the main French entrenchments. Karl had seen enough. The redoubt had fallen. He retraced his steps, but the rain had turned the steep slopes into a quagmire, and he had to pull on the long shoots of grass to hoist himself back up to the top. Several times trigger-happy militiamen fired at him—unable to discern his uniform in the downpour. Their aim was poor—no portent of things to come, he hoped. He reached Montcalm and Levis finally. They had moved forward toward the line, hoping to get some view of the events below.

Karl saluted the generals.

"Yes, Lieutenant?"

"The redoubts have fallen, sir," he said.

"Very well," said Montcalm kindly. "Monsieur le Comte," he said, turning toward Levis. "Please have our troops open fire immediately. The British will now attempt to storm our position on the bluffs."

Levis saluted and then climbed on his mount and rode off to the left. He was soon out of sight.

Within minutes, however, the whole left flank of the French position, mostly Canadian militia, exploded in a volley of musket fire, aimed blindly but massively against the Highlanders and Grenadiers as they slipped and tumbled in the grass, trying to reach the entrenched positions above. It was a slaughter. The English fell back into the cover of the redoubt.

Levis came riding back to Montcalm. "The English have withdrawn. Should we counterattack and drive them from the mud flats?"

"No," said Montcalm, smiling. "Wolfe would like that. No. I believe we should let the tides rise, and when the English realize that water separates the main army from the refugees in the redoubts, they will withdraw voluntarily. Remember,

Monsieur le Comte, we have all the time on our side. Tomorrow begins August; the nights will become chillier. By the end of the month we will see red in the leaves. And the admirals on those stout ships below will begin to become nervous and will pressure our worthy opponent, General Wolfe."

Stephen Nowell and William Vaughan had not witnessed the assault on the Beauport trenches. They were aboard the frigate *Southerland,* now anchored in the river past the town of Quebec. They heard the fury of the assault, but they could not see the defeat of Wolfe's army. Then the rains came and they were forced to go below.

Stephen walked to one side of his cabin and then walked back. His face was calm, but he could not fool Vaughan, who sat calmly on his bunk.

"What's got into you, Stephen?" asked the older man. "You've been pacing up and down, back and forth all day."

"You know what's got into me. It's inactivity. I want to get into Quebec, and our esteemed leader can't seem to find a way to do it. Wolfe has been at it over a month now, and no progress. The best he could come up with was a frontal assault on an entrenched position. I'm no soldier, and even I know that's not very clever, not against someone as competent as Montcalm. Good God! That's exactly what Abercrombie did last summer at Ticonderoga, and that's exactly what Pierce tried to force us to do at Louisbourg back in 1745. Where is the Wolfe who followed your plan to reduce Louisbourg so effectively last year?"

"Be patient, Stephen. Wolfe is not Abercrombie. He's a bold man searching for a plan. Look at the way he's tempting Montcalm. His army is split three ways, and if you count our little contingent up here beyond the city, it's four ways."

"But why hasn't he taken advantage of us? A whole new operation opened up to him when this ship sailed past the guns of the fortress and made it west of the city. He should transfer troops to this area. We'll force Montcalm out of his trenches if we attack from this side."

"But dammit, Stephen, we'd have to sail almost to Montreal to find a place along the north shore of the river level enough to land troops. Them bluffs over the river are damned steep, and each landing area with even the vaguest pathway up the cliffs has been fortified by Montcalm."

Stephen slapped his hand on the table in frustration. "But at least it's some action, and it would force Montcalm out of his trenches if we landed men west of the city. I can't help but feel that the *Southerland*'s passing Quebec was the most significant thing that has happened in this campaign, and no one has picked it up."

"What do you suggest that two visiting observers do about it?" said Vaughan.

"I don't know," said Stephen with a sigh. "I guess that I should be grateful that Wolfe allowed a one-armed observer to even come along. I don't suppose he would be terribly receptive to critical suggestions from civilians on how to win this campaign. But dammit, Willie, I want to get into the city. Katherine and Amy must be there. The house on the island had already been abandoned in a hurry. They got away. I'm sure of it."

"Yes, Stephen, they got away. Not like those poor blokes—their neighbors. I can't understand Wolfe letting his men behave like that."

"It's a tactic, Willie; they are burning out every Canadian farm and terrorizing the civilian population. They would have destroyed her farm, all the things she had there, if we hadn't claimed them as ours—and therefore British property."

"Pretty flimsy claim."

"They were my wife's and therefore mine under the law."

Vaughan said nothing. He did not have to remind Stephen that Karl's possessions had been discovered there as well. Stephen had irrefutable proof that his wife had taken up with another man—a man he regarded as a brother.

"I think the rain has stopped," Vaughan said finally.

"So have the cannons and the small-arms fire."

"I tell you, I know one of Wolfe's brigadiers better than I know Wolfe even, George Townshend. There is no way you could get me to make suggestions to the general—not after a failure like the one I expect he suffered today. But I suggest we go to see George and see what he says."

Two days later Vaughan and Nowell made their way back to the camp beside the falls where Wolfe's headquarters were located. The general had retired after the battle and had not made a reappearance. His health was always precarious, and his failure to reach Montcalm's lines and his failure to lure his opponent out of a seemingly impregnable position now affected his morale. Wolfe was suffering from colitis, said his doctor, and was in terrible agony.

George Townshend was a snob and a clever caricaturist. He had already been reprimanded by Wolfe for his devastating cartoon of the general, which he had passed about the officers' mess and which had come to Wolfe's attention. But he was also a good soldier. He listened carefully to William Vaughan's suggestion and then joked, "By God, Willie, I do believe you want to be remembered in history as the strategist who destroyed New France—first Louisbourg and now Quebec."

"Sir, history is not going to remember me at all—maybe a little for that Louisbourg attack back in '45, but that's all. Nowell and I are just talking common sense."

"No doubt about it. Wolfe simply has not yet understood the significance of passing by the *Southerland*. The navy now plans to send more and more ships upriver. Once our silly general gets over his sulking—he's threatened me with court martial after the campaign's over, all about my little drawing. Can you believe that? Goddamn nobody—but once he gets over his sulk, Brigadier General Monckton and I will bring this new proposal to him—that we move the army west of Quebec. God knows how long his ego and his bowels will keep us waiting, however. Here we are in August and no closer to success than we were in June. This is the last gamble. After this, if no success is forthcoming, the navy will leave, and I have no doubt the army will pack up and go with them. Wolfe's whole career is on the line."

"You're pretty hard on the general. He fought like a lion at Louisbourg."

"Yes he did, when someone else had the responsibility and told him what to do; he had Jeffrey Amherst over him there."

"Not fair," interrupted Vaughan. "Nowell here wasn't there, but I was, and if they had had to wait for Amherst to tell them what to do, the whole army would still be sitting outside the swamps around Louisbourg. The general did it himself. But he was healthier then—more vigorous."

"Ah, Vaughan, I can see you are a Wolfe supporter. I concede that the man has his talents. But he has absolutely no sense of humor." He reached into his desk and pulled out a scrap of paper. "Look at this—it's a copy of the offending cartoon." He showed them an almost sticklike figure of Wolfe, receding chin and hairline and all. "Don't see why he took offense," said Townshend. "Maybe he sees himself as handsome. He got engaged just before he left England for this campaign. Maybe he now fancies himself a handsome lady's man. My God, the man's legs are so skinny, they had to tie knots in them to make knees. Oh, well, if we're successful

I guess I won't have to worry about court martial, and if we're not, James Wolfe will be remembered only as a skinny and spiteful, failed general. I'll bring your suggestion to my colleague, gentlemen, and we in turn will take it to skinny Jimmy."

He rose; it was a clear signal to Vaughan and Nowell that their conversation was over. They left his office.

"What do you think?" Stephen asked.

"I think he doesn't like James Wolfe," responded Vaughan. 'But he's a good soldier and will do what he says. Now that I've done my good deed for today, I want to find a drink. Come with me, lad?"

Stephen shook his head. He grieved that Vaughan had gone back to the bottle after Pierce's death. Stephen made the long journey back to the *Southerland* alone.

The late summer gave way to early fall. The occasional splotch of orange magnified into forests of yellows, reds and oranges, interspersed with the drabness of evergreens. More and more ships of the royal navy, filled with troops, passed the guns of the fortress unharmed, and Wolfe accomplished the significant fourth diversion of forces—Montmorenci, Isle d'Orleans, Levis and an amphibious force of troops west of Quebec. And still Montcalm and his forces remained in their trenches. The only concession the marquis would make to the new threat was to dispatch Bougainville with a mobile force of three thousand to the bluffs west of the city to guard against a landing there.

But New France was imperiled from other directions as well. Ticonderoga and Crown Point were abandoned to Amherst, and a new position at the top of Lake Champlain on Isle aux Noix was prepared. Amherst took a look at it, dubbed it impregnable and switched to William Johnson's idea of a western campaign. Niagara fell, and Amherst now could approach Montreal down the St. Lawrence from the west. Montcalm sent the Comte de Levis to Montreal with a thousand men to defend that crucial commercial town.

But for all of these developments, New France's fate still depended on the game of cat and mouse before the capital city of Quebec. But now Wolfe had a plan.

Stephen and Vaughan were still aboard the *Southerland*. Sailors and soldiers alike ignored the presence of the two civilians. It was enough to know that they were friends of the general and that they were to be tolerated. Stephen's friendship with the late Lord Howe also endeared him to Colonel William Howe, the Irish peer's younger brother, and he was allowed close observation of preparations.

Within the past several days, the English plan had been put into operation. The camp at Montmorenci was abandoned, and three thousand men were placed aboard boats and brought upriver, west of Quebec.

The transports sailed upriver at high tide and floated back down toward Quebec at the ebb, while Bougainville marched his three thousand men back and forth to keep the English under observation.

On the night of September 12, it was clear to Stephen and to Vaughan that something was afoot. Naval ships had bombarded the cove at Samos, but no landing was attempted. Only feints were made here.

When darkness fell on the river, both the army and the navy came alive. Small boats were lowered into the river and began to load with troops.

Stephen desperately wanted to be involved. Here, was an assault on Quebec itself, and he wanted to enter that city with such an assault. He found Sir William Howe's cabin. It was filled with junior officers who took directions from Howe and scurried off, only to be replaced by new men.

Stephen stood off to the side and waited for his opportunity. As Howe rose to leave, Stephen intervened. "Colonel Howe."

"Ah, Nowell, you've been watching the preparations."

"I've noted," said Stephen, "that you will lead a force of volunteers. I'd like to be one."

Howe looked embarrassed for a moment. "I'm sorry, Nowell; only military men will be allowed to come with me."

"Please don't make that decision because of my handicap rather than my status. You may have need of one of my talents. I speak French rather well."

"I'm not so bad myself, you know," countered Howe.

"Do you speak it like a Canadien rather than a Paris gentleman?" Stephen asked in French.

Howe laughed. "No, you have a point. I can't manage that."

"I doubt if any of your volunteers could. Take me along. I'll not get in your way."

Howe thought for a moment and then shrugged his shoulders. "You could prove useful on the trip down. But there will be some sharp and hard climbing at the end—more than a one-armed man could manage. Maybe when we arrive you could stay with the boats."

Stephen smiled broadly. "Yes, sir," he said, snapping a salute to Howe.

"Remember, Nowell, you're a civilian."

"Yes, sir, but one more favor. Let William Vaughan come with me."

"Damn you, Nowell, you really push. What talent, other than rum guzzling, will he bring to the operation? No, I can't risk it. If he gets into the rum, he'll ruin everything. You get no Vaughan and that's final."

Stephen was disappointed, but he knew better than to argue. "I'd better leave right away, then. Vaughan will kick up a fuss if he knows I am going and he's not."

"Right away, and I want you in the lead boat in case we're sighted and challenged."

The night was dark and moonless. Shortly after midnight Stephen found himself in the lead boat with twenty other volunteers—light infantry and some Highlanders. Colonel Howe leapt the final two feet into the boat and crawled over some of his men to sit next to Stephen. "I've been thinking about your argument about speaking French, Nowell, and I believe I was had. My God, most of the French army here is directly from France. The argument about accent is pure poppycock. I should order you back up aboard ship."

"I can't climb back up with only one arm," said Stephen. He was smiling when he said it, but Howe did not respond to the humor.

"Dammit, I could have you lifted out of the boat bodily and thrown overboard. Let the navy pick you up."

"I can't swim with only one arm."

"Goddamn your arm. To hell with you. Sit here, and if you open your mouth I swear I'll have your other arm."

"I won't say a word."

At about two in the morning, two lanterns were hung in the shrouds of the *Southerland*. The tide was ebbing. The boats were to get underway. Current carried them along, and they did not have to do a great deal of rowing. Helmsmen steered and the volunteers tried to remain absolutely silent. Each man was determined to succeed. Wolfe and an army of 3,500 would follow the course they charted.

Stephen heard the man behind him recite the Lord's Prayer in a whisper. He was tempted to turn around and remind the man of Howe's command for silence, but he realized no one but he and Howe could have heard the prayer. The stillness of the night seemed to magnify every noise.

The current moved them downstream rapidly. As they moved along, they drew closer to the shore, and the tree covered cliffs overhead seemed to frown darkness down upon them.

Suddenly the stillness was cracked by a voice, calling in French. "Who goes there?"

Howe whispered to Stephen. "Is he asking for a password?"

"I thought you said you spoke French," said Stephen.

Before Howe could respond, the Highlander from the back of the boat called out in a good accent, "We're French."

"What is your regiment?"

Stephen translated the request to Howe, whether he needed it or not.

"I've heard that the Queen's regiment is serving here. How does he say it?" he asked of Stephen.

"De la Reine," said Stephen.

"Call it out!"

"De la Reine," yelled Stephen.

"Pass on," called the sentry.

Howe whistled relief under his breath.

"Damn careless or we're awfully lucky," whispered Stephen.

"Both," said Howe. "They're expecting provisions to come downriver to Quebec tonight. They're seeing what they expect to see—a lot of boats moving silently downstream toward the capital. But they should be shot for not asking the password."

They continued on in the dark. The helmsmen attempted to keep them close to the shore, but the river currents thwarted him. A few minutes later, another shout in French came down upon them—this time from the bluffs above. Once again careless sentries accepted the response that this was the first of the provision boats on the last leg of a long journey from Three Rivers and Montreal.

Then Howe pushed to the bow of the boat, peering into the black night. "We're passing it, helmsmen," he whispered sharply. "The cove, Anse au Foulon, is to port; bring us in immediately."

The helmsman brought the boat around to Howe's command. The river current caught the bow and thrust it forward toward the shore. They heard the sound of gravel and mud scraping the bottom of the boat. Howe leapt into the ankle-deep water, followed by his volunteers. Stephen was the last one out of the boat.

"You stay with the boat, Nowell," said Howe. "When the others arrive, you point out the path—the way up."

"Where is it?" asked Stephen innocently.

"Right in front of you," said Howe. "Nothing that a good old alpine goat couldn't handle with a few years' practice."

Howe was gone, leading the volunteers up the tree-strewn, ditch-covered path to the top of the cliffs above.

More boats arrived in the cove and Stephen pointed out the almost invisible path to the newcomers. They too started to climb. When the second boat's crew were halfway up the cliff, shots rang out from the cliff above, followed by a shout in French.

Stephen craned his neck upward to look into the star-covered night, trying to discern the edge of the cliff. But he could see nothing. Finally, after what seemed like an eternal delay, there was a call in English from the bluff. The French guard detail at Anse au Foulon had been surprised and taken. The bluff above was, for the moment at least, in English hands.

Several more boats arrived, and one of them contained both James Wolfe and William Vaughan.

"Willie," Stephen greeted him.

"Thought you could leave me behind, did you, boy?"

Stephen did not know how to respond, but Vaughan made it unnecessary. "We all have to find our own way, don't we? I've known Wolfe for some time. He's in a strange mood tonight—talking about dying the whole way downriver and reciting poetry—something about a 'lowing herd.' Damn strange man, if you ask me."

"I'm glad you're here, William. Now you can help me get to the top. I don't think I could have made it alone."

"Why the hell not? Wolfe's going to do it, and he is a sick and weak man."

"Why the hell not?" repeated Stephen, shrugging his shoulders. Stephen went first, followed by Vaughan. If Stephen fell backward, Vaughan intended to use his great bulk to block his fall.

The path was incredibly steep. Stephen grabbed at branches of bushes with his hand to pull himself upward. He began to breathe heavily. He had done little manual labor since the amputation, and his body had become much softer.

257

He broke out into a sweat very quickly. He stumbled over a tree branch that had not been cleared by those who had made it up ahead of him, and he fell forward. He broke his fall with his hand and tumbled onto his left side, grunting as breath was knocked from him.

Vaughan looked down at him. His chest was heaving in and out. His face was moist with sweat, but his disposition had not changed. "That was a cute trick," he said. "I'll bet you can't do it again."

He offered Stephen his arm and pulled him to his feet. Stephen rested a second with his arm on Vaughan's shoulder and then turned and started back up the path.

The climb became more and more difficult for him. He began to concentrate on taking one step at a time, trying to avoid any more falls. There were trenches and trees that had been placed in the pathway deliberately by the French to block any ascent. Most of them had been cleared, but the few obstacles that still remained were sufficient to force Stephen to slow down. Vaughan frequently placed his hand on Stephen's back and gave a gentle push.

"No offense meant, my boy," said Vaughan. "But James Wolfe is catching up to me, and I'll be damned if I'll let him beat me to the top."

Stephen tried to ignore Vaughan's humor. It was obvious, even to him, that Vaughan's hand went to his back as he approached an obstacle.

He could see the top now, and he continued to push his legs forward. He fell again, but this time only to his knees. He got to his feet before Vaughan could reach him. He turned to say the obvious—that they were almost at the top. But Vaughan had collapsed on his face and was lying still.

Stephen took two steps, two agonizing steps, backward and dropped down on the ground next to the older man, who lay there, not moving. "That's a cute trick," said Stephen. "I'll bet you can't do it again."

"You son of a bitch," laughed Vaughan. He got to his feet and swayed drunkenly.

"I think you're showing the effects of a little too much rum, my friend," chided Stephen, "while I'm showing the effects of soft living. If you hold me up, I'll try to do the same for you."

Together the two of them climbed the last few yards and fell on the ground. The morning was some hours off, and Stephen could not get much of a view, but he rested, content that he had finally reached the Plains of Abraham.

All during the night the Marquis de Montcalm paced restlessly in his headquarters tent at Beauport. Every half hour or so, he would leave the shelter of the tent to walk to the observation point on the fortifications. The English fleet seemed to be maneuvering to get close in to shore for another landing and another assault. Each time he rose from his bed and began to pace or walk about, Karl, who was sleeping upright in Montcalm's camp chair, would awaken with a start, get to his feet and follow the marquis outside. It was clear to Karl that the general was unnerved and desperate for company.

Karl stood behind Montcalm as he peered out into the dark river. "I don't trust it," Montcalm said aloud. "Why are they so obvious about intentions and suddenly so careless about things the British navy always takes care with? I must conclude that they will not strike here at our middle, at Beauport. Stiegler, send Gozin to Vaudreuil on the right wing and tell him to watch for a flanking movement on our right. Tell him also to alert Ramesay and his garrison in the city. Also, the word should be sent to Bougainville west of the city. Everyone must be alert. I think that this is Wolfe's last effort. If we can thwart it, New France is saved for another year."

Karl left him.

Montcalm continued to stare out into the river. Throughout the whole campaign he had been filled with a sense of security. He held a strong military position with superior forces, and he was doing what he did best—countering the enemy attack. Yet tonight he was filled with foreboding.

Karl returned ten minutes later. The messages were on their way.

"It's about an hour to dawn, sir," Karl said. "Perhaps you should try to sleep."

Montcalm shook his head. "There will be much time to sleep later—after the English have gone." He sighed and rested his elbows on the wooden beam that formed the top of the entrenched redoubts in which they stood.

"Did you speak with Charles, my nephew?"

"Yes, sir."

"I am sorry, Karl. I know that relations between you two have been strained concerning Mrs. Nowell."

Karl merely shifted his weight from one foot to another without comment.

"I do not intend to pry into your private business or the lady's. But this sort of arrangement, tolerable for young officers of France, simply cannot succeed here. If you continue to live with Mrs. Nowell, Karl, young men like my nephew will drive you from the army."

"I understand," said Karl. "I'm not much of a farmer, but I've been getting much practice over the past few years."

"That means you're determined to remain with the lady."

"Yes, sir."

"You must love her deeply."

"With all my heart."

"Then hold on to her, Karl, and don't let someone like Charles pry you apart."

"The lady has a husband, General. He is more likely to pry us apart than your Charles."

"He cares for her, then?"

"I'm not sure whether his pride can allow her to leave him."

"That is a dangerous situation."

Karl merely nodded his understanding of the danger. "I've said little about it, General, but Katherine and I have a son. I hope you will take no offense from the fact that we have named him Louis Joseph."

"After me? How could I take offense? I'm honored." His face broke into a broad smile.

"No, sir. It is rather my Louis Joseph who is honored."

They were silent for a few moments, and then the night quiet was shattered by the roar of cannon from the ramparts of Quebec. Montcalm was instantly alert. "What is Ramesay firing at?"

He paced some more minutes and then the cannon fire stopped. "I can't take this any longer," he said finally. "The English feint here. The attack will be west of here. Karl, get my black mare saddled. And get a mount for yourself. We will ride to Quebec. And send for the Chevalier Johnstone; he will accompany us. He's a Scot. He knows these people."

They rode with abandon along the road from Beauport toward the bridge that crossed the St. Charles River north of Quebec. Governor Vaudreuil's headquarters were on the way, and Montcalm hoped to reach the Governor before the sun rose.

Karl was a terrible horseman, but he knew he had to keep up with the expert Montcalm, and he abandoned all caution and practically gave the horse his head—hoping he would have sure feet in the dark.

The sun was turning the sky gold behind them when they reached Vaudreuil's tent. The Governor was asleep and clearly resented it when Montcalm awakened him.

"Why was Ramesay firing cannon?" Montcalm asked his political superior.

"Ach," said Vaudreuil, "he sees ghosts. Bougainville sent reports of English raids on Samos and Anse au Foulon and Ramesay's trigger-happy regulars fire at goats and cows grazing on the Plains of Abraham. Everyone is very jumpy, including you, *mon Général*," said Vaudreuil.

"Am I to understand from what you said that the English have been sighted on the plains?"

"There were scattered reports to that effect."

"Good God, man, why wasn't I informed?"

"The English have been west of Quebec for over a month, Louis. They've raided frequently. If I informed you of every one, expecting you to respond, you'd have little time for anything else."

Karl had never seen Montcalm so angry before. "The plains west of the city are Quebec's Achilles heel. The walls of the city can be breeched by cannon if the English put them on the plains. Quebec is doomed once they entrench there. If the English get there, we must abandon our defense and fight them out in the open field. I don't want to risk that. Vaudreuil, you never seem to understand the military necessities."

"I understand them better than you understand the political ones, and I understand Canadiens, something you have no inclination or ability to do."

"Nothing has changed," said an angry Montcalm. "We still have the same arguments—almost the same words we have exchanged since I first arrived in New France. I ride to Quebec via the St. Charles Bridge, and if I need your support, I'll send word to you. Remember, hold these trenches unless I send you word to the contrary."

He whipped his horse and was off to the west before Vaudreuil could respond.

When Karl and Montcalm arrived at the bridge, they found Ramesay, the garrison commander there, very agitated. "The English are here, General; they are on the Plains of Abraham."

"How many?"

"I have conflicting reports. You cannot see the whole plain from the city because of a knoll—the Buttes-a-Nevue—in the middle. The English are on the other side of the knoll."

"There is only one way to determine that. Karl, come with me and Johnstone. You too, Ramesay. We will get a better picture on the other side of the bridge."

On the west side of the St. Charles, the whole countryside

opened to their view. By now the sun was high enough in the sky to allow them to see all. "My God, this is serious," said Montcalm. "That's not a raiding party. It's a whole army."

The English ranks of redcoats stretched in parallel lines from the heights overlooking the St. Lawrence to the woods and underbrush of the Cote Ste. Genevieve—a width of about one mile.

"I estimate about 4,000 men, General."

"We are lost unless we drive them from the plains," said Montcalm. "They seem to have few heavy guns, but that is a matter of time. If Wolfe initiates a siege from the west, the walls of Quebec will fall faster than the walls of Jericho. They were never intended to withstand heavy guns. We must act immediately."

Johnstone nodded in agreement. "But surely, General, you will have to bring reinforcements from the Beauport trenches. We have only one regiment of regulars here, along with the garrison."

"We'll use what we have. Get to Beauport immediately, Johnstone, and tell Vaudreuil what you have seen. He is to empty our left flank of troops at Beauport and send them to me. Also, we'll use our Canadien militia in the city and, so help me God, I swore I would never do it again, as many Indians as we can get together. I want to occupy the buttes before the English do."

Johnstone saluted and started to walk along. Suddenly he stopped and turned back toward Montcalm. "Who will notify Bougainville?"

"We haven't time. We must strike before the English entrench. They've cut off our lines of communication and supply with Montreal and the relief supply ships at Sorel. Don't you understand, man, the situation is desperate."

"But he's behind Wolfe and may be closer than Beauport. If he attacks when we do, Wolfe is finished."

"We don't know where Bougainville is, monsieur. I have no intention of waiting to find out."

There was a note of desperation in Montcalm's voice that Karl had never heard before. It frightened him.

The regiments from France had unfurled their battle flags. The roll of drums called all to fall into ranks and face the red-clad army on the plains below. The white-uniformed army of French regulars, with ranks interspersed with homespun-clad militia, soon appeared on the knoll above the plains. Montcalm, still riding his black mare, rode through their

nks. Soldiers reached up to touch his mare or his boots, and
e mare shied away. The general stroked her flanks to calm
er down. The militia greeted the general with smiles and
ffectionate calls. "The English are goats, *mon Général*,"
alled the militiamen. "How else could they have climbed the
liffs?"

"They smell like goats," quipped another, to a chorus of
ughter.

"When you are finished with them, my friends, they will
ish they were pigeons or some other bird with wings so that
ey might fly off the plains back to their ships in the river,"
id Montcalm. He turned to Karl, who rode by his side.
Are all the troops in place?"

"We have not received the additional troops from the
overnor," responded Karl.

"I don't have time for him to make up his mind whether to
upport me or not. If I know my friend the Marquis Vau-
reuil, he'll wait until he can figure out whether I am winning
r losing. If I win, he'll appear on the scene to claim his
hare. If I lose, I'll not see him today."

"General," said Karl. "Let me ride behind the English lines
nd alert Bougainville and even Levis in Montreal to our
ituation. We could catch the English at the front and rear at
he same time."

"It won't work, Karl. The English must be given no time.
Ve must attack. Give out the word along the whole line. We
1ove off the buttes and advance onto the plains against the
nglish."

All were silent. They could almost hear the commands in
1e English ranks. Karl signaled the drummer, who gave a
oll on his drum. Harsh officers' voices interrupted the still-
ess. Muskets were loaded and bayonets were affixed to the
1uzzles of the muskets of the Regulars.

The French lines began to move forward. The Plains of
braham was mostly level, but it was dotted with occasional
ornfields and patches of bushes. The red-coated lines of
ritish troops remained motionless. The French marched
ward them. The command was given to halt and fire. The
anks of French troops fired, and small gaps were seen in the
ritish lines. But suddenly the white lines were staggered and
roken. The Canadien militia, after firing, had dropped to the
round to reload, as was their practice. Montcalm had inter-
persed the militia with the Regulars, and the white-coated
rofessionals moved forward, loading as they marched, fol-
owing the precise drill of the European training field. But

huge gaps broke in their lines. And the white now presented itself as a jagged front to the English.

As the French approached, the English muskets were aimed. Then came the command to fire. The red line exploded in a mass volley of iron that moved through the French ranks with devastating effects. The French advance was halted in its tracks. It staggered, as if punched between the eyes, and then came to a halt. Some soldiers got to their knees and fired at the English ranks.

Karl had been riding in the van when the first volley struck. He had become separated from Montcalm. His horse collapsed beneath him. A bullet had penetrated through its neck. He swung his foot over the saddle as the horse fell, preventing himself from being crushed beneath the weight of the horse. He grabbed his sword out of its scabbard and ran to a group of Canadians who, after the first volley, had fallen to the ground. "Get up," he yelled. "You must march forward and help the Regulars."

"This is insane," said one Canadian. "I didn't join the army to march straight into the English volley. That's for dull-witted Regulars. We'll wait until the English shoot off their second volley and then we'll advance until we feel they are about ready for a third."

The roar of another English volley violated Karl's ears. The firing was so precise that thousands of muskets sounded like the combined fire of a dozen cannons.

Now the Canadians rose to their feet and began to run toward the front. But everywhere white-coated soldiers fell back on them. Their faces were flushed, and their eyes were glazed with panic. Everywhere white-uniformed bodies lay face down in the grass, their coats gradually becoming the same color as those of their enemies.

Karl tried to use the flat side of his sword on the returning soldiers. "You can't run; you can't fail the general. Think of Canada—of New France. We are lost. Our country is lost if you run." He shouted until he was hoarse, but to no avail. Now the English fired sporadically at the fleeing French forces.

The Canadian militia was dazed. "Why do they run?"

"They're beaten," said Karl. "The battle is over. We must retreat back to the city."

"Over?" yelled a young militiaman. "It couldn't have lasted more than ten minutes, and it's over?"

"Let's charge the goddamned English," said another militiaman.

"The time for charging is past," said Karl bitterly. "It passed while you lay on the ground reloading. Now it's time to rally."

Karl led the militia back toward the buttes in good order. As they retreated, more and more militiamen came to join them. The Regulars were racing beyond the buttes, making for the safety of the walls of Quebec.

Karl felt someone tug at his sleeve. It was Antoine.

"Lieutenant, why are we fleeing the battle just as it began?" he asked.

"We've been beaten," answered Karl.

"Who's beaten?" said Henri Gingras, who joined his younger son, in the company of his two other sons. "We militia from St. Pierre didn't even get to fire a shot."

Karl caught sight of General Montcalm, caught in the melee of white-coated, panic-warped soldiers in front of him, and raced ahead. He saw Montcalm, tears in his eyes, trying to rally his troops. But, averting their eyes from him, they raced away from the devastating horror of the English volley.

Karl reached up for the reins of Montcalm's horse. "General, it's hopeless. Let them run."

Just at that moment, Montcalm's body stiffened. He cried out. "My God, I've been hit." The ball passed right through his body. He staggered and started to slip from his horse, but Karl kept him in his saddle.

"It's all right, Lieutenant. I'll be all right. I can keep in my saddle."

A great cheer rose from the English ranks on the plains. And with that were intermingled the howls of the Scottish Highlanders.

"The English charge," Karl yelled at the general.

"They will break through to the St. Charles if they make it to the bridge. If they take the bridge, they can fall on the rear of our position at Beauport. They must be stopped. Stiegler, the only force still intact is those militia who seem to be tagging after you." Montcalm started to cough and some blood oozed out of the corner of his mouth.

Karl was soldier enough to know he would never see the general alive again. "I'll do as you ask me, General."

Montcalm smiled resignedly. "You must. It may be Quebec's only hope."

Karl reached up and touched the top of Montcalm's boots. "Goodbye, General," he said, his eyes filling with tears.

"Don't let the others see what you and I both know, Stiegler. I'll ride into the city on this horse. It will be essential for morale. Goodbye, Karl." He dug his heels into the mare's side and it jumped away from Karl. Montcalm pulled on the reins and the horse began to trot toward the gates of Quebec —already filled with white-uniformed refugees.

Karl stood, staring at the retreating figure of the general he loved. Then, snapping out of his trance, he turned toward Henri Gingras. "We must hold the St. Charles bridge."

"Can't be done," said Gingras.

"What do you mean, can't be done? You heard Montcalm. Are you going to desert him too?"

"Hell, no," said Gingras. "But I for sure don't intend to get my ass shot off by the Anglais standing out there in the open at the bridge. Me and the St. Pierre men will get into the underbrush by the Côte Ste. Geneviève. It will take a hell of an army to drive us Canadien sharpshooters out of there."

"Let's move it, then. The English are coming on with a rush."

Karl and the St. Pierre men made it to the underbrush just before the English arrived on the scene. Stiegler looked at Henri and started to laugh.

"What's so funny?"

"You still have your pipe in your mouth. I don't think I have ever seen you without it."

"And you never will. When they bury me they'll bury me with it in my teeth."

His older sons lay on either side of him. Antoine crawled up next to Karl. They could hear the bagpipes skirl, and the British troops, mostly Highlanders, formed in front of them, readying for an attack that they anticipated would get them to the bridge across the river.

Karl looked at Antoine and saw the pain in Henri's eyes. "Antoine," he said. "I have an important mission for you."

The boy's eyes brightened. "Yes, sir," he said.

"You're to report to the Governor. You are to tell Vaudreuil that it is essential for him to occupy the earthworks defending the bridge."

"When do I do it?"

"Now."

"But I'll miss the fight."

"I'll put you in chains if you refuse."

"Behave yourself, Antoine," said his father. "Do as the lieutenant commands."

Antoine apologized and then slipped behind them, heading out of the dense underbrush toward the slope leading to the river.

266

When Antoine had disappeared, Henri looked over at Karl. "Thank you, Lieutenant," he said.

"He's a good boy," said Karl. "It was the least I could do for you after what you did for my family."

The Canadians lay on their stomachs at various vantage points in the underbrush. Some had even climbed into the low branches of the trees.

Suddenly the pipes grew louder, and a great cry went up from the ranks of the Scots in front of them. They fired a volley; shot poured through the trees and bushes, ripping off the foliage and sending dead limbs crashing on those below.

The Canadians held their fire until the last moment, and then each picked a target and fired. Karl saw soldier after soldier fall in his tracks.

The Scots retreated and regrouped. Karl heard a groan from the throat of Henri Gingras, next to him. On the other side of Gingras lay his older son. Half of his head had been shot away in the first volley. Gingras cried and held his head in his hands.

"Henri," said Karl, touching his shoulder. "They come again."

There was no volley this time, just the charge of infuriated Celts, their swords held in front of them. Again the Canadians fired in a devastating volley. But on came the Scots. They came into the woods, slashing at branches with their swords.

Karl thought the Canadians might panic before the awesome sight of kilted men slashing with giant swords. The Canadians did not run away, however. They rose as a man and charged the Scots with a yell of their own.

There was an actual sound of collision as Karl, Henri and the militia crashed into the Highlanders. Henri's tomahawk crashed into the side of a Scotsman's neck. "You son of a bitch. That is for my son, whom you have just killed." Then he swung his musket and fired the ball into the face of an officer who appeared just before him.

Karl fired his pistol. He saw the second Gingras boy fall, almost cut in half by a broadsword. He looked surprised and then fell into a lifeless heap.

A giant form loomed above Karl. He lunged at it with his sword. It was parried away. The Highlander swung his sword at Karl. He snapped Karl's officer's sword at the hilt. Karl threw his empty pistol at his adversary. The Scot came on toward him, his sword swinging back and forth. Karl saw the man's eyes; they seemed glazed with battle frenzy. He lunged

267

at Karl. Karl stepped backward and tripped over a tiny knob of a tree stump. He fell on his back; the wind was knocked out of him. He felt almost nothing when the great sword was plunged into his belly.

The Highlanders retreated a second time before the determined defense of the Canadian militia. Henri lifted Karl into his arms and poured some water into his throat. Karl awoke and coughed.

"Both of my boys and you too," cried Gingras. "The damned British are leaving a scar on my soul that time won't heal."

Karl's eyes struggled to focus. He saw several militiamen standing about him as he lay on the ground. He called to them. "The Scots may come again. Get back to the defenses."

"No," said Gingras. "They're coming again, but we can all see Vaudreuil's troops entering the bridge defenses. We've done our job. The British can't cross the St. Charles and attack Beauport. We're picking you up and taking you to Vaudreuil's line."

"No, you're not," said Karl. "This wound in the belly will open up and if you carry me I'll be dead before you go fifty feet. I'm a dead man, Henri."

Gingras knew that it was true, and great tears filled his eyes.

"You go," said Karl. "They come again, and there is no need for you all to die. Get away while you can. Henri, take care of Katherine for me. Protect her from a man named Stephen Nowell. He may try to harm her because of me."

Gingras nodded. He got up, after resting Karl's head against a fallen tree. The wild yell of the Scots was heard once again. The Canadians turned to leave. Gingras reached up to his mouth and felt his pipe. It was warm. He placed the stem between Karl's lips. "You smoke," he said. "One last smoke before the devil comes."

Stephen had remained at the rear of the English line of battle, along with Vaughan. But he was startled by the way the British volley had staggered the French advance, which he could see from the rear of the British lines. And then came the command for a British charge. He saw Wolfe himself lead the van of the army on the right in front of his Louisbourg grenadiers. Musket shot passed over the general's head. Vaughan called to Wolfe to have more care precisely at the moment when a ball smashed into Wolfe's wrist. The general looked dumbly at the blood pouring from the wound. He reached into his uniformed coat, wrapped a handkerchief about his wrist and paid it no more mind. He moved forward to catch up wtih the van of the advancing redcoats.

"Damn me, Stephen, but that man is determined to end the day a corpse."

"I have no doubt he'll achieve his goal," said Stephen. "His plan is that of a desperate man. If he loses, he dies in the effort. If he wins, he is the tragic hero. For a man predisposed to die, it is not a bad way to go."

A spent musket ball struck the ground in front of Vaughan, causing him to wince and duck. "I don't share the general's predisposition," Vaughan said with a grin. "As long as we're not fighters in this battle, Stephen, why don't we retire to a safer distance?"

Stephen shook his head. "I'm moving ahead with the army," he said stubbornly. "If there's any chance of getting into the city, I'm going to take it."

Vaughan sighed. "Then I'm coming with you."

He had tried to draw Stephen away from the hostilities, but failing in that, he could not allow Sarah Nowell's son to step into the path of danger alone.

All along the front, the British army moved forward, through the cornfields and patches of bushes up to the buttes and on beyond. They could now see the grey stone walls of the fortress of Quebec, at last.

The French troops were in a panic, trying to force their way through the gates of St. Louis. Then suddenly the attention of the British swung toward Côte Ste. Geneviève.

At first it began as a vague rumor, but then it became a loud cry up and down the British lines. Wolfe had been hit; he was seen being carried toward the rear; the wound was mortal; and finally the leader was dead. Anger swelled through the army. The hero—the funny skinny man was dead. His last command had been to seize the bridge across the St. Charles. His grieving men threw their entire strength against a small contingent of Canadian militia who blocked their path.

Stephen followed the Scottish Highlanders across the field. He searched every white-uniformed face, whether dead or wounded, that he came across on the plains. He knew that Karl would be in the forefront of battle, and casualties among the French had been high.

The Highlanders charged into the woods of the Côte and came out again, bleeding and beaten. The officers turned their men around, screaming at them in the tongue of those northern hills of Scotland. The pipes took up the cry and again, with a roar of pent-up Celtic anger, they charged into the Canadian position, and again they came back out of the woods.

The third charge was anticlimactic. The French Regulars in their white uniforms could be seen coming in force to occupy the trenches on the Quebec side of the St. Charles, and the militia could be seen withdrawing to join them. The stubborn resistance had saved the bridge and the French rear at Beauport. But the Highlanders would make a third assault —if only to save their honor. The Côte Ste. Genevieve would not remain unoccupied. The pipes skirled and for the third time the kilted troops marched forward.

Vaughan stayed close to Stephen, and they followed close behind the troops. "Stephen, what's the point of all of this?" asked Vaughan. "You're not going to get into Quebec this way."

"I've got to check," Stephen responded. "I've got to make sure he lives."

"I thought you hated the bastard," said Vaughan.

"I do, and I love him. I don't want him hurt. I want everything to go back to the way it was. But I know it can't, and I don't know what it is that I want. I want Karl and Katherine to tell me that they are sorry and to ask forgiveness, and maybe it could be all right again."

Vaughan looked at him incredulously.

"I started out hating Karl. Now I'm searching every face, deathly afraid that the next one I turn over might be him."

They entered the underbrush of the Côte Ste. Genevieve. The Highlanders were in a rage. Their losses had been great, and several were taking their rage out on a few corpses of Canadians that had been left behind. One of the Scotsmen let out a yell of triumph. "I found one alive. He's a bloody officer."

Several of the soldiers near Stephen and William began to run toward the cry.

"I think we better head on over with them. They're in a foul mood."

William began to run toward where the commotion was developing. Stephen followed right behind. They pushed their way through the crowd of men and saw one of the soldiers,

270

his great sword in hand, its point striking the deathly pale face of a man in a white uniform. Stephen shouted out, "Don't harm him!"

"Who the hell are you?" said a soldier with a heavy Scottish accent. "Some goddamned civilian is going to tell us what to do? And English to boot?"

"Not English at all, lads," said Vaughan. "We're Americans—exploited by the bloody English just like you boys and your folks."

"Exploited ain't the half of it. I know you," said the soldier with the sword to Vaughan. "You're a friend of Jimmy Wolfe, ain't you? Is it true he's dead?"

"I don't know," said Vaughan. "But if he's alive, he'll skin you with the cat if you kill this wounded officer, and if he's dead you'll disgrace his memory by the deed."

Vaughan's words had their effect. The sword's point moved several inches away from Karl's white, bloodless face, and several of the Highlanders backed away some feet. They all had respect for James Wolfe, living or dead.

Stephen fell to his knees beside Karl. He looked up at one of the soldiers. The man passed an animal skin of whiskey to him. Stephen pulled an old pipe out of Karl's hand and lifted his head, pouring some of the whiskey between his lips.

The burning sensation caused Karl to awaken, and his eyes fluttered open. He could not recognize Stephen at first, but Stephen continued to call him and cajole him in French and in English to wake up. "Karl, you're not getting away from me; wake up. Look at me. It's Stephen."

Finally Karl mumbled his name. "Stefan, the little priest."

He groaned and held on to his belly. Vaughan knelt down and with his knife sliced away the upper front of Karl's breeches. He looked away in horror as a portion of Karl's lacerated intestines oozed through the wound. He placed the cloth back in place to cover the obscenity. He looked at Stephen, whose face had gone white, and merely shook his head.

"Stefan," Karl called. "You've come after Katherine. Don't be harsh with her. Love her. Love her as I have."

Stephen started to cry. "Where is she?" he said finally, wiping the tears off his cheeks.

"I left her in the city at the home of the surgeon Arnoux. She's safe there." He gasped in pain, and his hand grabbed for his stomach. "God," he called. "How I hurt." The spasms subsided and a daze seemed to fall over his eyes; they closed.

271

Stephen pushed the sweaty blond hair off his forehead. Karl opened his eyes again. "I always wanted a little brother," he said softly, and then he died.

Night settled on the city of Quebec. In parts of the town there were feverish conferences among officers attempting to determine what was the next course of action, and in other parts of town panic had set in.

Stephen landed his small boat at the wharf in the lower town. It had been tricky to handle the boat one-handed, but he had used the oar as a rudder, and he finally arrived at his destination, completely exhausted.

He went unchallenged through the checkpoint. He wore the clothes of an ordinary citizen, and he spoke their language.

The lower town was in shambles. The bombardment from Point Levy throughout the summer had destroyed most of the houses and shops. People roamed from bombed-out building to bombed-out building, scavenging for food and any usable clothing. Winter would soon be on them, and it was clear that by then they would be under siege or in enemy hands.

Stephen asked for the house of Dr. Arnoux. The first two persons looked at him furtively when he stopped them on the street. They had fear in their eyes and thought he was some sort of official or worse. Rumor had it that the pox had broken out in the city. Maybe he was an infected person seeking medical attention. They stared at him and then ran away. Finally Stephen stopped a soldier and asked for Arnoux.

"Just look for a crowd in the upper town. That will be the place. They have brought the general there."

Stephen climbed the stairs that led to the upper town. He was totally out of breath when he reached the top. The climb had been as steep, if not as rugged, as yesterday's climb up Anse au Foulon. He continued down the street, asking for Arnoux' house. Finally he asked a nun who was scurrying along the street.

"Follow me," she said sharply. "That's where I am headed. The general's wound is mortal, you know. Monseigneur Pointbriand, the bishop, is on his way to give the last rites. Poor man, he will need them himself before many more days go by. He wastes away. He has a cancer of some kind, I'm sure of it. He is in such pain. The general at least seems at peace. Hurry along, young man We have no time to waste. What is your business at the doctor's?"

"I've a message for a Katherine—" Stephen hesitated. He did not know what last name Katherine was using.

"Ah! Madame Nowell—that's who you want—lovely woman, a kind nurse. She hasn't left the general's side since they brought him into the city. I can't believe the rumors they spread about her. She is too good to be the whore that some have said she is."

Stephen said nothing but followed the nun down the dark street. They came to an intersection and turned onto a street crowded with silent people. It was a vigil. They stood on the street in front of a modest two-story house. There were some soldiers, but mostly they were common folk of the town.

The entryway was crowded, but the nun pushed her way in. Most stepped aside when they saw her coming, and Stephen stayed one step behind her; soon he found himself at the deathbed of the Marquis de Montcalm.

He saw her before she saw him. She sat in a chair next to the head of the bed. She placed a cool cloth on the marquis' head and wiped the perspiration from his face. Montcalm looked deathly, but he was not suffering. She looked from the dying general across the room to the nun whom Stephen had followed. Her eyes fixed on his and she did not even seem surprised to see him.

"The bishop is right behind," said the nun.

Katherine nodded. She whispered in the general's ear. He smiled wanly.

"Monsieur le Marquis," said an officer on the other side of the bed in a strangely accented French.

Montcalm opened his eyes and focused them on the speaker. "Ah, my Scot, Johnstone, you should be with Vaudreuil. He'll need every bit of help he can get."

"I've just come from him, sir. He's betraying the cause. He's abandoning the Beauport works. We are in full flight across the St. Charles. All Vaudreuil can think of is to join forces with Bougainville and flee to the Comte de Levis at Montreal. He has told Ramesay to surrender Quebec as soon as he is out of provisions, or as soon as the English offer terms or attempt to take the city by storm."

"The city is doomed," said Montcalm feebly. "Perhaps the Governor is right to spare lives. Our people—the Canadiens—have suffered so much. I think of them as my children. I want them not to suffer any more. Besides, Johnstone," he said wearily, "why do you bring this to me? I'm dying. I'll be before my Maker before the morning comes. Give me time to make peace with my God. I've made war enough."

Johnstone turned away. His face was flushed with sorrow and bitterness. He rose from the chair and spoke to the officer who stood next to him. "Everyone has lost their minds without his steady hand. Your uncle's loss has meant the destruction of New France."

Stephen recognized Charles Gozin finally.

Katherine left her chair and walked to Stephen. "There's another room that is being prepared for the bishop," she said to him in English. "We can go in there."

Stephen followed her out the door, into the anteroom. The nun whom Stephen had followed smiled at him and stepped back outside, into the bedroom of the general.

"Hello, Stephen," Katherine said softly. "I expected you to come, but not so soon."

"I've some dreadful news for you, Katherine," he said, his eyes filling.

She looked away from him. "Karl is dead," she said. "My friend Henri Gingras told me earlier today."

"I spoke to him before he died," Stephen said. She turned to him, her face indicating genuine surprise.

"He told me that he loved you and asked me to love you as he did."

Katherine's face filled with pain and she looked away, again biting her lip. Then he handed her the pipe that he had found in Karl's grasp.

"Did he tell you of our son?" she asked.

This time it was Stephen's face that showed the surprise.

"I see he didn't. Well, Louis Joseph Stiegler exists, and I am not ashamed of him and that his father was Karl Stiegler, whom I loved with all my heart."

"Katherine, I want you back," said Stephen, after some moments of silence.

"Why?" she asked.

"Because you are my wife, the mother of my daughter; I need you."

She smiled softly at him.

The door opened and a plain, thin man in clerical garb entered the room. "Pardon me," he said, "they told me I could prepare here."

Katherine bowed to the bishop. "Monseigneur, it is quite correct. This room has been prepared for you. I must go back to my vigil."

She stepped by Stephen, out into the crowded bedchamber. Stephen followed her and felt a hand touch his arm. He turned and looked into the face of Charles Gozin.

"LaGarde? Is that you?" Charles asked. Stephen smiled at his college roommate of so many years before.

"Yes, Charles, except that name is one I have not responded to in many years. My name is Stephen Nowell."

"I know," said Charles. "I had a falling out with Stiegler about your wife. I did not wish to cause the lady embarrassment, but I had hoped that Karl would come to his senses and send her home to you. I failed."

Stephen looked at Charles. He was clearly in agony from the loss of his beloved uncle, about whom they had talked so often. It was ironic that Stephen would see the man for the first time as he lay dying.

"Charles, go sit with your uncle and don't worry about my problems."

Charles smiled meekly. "Not the least of which, Etienne, is that you are a British subject inside a French fortress and dressed in civilian clothes."

"I am no spy, Charles. I came only to speak with my wife."

"I am not about to betray you, Etienne; I am just warning you to take care. This will not be a French fortress tomorrow. If I were to have you arrested tonight, you'd be able to watch my surrender in the morning. Besides, I have no heart left for war and hatred, not with him lying there."

There was a tinkling of a little bell. The door to the anteroom opened and the bishop, dressed in surplice and stole, entered the room, carrying a small gold case. All in the room fell to their knees. The bishop approached the bed of the dying marquis. Katherine stood and pulled the chair away from the bedside to make room. The bishop rested his head close to Montcalm, who made his confession, and when he had finished, Pointbriand raised his arm and made the sign of the cross. *"Ego te absolvo. . . ."*

Then, taking the host from the golden case, he held it high in the air. *"Corpus Domine Nostri Jesu Christi,"* said the bishop, in the ancient words of the communion service of the Church.

Montcalm opened his eyes and looked up with devotion at the wafer of unleavened bread that he believed to be the body of his savior. He opened his mouth and the bishop placed the bread on his tongue.

Montcalm was too weak to do it for himself, but Charles reached over and carefully made the sign of the cross on the general's forehead. Then the bishop took holy oils and anointed the general's head, feet, hands and breast. When he had finished, the bishop retreated to a corner of the room and waited with the others. Two hours before dawn, the Marquis de Montcalm slipped away peacefully in his sleep.

"He is gone," said Charles, feeling for a pulse. There were several sobs in the room, from both men and women.

Gozin rose and walked away from the bed. He was in agony. Several officers went to his side to console him, but he pushed them away.

"I want him to be buried in a French Quebec," he said loudly. "That does not give us much time."

The nun stepped from the corner of the room and approached Charles. "You don't have to dig a grave if you bury the marquis in the cellar of the convent. There is already a bomb hole big enough for a coffin, and it is not far away."

Charles nodded assent. "And your sisters will pray for his soul as well," he said.

Several persons lifted the limp body of the marquis from his bed and bore it out the front door. The crowd in the street reverently stepped aside and helped to form the torchlight funeral cortege down the streets to the convent.

Once in the convent, they descended a flight of stone stairs into the damp basement. The old caretaker of the convent had nailed together a large wooden box of pine, which would have to serve as a coffin.

Stephen and Katherine walked side by side in the procession and went down into the cellar. They did not speak to each other.

The bishop recited the prayers for the dead. Charles and two other officers lifted the body of Montcalm and placed it into the box at the bottom of the bomb hole. The lid was then put in place. Charles raised his hand in a salute. "To a true hero of France and to a father of Canada," he said, in a voice choking with emotion.

Stephen walked away from the gravesite and up the stairs to the street above. Katherine followed him.

When they were out in the street, they could see the first light of dawn breaking over the abandoned trenches of Beauport.

"You've been very silent about coming back with me, Katherine. I'm very rich now. We, that is you, Amy, your son and I, could live in Boston. You could have the finest."

She interrupted him. "I'm going back to Isle d'Orleans—to my farm. I'm going to live there with my children," she said. "We were happy there, happier than I have ever been in my life. Karl won't be there, but the memory of him will be."

Stephen was thunderstruck. "Don't you love me?" he asked.

She looked at him and then spoke softly. "Yes, I do, Stephen. I always have. That will never change. But bringing the son of another man into your home—even the son of a man like Karl, whom you loved—would be too much of a burden to place on you and on him. I'll not risk damage to my son because his father was not my husband. I've lived through that myself. On the island, the people will come to accept me as Karl's wife; some already have."

"Katherine, I love you," he said in desperation.

Katherine smiled softly. "Finally, I hear those words. I think you mean them, Stephen, but your love is very weak and too late. You were always running away from love especially when those who loved you needed you. It doesn't sustain through disappointment or despair. It turns ugly when thwarted. I wish you well, husband, and I love you still, but for now I am going back to my island."

She walked away from him and started down the stairs to the lower town. From out of the shadows stepped an older man, dressed in the clothes of a Canadian habitant. She smiled at him and handed him "Karl's" pipe.

ABOUT THE AUTHOR

ROBERT E. WALL was born in Brooklyn, New York, in 1937. He received his education at American schools— B.A. at Holy Cross College, Worcester, Massachusetts, and an M.A. and Ph.D. in History from Yale University. He has taught history at Duke University and Michigan State University. In 1970 Wall moved his family to Canada where he became chairman of the History Department and, later, Provost of the Faculty of Arts & Sciences at Montreal's Concordia University. In 1976 he became a Canadian citizen.

Wall perceives the histories of his adopted land and the land of his birth as deeply entwined. Influenced by the writings of such figures as Kenneth Roberts, he seeks to teach those histories through the historical novel. Wall is the author of the seven-volume series, THE CANADIANS and the novel, THE ACADIANS.

Wall is married and has five children. He recently left the academic field in order to devote all of his attention to writing full-time.

The fabulous saga of the taming of a continent
that began in **Blackrobe** and **Bloodbrothers**
continues.

Now read the thrilling opening pages of

Book Three
THE CANADIANS

BIRTHRIGHT

by
Robert E. Wall

Among his people a nineteen-year-old was a man, and Kenonranon had been taught by his uncle and his grandfather to behave like a warrior. But most of all it was his mother who had taught him what it meant to be a Mohawk. She said little, but he could see it in her eyes when she looked at him or in the way she straightened her shoulders and stood proud when he brought game to the longhouse or honor to the clan. It mattered little to him, or to her for that matter, that her husband was white and that Kenonranon's own father was a white man. She had rejected his father, the blackrobe, because his ways were the ways of the whites; her husband, the white man Johnson, was in his heart as much a Mohawk as Kenonranon's mother or his uncle.

Kenonranon was tall, almost six feet. His legs were short and stubby, but his waist was long and narrow and his shoulders broad. His chest was thick with muscles. His golden skin was darkened by the sun and by the bear grease with which he covered his body to ward off insects. It was his eyes that made him different from all the others. They were a striking light blue.

He had come to the land of the Inland Seas, far away from the river of his people, at the request of his stepfather and his uncle. He was to observe the behavior of the western Indians and to report back. Johnson had heard the stories, and even the Seneca people of the longhouse, cousins to Kenonranon, were restive. The tribes of the west had always loved the French and had never accepted their defeat and their expulsion from Canada.

The council fire grew brighter as warriors heaved great logs upon it. In the rear of the dark clearing, drums began to beat softly to summon the tribal leaders together. The council members entered the clearing and then parted to allow a pathway for their leader to join them.

The chief of the Ojibwa was named Minavavana. He was the leader of the largest band of his people dwelling near the fort at Michilinackinac, guarding the straits that connected Lake Michigan and Lake Huron. He was tall and, although he was only about fifty years old, his face was lined with wrinkles and his long, braided hair was streaked with grey. He spoke in the language that Kenonranon did not understand, but an Ojibwa who had known his uncle, Joseph Brant, at Dr. Wheelock's English school translated the speech for him.

Minavavana held the long wampum belt of war in his hand. It had come from Pontiac of the Ottawa earlier in the week. The great council of the tribes near Detroit had decided on war and that all the forts would be attacked, their garrisons destroyed; then the Indians would fall on the English settlers and destroy every man, woman and child.

The Ojibwa sat in council to render their decision on the fate of the English garrison at the fort on the straits.

The fire was large and yet Kenonranon could barely make out the outline of the elders and warriors who sat about it. The heat was intense enough to drive the council members into the shadows to escape it. But Minavavana could be heard.

"You know that the French king promised to be father to the Ojibwa," he shouted. "We became his children and we have been his loyal sons." He paused to await the grunts of assent that came from the shadows. "The English made war on our father. Our father was old and tired and he slept when his treacherous enemies stole Canada from him. But now our father's sleep is over. I can hear him stirring and stretching as he awakens.

He asks for us: 'Where are my children?' When he awakes fully he will call on us to destroy his enemies—the English.

"The English have conquered the soldiers of our father. The Canadians are docile and accept the foreign yoke. But the Ojibwa are unconquered. We still own the forests and the lakes. These we cannot allow the English to take from us. We must strike before they become strong enough to try. The spirits of our people killed by the English must be avenged. We must kill the English. We must drive them from our land. We must dig up the bones of their dead. They can have no peace in the soil of our fathers. It is war now. It is war until the English are gone forever."

Minavavana threw off his blanket. His torso glistened in the firelight. His body was painted red and black. He was naked except for the cloth that covered his loins. The drums began to beat loudly. The chief took the belt of wampum and carried it to each elder and each warrior. One by one they touched it. When all had signaled acceptance of Pontiac's war of extermination, Minavavana gave a great yell and, picking up his war axe, he raced to the pole beyond the light of the fire and struck it with a great blow. The axe sank into the wooden post. It would take an arm stronger than most to retrieve it. It would remain there as long as the Ojibwa made war on Louis XV's enemies.

Kenonranon studied the scene carefully. He

would have to repeat these words for his step-father. Johnson would want to know all. But if he could not leave the camp tonight, it would be too late. Tomorrow the Ojibwa would attack the fort. He stepped more deeply into the shadows. When he was sure that he could be seen by no one, he began to move quietly away from the council site.

He must exercise all the care and stealth that his uncle Joseph Brant had taught him. He moved through the underbrush noiselessly. He knew there would be a scout posted, but the scout would be thinking of keeping people away from the council instead of stopping someone coming from the fire. Kenonranon saw the sentry hiding in the brush by the stream that flowed into the Great Lake. He had not covered his back, and he was fully visible in the moonlight. Kenonranon sneaked up behind him. He raised his tomahawk and brought the flat face of it down on the back of the Ojibwa's skull with a dull thud. The sentry moaned and then fell forward into the bushes. He would not know who had struck him. Kenonranon checked to see if he were still breathing. The man lived, but he would be unconscious for some time. Kenonranon stepped over his body and waded into the stream. The water was frigid and his feet inside his moccasins were soon numb with the cold. He walked until he reached the waters of the lake. He turned south in the water to hide his footprints. He would warn the English because that was what Molly, his mother; Johnson, his father; and Joseph, his uncle would want of him.

Captain Etherington had only recently received possession of the fort at Michilinackinac from the French. He had thirty-five men and several officers under his command. It was his first independent post and he was determined to do well. He had followed the commanding general's instructions to give up the French practice of bribing the tribes with gifts, and he had personally removed the warriors who lolled about the fort parade ground, drinking and carrying on. An English fort would be strictly run, like a proper military base. The slovenly Canadians who still ran the trading posts and stores very much wanted to continue the old ways, but he was a British officer and he knew the meaning of discipline. Tomorrow, the King's birthday, June 4, 1763, he would open the gates and allow the red men and their squaws to enter, but then he would awe them with a parade and fireworks. Certainly he would fire his cannon in honor of the King. The Ojibwa had invited his men to watch a ballgame they would play against their cousins the Sauk from Wisconsin. Etherington would normally not have allowed it. But he was a good officer, and he knew that the decision to allow the game on the King's birthday would be good for the morale of his men, who had so little to do in the middle of this godforsaken wilderness. There was a knock on the door and Corporal Davies entered.

"There's a young Indian outside to see you, sir."

"How did he enter the fort?"

"I don't know, sir. All I know is that he's here. He speaks English. Claims to be from Sir William Johnson."

"Oh Christ, that crowd," said Etherington, shaking his head in disgust. "Johnson just pours gifts onto these flea-bitten wastrels while they sit around trying to figure out ways to stay neutral. If the bugger is looking for a handout, throw him out on his arse."

"He won't say what he wants, sir," said Davies. "Only that he must see the captain."

"All right, send him in."

Kenonranon walked into Etherington's office before the corporal could turn around and ask him in; he wasted no time on introductions. "Captain," he said in his best school English, just like his uncle had taught him, "this fort is in jeopardy. The Ojibwa plan to destroy it tomorrow."

"How do they plan to do that?" asked Etherington, rather sarcastically.

"I don't know," said Kenonranon, "but you will be attacked tomorrow in force and the plan is to destroy you."

"How much rum have you imbibed this evening, young man?" said the British officer.

Kenonranon looked at him without comprehension.

"You're drunk! Just like all you bloody savages. You can't keep away from the firewater —poor bastards."

"I've not tasted whisky," said Kenonranon, "not ever."

"Davies, get this lying savage out of my office. No telling what kind of vermin he has tracked in with him."

The corporal took Kenonranon's arm. But the Indian, with one turn of his powerful shoulders, twisted out of his grasp. "Don't touch me again," said Kenonranon. "I came here to warn you, as I have been trained to do. And yet you insult me and call me foul names. I don't agree with the sentiments of my Ojibwa cousins, but I understand their feelings better than you do. Captain, you need training from my father, Johnson, about the way to treat Indians." He turned and walked from the room without looking back. He had done what his family and his clan would have expected of him. It was not his fault that the English chief was a fool.

The next day was the King's birthday. The British garrison, except for those with sentry duty, was placed on a holiday standing. The great wooden gates of the stockade were opened wide. The Indians encamped about the fort strolled in and stopped at the trading post to purchase blankets and kettles, powder and shot—and for the lucky few who knew a Canadian trader who would bend the rules, some whiskey, all paid for with the richest beaver furs to be found in the region of the lakes.

Kenonranon strolled along the company street and parade ground to the fort. He could feel the tension in the air, even if the British were oblivious to it. The Canadian shopkeepers had opened their stores, but nowhere could one see the white women and children. All had been carefully hidden away in cellars or in locked rooms on the second-floor living quarters above the shops. But Kenonranon noted the presence of large numbers of Ojibwa squaws inside the fort, and it did not escape his notice that all were wrapped in heavy woolen blankets on a hot June day. Minavavana came into the fort, dressed in his finest eagle feathers and a European coat frayed at the sleeves and elbows—a coat that had been a gift from an earlier commandant of this same fort, when it had been a French fort at the Straits of Mackinaw. He called on Etherington in a loud voice. The captain came to the front porch of his headquarters building. "Etherington," said the Ojibwa in French. "My people play a game against the men of our cousins from the west, the Sauk. We invite all to watch."

Etherington waited until Lieutenant Leslie, his second in command, translated. He then nodded to the chief. "My men celebrate the birthday of our father the King. It pleases me that our brothers should choose to treat this day as a day of celebration."

Minavavana stared at Etherington while his words were turned into a poorly accented French by Leslie. And then he turned and walked out of the fort without comment.

Kenonranon joined his Ojibwa friends of last night's council. He was stripped to his loincloth, his hair tied in a knot, and he carried two wooden sticks curved at the bottom into clublike instruments. "Are the Mohawk familiar with our game, Baggataway?" Kenonranon knew of it by a different name, but he had never played it.

The Ojibwa handed him one of the bats. "Strip!" he said, "and join us. If you're strong and can run, you can play."

Kenonranon took off his loincloth and laid it in a pile with the clothing of all the other players. A large field in front of the fort had been marked off, and a goal stake had been driven into the ground at each end. Kenonranon joined the Ojibwa side in front of their stake. They numbered about a hundred. An equal number of Sauks stood at the opposite end. Minavavana walked onto the field. He held a wooden ball in his hand. With a big yell he hurled it high into the sky. From two hundred throats came a cheer, and all two hundred men ran screaming toward the spot where they thought the ball would land.

Kenonranon raced ahead, holding his bat with both hands. He was a fast runner, and he soon reached the front of the Ojibwa line. The ball had rolled after hitting the ground, however, and it had rolled in the direction of the charging Sauks.

The leading opponent, a man with an upright crest of hair on his otherwise shaven skull, smashed the ball backward toward a line of Sauk players. Kenonranon rushed by the first Sauk and then felt the smash of a bat against his shin. He doubled over in pain and fell face forward on the ground. His Ojibwa friend came up behind him and helped him to his feet. Kenonranon hobbled about, holding his shin and howling in pain. He put his weight on his leg gingerly and found that it was numb. He looked in anger about him for his assailant, but he was gone.

The Sauks had cleverly pushed the ball toward the rear, where their faster runners were now trying to outrace the Ojibwas on their right flank. The Sauk onlookers cheered their team. Kenonranon could now feel the throb in his leg, but he placed more and more pressure on it and found that he could run—not fast, but he would leave that to others. The Ojibwas were not without skills at this ballgame. Their fastest runners had cut off the Sauks and a mad melee of bodies falling on each other had now developed, causing most of the players to lose sight of the ball. Kenonranon ran toward the pile of bodies. He could see players plucking at each other and pulling hair to force their opponents away from where they thought the ball ought to be.

Finally there was a yell, and one of the Sauks pulled away from the pile and smacked the loosened ball back toward his own goal stick. Kenonranon saw that he was the Sauk's closest opponent—that, in fact, the Sauk had made an error in strategy. Kenonranon was closer to the ball than the Sauk himself. Kenonranon began to race for the ball. He cursed the pain in his leg, but the faster he ran the more excited he became and the less he felt the pain.

The path to the Sauk goal was clear. No one had lingered behind to defend it. Kenonranon held the bat in his right hand and dove forward toward the ball. He felt the Sauk coming up behind him and knew that he would attempt to hit him with his bat before he could reach the ball. His opponent's bat squeezed between Kenonranon's legs, forcing him to fall just as his own bat struck the ball and sent it whirling toward the goal stick. Kenonranon was lying face forward on the ground when he heard the cheer go up from the Ojibwas as the ball crossed the Sauk goal line.

His new friends crowded around Kenonranon and pounded him on the back. There were some who would have preferred the goal to have been scored by one of their own rather than by a visitor from the Six Nations, but a goal was a goal.

The Ojibwas now walked back toward their

own goal line. As Kenonranon joined them, he could see that most of the British soldiers had left the fort and were standing outside the stockade to get a better view of the game.

Now the Sauks came forward with the ball. Once again they tried an outflanking tactic. This time the same Sauk who had first slammed Kenonranon with his stick gave a great yell and smashed the ball with all of his might. The ball rose high in the air and sailed well over the heads of the Ojibwa defenders, beyond the Ojibwa goal, and began to roll toward the open gate of the fort. Two hundred screaming, naked players began to race after it. Kenonranon, still limping, could not keep up with the rest.

But he stopped dead in his tracks when he realized that the players were ignoring the ball altogether. They raced toward the English soldiers, who stood or lounged on the ground, weaponless. Some ran past the soldiers into the fort, where Ojibwa and Sauk squaws opened their blankets and handed their men muskets and tomahawks and knives. Others began to smash the soldiers with their bats, knocking them senseless. The slaughter began. An Ojibwa holding a living, conscious English soldier between his knees tore off the scalp of his screaming prisoner with his scalping knife.

Kenonranon stopped in the field. The screams of the soldiers could be heard from within the fort, and every soldier outside who was not already dead would face an even more horrible fate that night in the fires. The stores of the Canadians remained untouched; the wives and children of the traders remained safe, if frightened, in the security of their homes. Minavavana was true to his word. The children of his father, the awakening King of France, were unharmed. But the English had paid a horrible price for ignoring the warnings of a son of the Six Nations of the Iroquois.

SEAL BOOKS

Offers you a list of outstanding fiction, non-fiction and classics of
Canadian literature in paperback by Canadian authors, available
at all good bookstores throughout Canada.

The Mark of Canadian Bestsellers